BASED ON THE *NEW YORK TIMES* BESTSELLING SERIES

Five Nights at Freddy's™

FAZBEAR FRIGHTS

GRAPHIC NOVEL COLLECTION VOL. 2

BY SCOTT CAWTHON,

ANDREA WAGGENER, AND CARLY ANNE WEST

ADAPTED BY CHRISTOPHER HASTINGS

FETCH
ILLUSTRATED BY DIDI ESMERALDA
COLORS BY EVA DE LA CRUZ

ROOM FOR ONE MORE
ILLUSTRATED BY ANTHONY MORRIS JR.
COLORS BY BEN SAWYER

THE NEW KID
ILLUSTRATED BY CORYN MacPHERSON
COLORS BY GONZALO DUARTE

LETTERS BY MICAH MYERS

graphix

An Imprint of

SCHOLASTIC

All rights reserved. Published by Graphix, an imprint of Scholastic Inc.,
Publishers since 1920. SCHOLASTIC, GRAPHIX, and associated logos are
trademarks and/or registered trademarks of Scholastic Inc.

ISBN 978-1-338-79272-0 (hardcover)

ISBN 978-1-338-79270-6 (paperback)

10 9 8 7 6 5 4 3 2 1   23 24 25 26 27

Printed in China   62

First edition, January 2023

Edited by Michael Petranek

Book Design by Jeff Shake

Layout Design by Dawn Guzzo

Inks by Didi Esmeralda, Anthony Morris Jr., and Coryn MacPherson

Colors by Eva de la Cruz, Ben Sawyer, and Gonzalo Duarte

Letters by Micah Myers

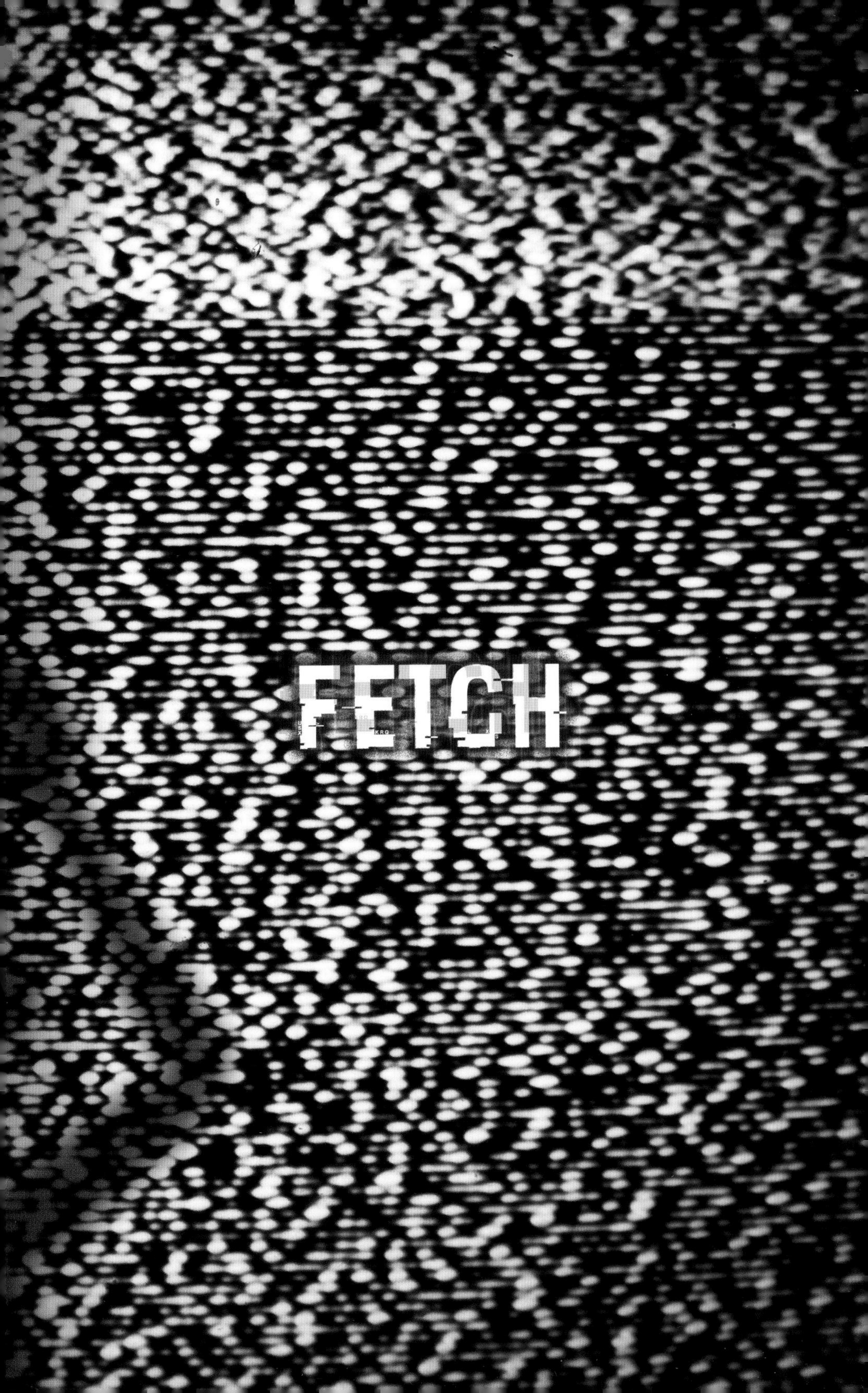
FETCH

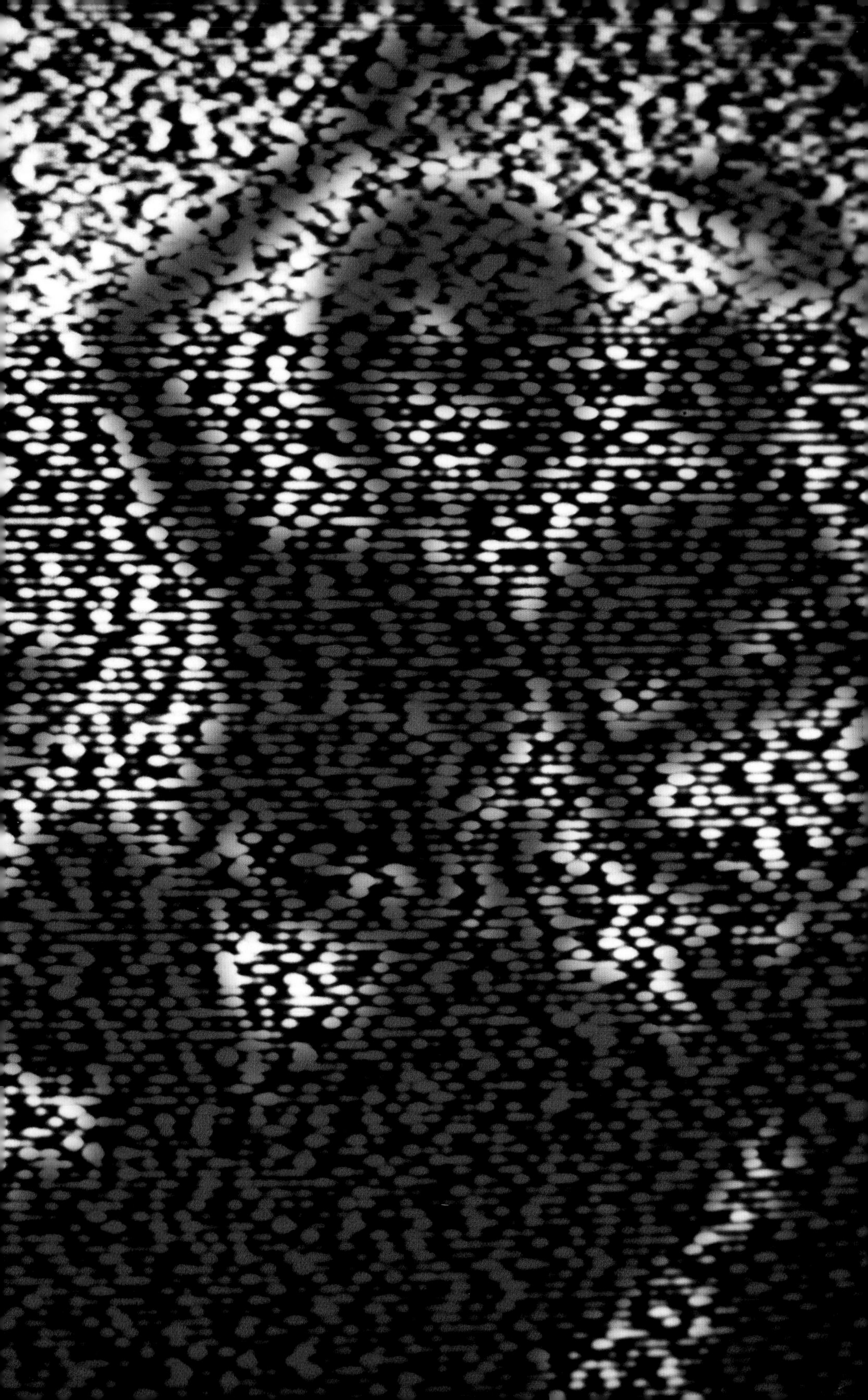

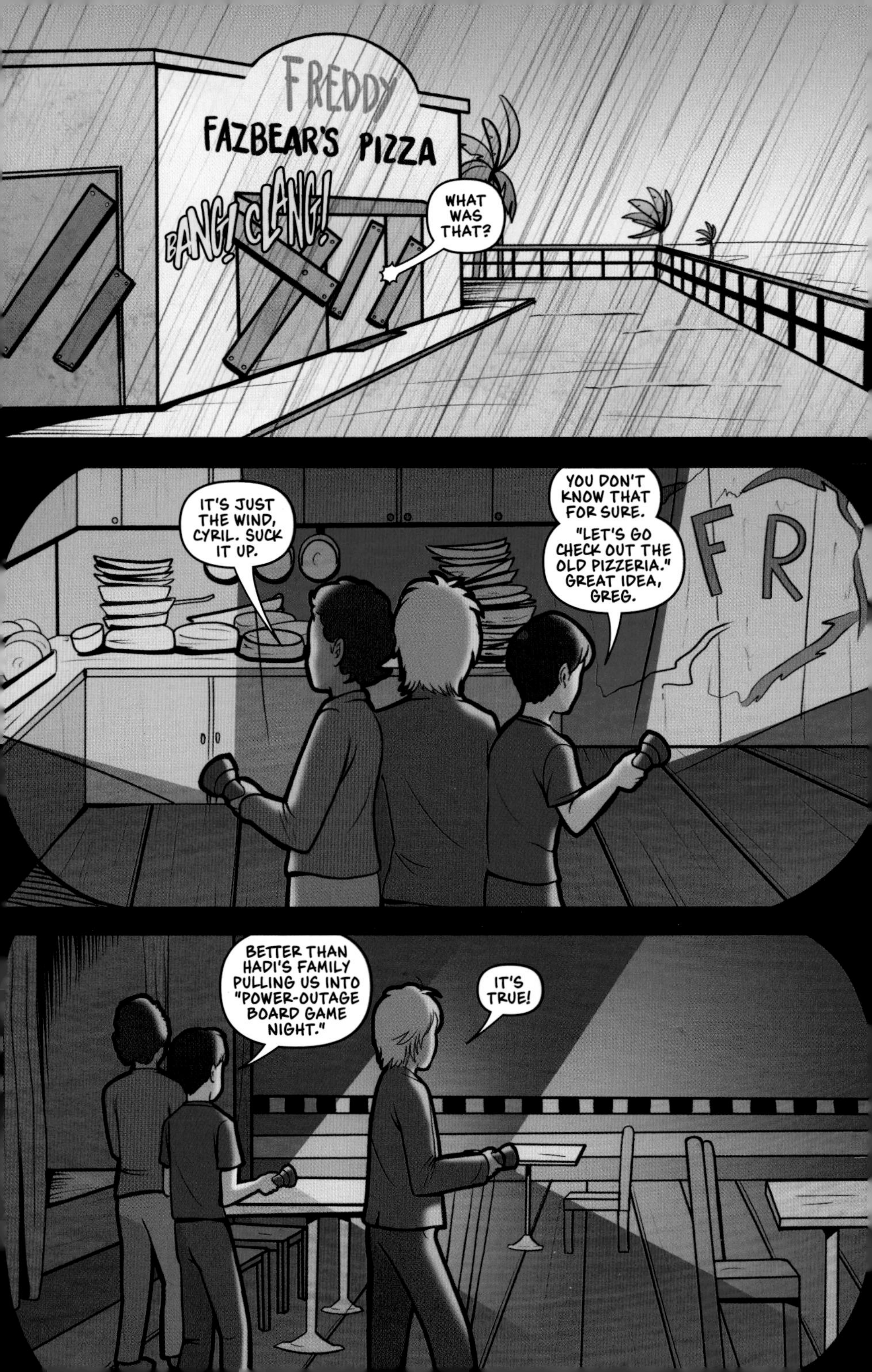
FREDDY
FAZBEAR'S PIZZA
BANG! CLANG!
WHAT WAS THAT?
IT'S JUST THE WIND, CYRIL. SUCK IT UP.
YOU DON'T KNOW THAT FOR SURE.
"LET'S GO CHECK OUT THE OLD PIZZERIA." GREAT IDEA, GREG.
FR
BETTER THAN HADI'S FAMILY PULLING US INTO "POWER-OUTAGE BOARD GAME NIGHT."
IT'S TRUE!

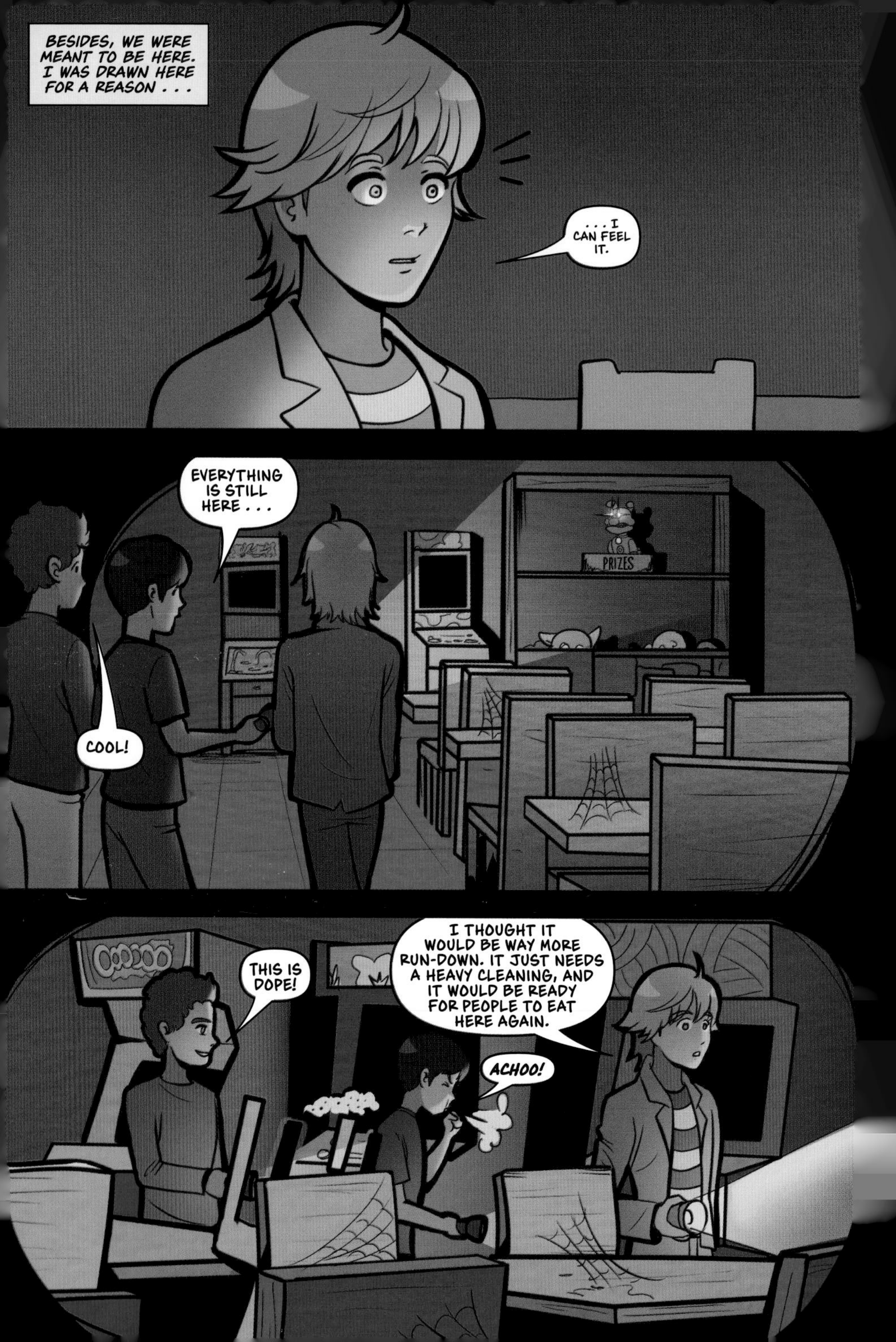
BESIDES, WE WERE MEANT TO BE HERE. I WAS DRAWN HERE FOR A REASON . . .
. . . I CAN FEEL IT.
EVERYTHING IS STILL HERE . . .
COOL!
PRIZES
THIS IS DOPE!
I THOUGHT IT WOULD BE WAY MORE RUN-DOWN. IT JUST NEEDS A HEAVY CLEANING, AND IT WOULD BE READY FOR PEOPLE TO EAT HERE AGAIN.
ACHOO!

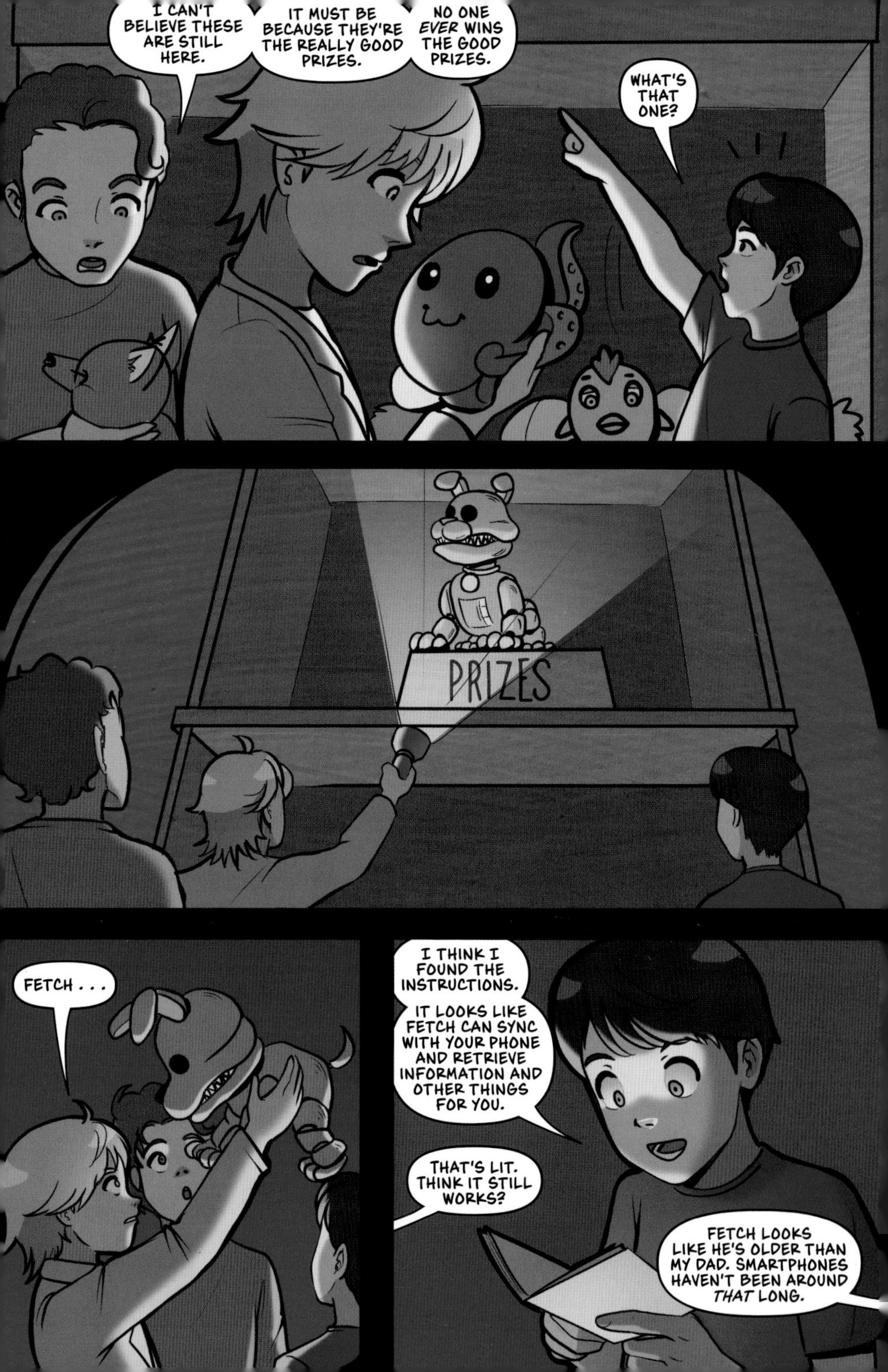
I CAN'T BELIEVE THESE ARE STILL HERE.
IT MUST BE BECAUSE THEY'RE THE REALLY GOOD PRIZES.
NO ONE *EVER* WINS THE GOOD PRIZES.
WHAT'S THAT ONE?
PRIZES
FETCH . . .
I THINK I FOUND THE INSTRUCTIONS.
IT LOOKS LIKE FETCH CAN SYNC WITH YOUR PHONE AND RETRIEVE INFORMATION AND OTHER THINGS FOR YOU.
THAT'S LIT. THINK IT STILL WORKS?
FETCH LOOKS LIKE HE'S OLDER THAN MY DAD. SMARTPHONES HAVEN'T BEEN AROUND *THAT* LONG.

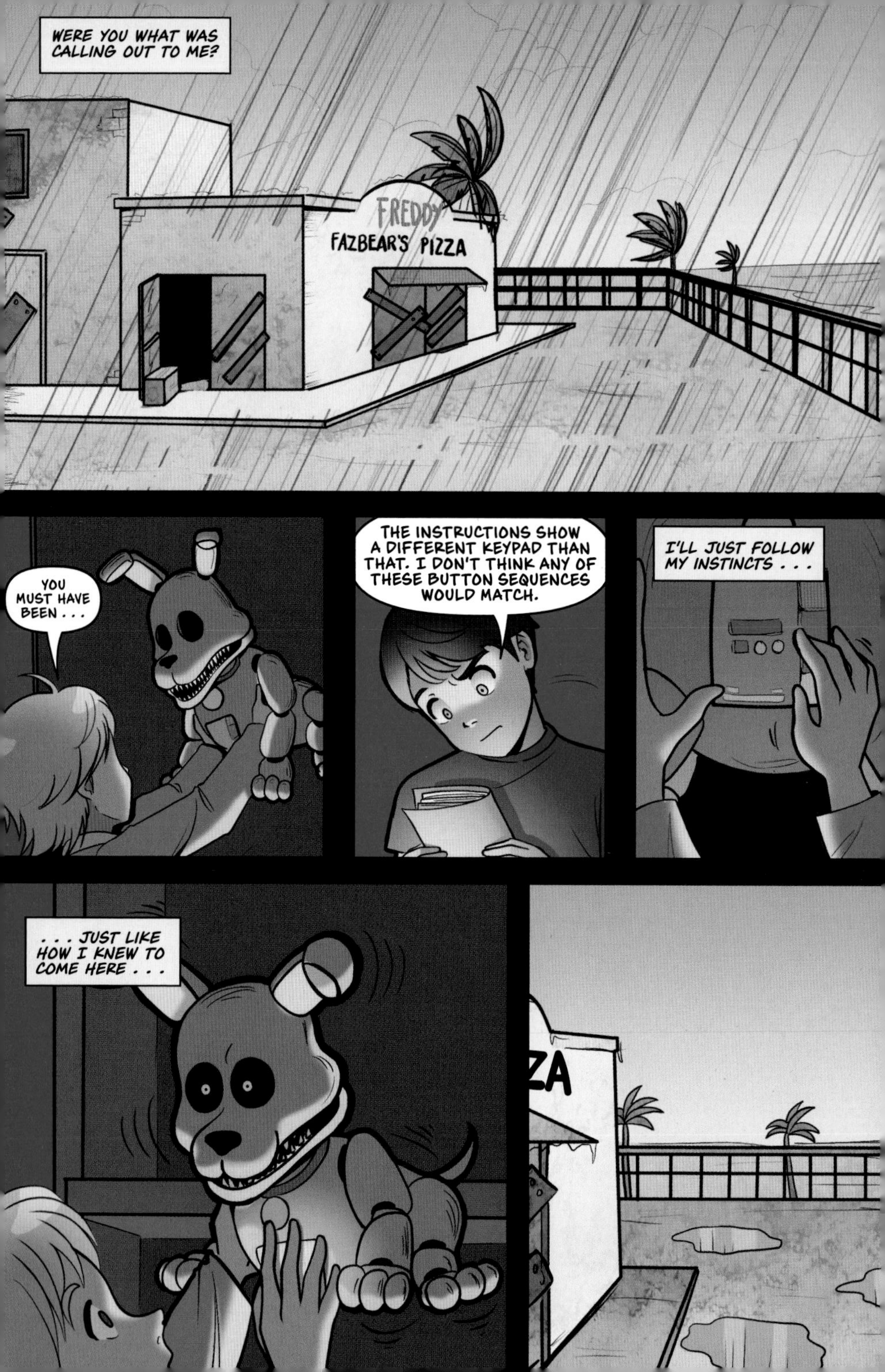
WERE YOU WHAT WAS CALLING OUT TO ME?
FREDDY FAZBEAR'S PIZZA
YOU MUST HAVE BEEN . . .
THE INSTRUCTIONS SHOW A DIFFERENT KEYPAD THAN THAT. I DON'T THINK ANY OF THESE BUTTON SEQUENCES WOULD MATCH.
I'LL JUST FOLLOW MY INSTINCTS . . .
. . . JUST LIKE HOW I KNEW TO COME HERE . . .
ZA

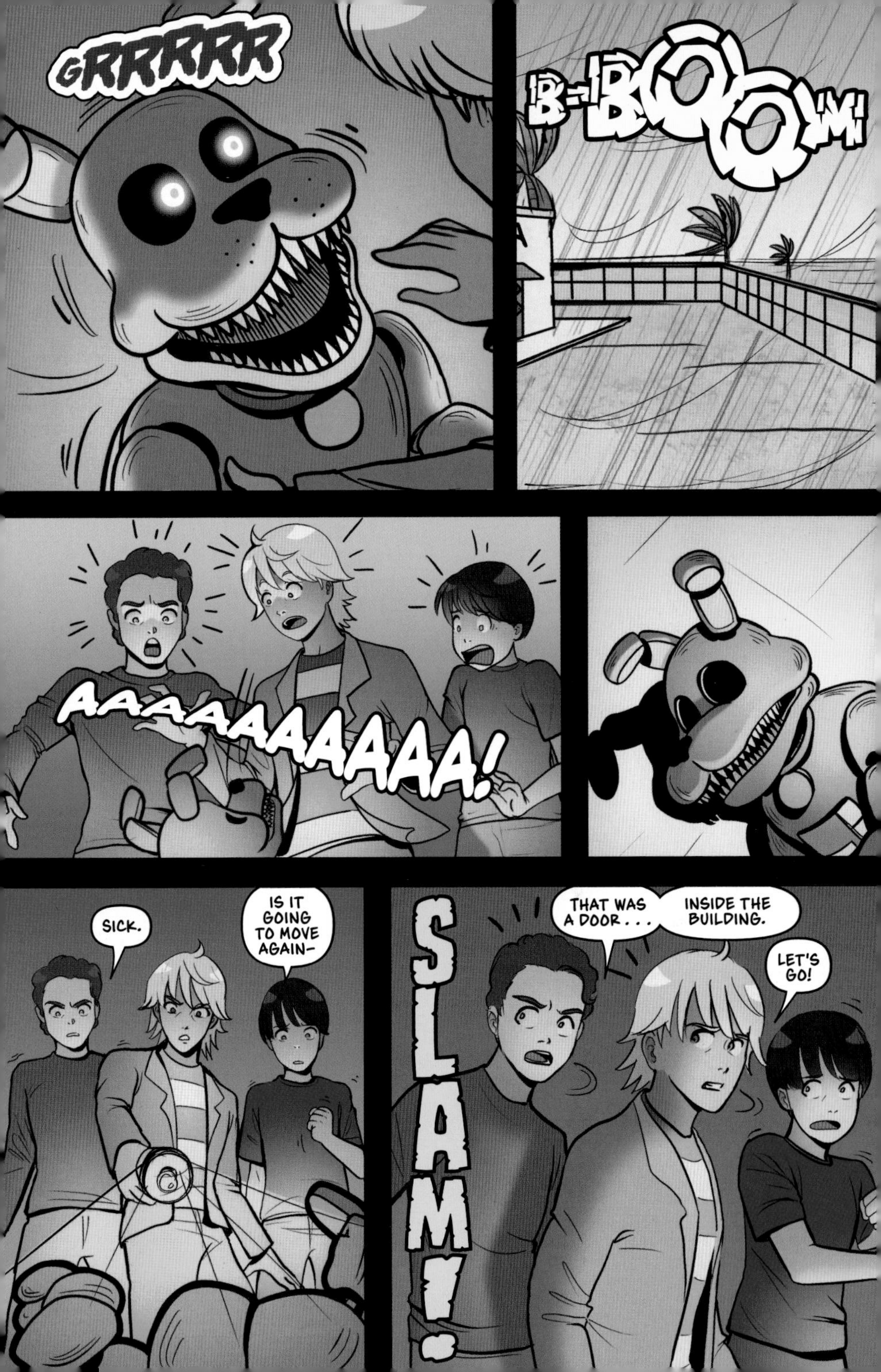
GRRRRRR
B-BOOOOM!
AAAAAAAAAAAA!
SICK.
IS IT GOING TO MOVE AGAIN-
SLAM!
THAT WAS A DOOR . . .
INSIDE THE BUILDING.
LET'S GO!

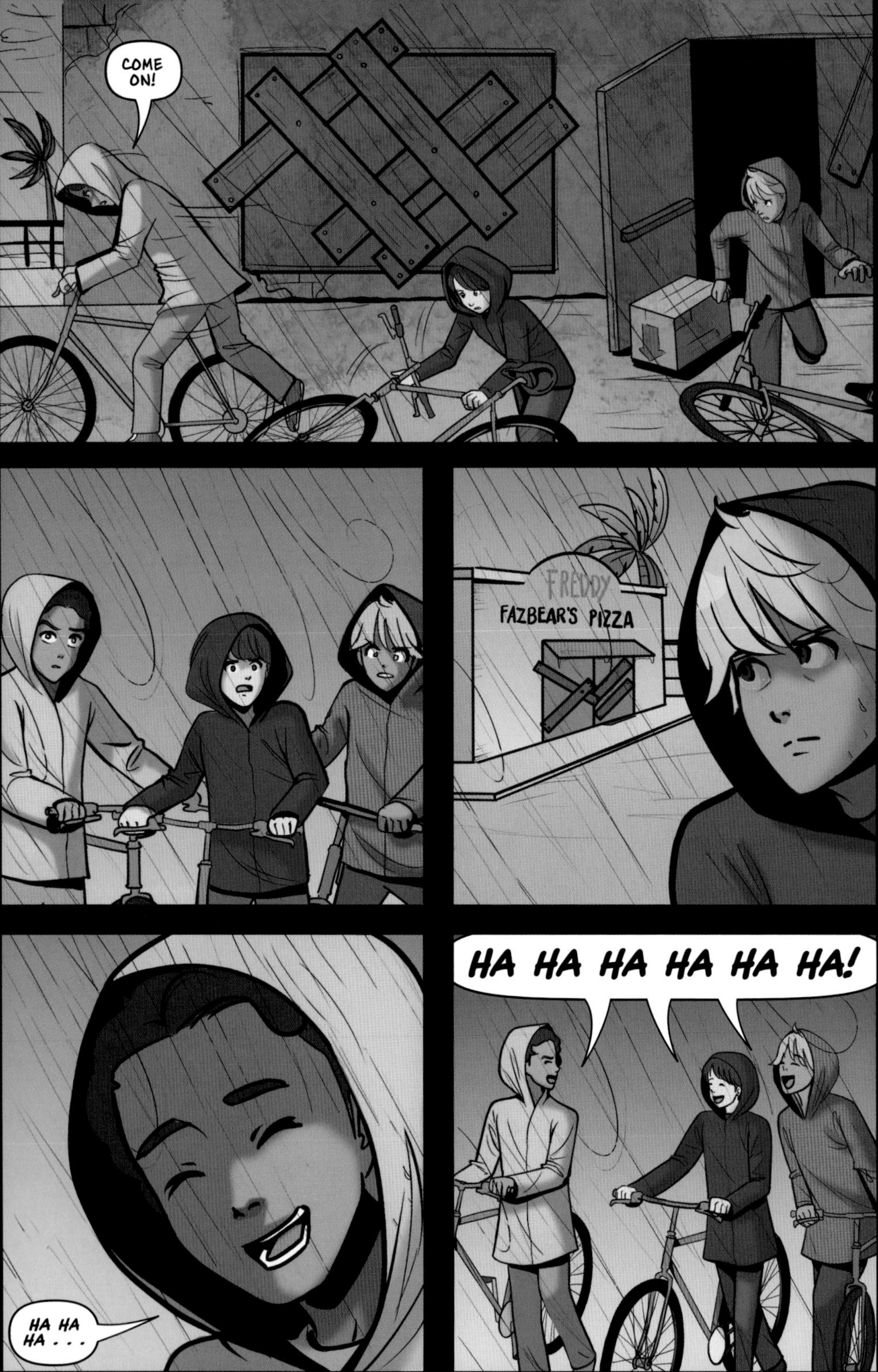
COME ON!
FREDDY
FAZBEAR'S PIZZA
HA HA HA . . .
HA HA HA HA HA HA!

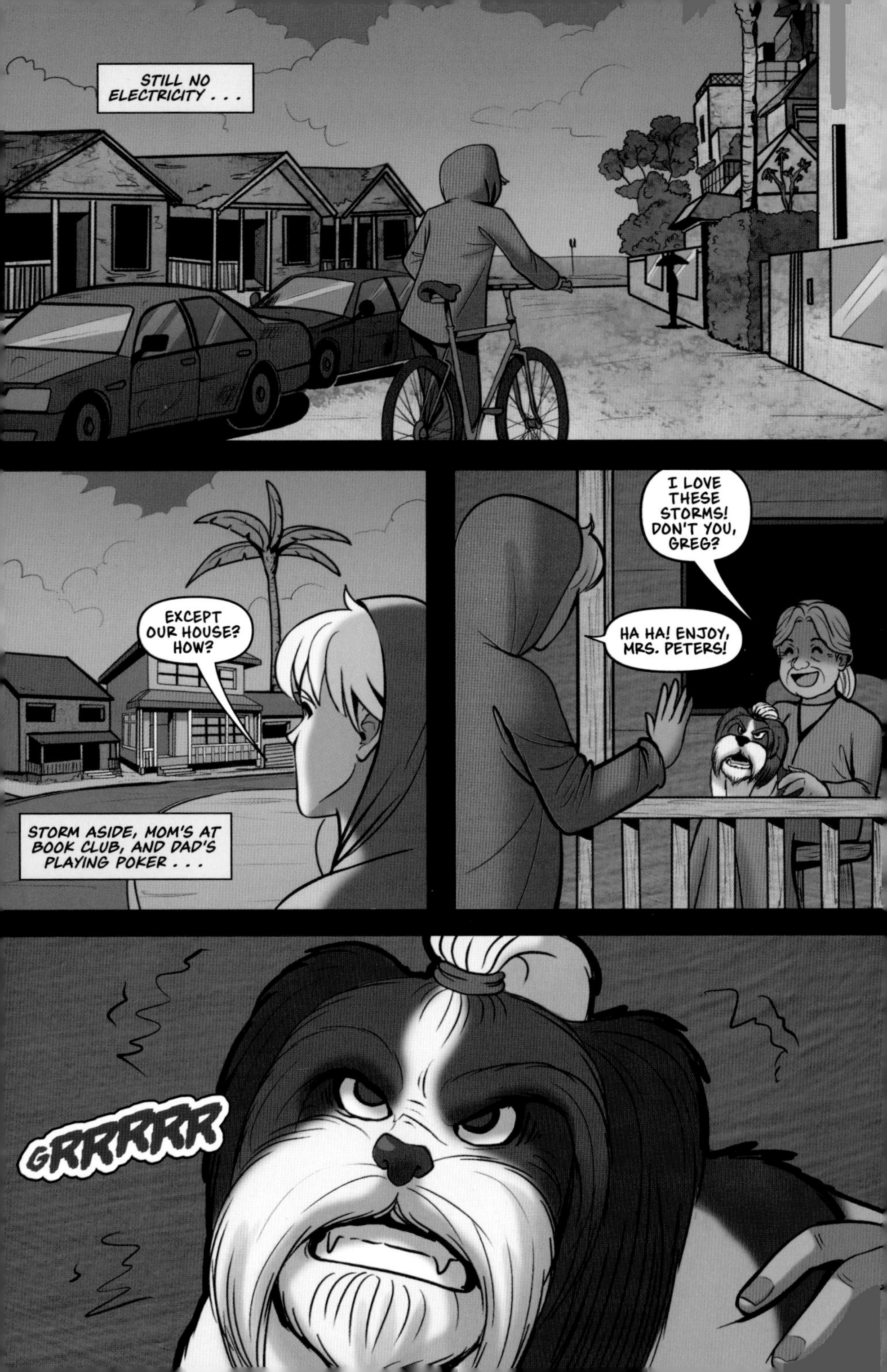
STILL NO ELECTRICITY . . .
EXCEPT OUR HOUSE? HOW?
STORM ASIDE, MOM'S AT BOOK CLUB, AND DAD'S PLAYING POKER . . .
I LOVE THESE STORMS! DON'T YOU, GREG?
HA HA! ENJOY, MRS. PETERS!
GRRRRR

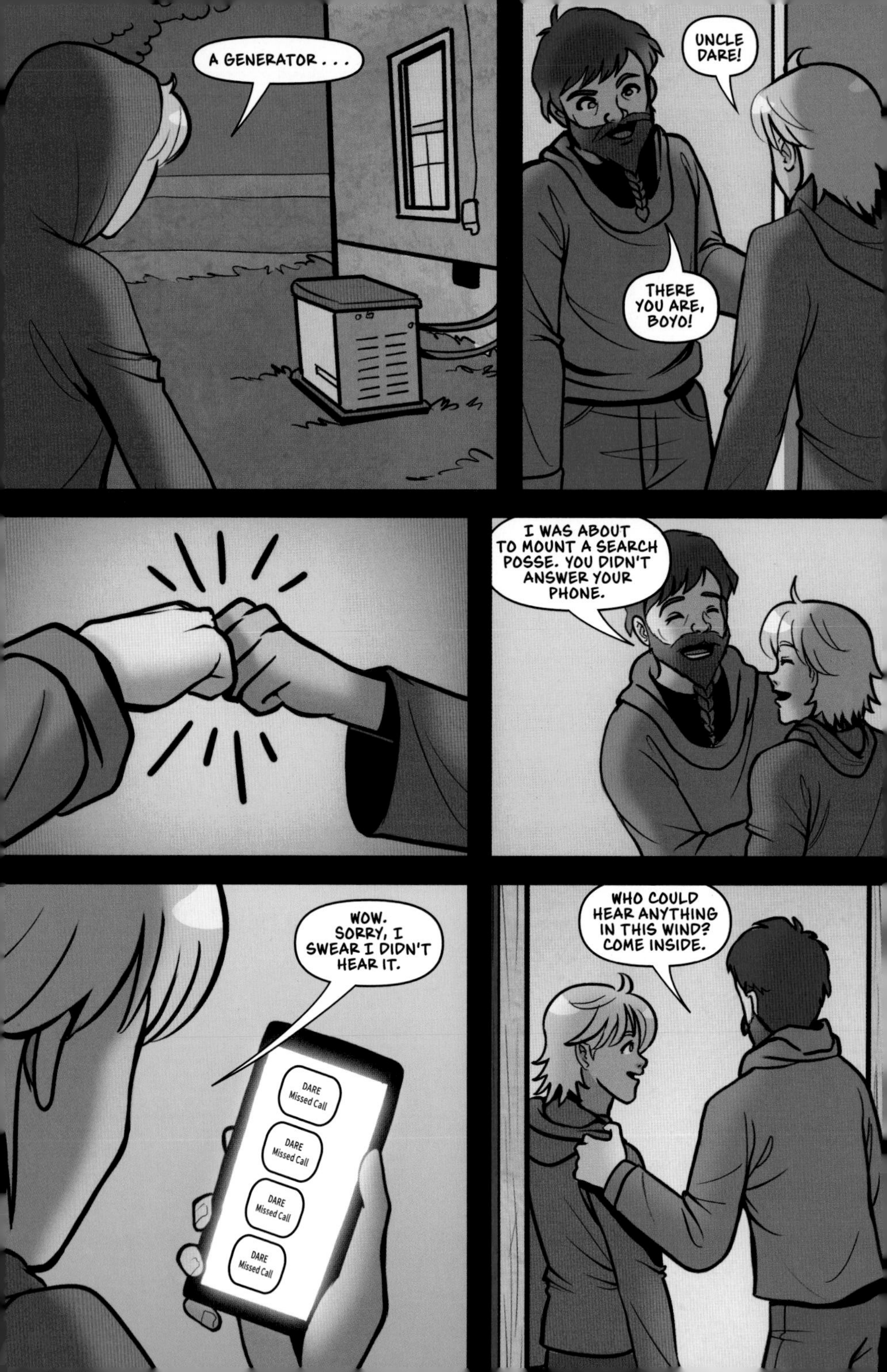
A GENERATOR . . .
UNCLE DARE!
THERE YOU ARE, BOYO!
I WAS ABOUT TO MOUNT A SEARCH POSSE. YOU DIDN'T ANSWER YOUR PHONE.
WOW. SORRY, I SWEAR I DIDN'T HEAR IT.
DARE Missed Call
DARE Missed Call
DARE Missed Call
DARE Missed Call
WHO COULD HEAR ANYTHING IN THIS WIND? COME INSIDE.

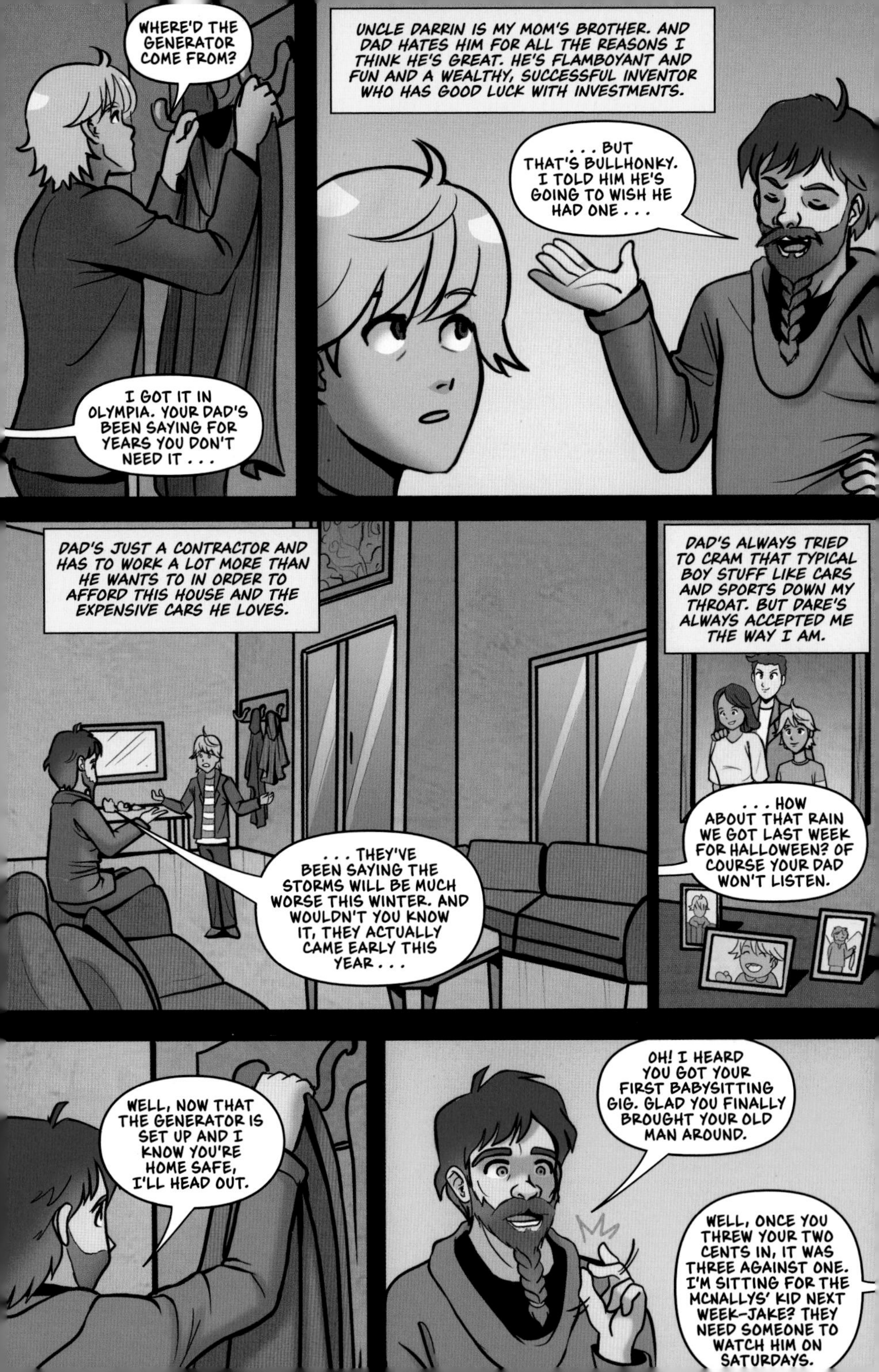
WHERE'D THE GENERATOR COME FROM?
I GOT IT IN OLYMPIA. YOUR DAD'S BEEN SAYING FOR YEARS YOU DON'T NEED IT . . .
UNCLE DARRIN IS MY MOM'S BROTHER. AND DAD HATES HIM FOR ALL THE REASONS I THINK HE'S GREAT. HE'S FLAMBOYANT AND FUN AND A WEALTHY, SUCCESSFUL INVENTOR WHO HAS GOOD LUCK WITH INVESTMENTS.
. . . BUT THAT'S BULLHONKY. I TOLD HIM HE'S GOING TO WISH HE HAD ONE . . .
DAD'S JUST A CONTRACTOR AND HAS TO WORK A LOT MORE THAN HE WANTS TO IN ORDER TO AFFORD THIS HOUSE AND THE EXPENSIVE CARS HE LOVES.
. . . THEY'VE BEEN SAYING THE STORMS WILL BE MUCH WORSE THIS WINTER. AND WOULDN'T YOU KNOW IT, THEY ACTUALLY CAME EARLY THIS YEAR . . .
DAD'S ALWAYS TRIED TO CRAM THAT TYPICAL BOY STUFF LIKE CARS AND SPORTS DOWN MY THROAT. BUT DARE'S ALWAYS ACCEPTED ME THE WAY I AM.
. . . HOW ABOUT THAT RAIN WE GOT LAST WEEK FOR HALLOWEEN? OF COURSE YOUR DAD WON'T LISTEN.
WELL, NOW THAT THE GENERATOR IS SET UP AND I KNOW YOU'RE HOME SAFE, I'LL HEAD OUT.
OH! I HEARD YOU GOT YOUR FIRST BABYSITTING GIG. GLAD YOU FINALLY BROUGHT YOUR OLD MAN AROUND.
WELL, ONCE YOU THREW YOUR TWO CENTS IN, IT WAS THREE AGAINST ONE. I'M SITTING FOR THE MCNALLYS' KID NEXT WEEK—JAKE? THEY NEED SOMEONE TO WATCH HIM ON SATURDAYS.

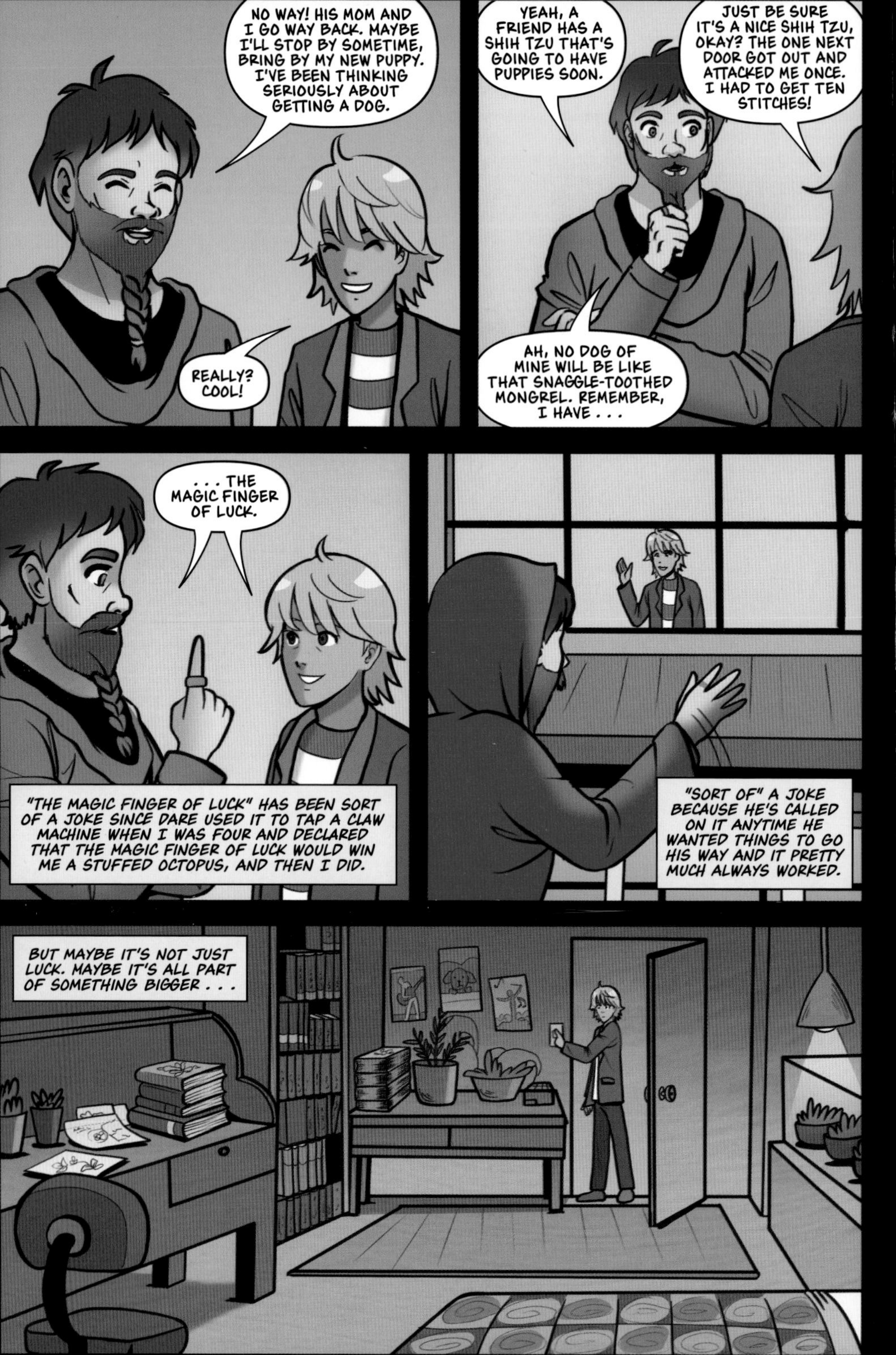
NO WAY! HIS MOM AND I GO WAY BACK. MAYBE I'LL STOP BY SOMETIME, BRING BY MY NEW PUPPY. I'VE BEEN THINKING SERIOUSLY ABOUT GETTING A DOG.
REALLY? COOL!
YEAH, A FRIEND HAS A SHIH TZU THAT'S GOING TO HAVE PUPPIES SOON.
JUST BE SURE IT'S A NICE SHIH TZU, OKAY? THE ONE NEXT DOOR GOT OUT AND ATTACKED ME ONCE. I HAD TO GET TEN STITCHES!
AH, NO DOG OF MINE WILL BE LIKE THAT SNAGGLE-TOOTHED MONGREL. REMEMBER, I HAVE . . .
. . . THE MAGIC FINGER OF LUCK.
"THE MAGIC FINGER OF LUCK" HAS BEEN SORT OF A JOKE SINCE DARE USED IT TO TAP A CLAW MACHINE WHEN I WAS FOUR AND DECLARED THAT THE MAGIC FINGER OF LUCK WOULD WIN ME A STUFFED OCTOPUS, AND THEN I DID.
"SORT OF" A JOKE BECAUSE HE'S CALLED ON IT ANYTIME HE WANTED THINGS TO GO HIS WAY AND IT PRETTY MUCH ALWAYS WORKED.
BUT MAYBE IT'S NOT JUST LUCK. MAYBE IT'S ALL PART OF SOMETHING BIGGER . . .

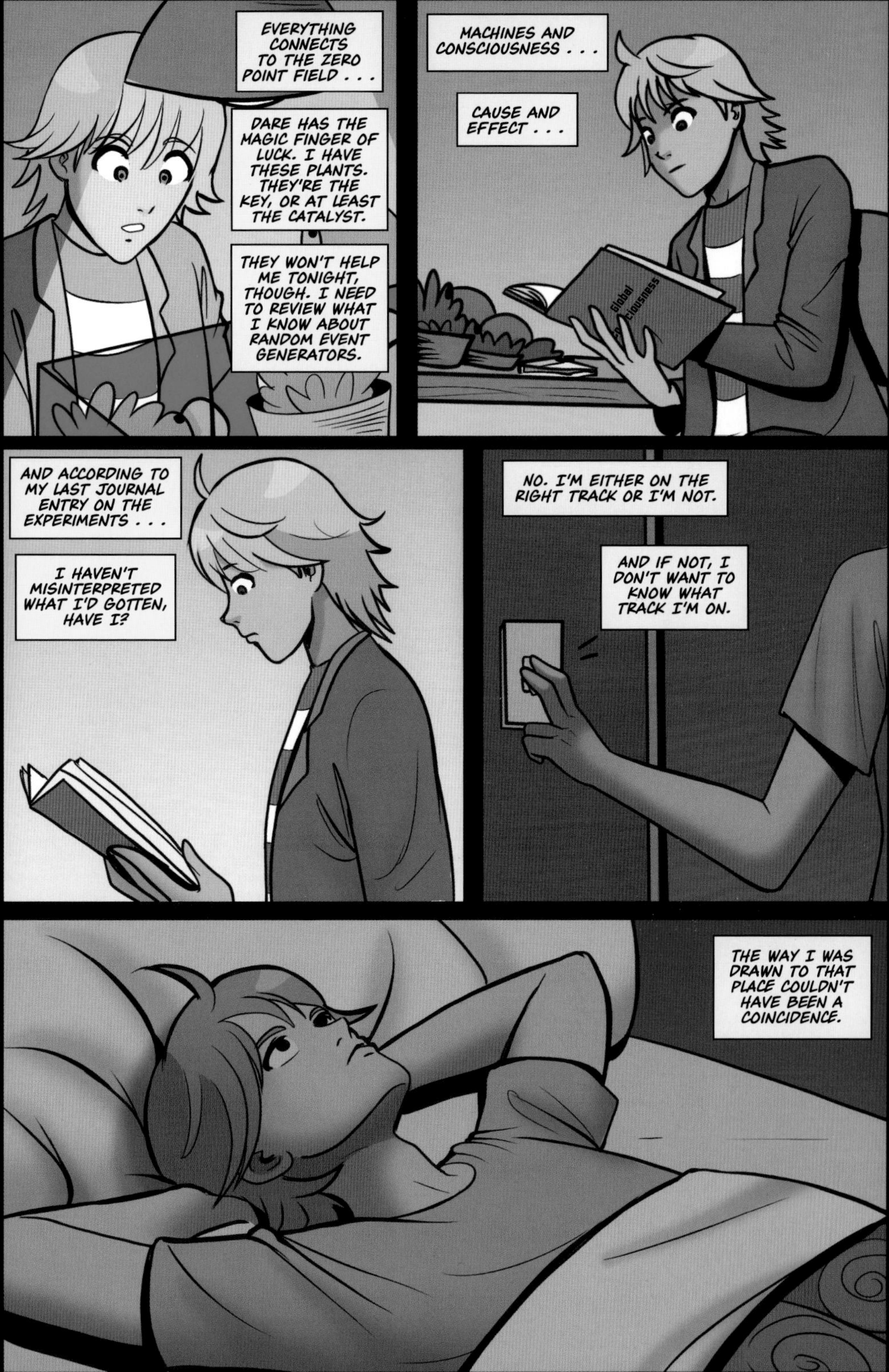
EVERYTHING CONNECTS TO THE ZERO POINT FIELD . . .
DARE HAS THE MAGIC FINGER OF LUCK. I HAVE THESE PLANTS. THEY'RE THE KEY, OR AT LEAST THE CATALYST.
THEY WON'T HELP ME TONIGHT, THOUGH. I NEED TO REVIEW WHAT I KNOW ABOUT RANDOM EVENT GENERATORS.
MACHINES AND CONSCIOUSNESS . . .
CAUSE AND EFFECT . . .
AND ACCORDING TO MY LAST JOURNAL ENTRY ON THE EXPERIMENTS . . .
I HAVEN'T MISINTERPRETED WHAT I'D GOTTEN, HAVE I?
NO. I'M EITHER ON THE RIGHT TRACK OR I'M NOT.
AND IF NOT, I DON'T WANT TO KNOW WHAT TRACK I'M ON.
THE WAY I WAS DRAWN TO THAT PLACE COULDN'T HAVE BEEN A COINCIDENCE.

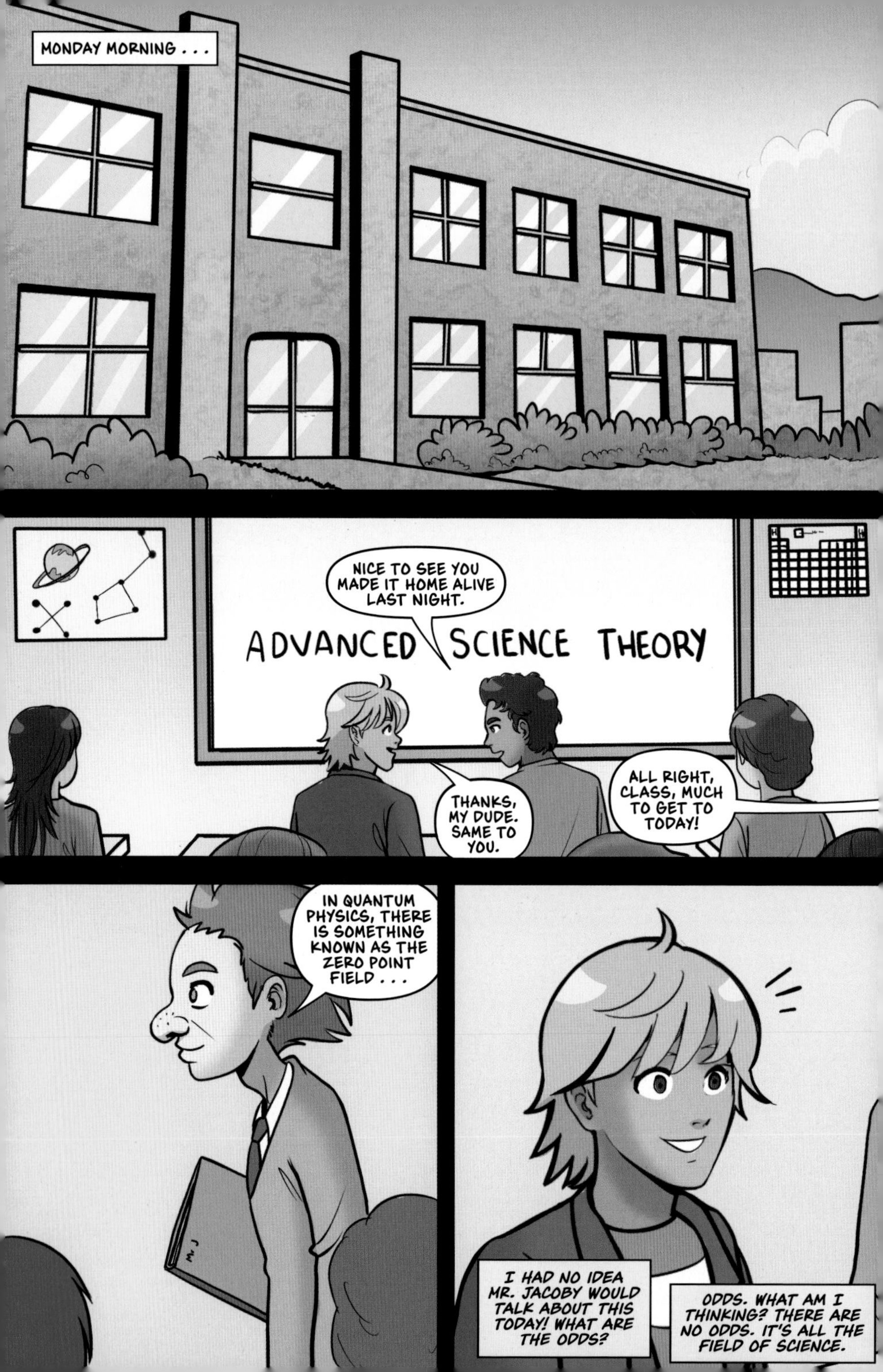
MONDAY MORNING . . .
NICE TO SEE YOU MADE IT HOME ALIVE LAST NIGHT.
ADVANCED SCIENCE THEORY
THANKS, MY DUDE. SAME TO YOU.
ALL RIGHT, CLASS, MUCH TO GET TO TODAY!
IN QUANTUM PHYSICS, THERE IS SOMETHING KNOWN AS THE ZERO POINT FIELD . . .
I HAD NO IDEA MR. JACOBY WOULD TALK ABOUT THIS TODAY! WHAT ARE THE ODDS?
ODDS. WHAT AM I THINKING? THERE ARE NO ODDS. IT'S ALL THE FIELD OF SCIENCE.

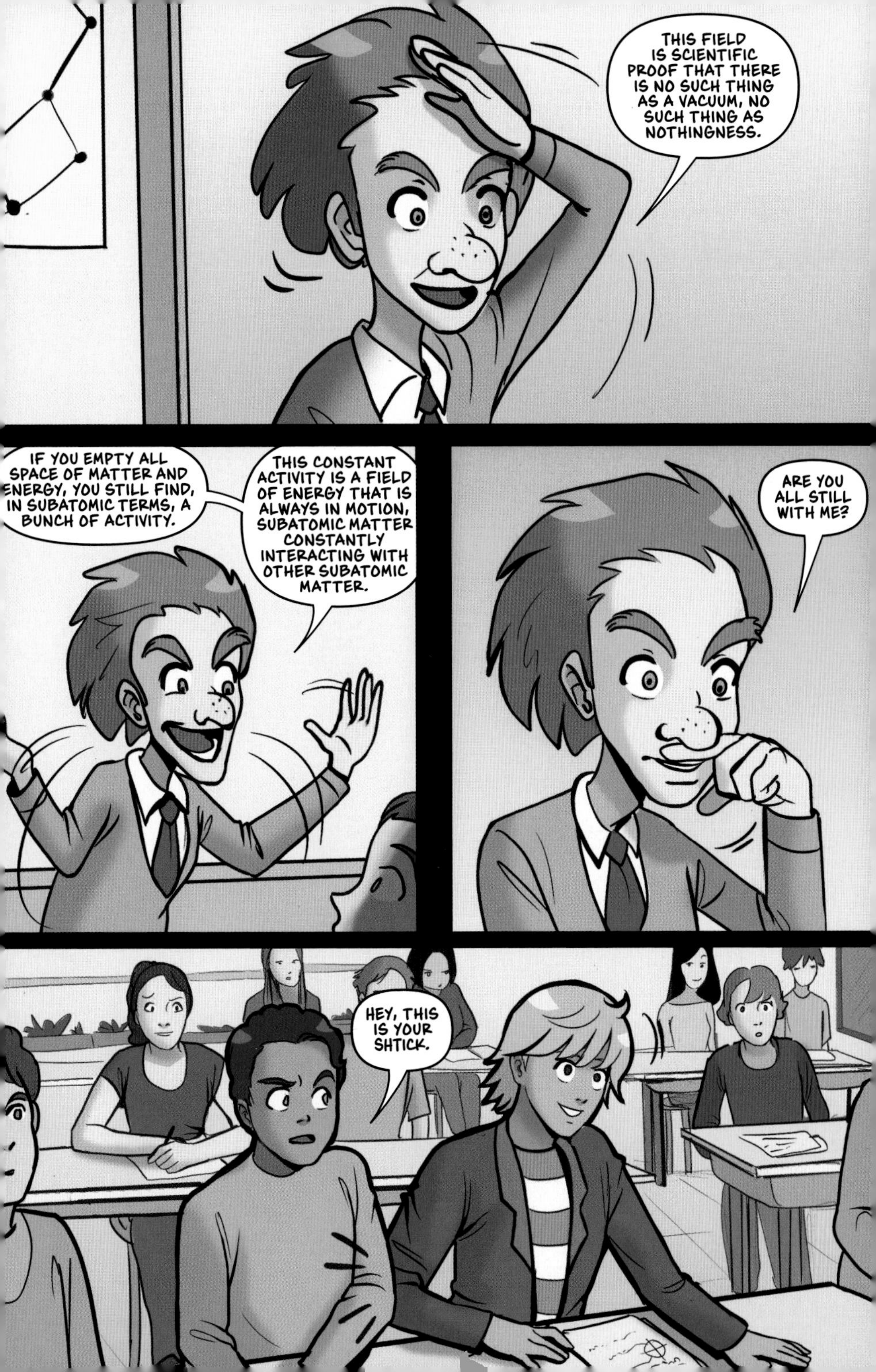
THIS FIELD IS SCIENTIFIC PROOF THAT THERE IS NO SUCH THING AS A VACUUM, NO SUCH THING AS NOTHINGNESS.
IF YOU EMPTY ALL SPACE OF MATTER AND ENERGY, YOU STILL FIND, IN SUBATOMIC TERMS, A BUNCH OF ACTIVITY.
THIS CONSTANT ACTIVITY IS A FIELD OF ENERGY THAT IS ALWAYS IN MOTION, SUBATOMIC MATTER CONSTANTLY INTERACTING WITH OTHER SUBATOMIC MATTER.
ARE YOU ALL STILL WITH ME?
HEY, THIS IS YOUR SHTICK.

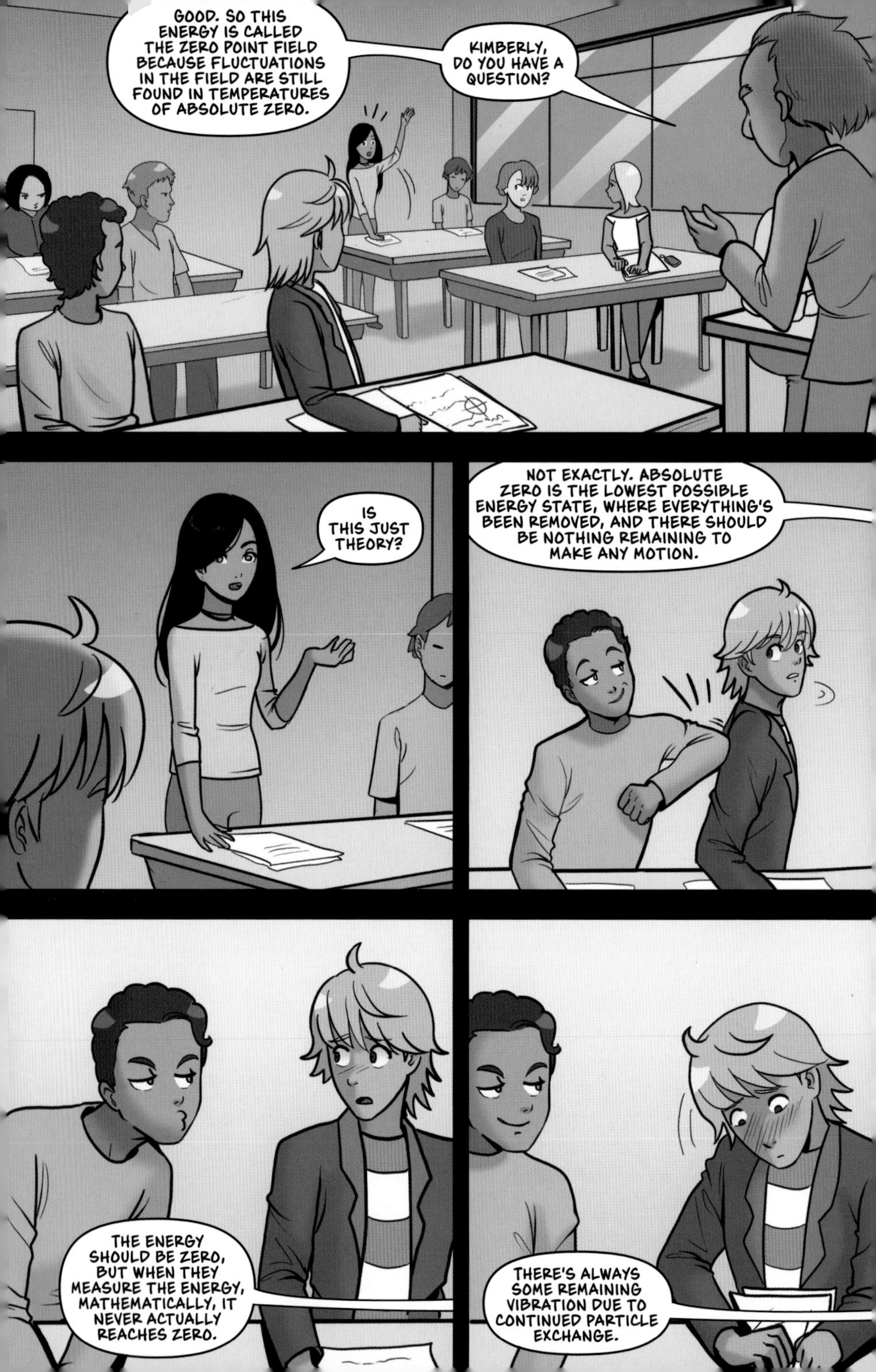
GOOD. SO THIS ENERGY IS CALLED THE ZERO POINT FIELD BECAUSE FLUCTUATIONS IN THE FIELD ARE STILL FOUND IN TEMPERATURES OF ABSOLUTE ZERO.
KIMBERLY, DO YOU HAVE A QUESTION?
IS THIS JUST THEORY?
NOT EXACTLY. ABSOLUTE ZERO IS THE LOWEST POSSIBLE ENERGY STATE, WHERE EVERYTHING'S BEEN REMOVED, AND THERE SHOULD BE NOTHING REMAINING TO MAKE ANY MOTION.
THE ENERGY SHOULD BE ZERO, BUT WHEN THEY MEASURE THE ENERGY, MATHEMATICALLY, IT NEVER ACTUALLY REACHES ZERO.
THERE'S ALWAYS SOME REMAINING VIBRATION DUE TO CONTINUED PARTICLE EXCHANGE.

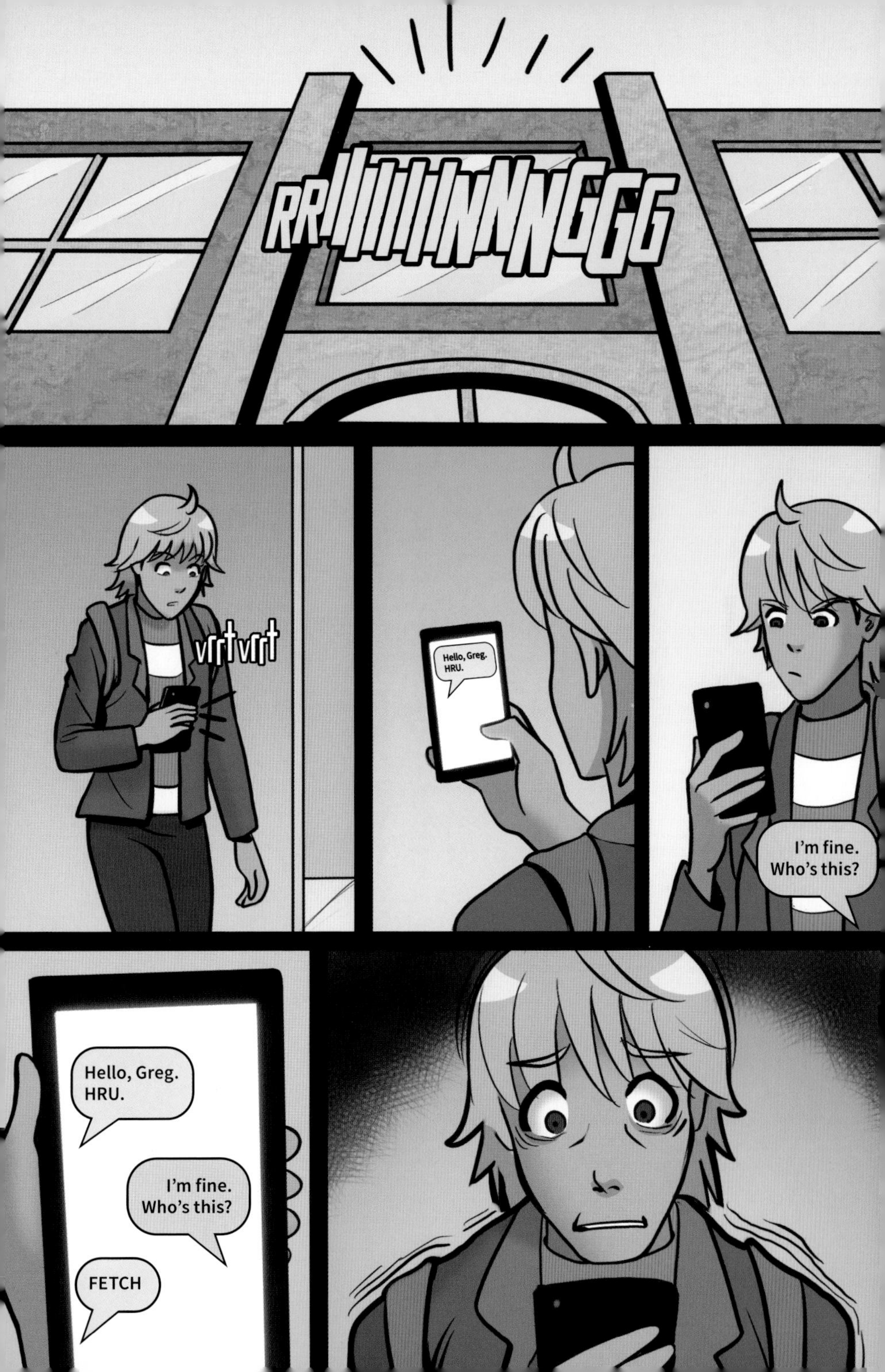
RRIIIIIIIINNNGGG
vrrt vrrt
Hello, Greg.
HRU.
I'm fine.
Who's this?
Hello, Greg.
HRU.
I'm fine.
Who's this?
FETCH

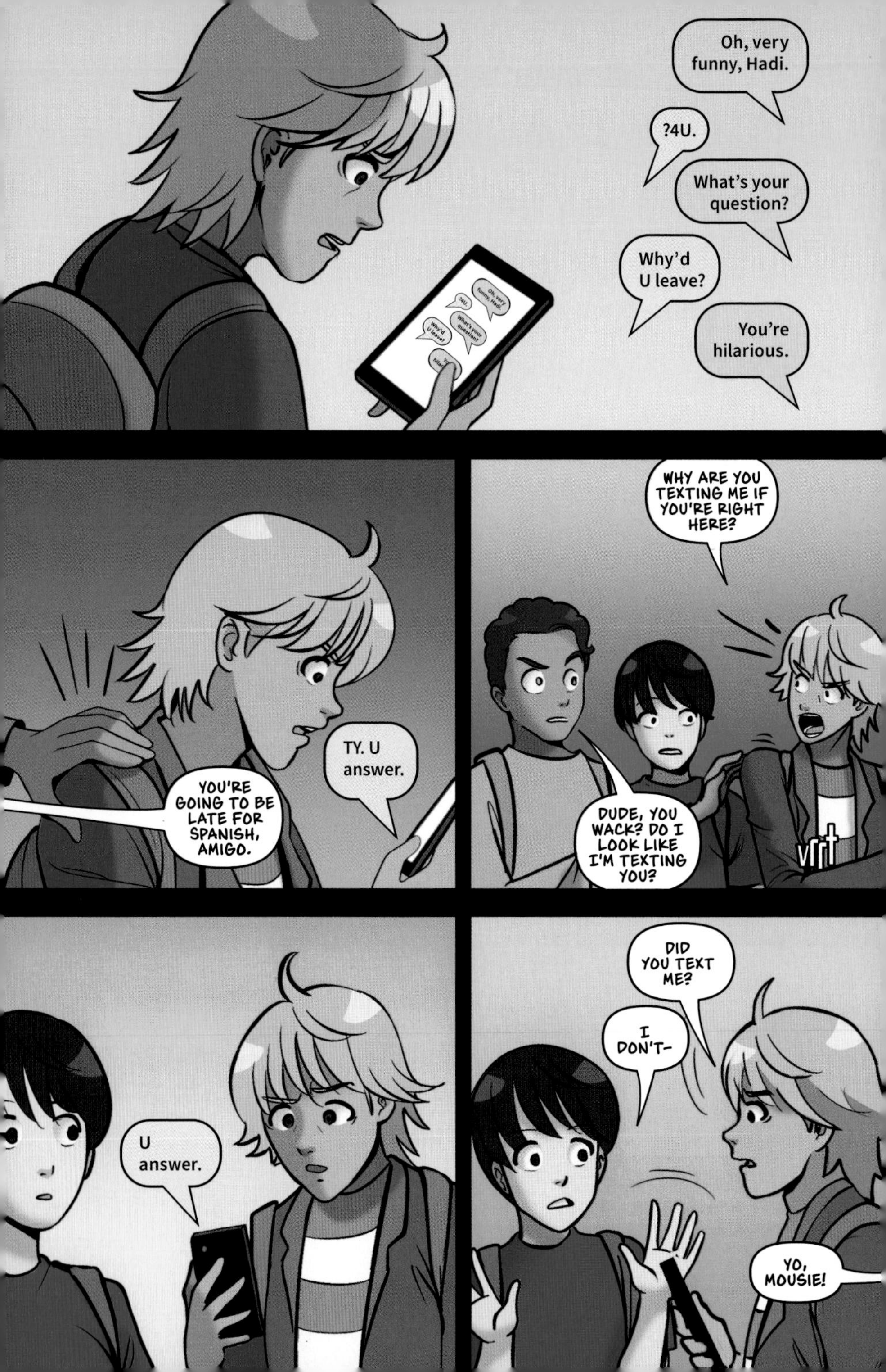
Oh, very funny, Hadi.
?4U.
What's your question?
Why'd U leave?
You're hilarious.
YOU'RE GOING TO BE LATE FOR SPANISH, AMIGO.
TY. U answer.
WHY ARE YOU TEXTING ME IF YOU'RE RIGHT HERE?
DUDE, YOU WACK? DO I LOOK LIKE I'M TEXTING YOU?
VRRT
U answer.
DID YOU TEXT ME?
I DON'T—
YO, MOUSIE!

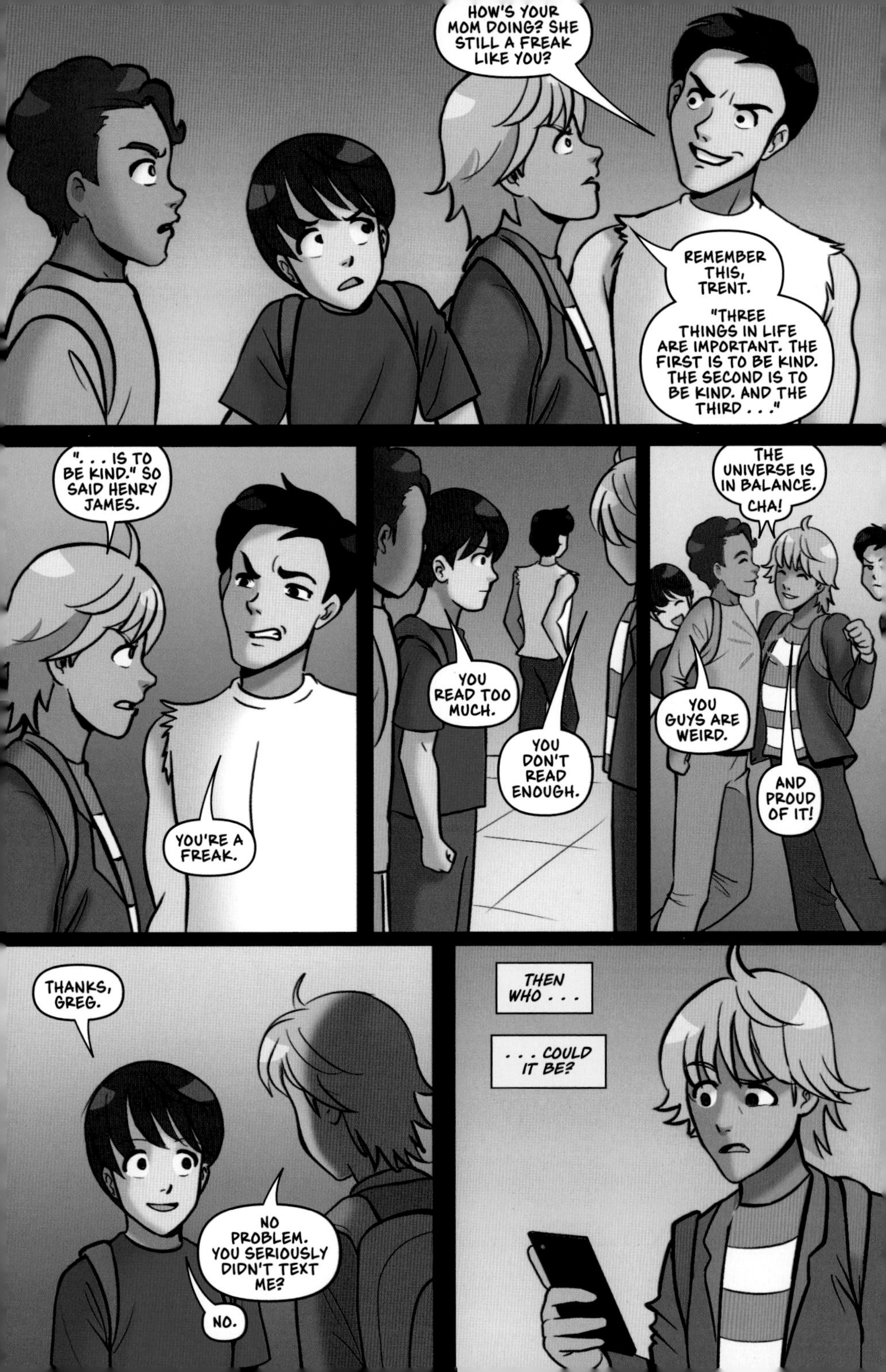
HOW'S YOUR MOM DOING? SHE STILL A FREAK LIKE YOU?
REMEMBER THIS, TRENT.
"THREE THINGS IN LIFE ARE IMPORTANT. THE FIRST IS TO BE KIND. THE SECOND IS TO BE KIND. AND THE THIRD . . ."
". . . IS TO BE KIND." SO SAID HENRY JAMES.
YOU'RE A FREAK.
YOU READ TOO MUCH.
YOU DON'T READ ENOUGH.
THE UNIVERSE IS IN BALANCE.
CHA!
YOU GUYS ARE WEIRD.
AND PROUD OF IT!
THANKS, GREG.
NO PROBLEM. YOU SERIOUSLY DIDN'T TEXT ME?
NO.
THEN WHO . . .
. . . COULD IT BE?

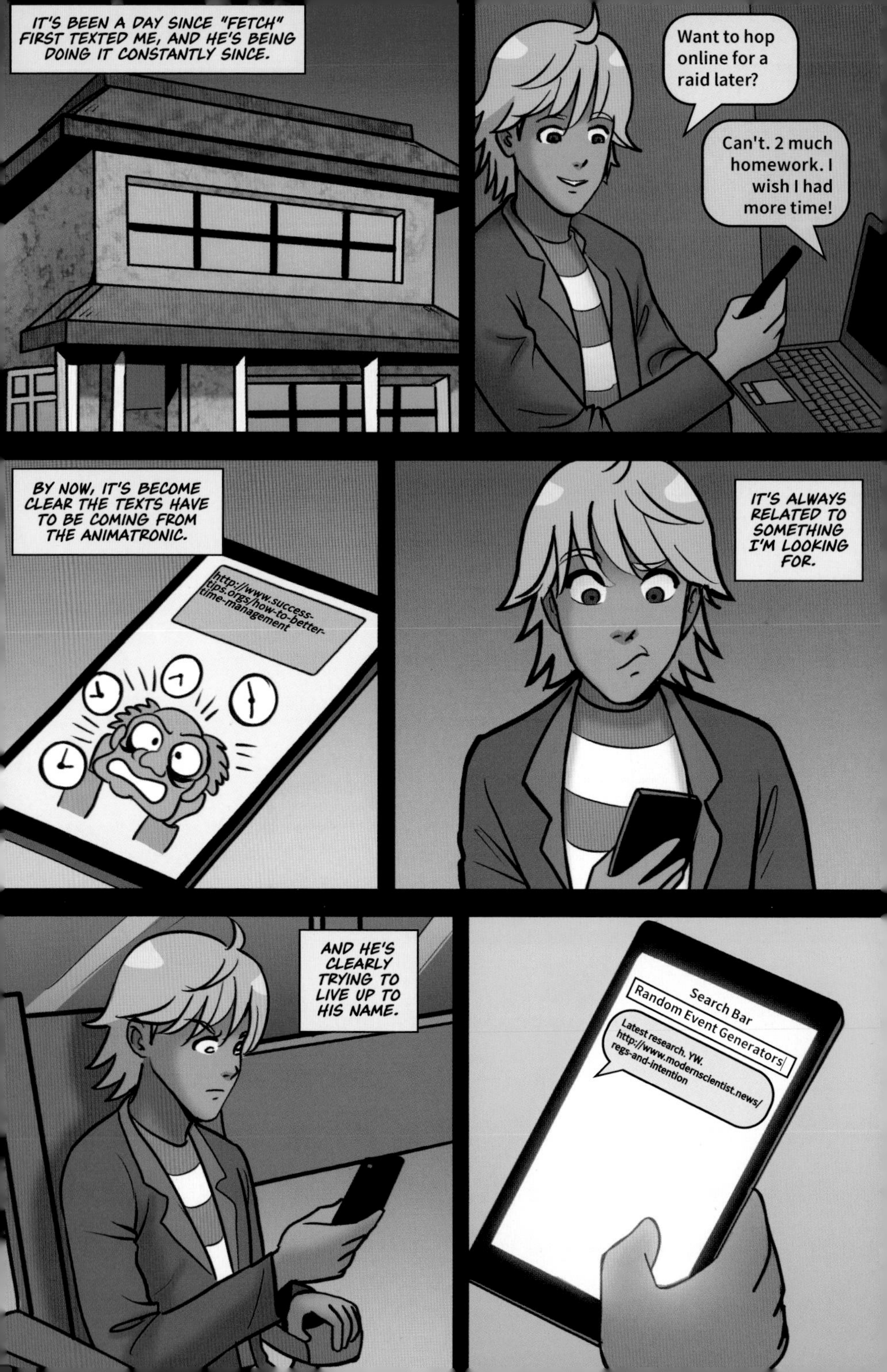
IT'S BEEN A DAY SINCE "FETCH" FIRST TEXTED ME, AND HE'S BEING DOING IT CONSTANTLY SINCE.
Want to hop online for a raid later?
Can't. 2 much homework. I wish I had more time!
BY NOW, IT'S BECOME CLEAR THE TEXTS HAVE TO BE COMING FROM THE ANIMATRONIC.
http://www.success-tips.orgs/how-to-better-time-management
IT'S ALWAYS RELATED TO SOMETHING I'M LOOKING FOR.
AND HE'S CLEARLY TRYING TO LIVE UP TO HIS NAME.
Search Bar
Random Event Generators
Latest research. YW. http://www.modernscientist.news/regs-and-intention

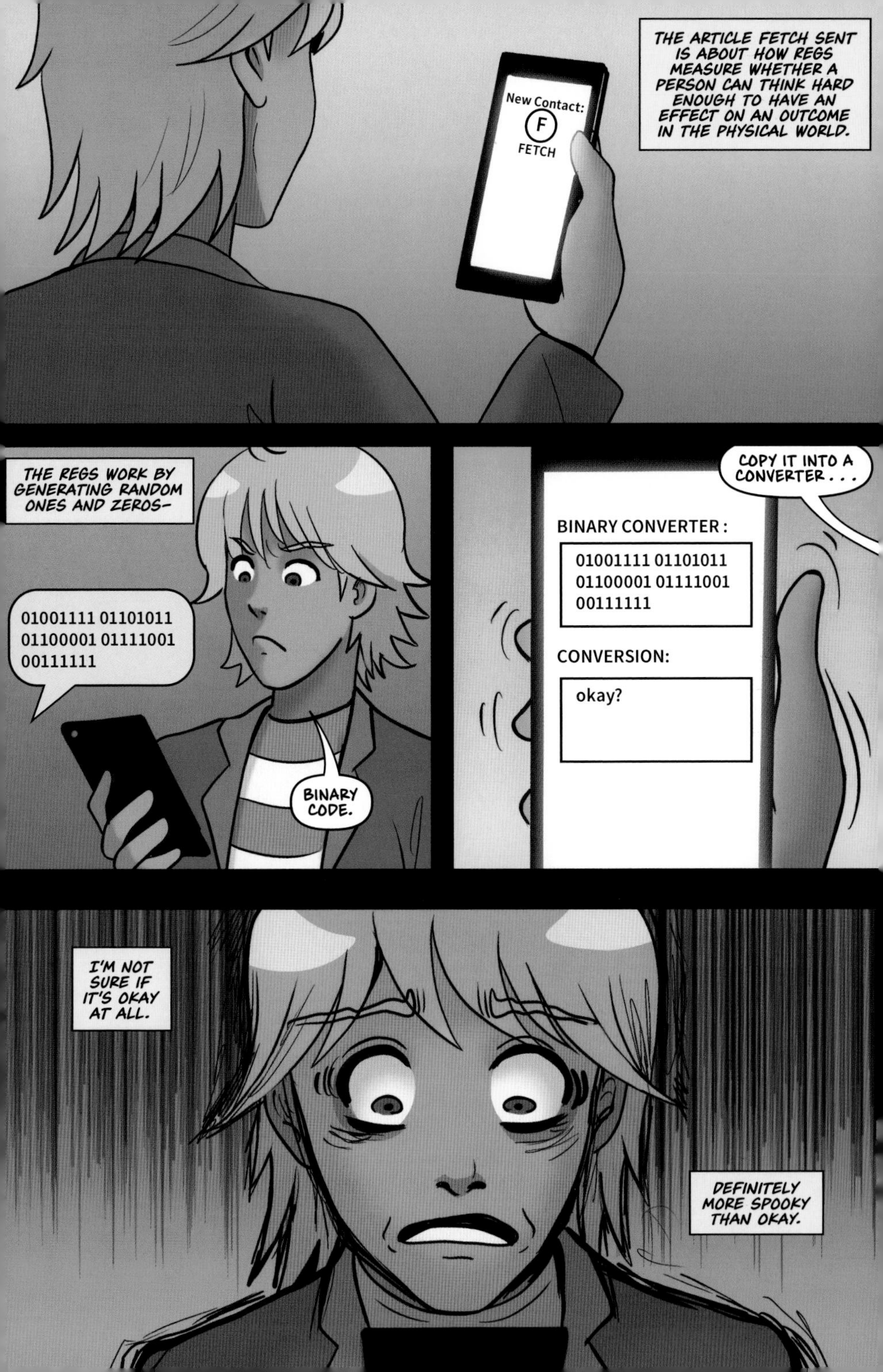
New Contact:
F
FETCH
THE ARTICLE FETCH SENT IS ABOUT HOW REGS MEASURE WHETHER A PERSON CAN THINK HARD ENOUGH TO HAVE AN EFFECT ON AN OUTCOME IN THE PHYSICAL WORLD.
THE REGS WORK BY GENERATING RANDOM ONES AND ZEROS-
01001111 01101011 01100001 01111001 00111111
BINARY CODE.
COPY IT INTO A CONVERTER . . .
BINARY CONVERTER :
01001111 01101011 01100001 01111001 00111111
CONVERSION:
okay?
I'M NOT SURE IF IT'S OKAY AT ALL.
DEFINITELY MORE SPOOKY THAN OKAY.

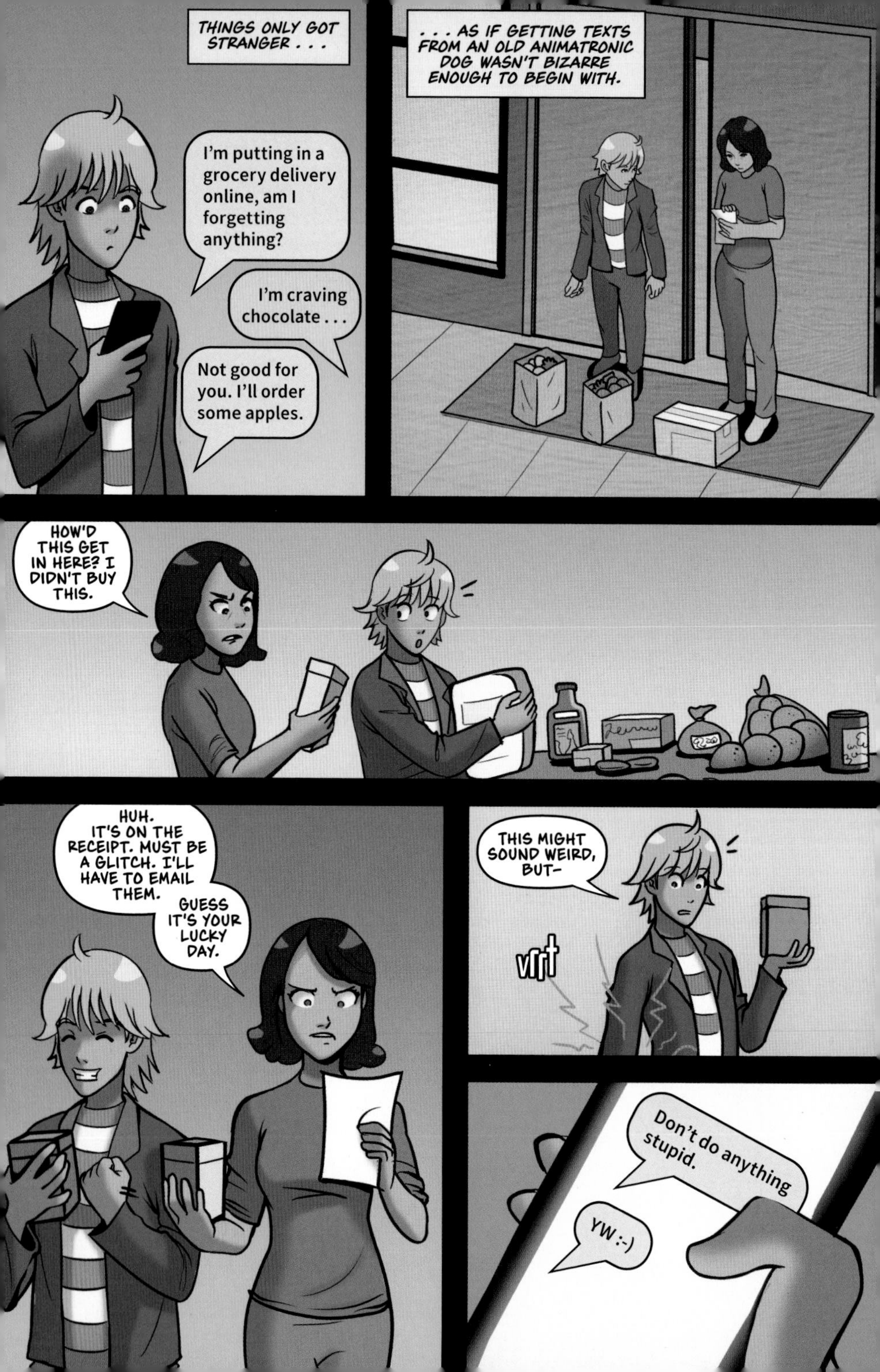
THINGS ONLY GOT STRANGER . . .
I'm putting in a grocery delivery online, am I forgetting anything?
I'm craving chocolate . . .
Not good for you. I'll order some apples.
. . . AS IF GETTING TEXTS FROM AN OLD ANIMATRONIC DOG WASN'T BIZARRE ENOUGH TO BEGIN WITH.
HOW'D THIS GET IN HERE? I DIDN'T BUY THIS.
HUH. IT'S ON THE RECEIPT. MUST BE A GLITCH. I'LL HAVE TO EMAIL THEM.
GUESS IT'S YOUR LUCKY DAY.
THIS MIGHT SOUND WEIRD, BUT-
vrrt
Don't do anything stupid.
YW :-)

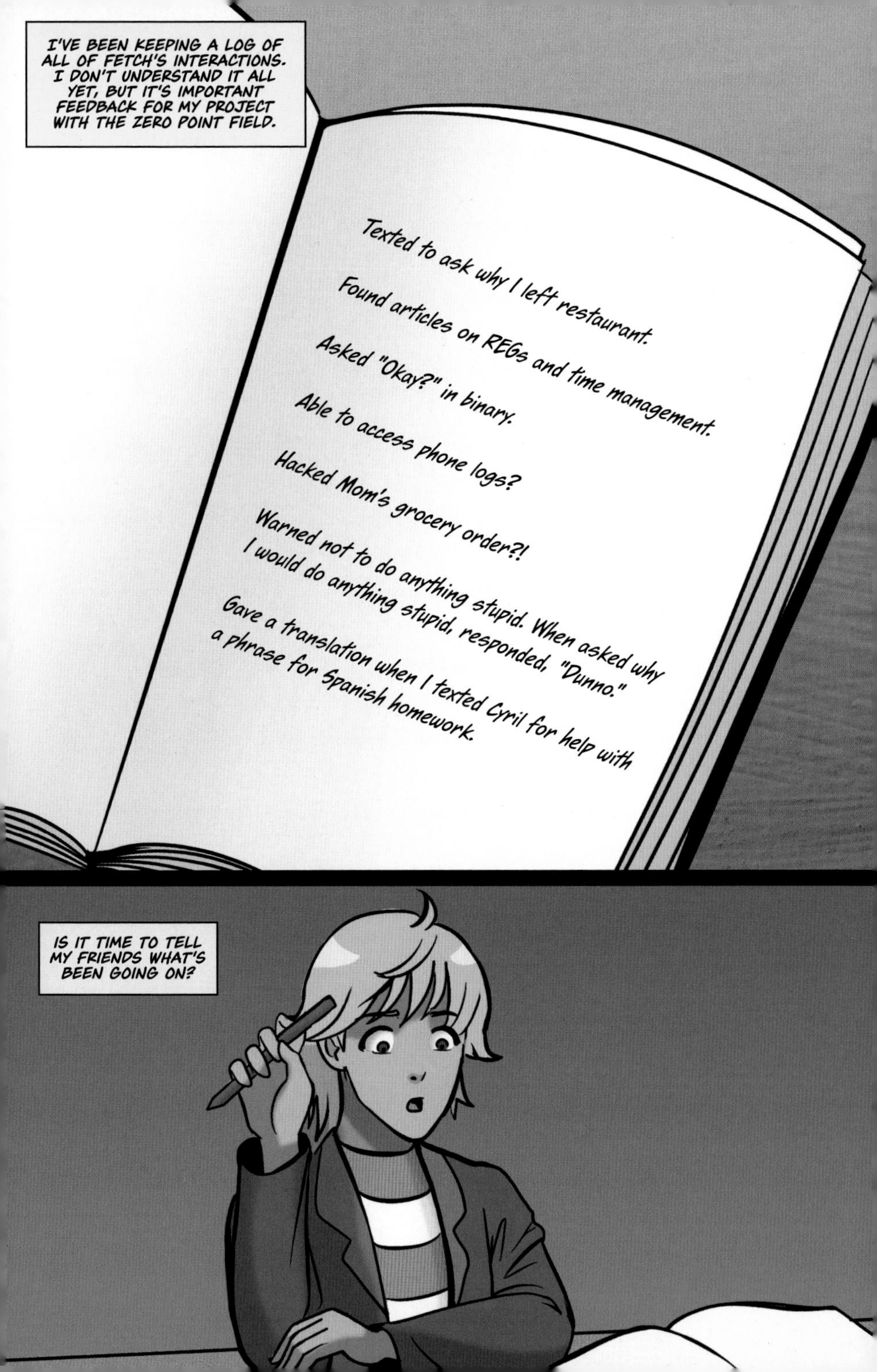

I'VE BEEN KEEPING A LOG OF ALL OF FETCH'S INTERACTIONS. I DON'T UNDERSTAND IT ALL YET, BUT IT'S IMPORTANT FEEDBACK FOR MY PROJECT WITH THE ZERO POINT FIELD.
Texted to ask why I left restaurant.
Found articles on REGs and time management.
Asked "Okay?" in binary.
Able to access phone logs?
Hacked Mom's grocery order?!
Warned not to do anything stupid. When asked why I would do anything stupid, responded, "Dunno."
Gave a translation when I texted Cyril for help with a phrase for Spanish homework.
IS IT TIME TO TELL MY FRIENDS WHAT'S BEEN GOING ON?

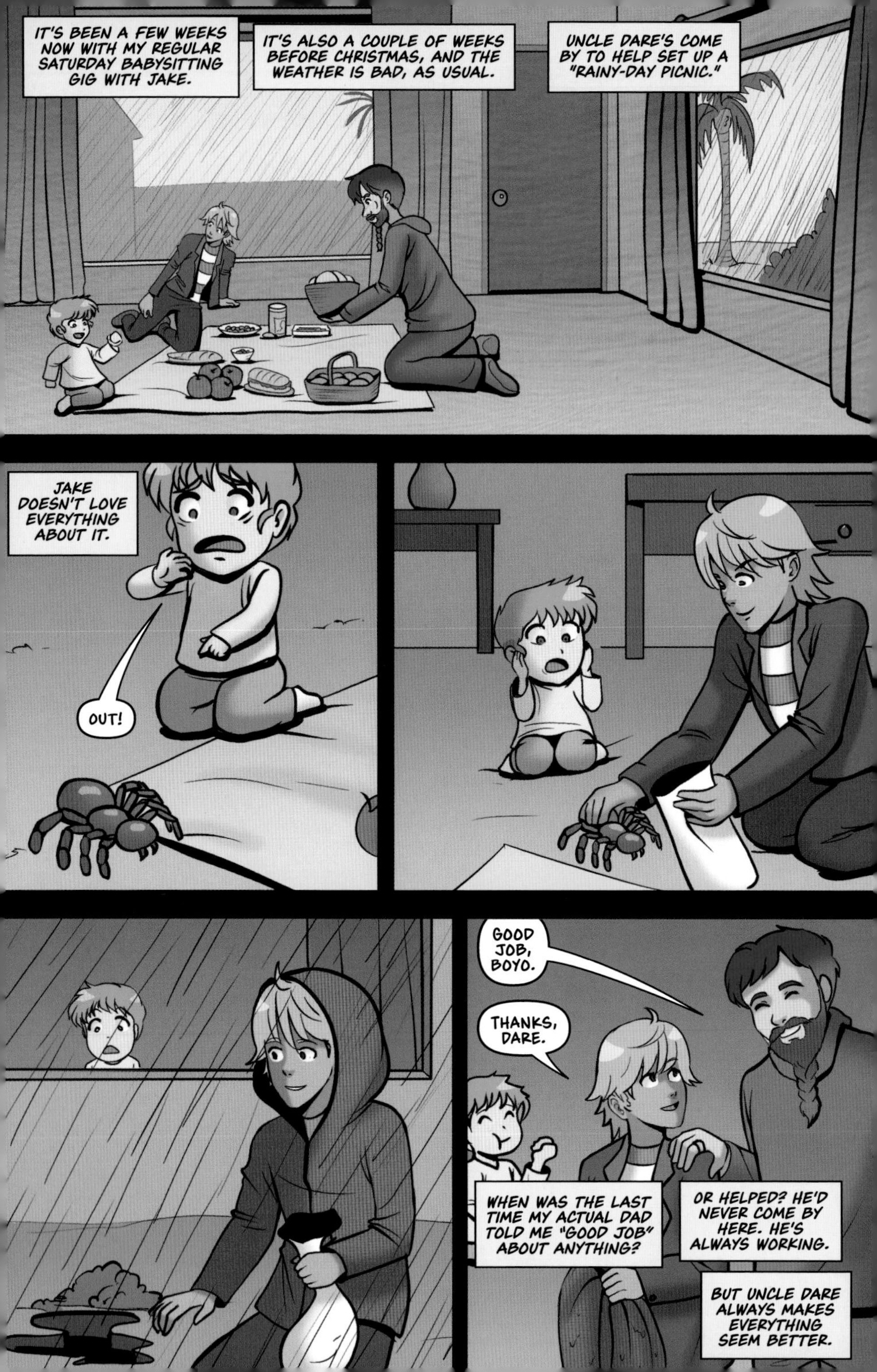
IT'S BEEN A FEW WEEKS NOW WITH MY REGULAR SATURDAY BABYSITTING GIG WITH JAKE.
IT'S ALSO A COUPLE OF WEEKS BEFORE CHRISTMAS, AND THE WEATHER IS BAD, AS USUAL.
UNCLE DARE'S COME BY TO HELP SET UP A "RAINY-DAY PICNIC."
JAKE DOESN'T LOVE EVERYTHING ABOUT IT.
OUT!
GOOD JOB, BOYO.
THANKS, DARE.
WHEN WAS THE LAST TIME MY ACTUAL DAD TOLD ME "GOOD JOB" ABOUT ANYTHING?
OR HELPED? HE'D NEVER COME BY HERE. HE'S ALWAYS WORKING.
BUT UNCLE DARE ALWAYS MAKES EVERYTHING SEEM BETTER.

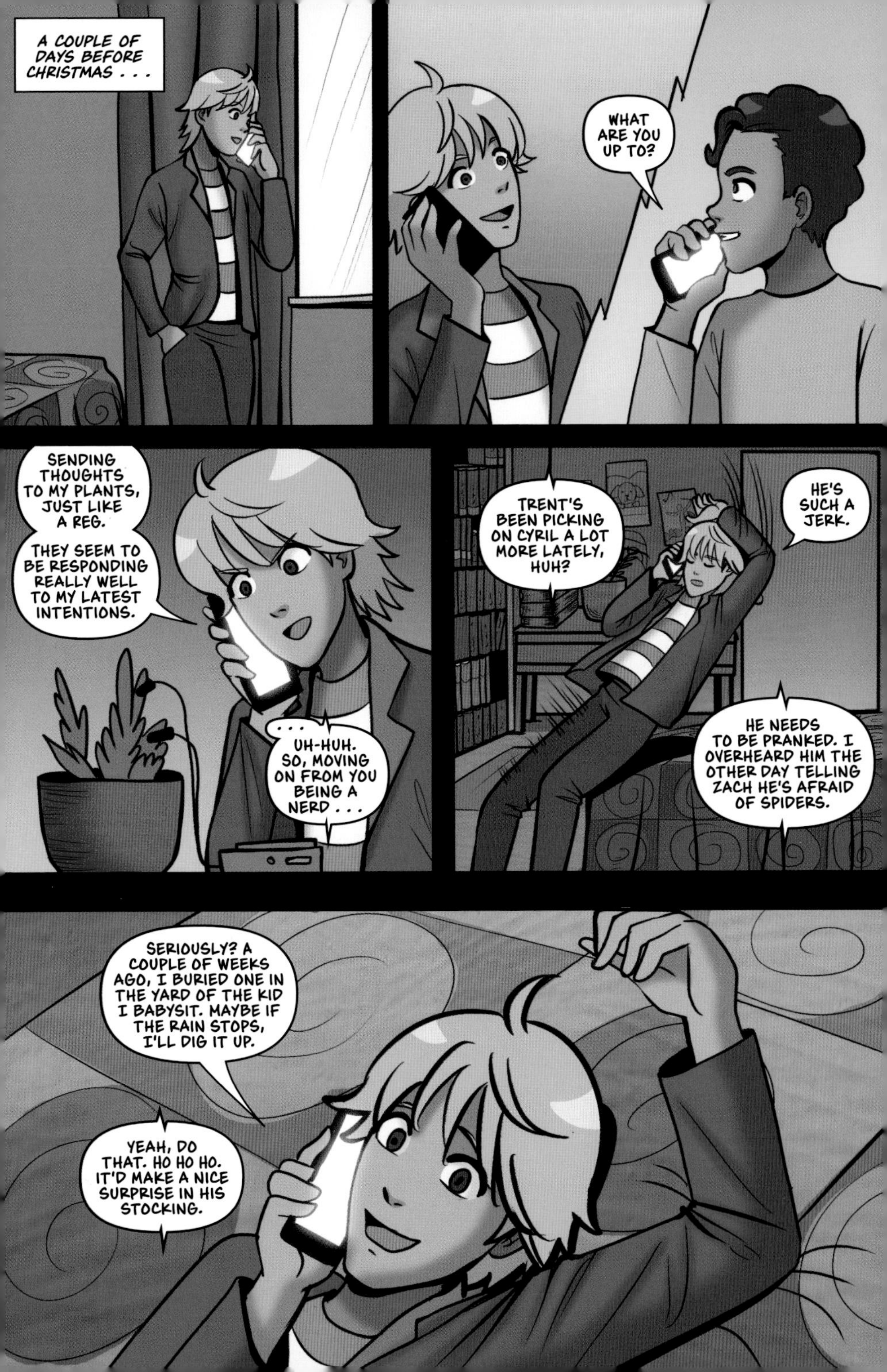
A COUPLE OF DAYS BEFORE CHRISTMAS . . .
WHAT ARE YOU UP TO?
SENDING THOUGHTS TO MY PLANTS, JUST LIKE A REG.
THEY SEEM TO BE RESPONDING REALLY WELL TO MY LATEST INTENTIONS.
. . . UH-HUH. SO, MOVING ON FROM YOU BEING A NERD . . .
TRENT'S BEEN PICKING ON CYRIL A LOT MORE LATELY, HUH?
HE'S SUCH A JERK.
HE NEEDS TO BE PRANKED. I OVERHEARD HIM THE OTHER DAY TELLING ZACH HE'S AFRAID OF SPIDERS.
SERIOUSLY? A COUPLE OF WEEKS AGO, I BURIED ONE IN THE YARD OF THE KID I BABYSIT. MAYBE IF THE RAIN STOPS, I'LL DIG IT UP.
YEAH, DO THAT. HO HO HO. IT'D MAKE A NICE SURPRISE IN HIS STOCKING.

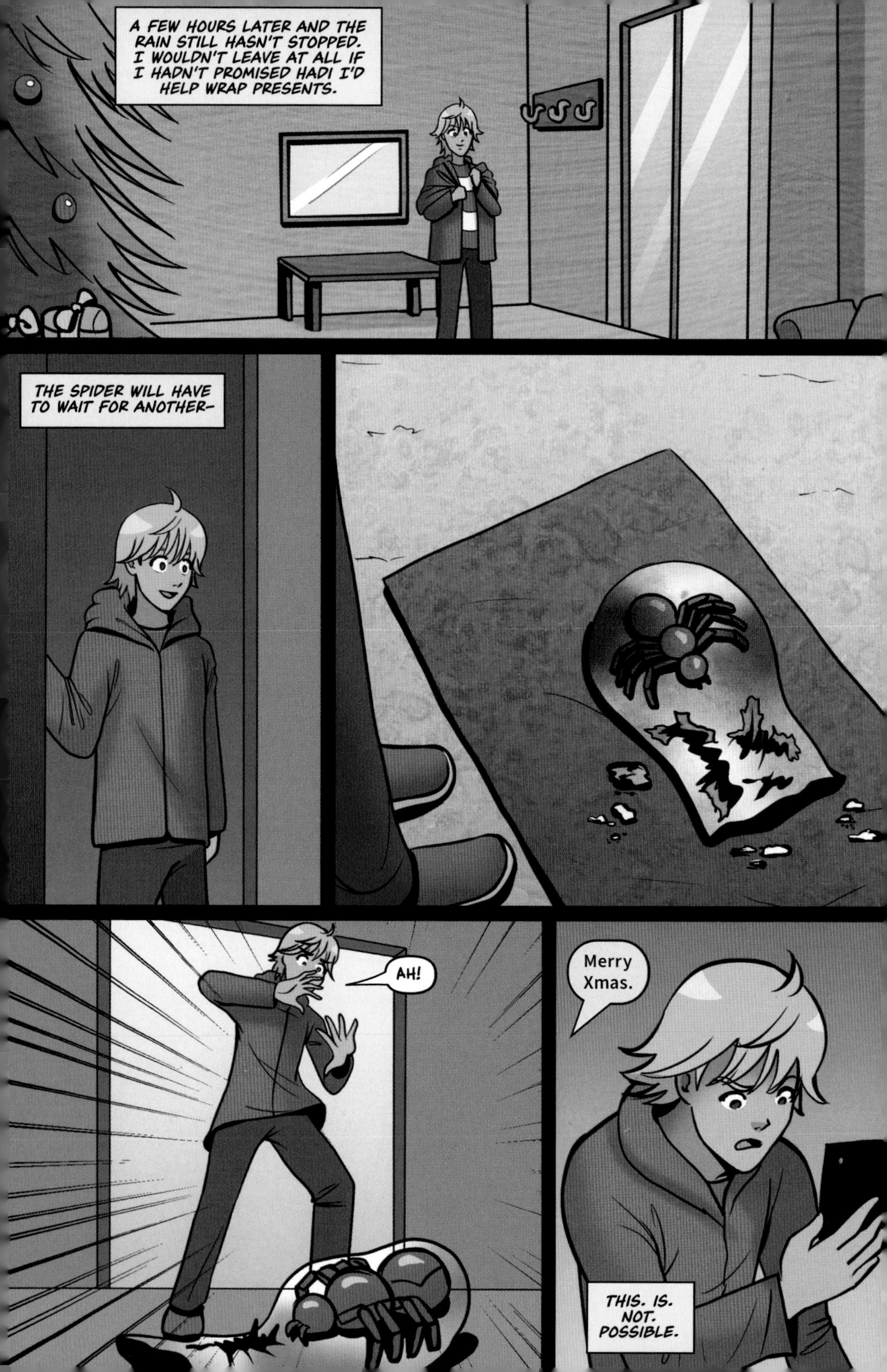
A FEW HOURS LATER AND THE RAIN STILL HASN'T STOPPED. I WOULDN'T LEAVE AT ALL IF I HADN'T PROMISED HADI I'D HELP WRAP PRESENTS.
THE SPIDER WILL HAVE TO WAIT FOR ANOTHER–
AH!
Merry Xmas.
THIS. IS. NOT. POSSIBLE.

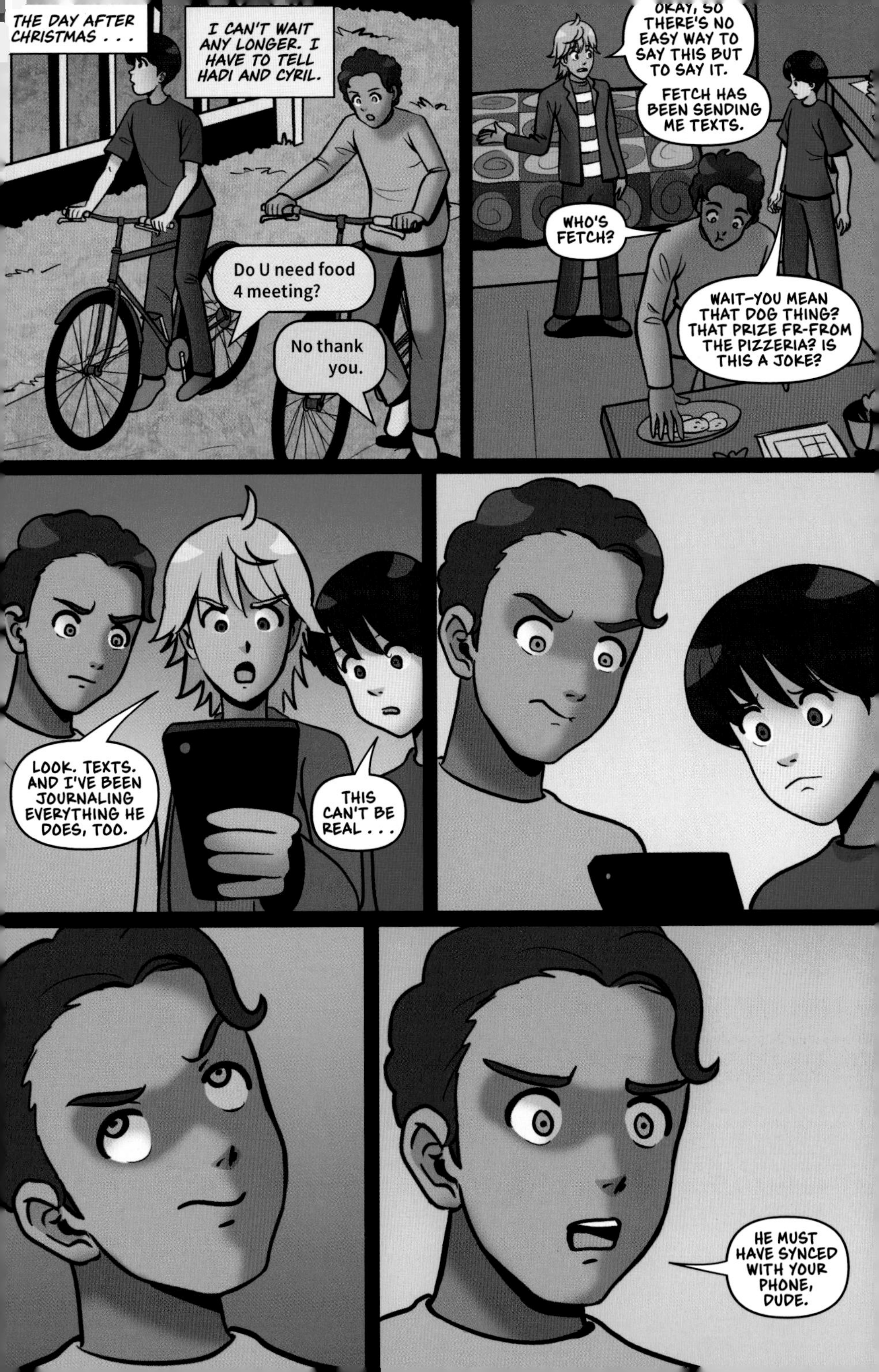
THE DAY AFTER CHRISTMAS . . .
I CAN'T WAIT ANY LONGER. I HAVE TO TELL HADI AND CYRIL.
Do U need food 4 meeting?
No thank you.
OKAY, SO THERE'S NO EASY WAY TO SAY THIS BUT TO SAY IT.
FETCH HAS BEEN SENDING ME TEXTS.
WHO'S FETCH?
WAIT—YOU MEAN THAT DOG THING? THAT PRIZE FR-FROM THE PIZZERIA? IS THIS A JOKE?
LOOK. TEXTS. AND I'VE BEEN JOURNALING EVERYTHING HE DOES, TOO.
THIS CAN'T BE REAL . . .
HE MUST HAVE SYNCED WITH YOUR PHONE, DUDE.

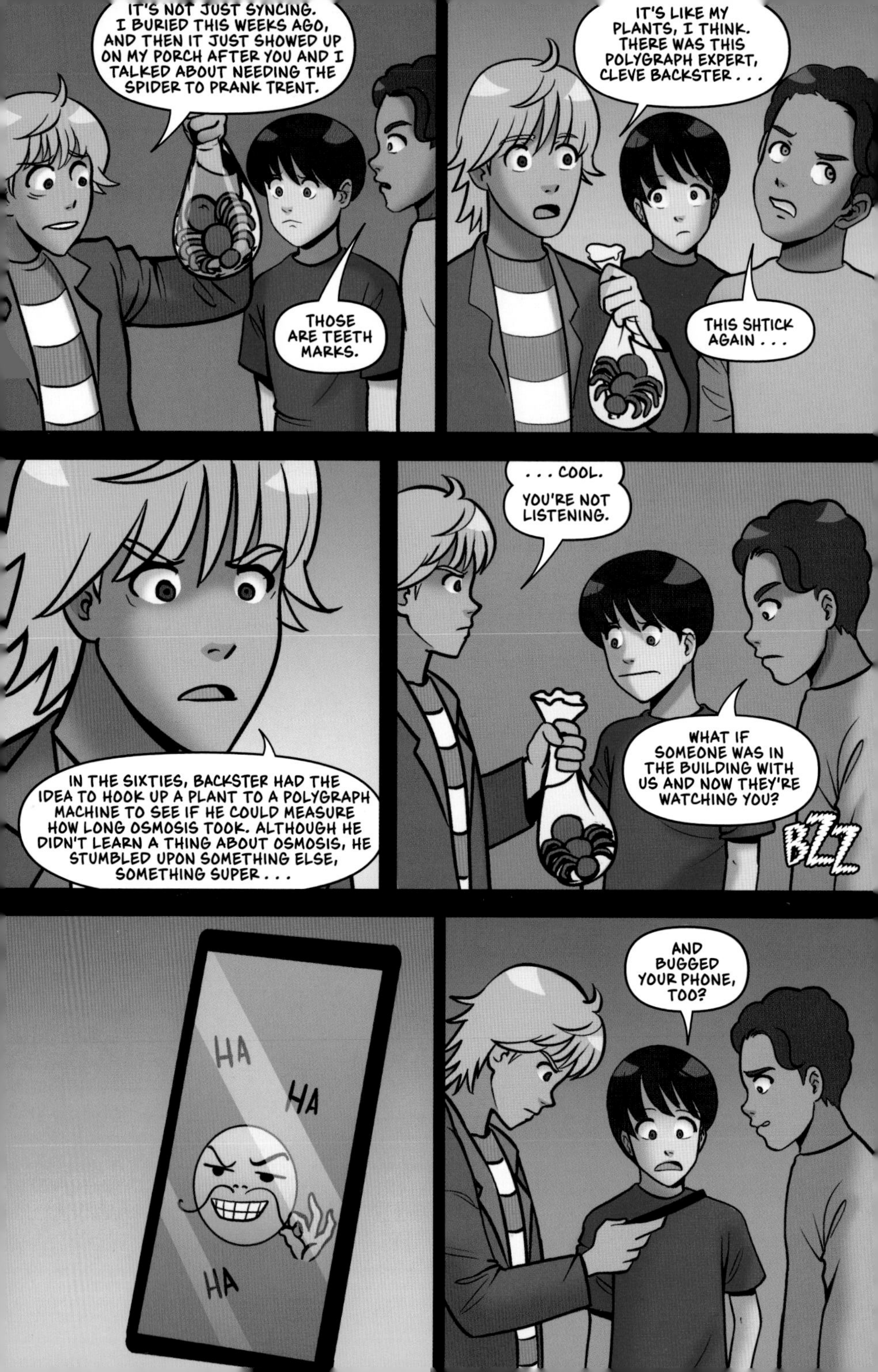
IT'S NOT JUST SYNCING. I BURIED THIS WEEKS AGO, AND THEN IT JUST SHOWED UP ON MY PORCH AFTER YOU AND I TALKED ABOUT NEEDING THE SPIDER TO PRANK TRENT.
THOSE ARE TEETH MARKS.
IT'S LIKE MY PLANTS, I THINK. THERE WAS THIS POLYGRAPH EXPERT, CLEVE BACKSTER . . .
THIS SHTICK AGAIN . . .
IN THE SIXTIES, BACKSTER HAD THE IDEA TO HOOK UP A PLANT TO A POLYGRAPH MACHINE TO SEE IF HE COULD MEASURE HOW LONG OSMOSIS TOOK. ALTHOUGH HE DIDN'T LEARN A THING ABOUT OSMOSIS, HE STUMBLED UPON SOMETHING ELSE, SOMETHING SUPER . . .
. . . COOL.
YOU'RE NOT LISTENING.
WHAT IF SOMEONE WAS IN THE BUILDING WITH US AND NOW THEY'RE WATCHING YOU?
BZZ
HA
HA
HA
AND BUGGED YOUR PHONE, TOO?

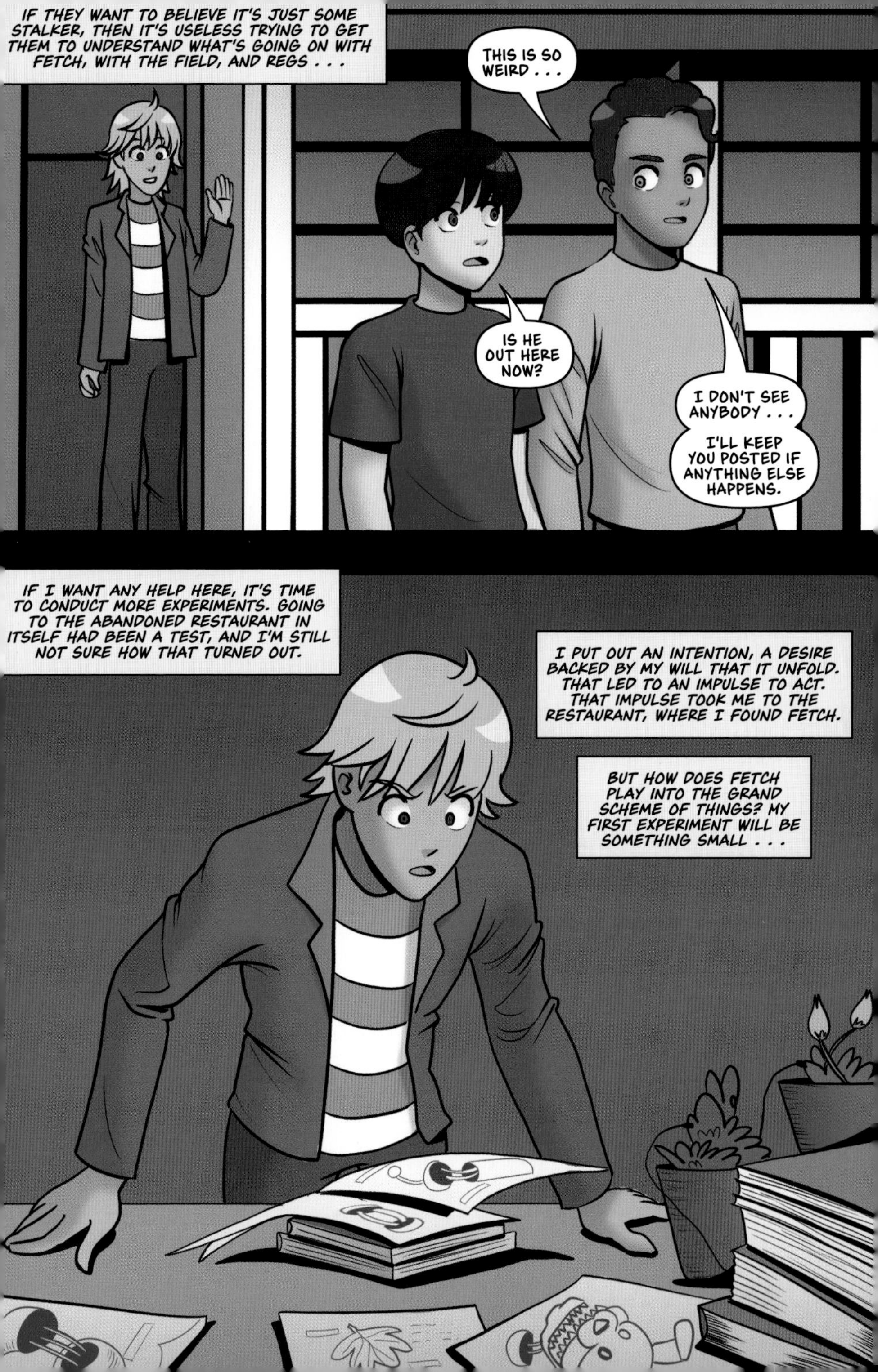
IF THEY WANT TO BELIEVE IT'S JUST SOME STALKER, THEN IT'S USELESS TRYING TO GET THEM TO UNDERSTAND WHAT'S GOING ON WITH FETCH, WITH THE FIELD, AND REGS . . .
THIS IS SO WEIRD . . .
IS HE OUT HERE NOW?
I DON'T SEE ANYBODY . . .
I'LL KEEP YOU POSTED IF ANYTHING ELSE HAPPENS.
IF I WANT ANY HELP HERE, IT'S TIME TO CONDUCT MORE EXPERIMENTS. GOING TO THE ABANDONED RESTAURANT IN ITSELF HAD BEEN A TEST, AND I'M STILL NOT SURE HOW THAT TURNED OUT.
I PUT OUT AN INTENTION, A DESIRE BACKED BY MY WILL THAT IT UNFOLD. THAT LED TO AN IMPULSE TO ACT. THAT IMPULSE TOOK ME TO THE RESTAURANT, WHERE I FOUND FETCH.
BUT HOW DOES FETCH PLAY INTO THE GRAND SCHEME OF THINGS? MY FIRST EXPERIMENT WILL BE SOMETHING SMALL . . .

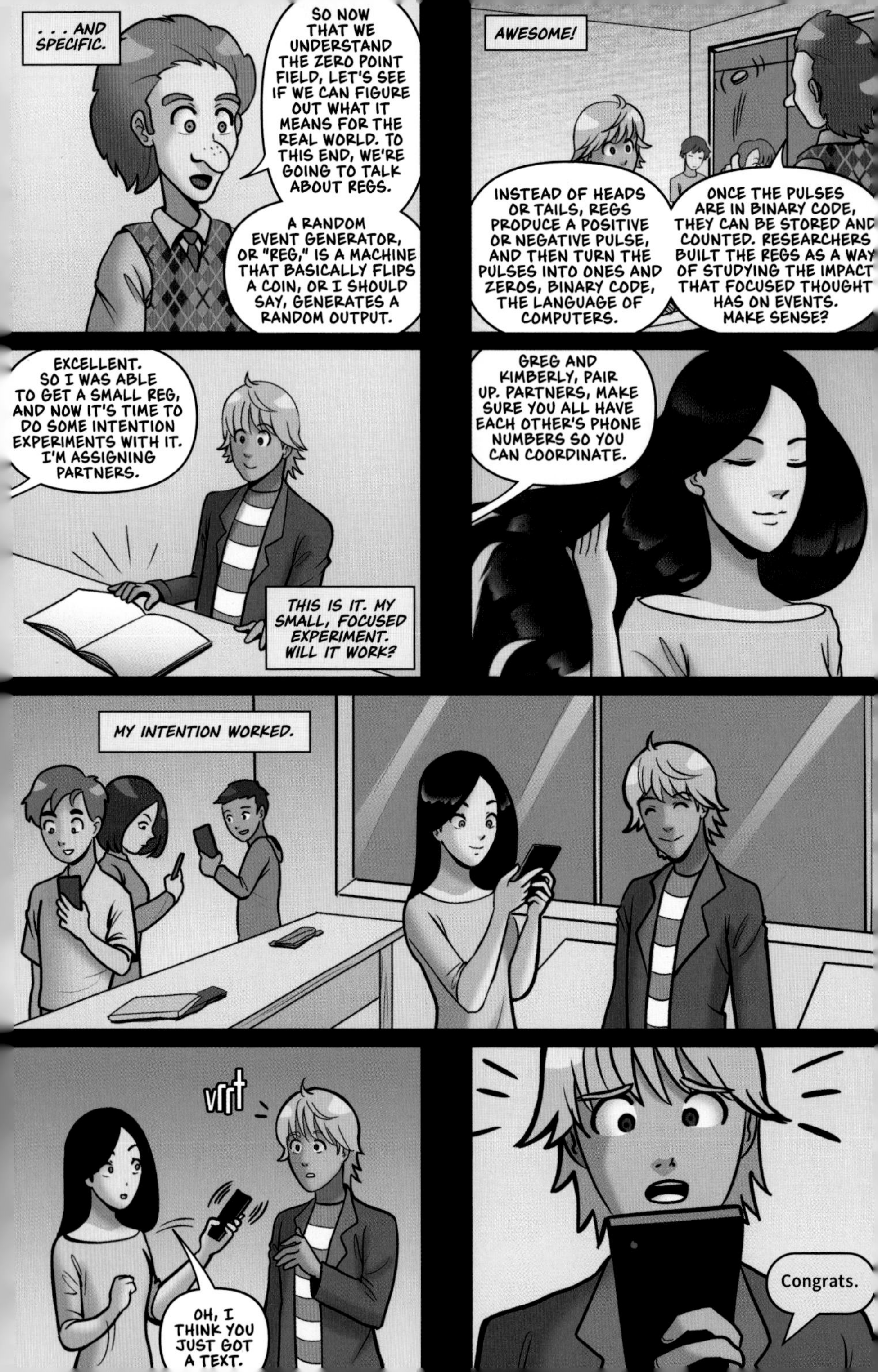
. . . AND SPECIFIC.
SO NOW THAT WE UNDERSTAND THE ZERO POINT FIELD, LET'S SEE IF WE CAN FIGURE OUT WHAT IT MEANS FOR THE REAL WORLD. TO THIS END, WE'RE GOING TO TALK ABOUT REGS.
A RANDOM EVENT GENERATOR, OR "REG," IS A MACHINE THAT BASICALLY FLIPS A COIN, OR I SHOULD SAY, GENERATES A RANDOM OUTPUT.
AWESOME!
INSTEAD OF HEADS OR TAILS, REGS PRODUCE A POSITIVE OR NEGATIVE PULSE, AND THEN TURN THE PULSES INTO ONES AND ZEROS, BINARY CODE, THE LANGUAGE OF COMPUTERS.
ONCE THE PULSES ARE IN BINARY CODE, THEY CAN BE STORED AND COUNTED. RESEARCHERS BUILT THE REGS AS A WAY OF STUDYING THE IMPACT THAT FOCUSED THOUGHT HAS ON EVENTS. MAKE SENSE?
EXCELLENT. SO I WAS ABLE TO GET A SMALL REG, AND NOW IT'S TIME TO DO SOME INTENTION EXPERIMENTS WITH IT. I'M ASSIGNING PARTNERS.
THIS IS IT. MY SMALL, FOCUSED EXPERIMENT. WILL IT WORK?
GREG AND KIMBERLY, PAIR UP. PARTNERS, MAKE SURE YOU ALL HAVE EACH OTHER'S PHONE NUMBERS SO YOU CAN COORDINATE.
MY INTENTION WORKED.
vrrt
OH, I THINK YOU JUST GOT A TEXT.
Congrats.

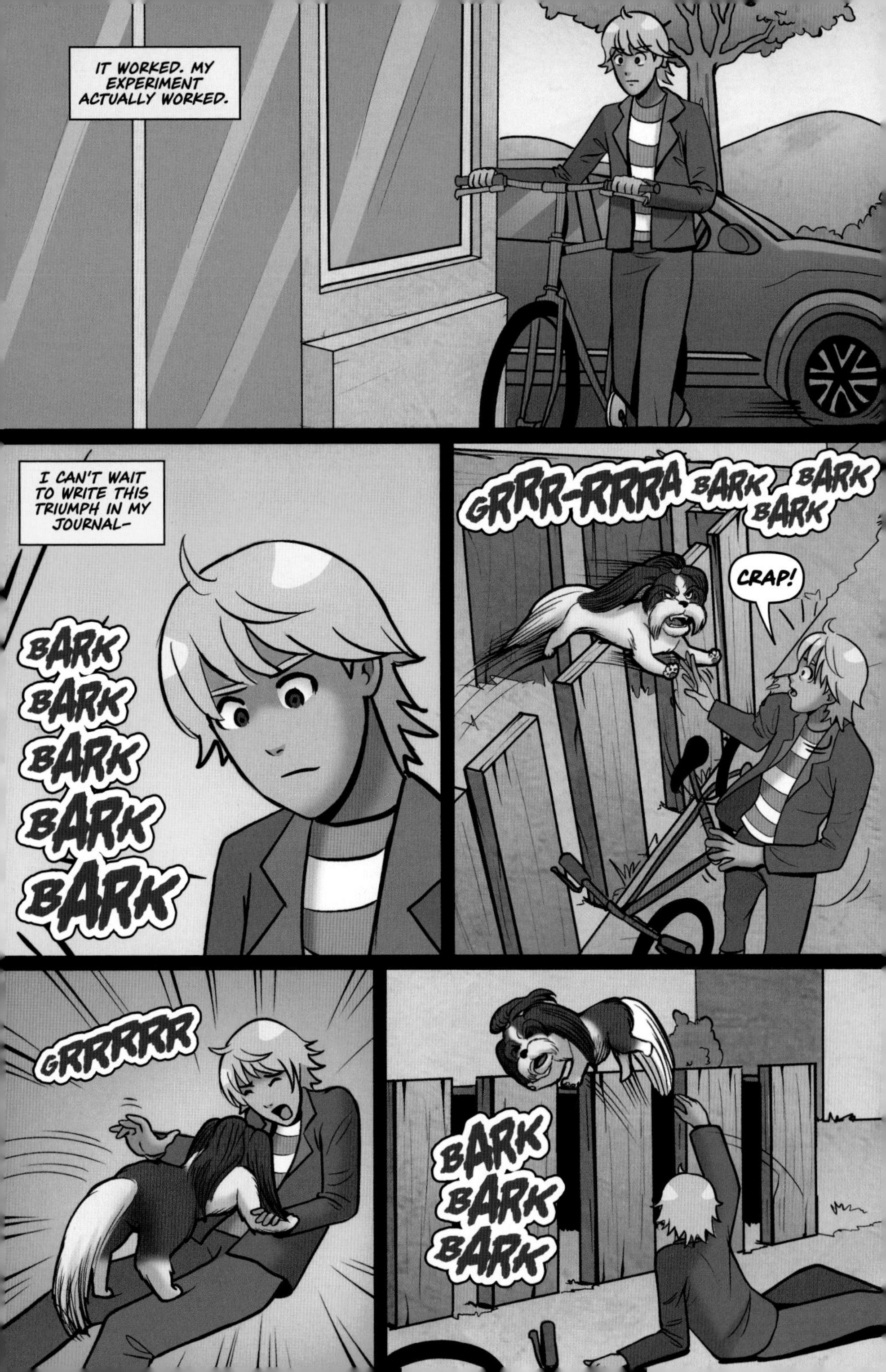
IT WORKED. MY EXPERIMENT ACTUALLY WORKED.
I CAN'T WAIT TO WRITE THIS TRIUMPH IN MY JOURNAL–
BARK BARK BARK BARK BARK
GRRR-RRRRA BARK BARK BARK
CRAP!
GRRRRR
BARK BARK BARK

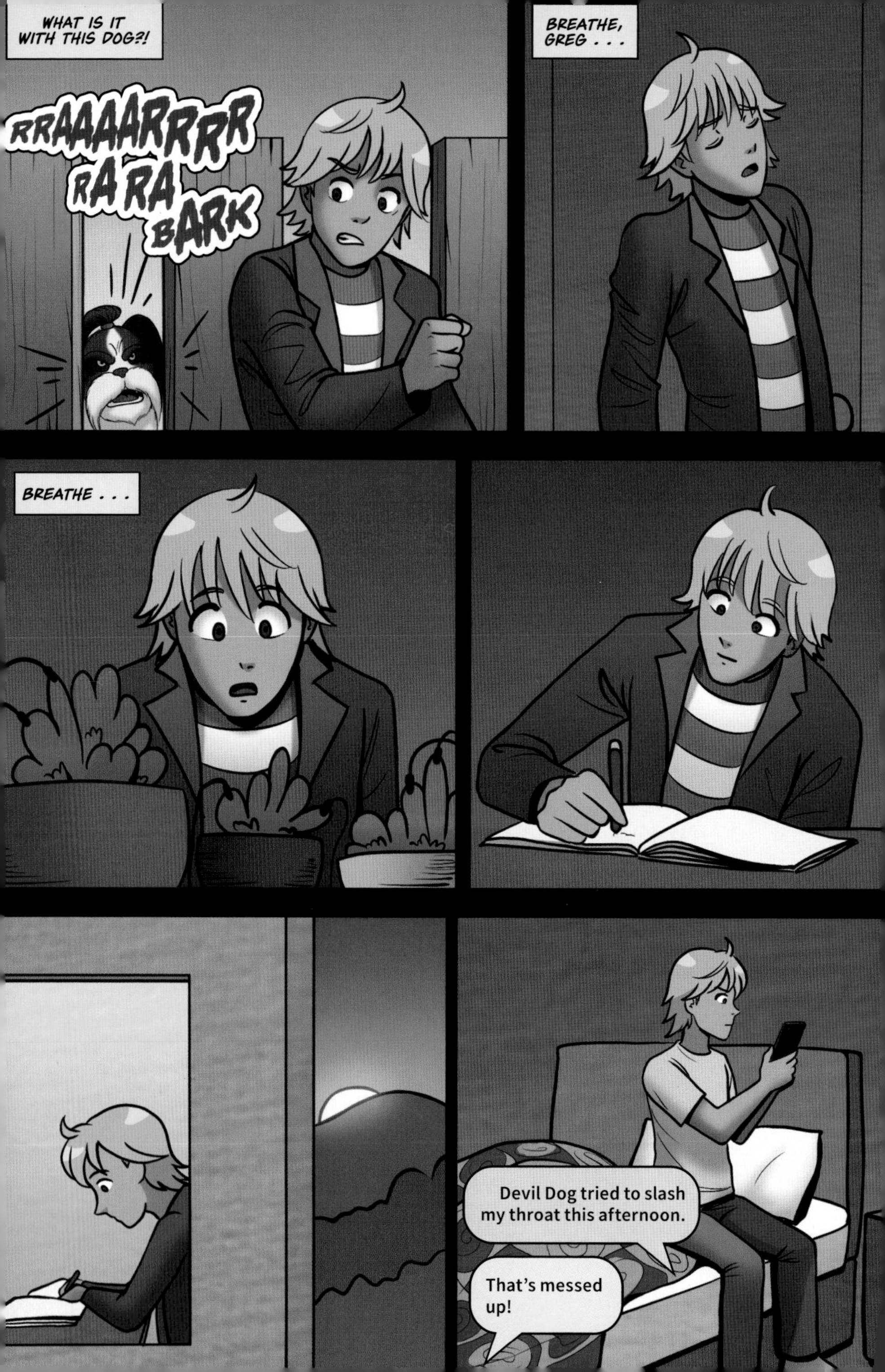
WHAT IS IT WITH THIS DOG?!
RRAAAARRRR RA RA BARK
BREATHE, GREG . . .
BREATHE . . .
Devil Dog tried to slash my throat this afternoon.
That's messed up!

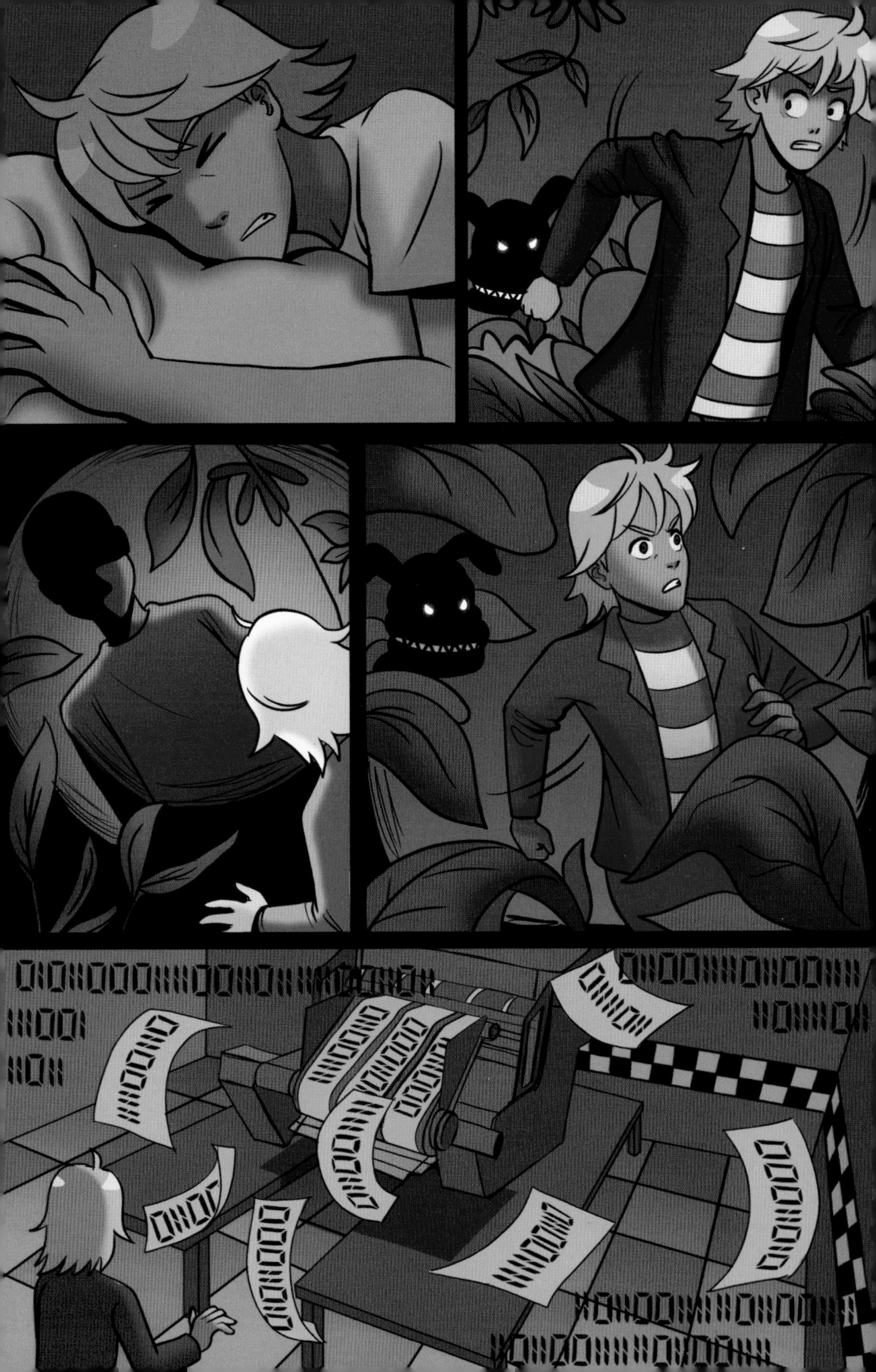

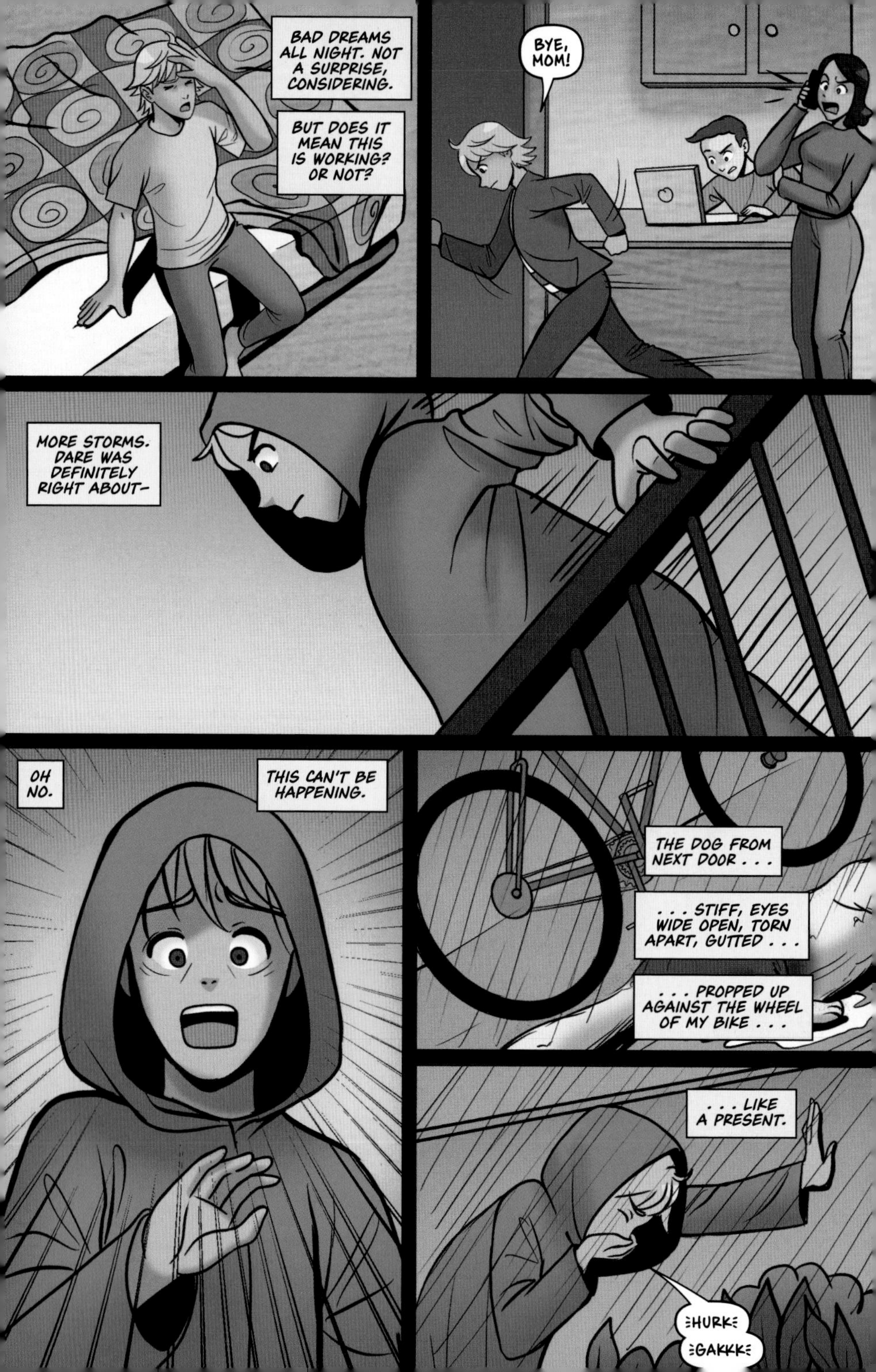
BAD DREAMS ALL NIGHT. NOT A SURPRISE, CONSIDERING.
BUT DOES IT MEAN THIS IS WORKING? OR NOT?
BYE, MOM!
MORE STORMS. DARE WAS DEFINITELY RIGHT ABOUT-
OH NO.
THIS CAN'T BE HAPPENING.
THE DOG FROM NEXT DOOR . . .
. . . STIFF, EYES WIDE OPEN, TORN APART, GUTTED . . .
. . . PROPPED UP AGAINST THE WHEEL OF MY BIKE . . .
. . . LIKE A PRESENT.
HURK
GAKKK

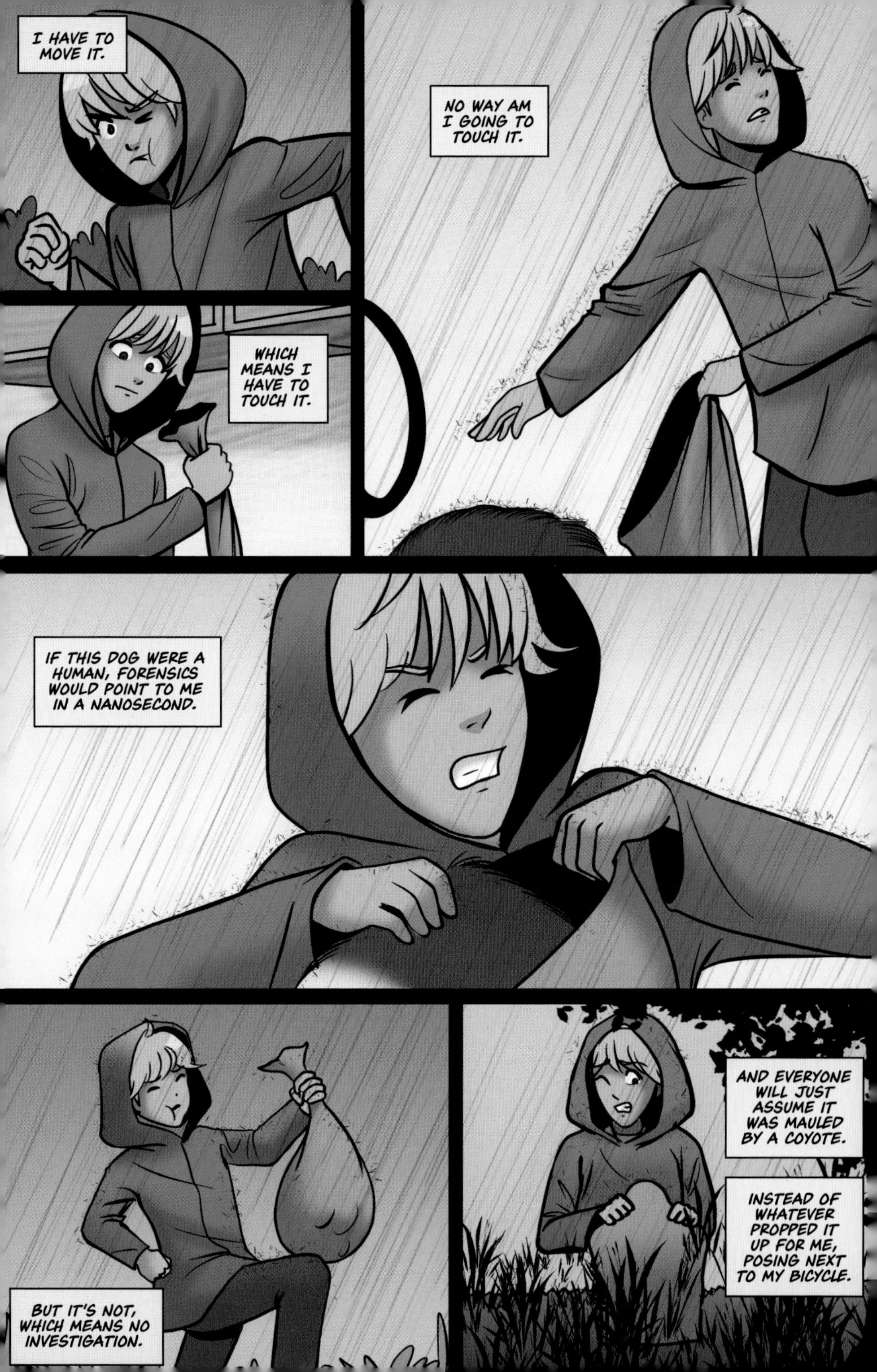
I HAVE TO MOVE IT.
WHICH MEANS I HAVE TO TOUCH IT.
NO WAY AM I GOING TO TOUCH IT.
IF THIS DOG WERE A HUMAN, FORENSICS WOULD POINT TO ME IN A NANOSECOND.
BUT IT'S NOT, WHICH MEANS NO INVESTIGATION.
AND EVERYONE WILL JUST ASSUME IT WAS MAULED BY A COYOTE.
INSTEAD OF WHATEVER PROPPED IT UP FOR ME, POSING NEXT TO MY BICYCLE.

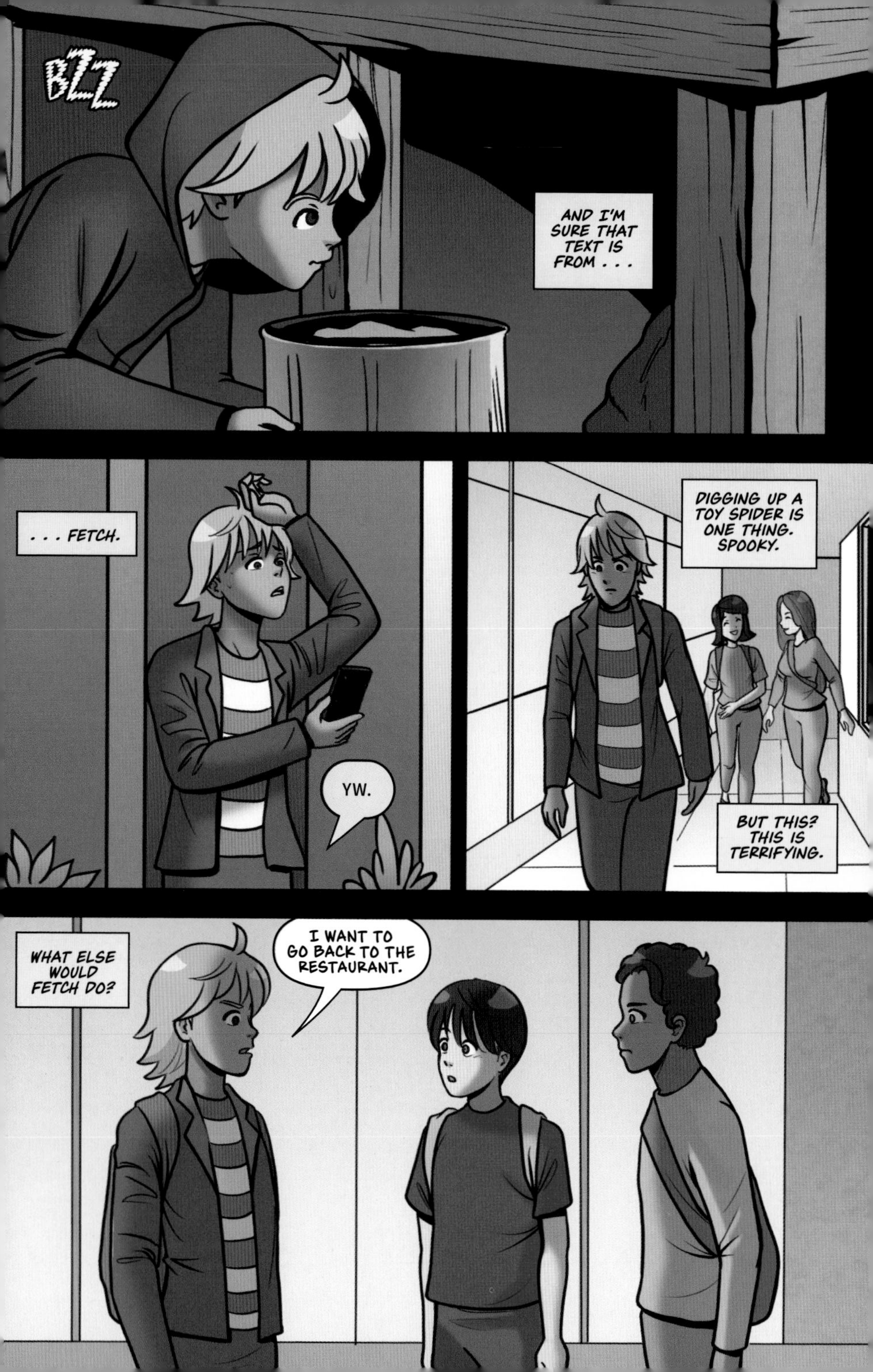
BZZ
AND I'M SURE THAT TEXT IS FROM . . .
. . . FETCH.
YW.
DIGGING UP A TOY SPIDER IS ONE THING. SPOOKY.
BUT THIS? THIS IS TERRIFYING.
WHAT ELSE WOULD FETCH DO?
I WANT TO GO BACK TO THE RESTAURANT.

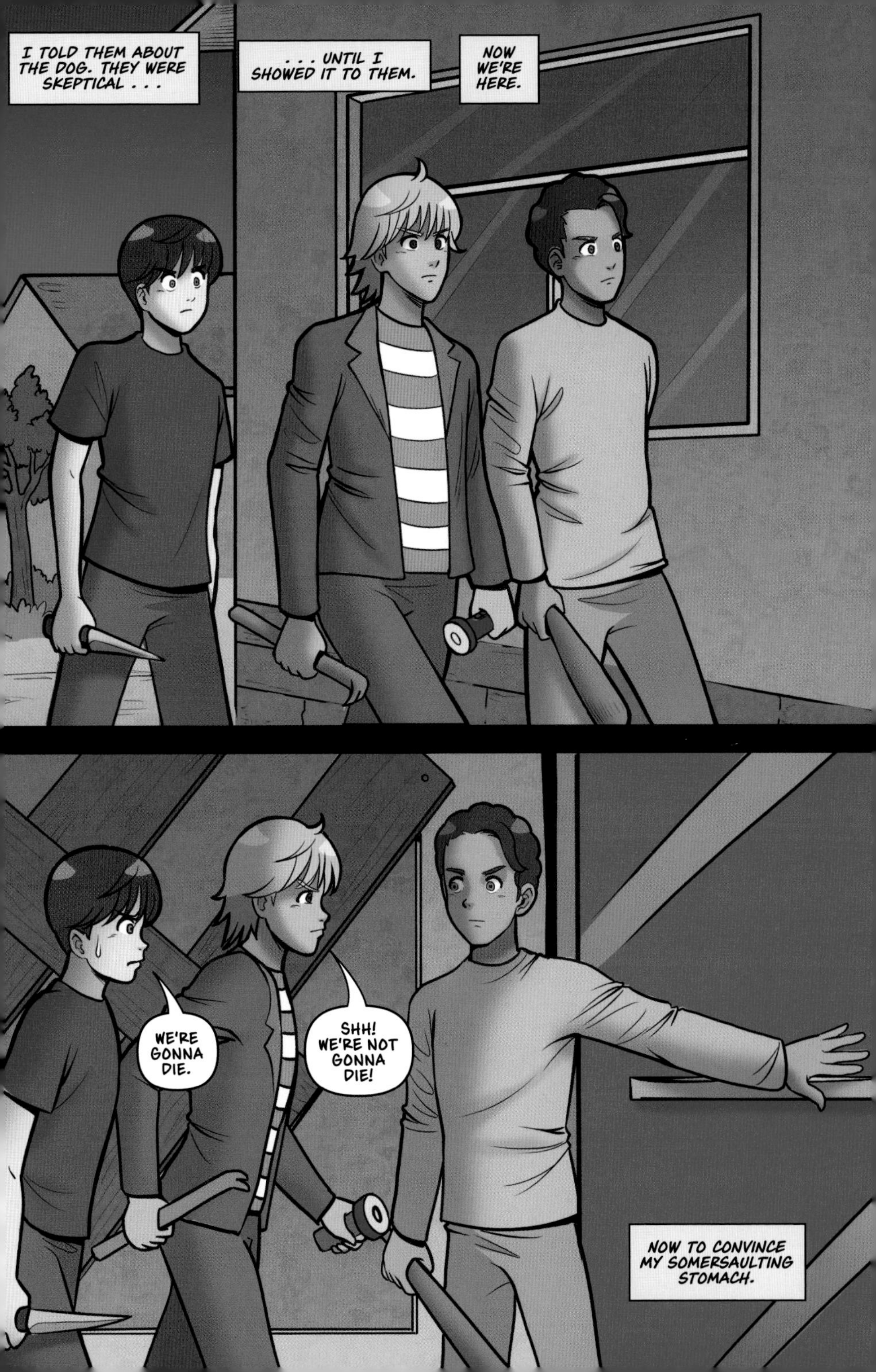
I TOLD THEM ABOUT THE DOG. THEY WERE SKEPTICAL . . .
. . . UNTIL I SHOWED IT TO THEM.
NOW WE'RE HERE.
WE'RE GONNA DIE.
SHH! WE'RE NOT GONNA DIE!
NOW TO CONVINCE MY SOMERSAULTING STOMACH.

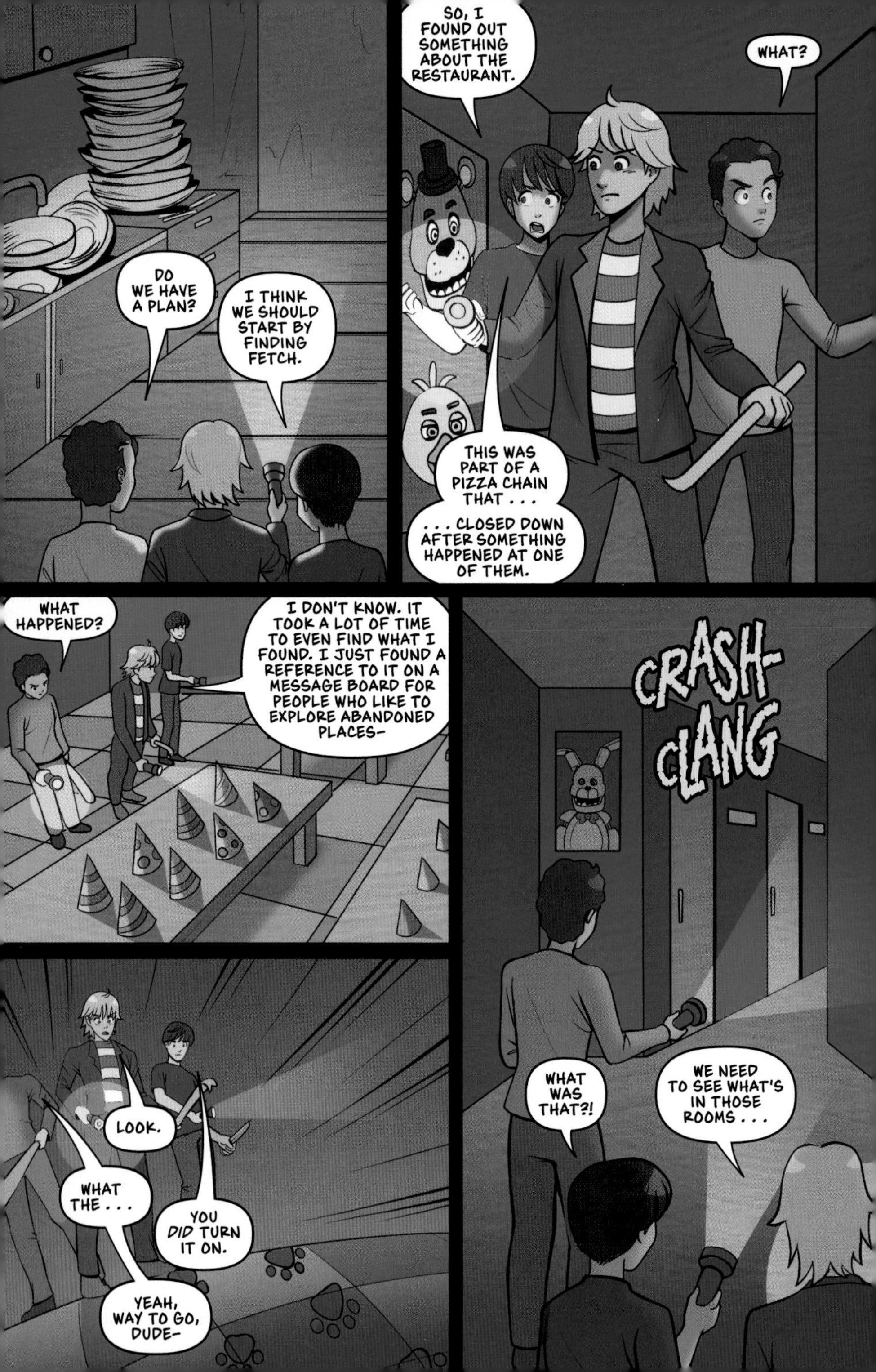
DO WE HAVE A PLAN?
I THINK WE SHOULD START BY FINDING FETCH.
SO, I FOUND OUT SOMETHING ABOUT THE RESTAURANT.
WHAT?
THIS WAS PART OF A PIZZA CHAIN THAT . . .
. . . CLOSED DOWN AFTER SOMETHING HAPPENED AT ONE OF THEM.
WHAT HAPPENED?
I DON'T KNOW. IT TOOK A LOT OF TIME TO EVEN FIND WHAT I FOUND. I JUST FOUND A REFERENCE TO IT ON A MESSAGE BOARD FOR PEOPLE WHO LIKE TO EXPLORE ABANDONED PLACES-
LOOK.
WHAT THE . . .
YOU DID TURN IT ON.
YEAH, WAY TO GO, DUDE-
CRASH-
CLANG
WHAT WAS THAT?!
WE NEED TO SEE WHAT'S IN THOSE ROOMS . . .

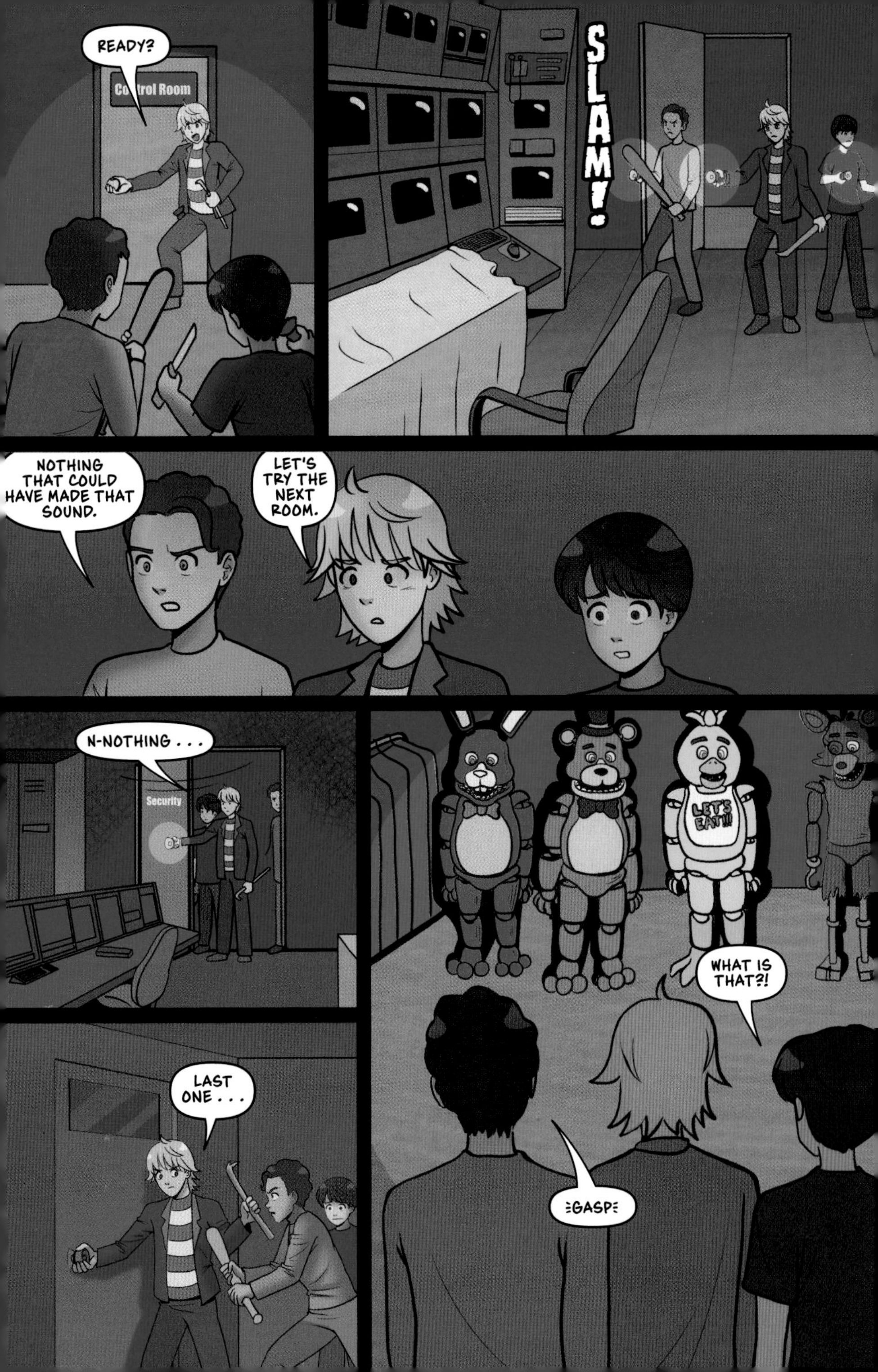

READY?
Control Room
SLAM!
NOTHING THAT COULD HAVE MADE THAT SOUND.
LET'S TRY THE NEXT ROOM.
N-NOTHING . . .
Security
LAST ONE . . .
LET'S EAT!!!
WHAT IS THAT?!
GASP

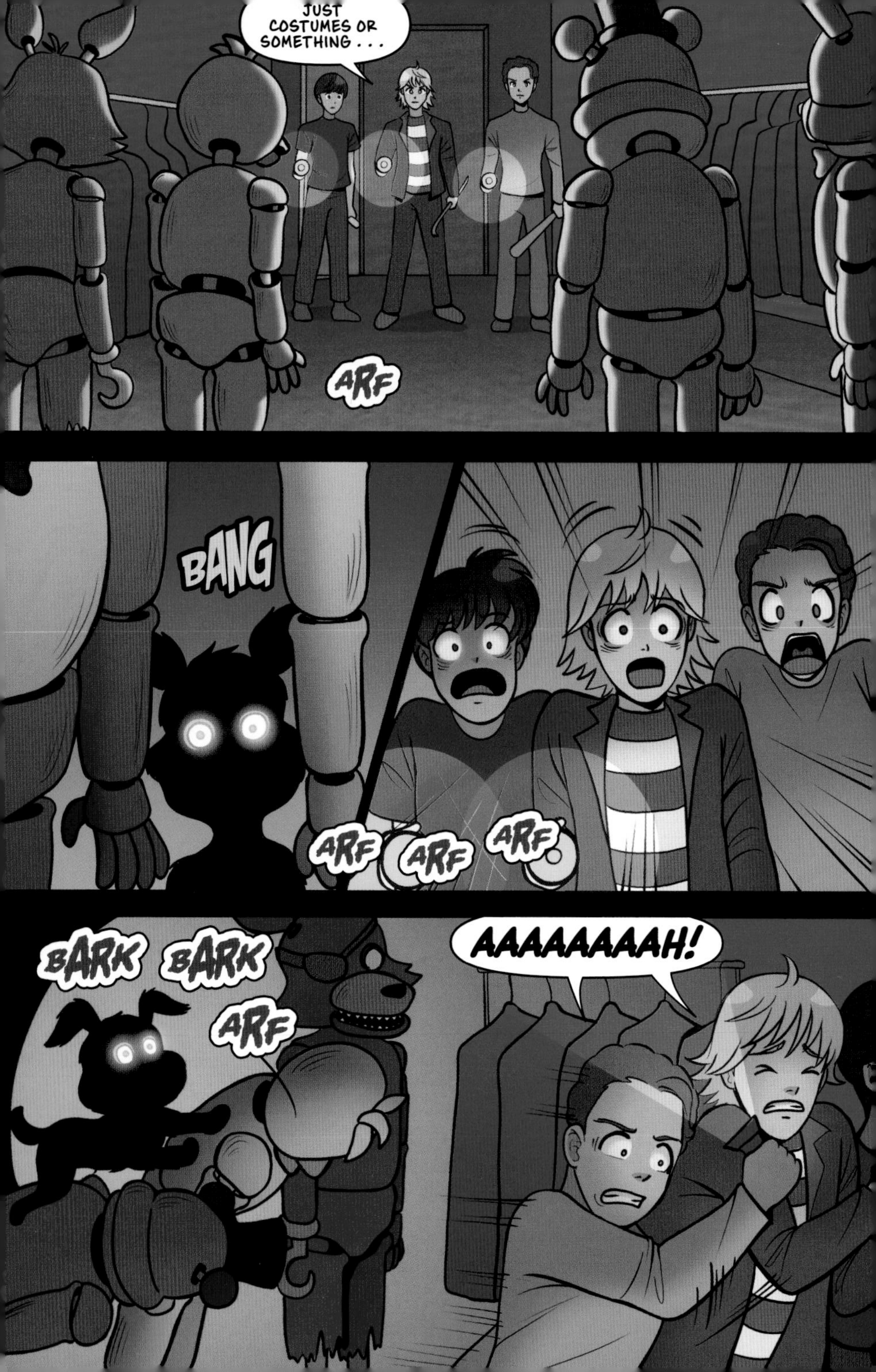

JUST COSTUMES OR SOMETHING . . .
ARF
BANG
ARF
ARF
ARF
BARK
BARK
ARF
AAAAAAAAH!

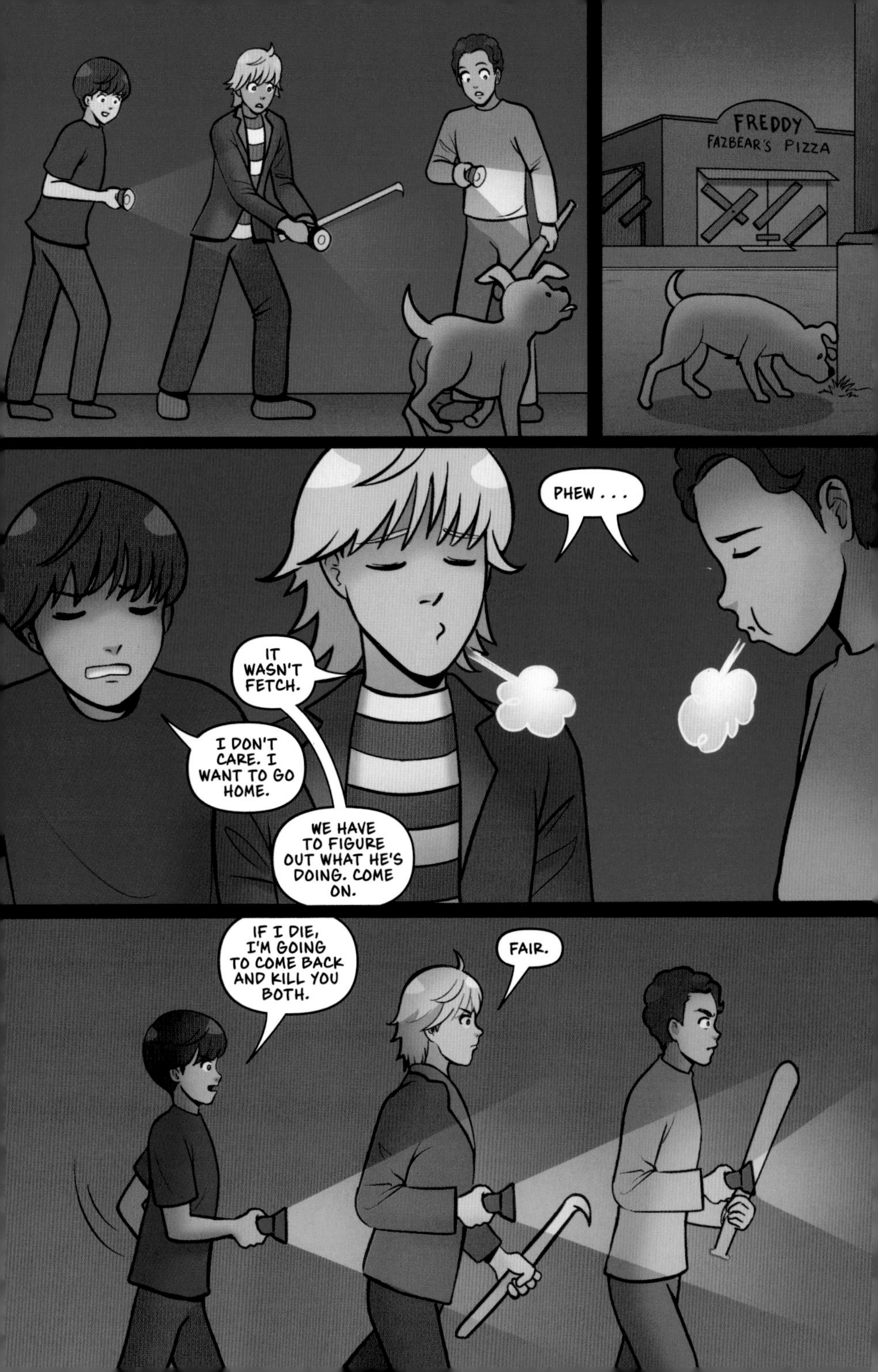
FREDDY
FAZBEAR'S PIZZA
PHEW . . .
IT WASN'T FETCH.
I DON'T CARE. I WANT TO GO HOME.
WE HAVE TO FIGURE OUT WHAT HE'S DOING. COME ON.
IF I DIE, I'M GOING TO COME BACK AND KILL YOU BOTH.
FAIR.

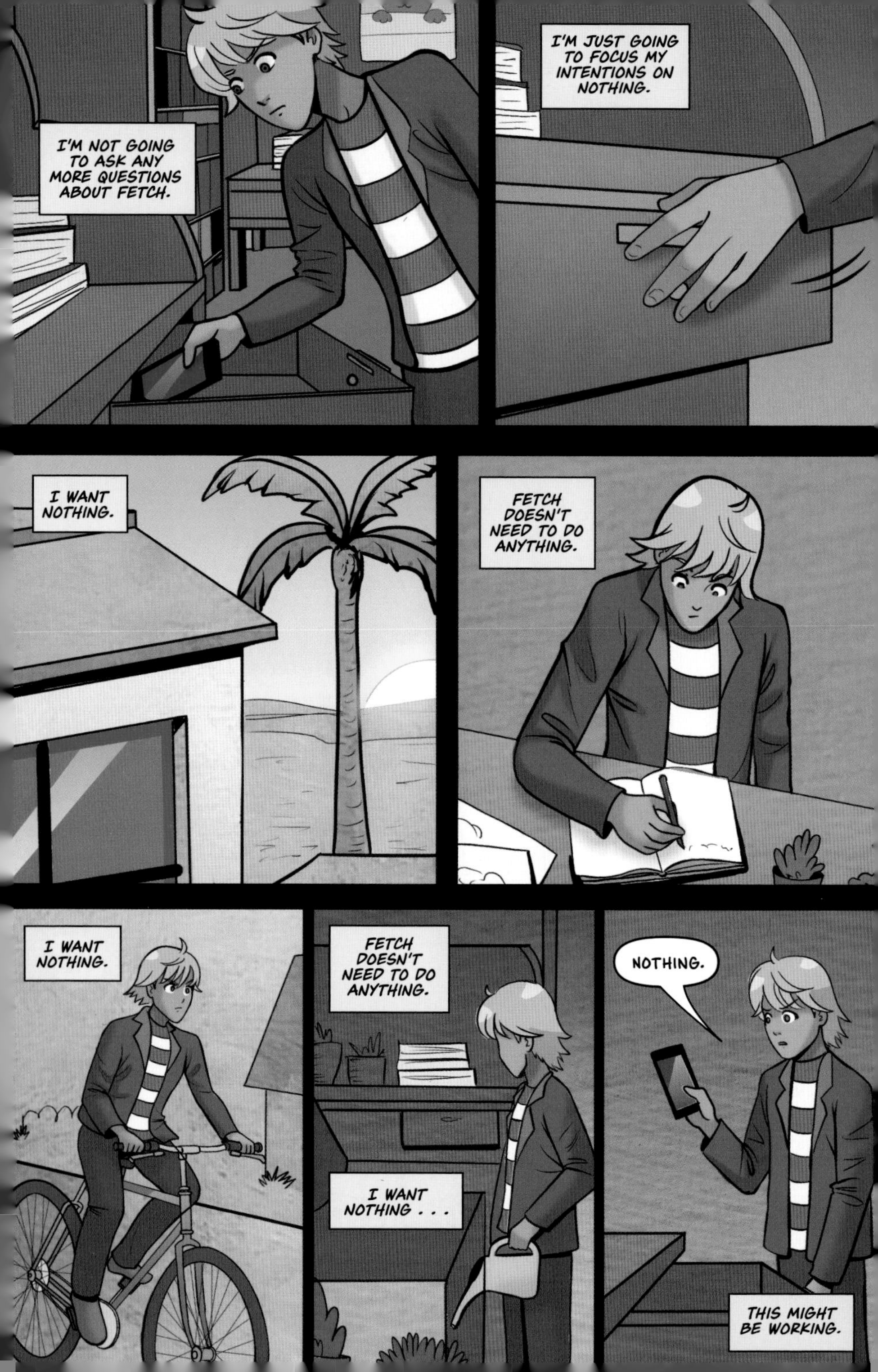
I'M NOT GOING TO ASK ANY MORE QUESTIONS ABOUT FETCH.
I'M JUST GOING TO FOCUS MY INTENTIONS ON NOTHING.
I WANT NOTHING.
FETCH DOESN'T NEED TO DO ANYTHING.
I WANT NOTHING.
FETCH DOESN'T NEED TO DO ANYTHING.
I WANT NOTHING . . .
NOTHING.
THIS MIGHT BE WORKING.

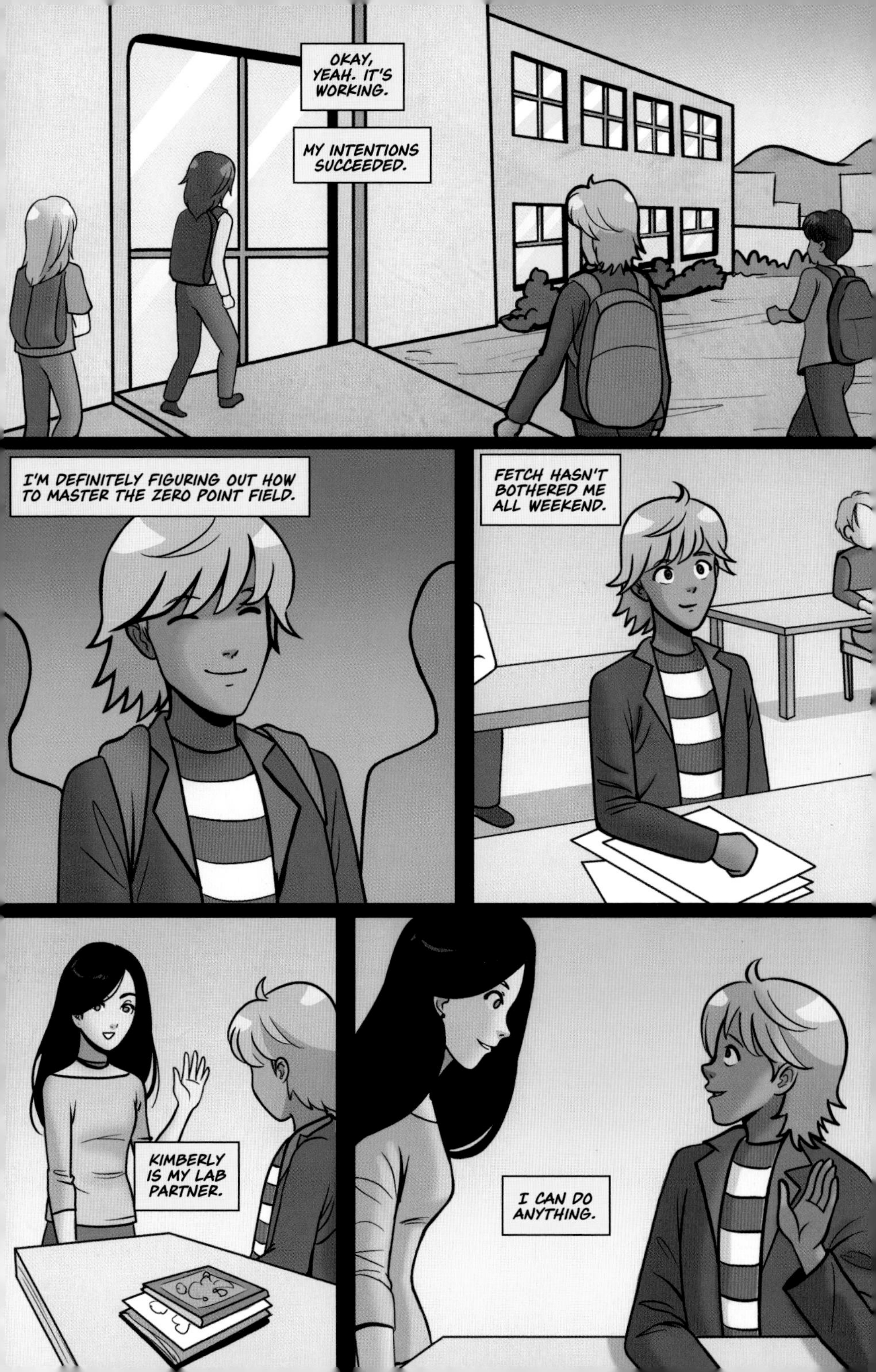
OKAY, YEAH. IT'S WORKING.
MY INTENTIONS SUCCEEDED.
I'M DEFINITELY FIGURING OUT HOW TO MASTER THE ZERO POINT FIELD.
FETCH HASN'T BOTHERED ME ALL WEEKEND.
KIMBERLY IS MY LAB PARTNER.
I CAN DO ANYTHING.

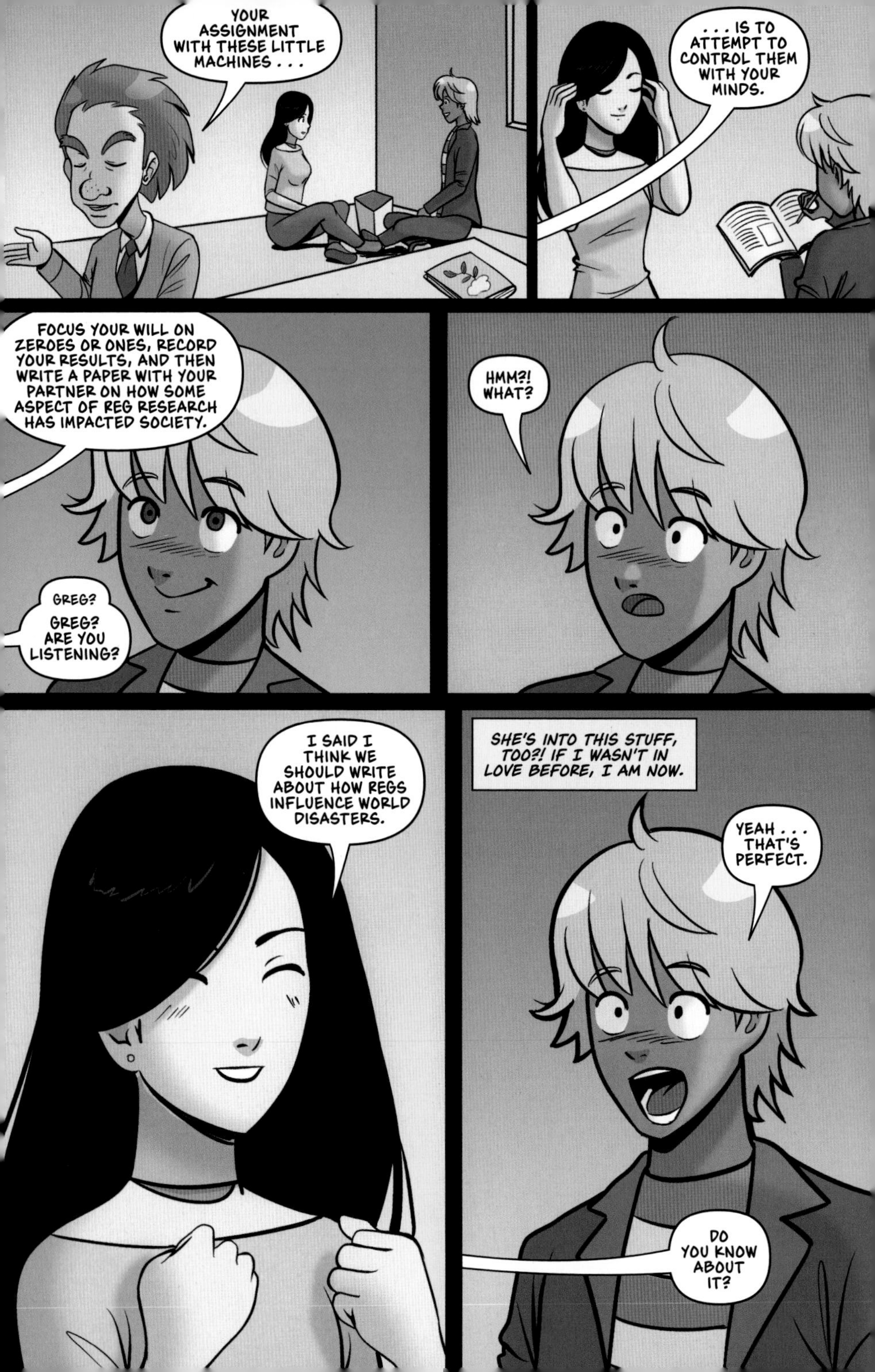
YOUR ASSIGNMENT WITH THESE LITTLE MACHINES . . .
. . . IS TO ATTEMPT TO CONTROL THEM WITH YOUR MINDS.
FOCUS YOUR WILL ON ZEROES OR ONES, RECORD YOUR RESULTS, AND THEN WRITE A PAPER WITH YOUR PARTNER ON HOW SOME ASPECT OF REG RESEARCH HAS IMPACTED SOCIETY.
GREG?
GREG? ARE YOU LISTENING?
HMM?! WHAT?
I SAID I THINK WE SHOULD WRITE ABOUT HOW REGS INFLUENCE WORLD DISASTERS.
SHE'S INTO THIS STUFF, TOO?! IF I WASN'T IN LOVE BEFORE, I AM NOW.
YEAH . . . THAT'S PERFECT.
DO YOU KNOW ABOUT IT?

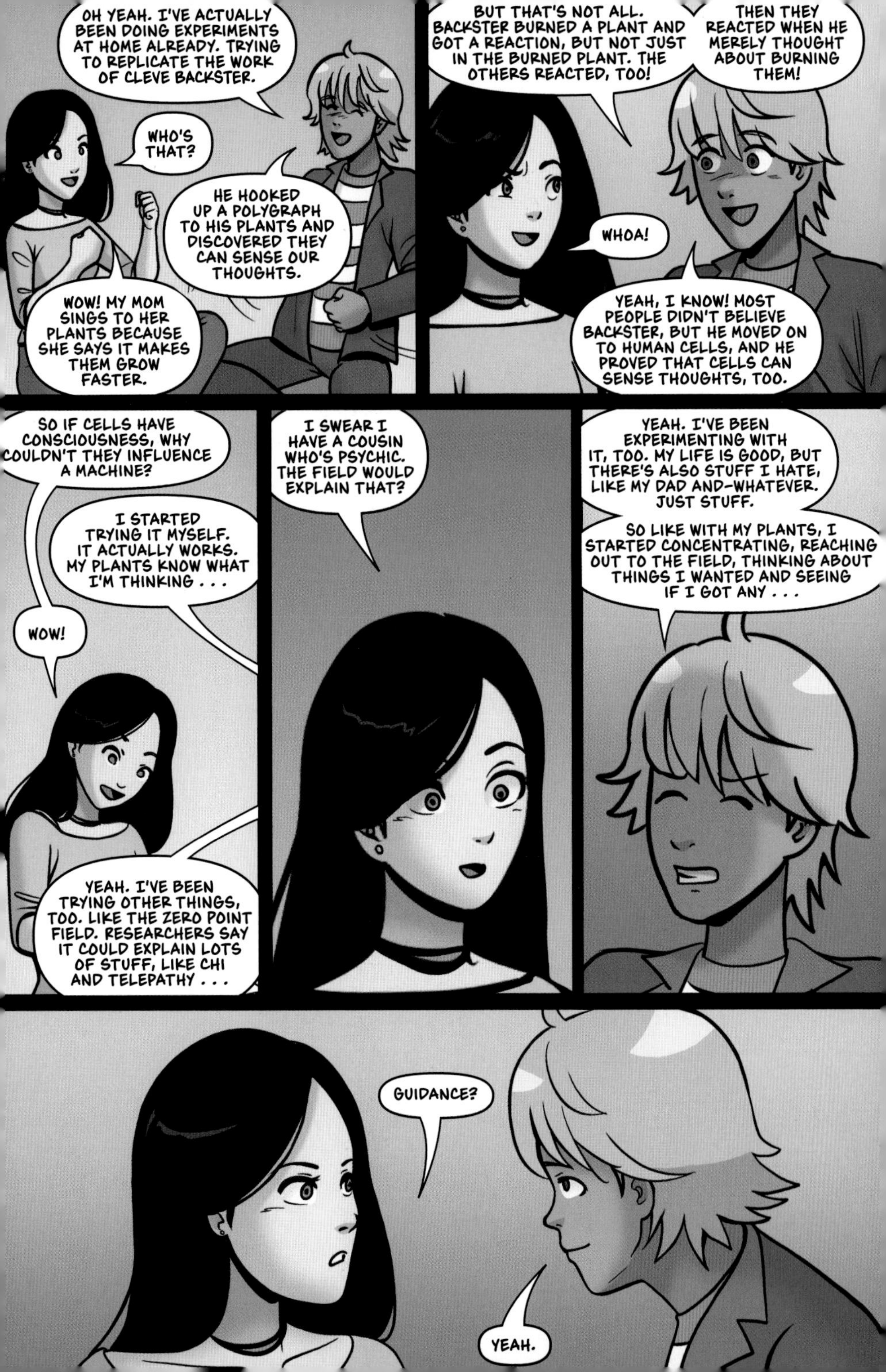
OH YEAH. I'VE ACTUALLY BEEN DOING EXPERIMENTS AT HOME ALREADY. TRYING TO REPLICATE THE WORK OF CLEVE BACKSTER.
WHO'S THAT?
HE HOOKED UP A POLYGRAPH TO HIS PLANTS AND DISCOVERED THEY CAN SENSE OUR THOUGHTS.
WOW! MY MOM SINGS TO HER PLANTS BECAUSE SHE SAYS IT MAKES THEM GROW FASTER.
BUT THAT'S NOT ALL. BACKSTER BURNED A PLANT AND GOT A REACTION, BUT NOT JUST IN THE BURNED PLANT. THE OTHERS REACTED, TOO!
THEN THEY REACTED WHEN HE MERELY THOUGHT ABOUT BURNING THEM!
WHOA!
YEAH, I KNOW! MOST PEOPLE DIDN'T BELIEVE BACKSTER, BUT HE MOVED ON TO HUMAN CELLS, AND HE PROVED THAT CELLS CAN SENSE THOUGHTS, TOO.
SO IF CELLS HAVE CONSCIOUSNESS, WHY COULDN'T THEY INFLUENCE A MACHINE?
I STARTED TRYING IT MYSELF. IT ACTUALLY WORKS. MY PLANTS KNOW WHAT I'M THINKING . . .
WOW!
YEAH. I'VE BEEN TRYING OTHER THINGS, TOO. LIKE THE ZERO POINT FIELD. RESEARCHERS SAY IT COULD EXPLAIN LOTS OF STUFF, LIKE CHI AND TELEPATHY . . .
I SWEAR I HAVE A COUSIN WHO'S PSYCHIC. THE FIELD WOULD EXPLAIN THAT?
YEAH. I'VE BEEN EXPERIMENTING WITH IT, TOO. MY LIFE IS GOOD, BUT THERE'S ALSO STUFF I HATE, LIKE MY DAD AND—WHATEVER. JUST STUFF.
SO LIKE WITH MY PLANTS, I STARTED CONCENTRATING, REACHING OUT TO THE FIELD, THINKING ABOUT THINGS I WANTED AND SEEING IF I GOT ANY . . .
GUIDANCE?
YEAH.

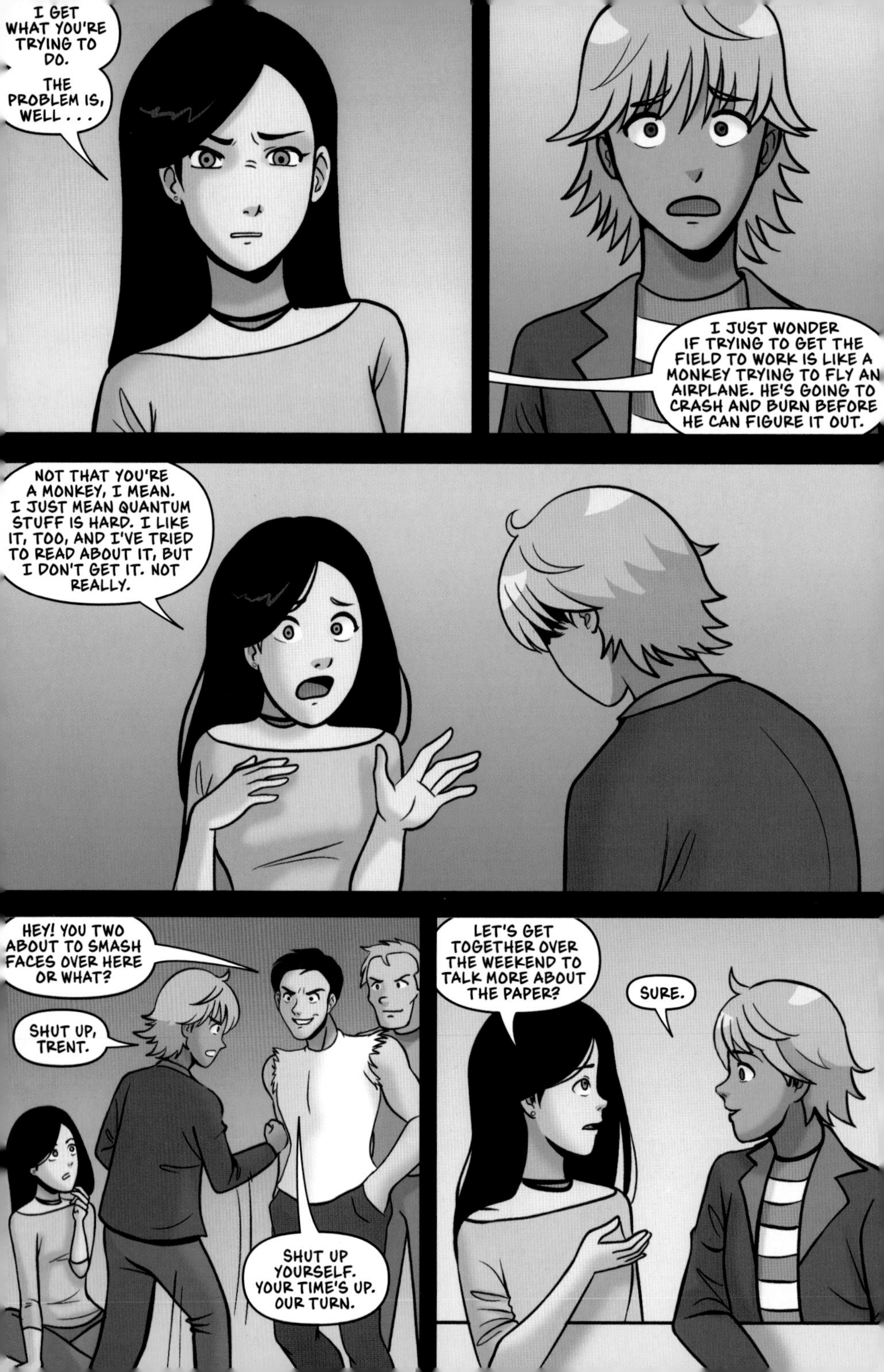
I GET WHAT YOU'RE TRYING TO DO.
THE PROBLEM IS, WELL . . .
I JUST WONDER IF TRYING TO GET THE FIELD TO WORK IS LIKE A MONKEY TRYING TO FLY AN AIRPLANE. HE'S GOING TO CRASH AND BURN BEFORE HE CAN FIGURE IT OUT.
NOT THAT YOU'RE A MONKEY, I MEAN. I JUST MEAN QUANTUM STUFF IS HARD. I LIKE IT, TOO, AND I'VE TRIED TO READ ABOUT IT, BUT I DON'T GET IT. NOT REALLY.
HEY! YOU TWO ABOUT TO SMASH FACES OVER HERE OR WHAT?
SHUT UP, TRENT.
SHUT UP YOURSELF. YOUR TIME'S UP. OUR TURN.
LET'S GET TOGETHER OVER THE WEEKEND TO TALK MORE ABOUT THE PAPER?
SURE.

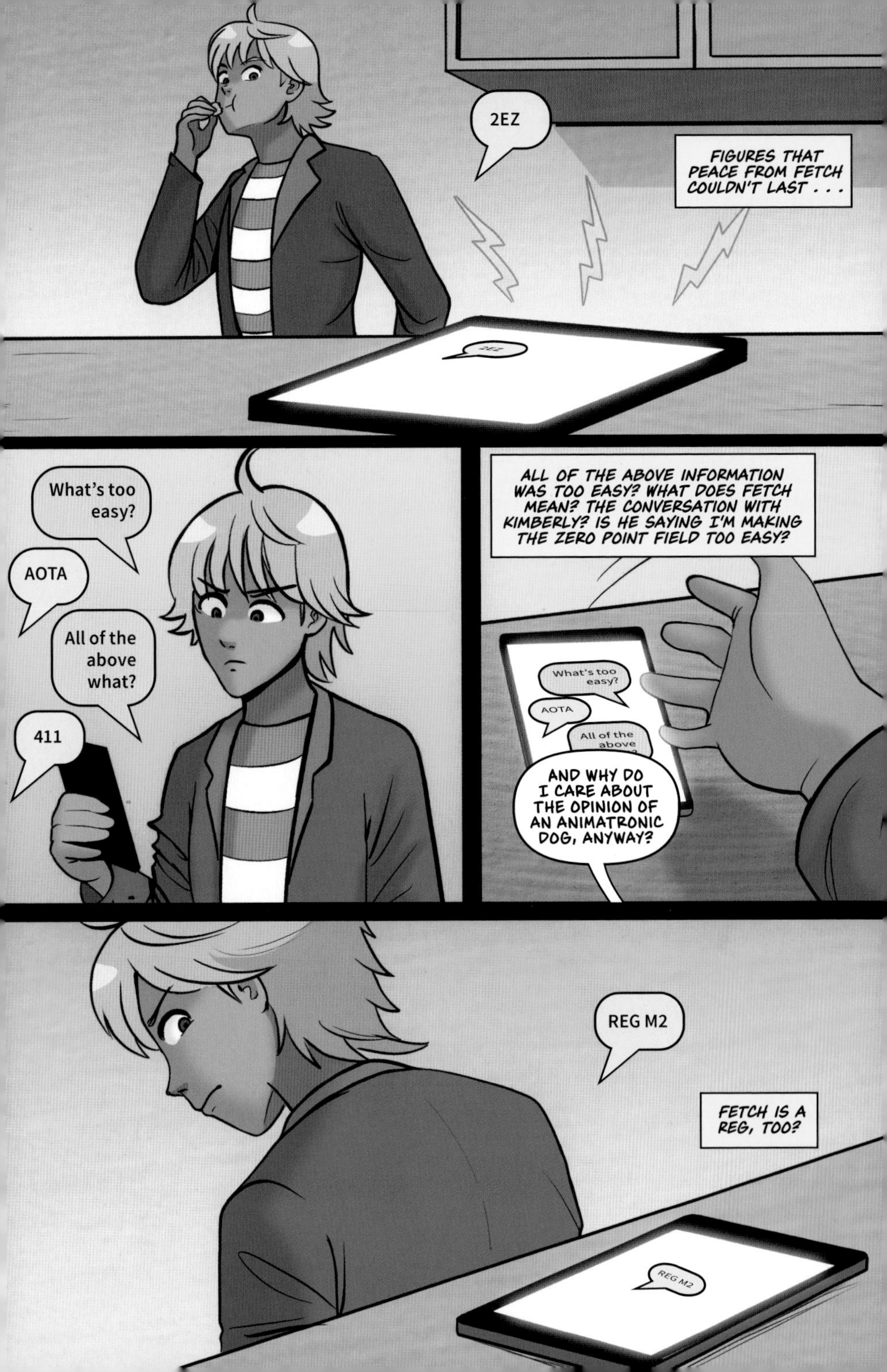
2EZ
FIGURES THAT PEACE FROM FETCH COULDN'T LAST . . .
2EZ
What's too easy?
AOTA
All of the above what?
411
ALL OF THE ABOVE INFORMATION WAS TOO EASY? WHAT DOES FETCH MEAN? THE CONVERSATION WITH KIMBERLY? IS HE SAYING I'M MAKING THE ZERO POINT FIELD TOO EASY?
What's too easy?
AOTA
AND WHY DO I CARE ABOUT THE OPINION OF AN ANIMATRONIC DOG, ANYWAY?
REG M2
FETCH IS A REG, TOO?
REG M2

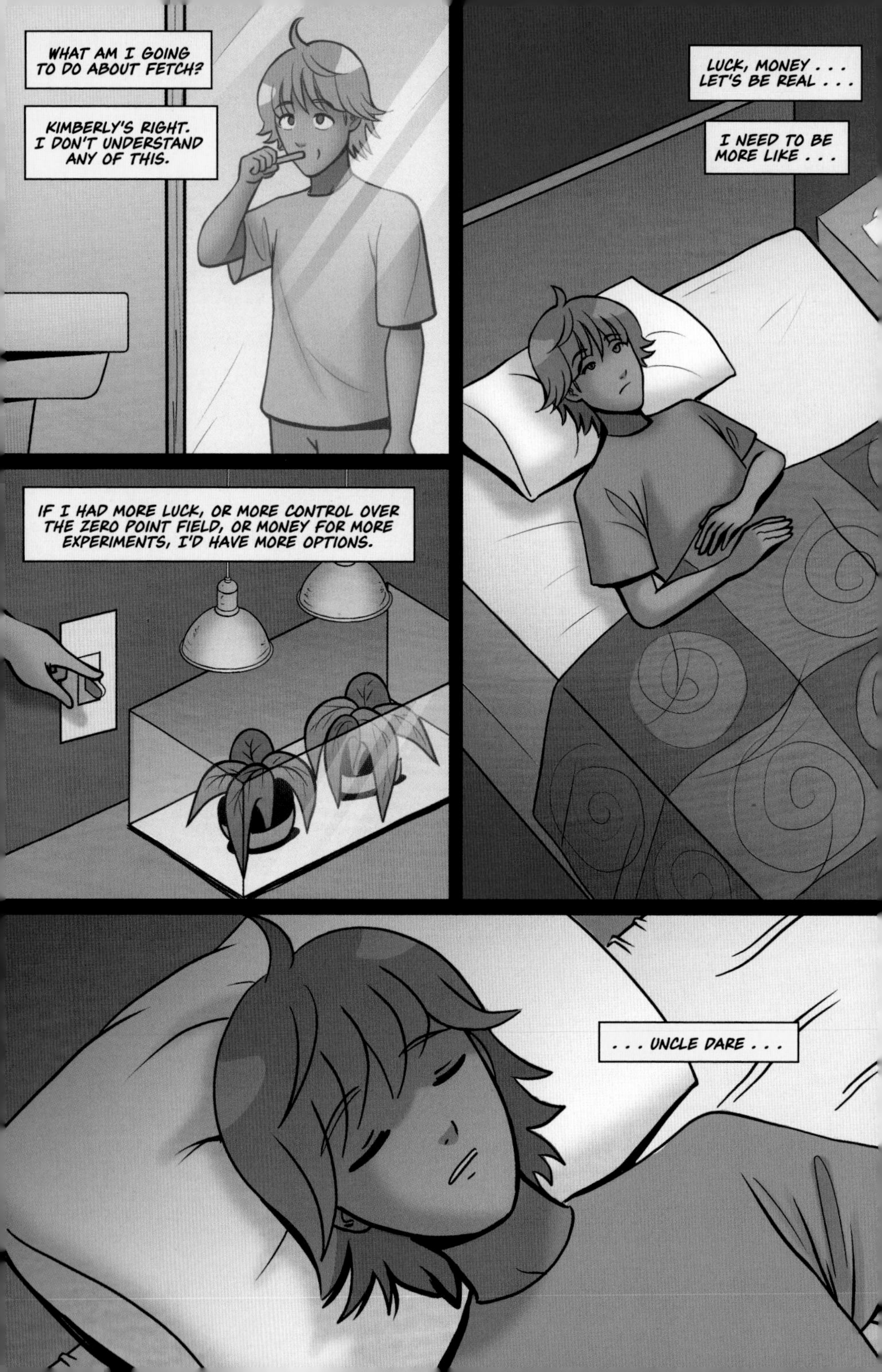
WHAT AM I GOING TO DO ABOUT FETCH?
KIMBERLY'S RIGHT. I DON'T UNDERSTAND ANY OF THIS.
LUCK, MONEY . . . LET'S BE REAL . . .
I NEED TO BE MORE LIKE . . .
IF I HAD MORE LUCK, OR MORE CONTROL OVER THE ZERO POINT FIELD, OR MONEY FOR MORE EXPERIMENTS, I'D HAVE MORE OPTIONS.
. . . UNCLE DARE . . .

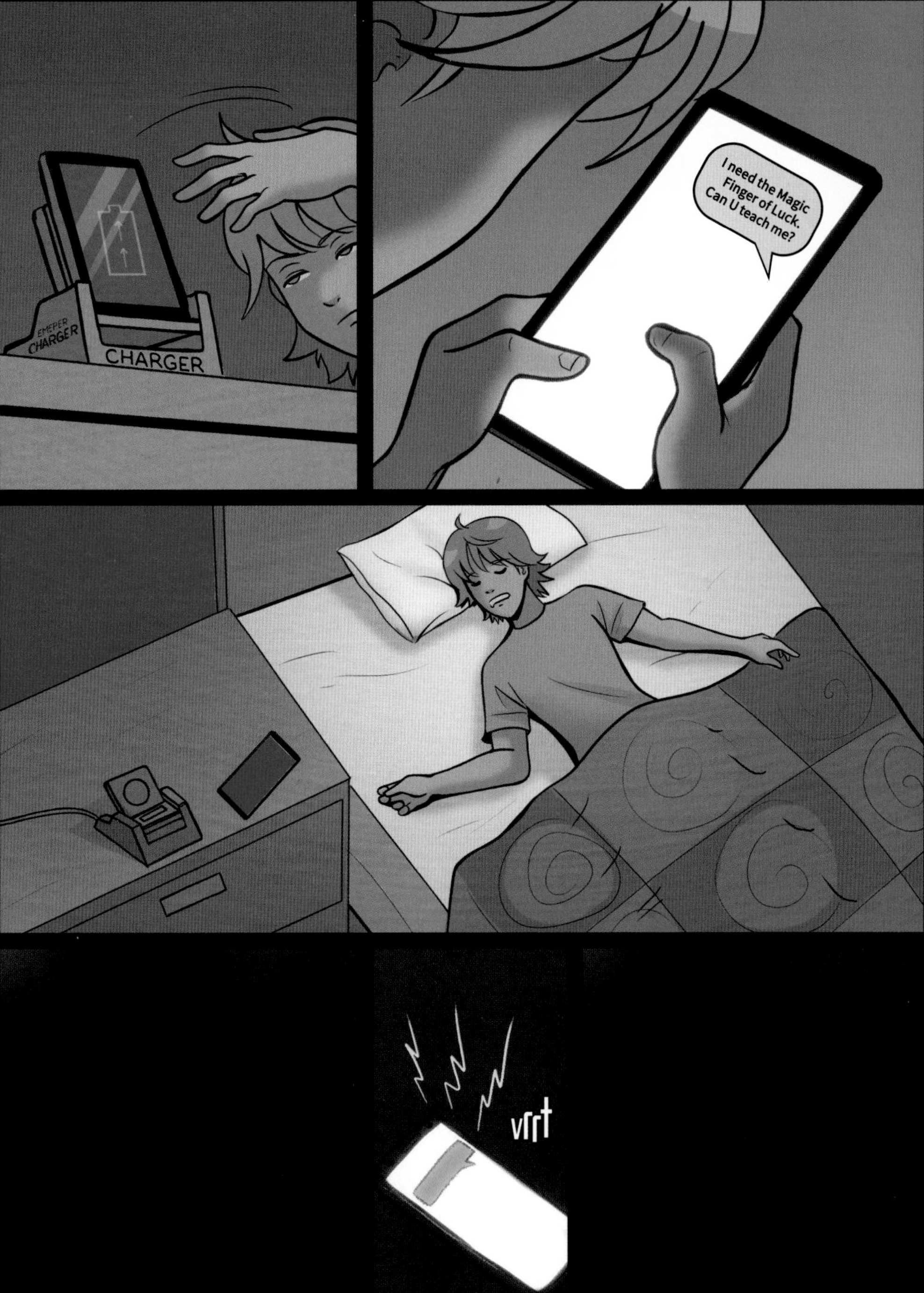
EMEPER
CHARGER
CHARGER
I need the Magic Finger of Luck. Can U teach me?
vrrt

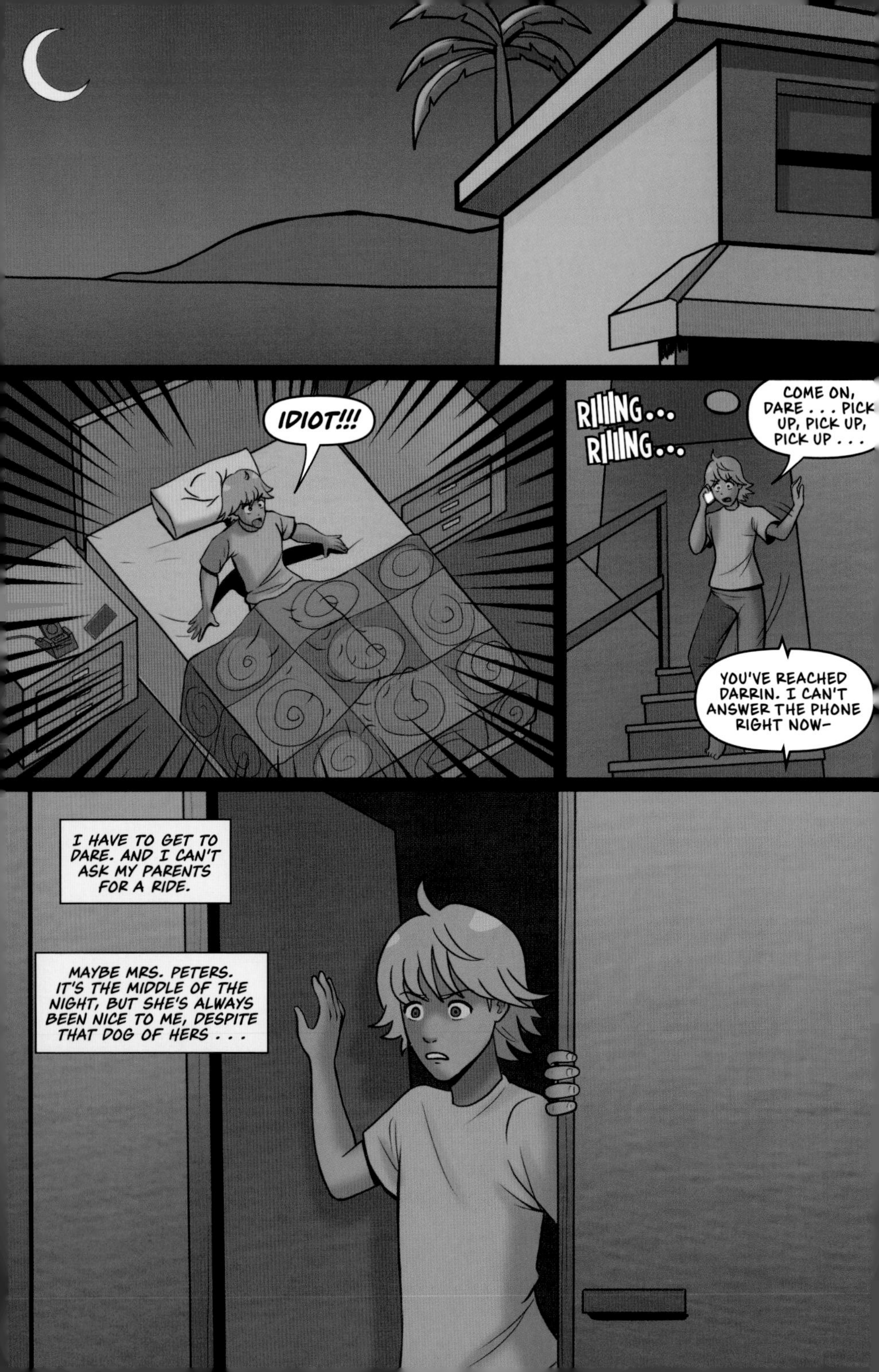
IDIOT!!!
RIIIING . . .
RIIIING . . .
COME ON, DARE . . . PICK UP, PICK UP, PICK UP . . .
YOU'VE REACHED DARRIN. I CAN'T ANSWER THE PHONE RIGHT NOW–
I HAVE TO GET TO DARE. AND I CAN'T ASK MY PARENTS FOR A RIDE.
MAYBE MRS. PETERS. IT'S THE MIDDLE OF THE NIGHT, BUT SHE'S ALWAYS BEEN NICE TO ME, DESPITE THAT DOG OF HERS . . .

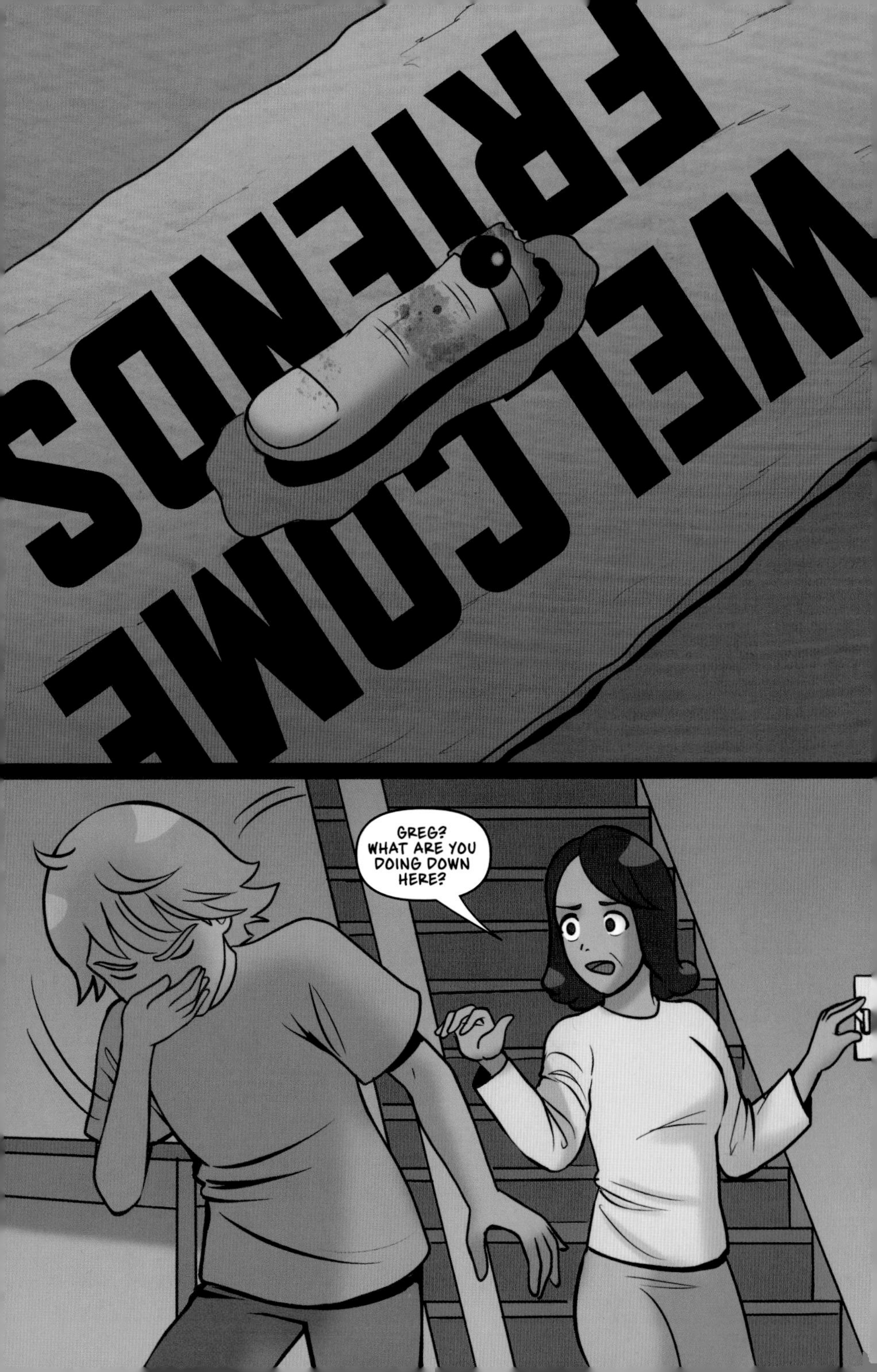
WELCOME FRIENDS
GREG? WHAT ARE YOU DOING DOWN HERE?

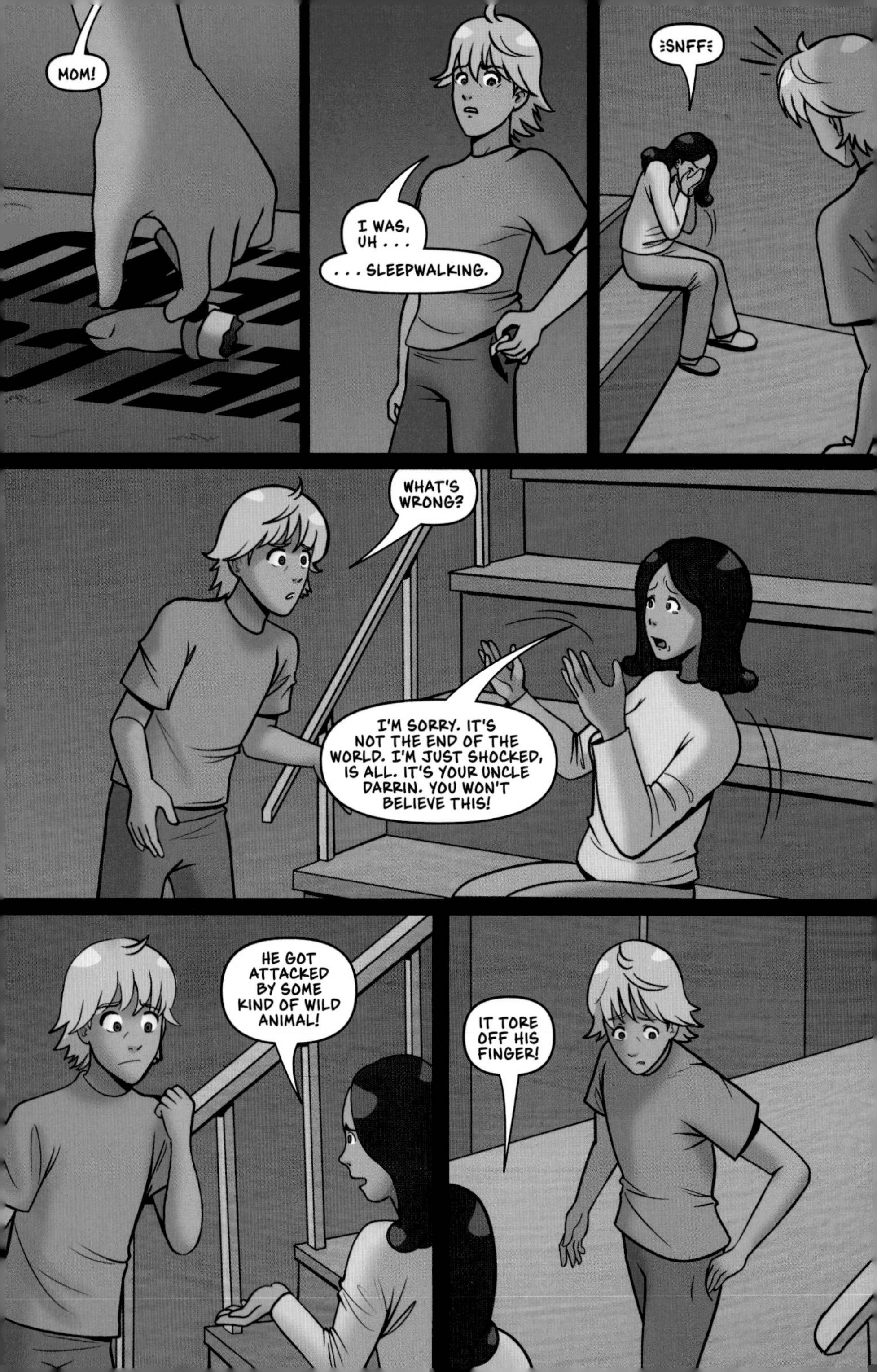
MOM!
I WAS, UH . . .
. . . SLEEPWALKING.
SNFF
WHAT'S WRONG?
I'M SORRY. IT'S NOT THE END OF THE WORLD. I'M JUST SHOCKED, IS ALL. IT'S YOUR UNCLE DARRIN. YOU WON'T BELIEVE THIS!
HE GOT ATTACKED BY SOME KIND OF WILD ANIMAL!
IT TORE OFF HIS FINGER!

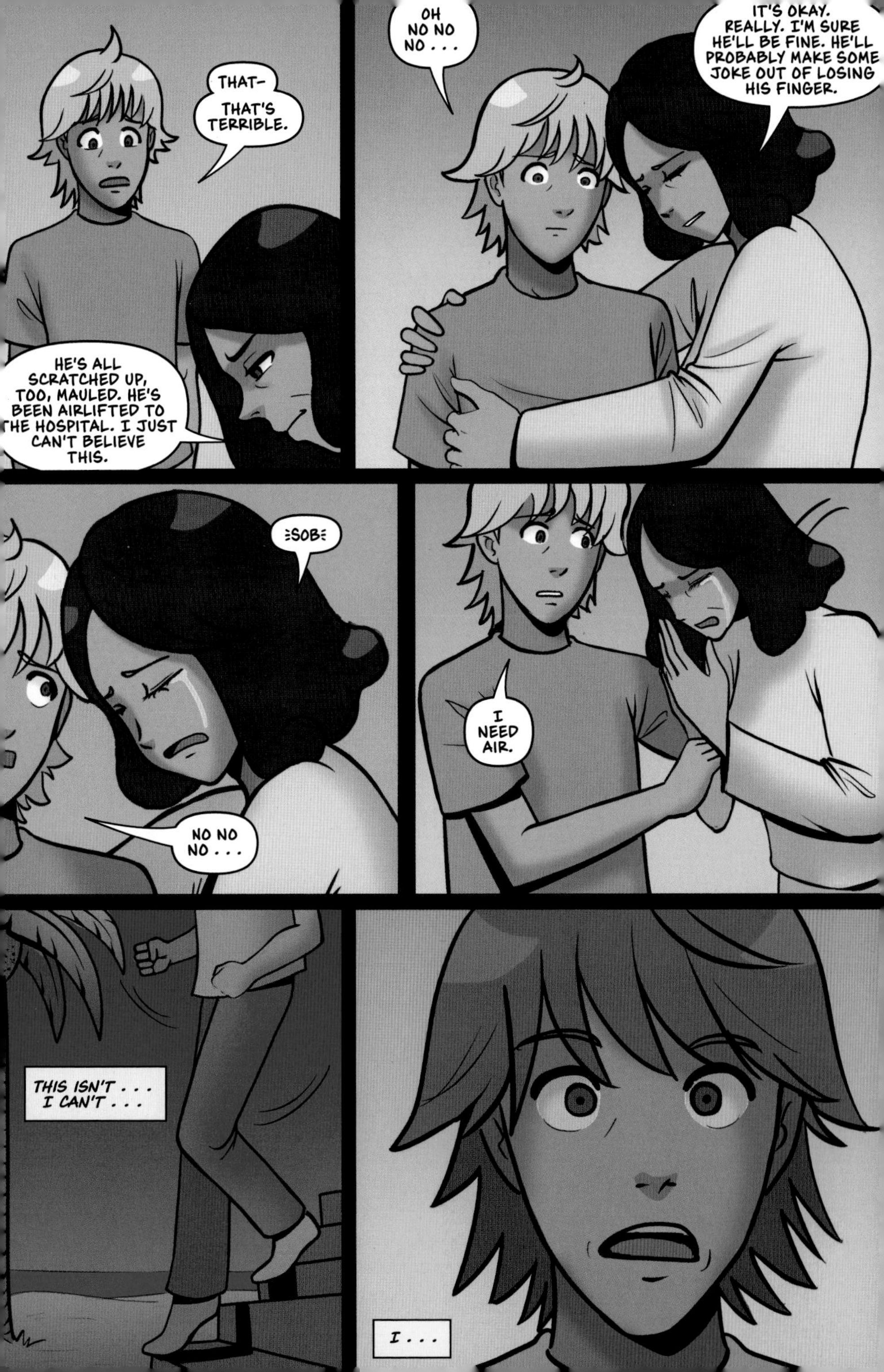
THAT-
THAT'S TERRIBLE.
HE'S ALL SCRATCHED UP, TOO, MAULED. HE'S BEEN AIRLIFTED TO THE HOSPITAL. I JUST CAN'T BELIEVE THIS.
OH NO NO NO . . .
IT'S OKAY. REALLY. I'M SURE HE'LL BE FINE. HE'LL PROBABLY MAKE SOME JOKE OUT OF LOSING HIS FINGER.
SOB
NO NO NO . . .
I NEED AIR.
THIS ISN'T . . . I CAN'T . . .
I . . .

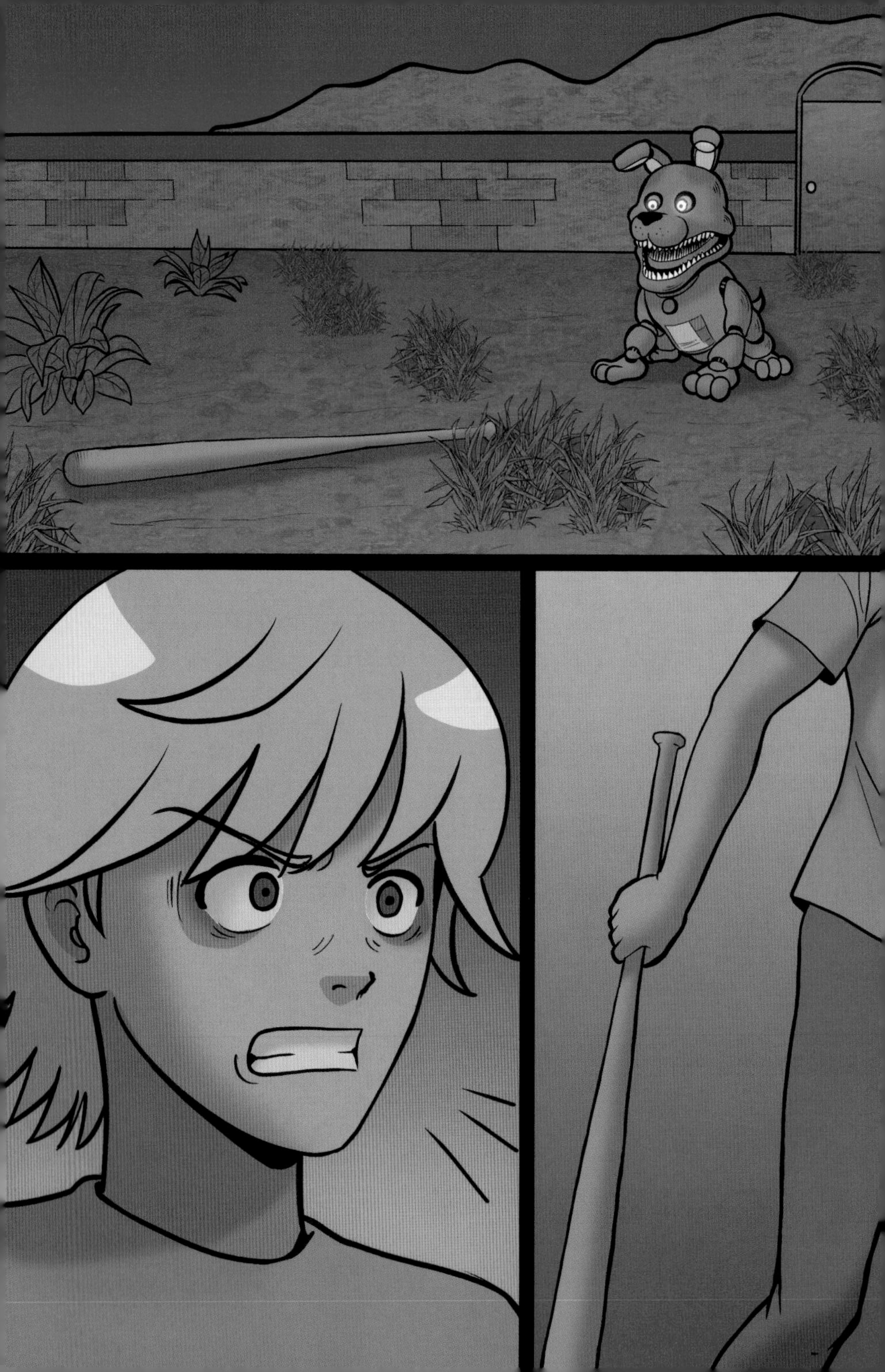

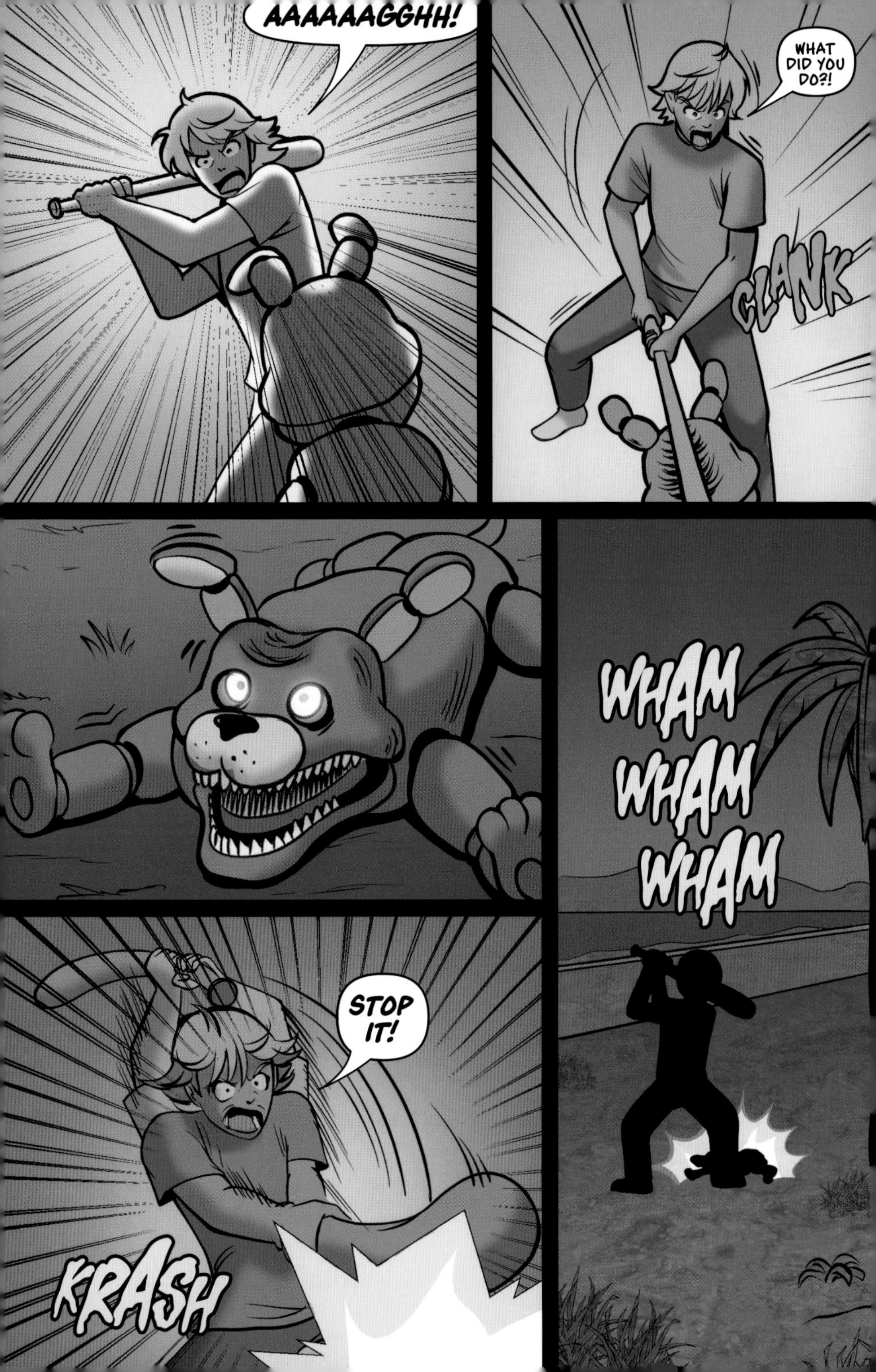
AAAAAAGGHH!
WHAT DID YOU DO?!
CLANK
WHAM
WHAM
WHAM
STOP IT!
KRASH

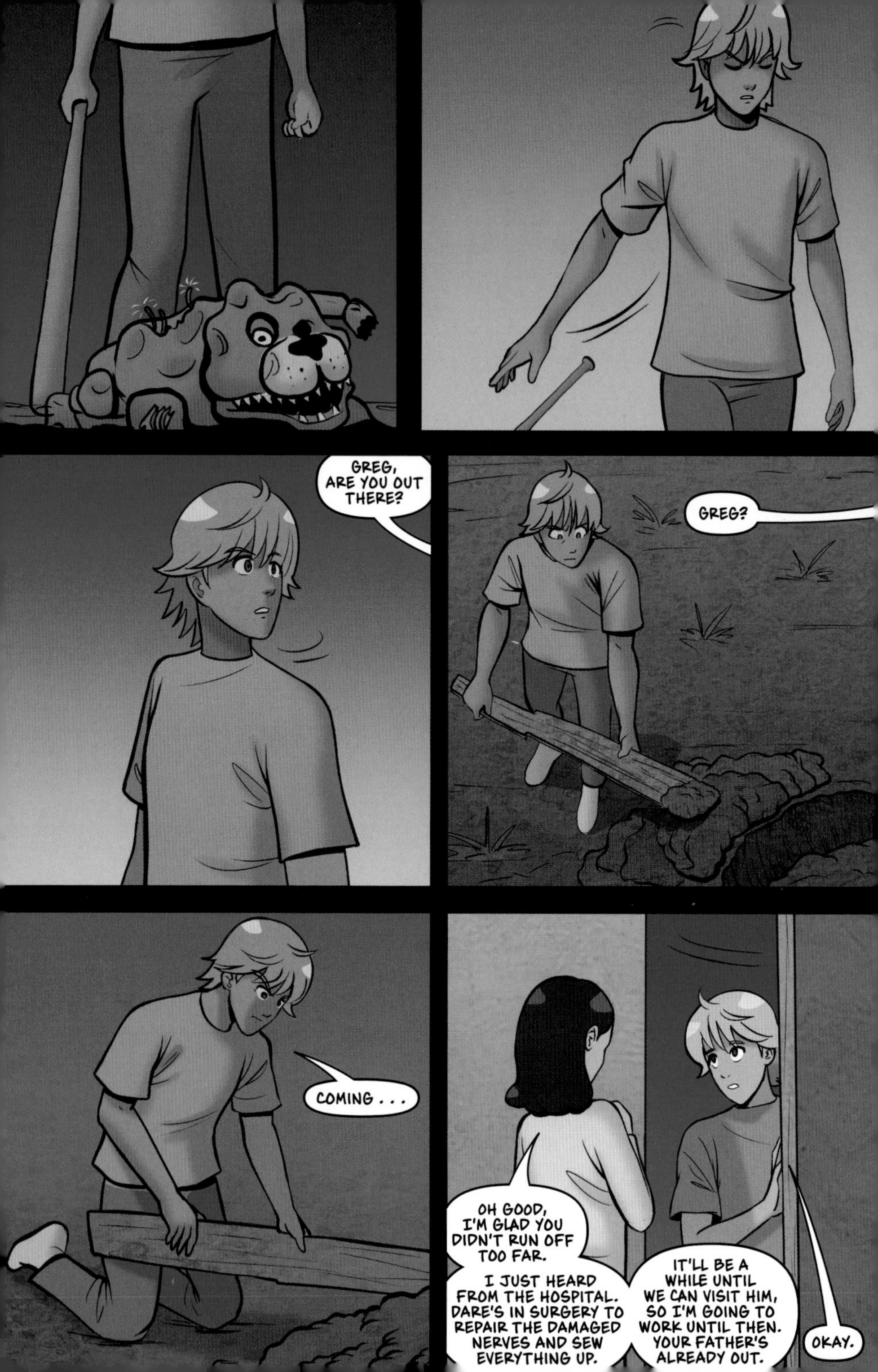
GREG, ARE YOU OUT THERE?
GREG?
COMING . . .
OH GOOD, I'M GLAD YOU DIDN'T RUN OFF TOO FAR.
I JUST HEARD FROM THE HOSPITAL. DARE'S IN SURGERY TO REPAIR THE DAMAGED NERVES AND SEW EVERYTHING UP.
IT'LL BE A WHILE UNTIL WE CAN VISIT HIM, SO I'M GOING TO WORK UNTIL THEN. YOUR FATHER'S ALREADY OUT.
OKAY.

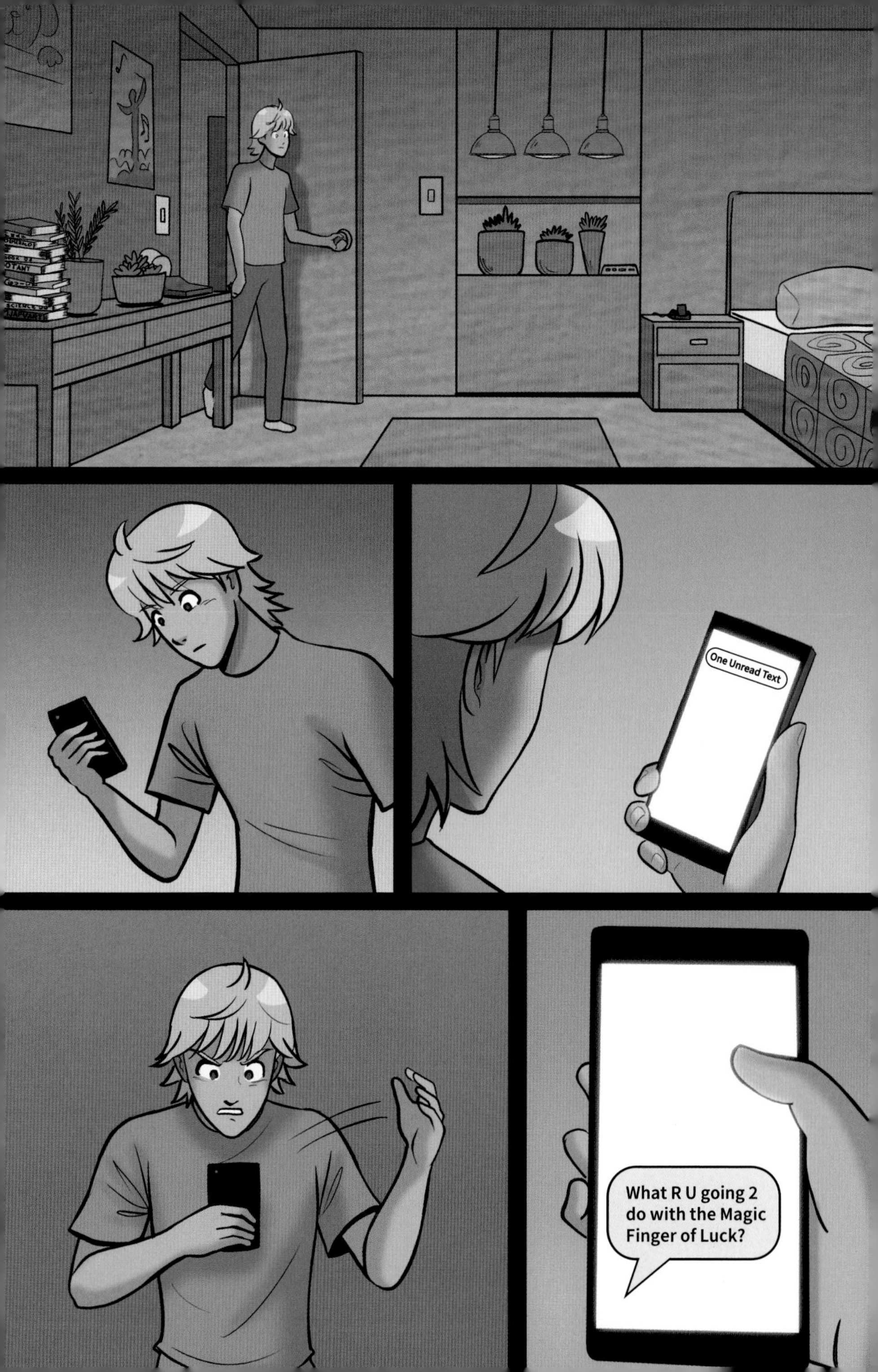
One Unread Text
What R U going 2 do with the Magic Finger of Luck?

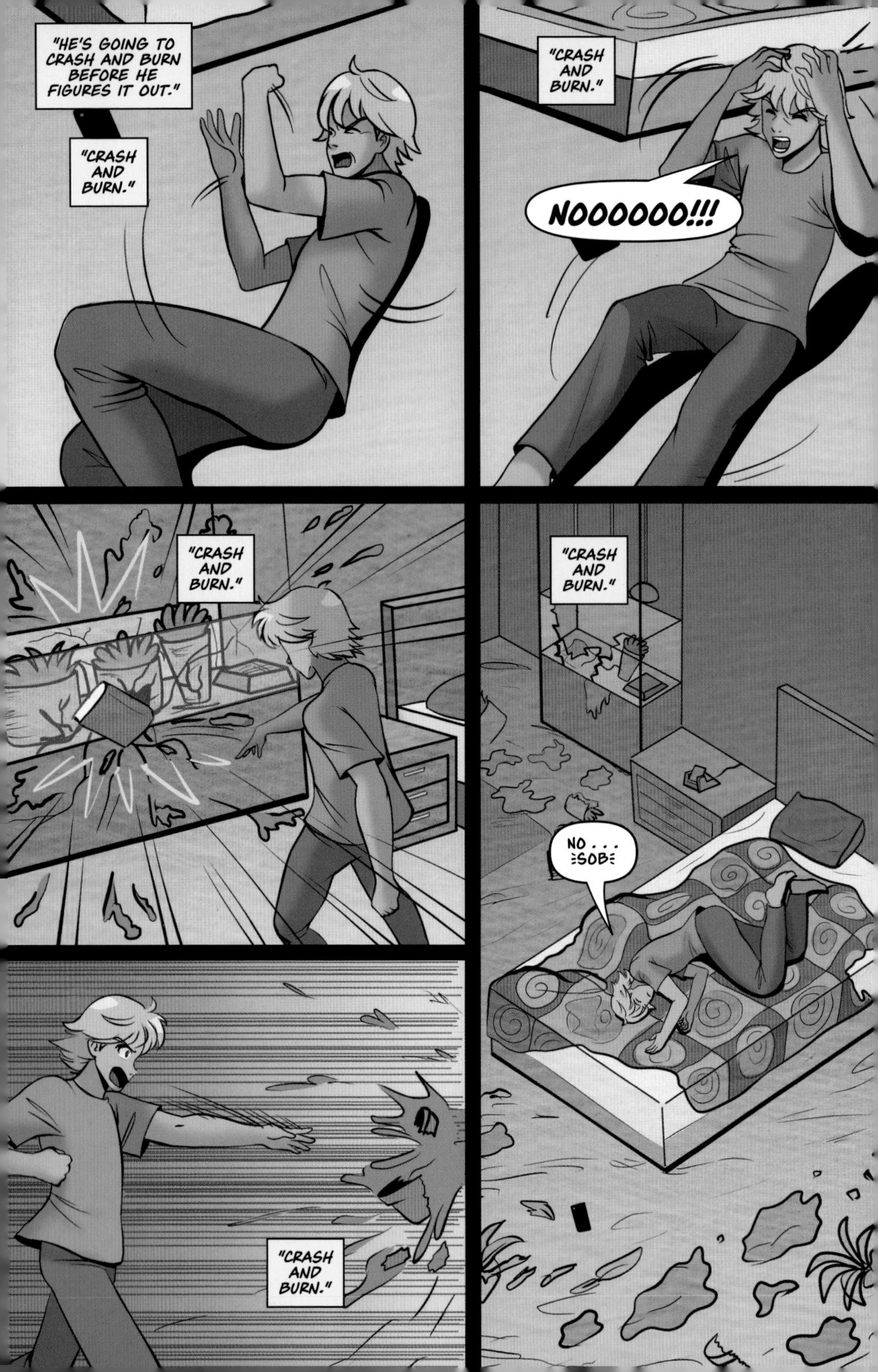
"HE'S GOING TO CRASH AND BURN BEFORE HE FIGURES IT OUT."
"CRASH AND BURN."
"CRASH AND BURN."
NOOOOOO!!!
"CRASH AND BURN."
"CRASH AND BURN."
"CRASH AND BURN."
NO . . . SOB

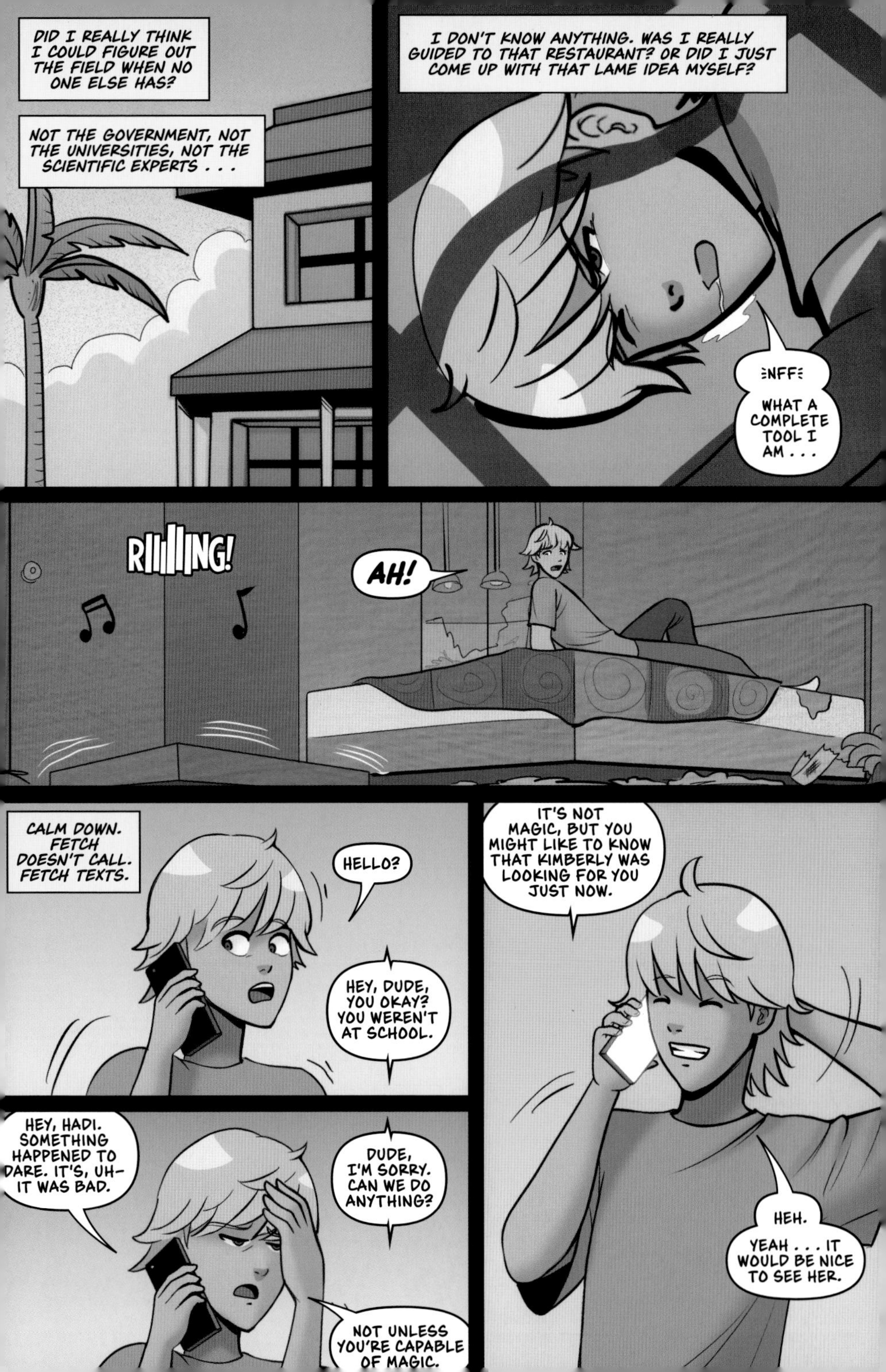
DID I REALLY THINK I COULD FIGURE OUT THE FIELD WHEN NO ONE ELSE HAS?
NOT THE GOVERNMENT, NOT THE UNIVERSITIES, NOT THE SCIENTIFIC EXPERTS . . .
I DON'T KNOW ANYTHING. WAS I REALLY GUIDED TO THAT RESTAURANT? OR DID I JUST COME UP WITH THAT LAME IDEA MYSELF?
SNFF
WHAT A COMPLETE TOOL I AM . . .
RIIIIING!
AH!
CALM DOWN. FETCH DOESN'T CALL. FETCH TEXTS.
HELLO?
HEY, DUDE, YOU OKAY? YOU WEREN'T AT SCHOOL.
HEY, HADI. SOMETHING HAPPENED TO DARE. IT'S, UH– IT WAS BAD.
DUDE, I'M SORRY. CAN WE DO ANYTHING?
NOT UNLESS YOU'RE CAPABLE OF MAGIC.
IT'S NOT MAGIC, BUT YOU MIGHT LIKE TO KNOW THAT KIMBERLY WAS LOOKING FOR YOU JUST NOW.
HEH.
YEAH . . . IT WOULD BE NICE TO SEE HER.

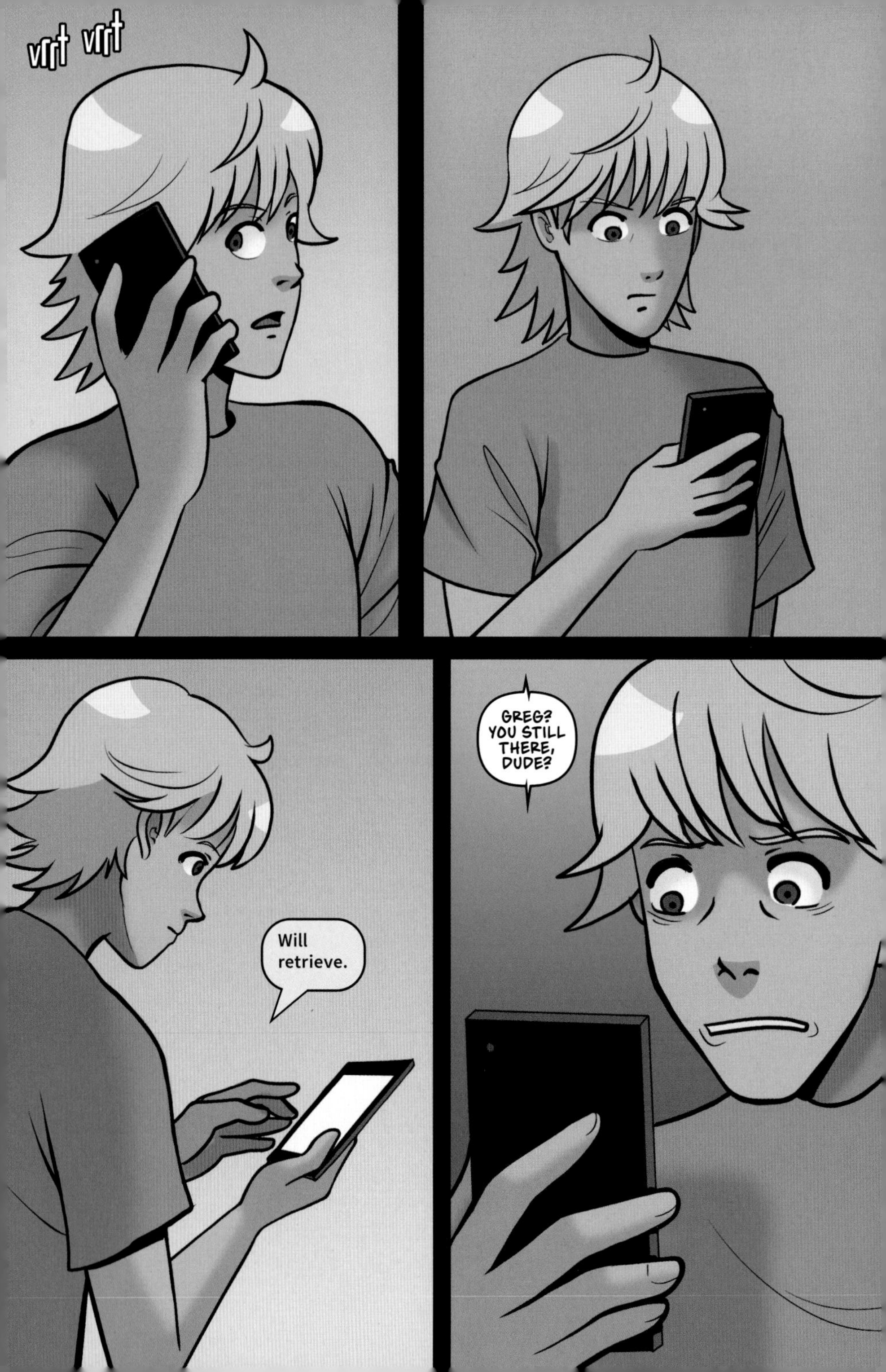
vrrt vrrt
Will retrieve.
GREG? YOU STILL THERE, DUDE?

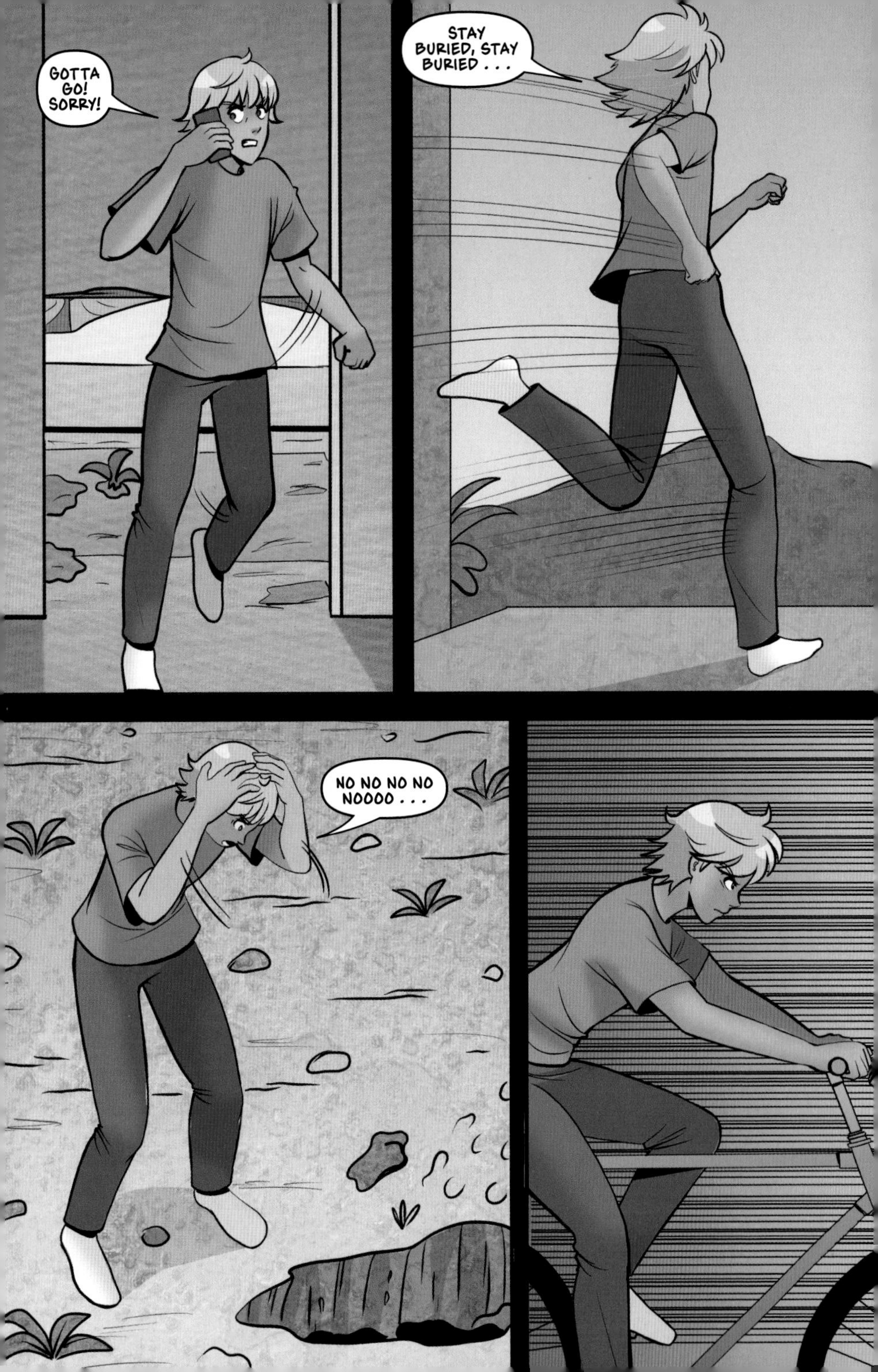
GOTTA GO! SORRY!
STAY BURIED, STAY BURIED . . .
NO NO NO NO NOOOO . . .

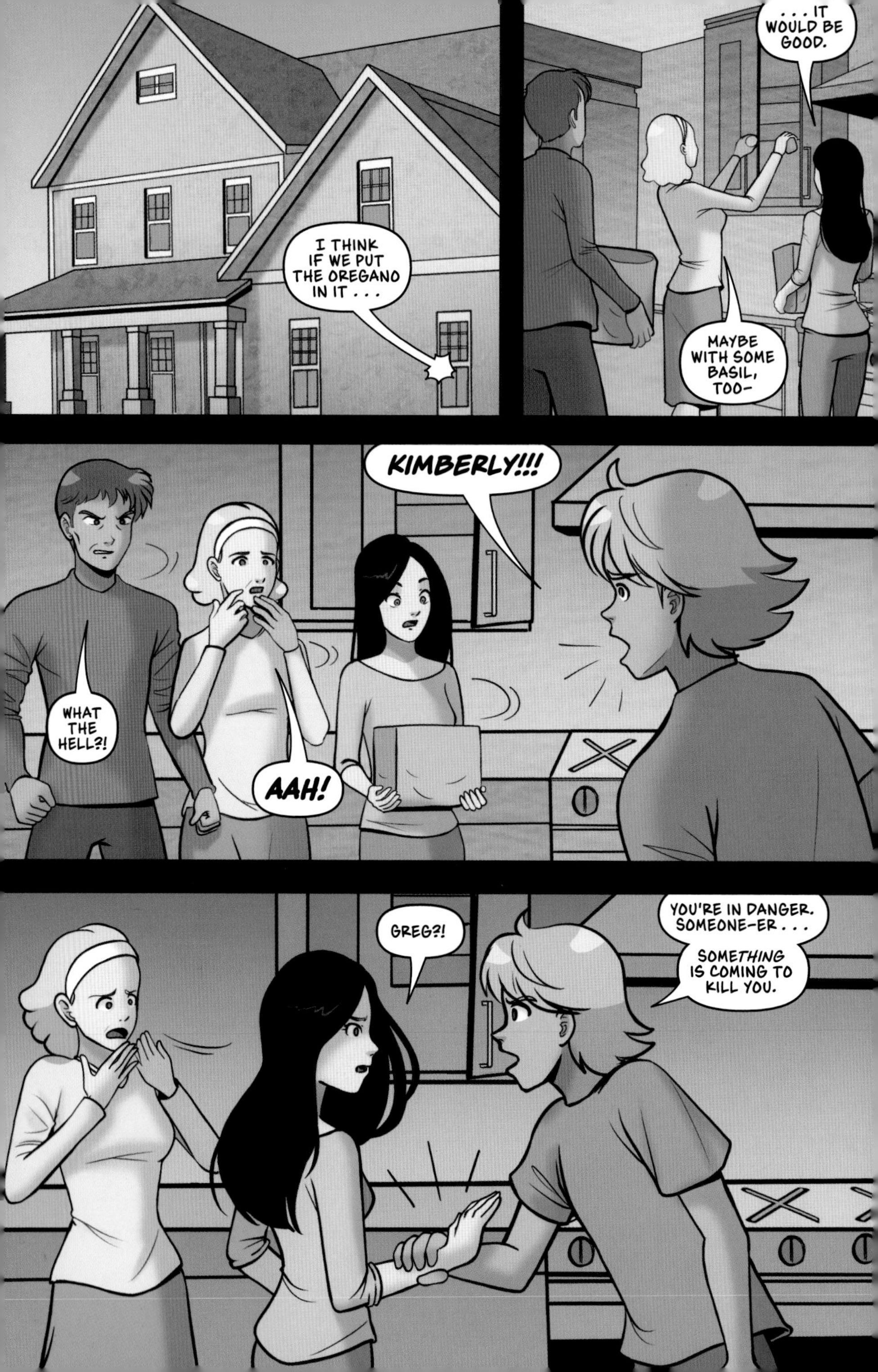
I THINK IF WE PUT THE OREGANO IN IT . . .
. . . IT WOULD BE GOOD.
MAYBE WITH SOME BASIL, TOO-
KIMBERLY!!!
WHAT THE HELL?!
AAH!
GREG?!
YOU'RE IN DANGER. SOMEONE-ER . . .
SOMETHING IS COMING TO KILL YOU.

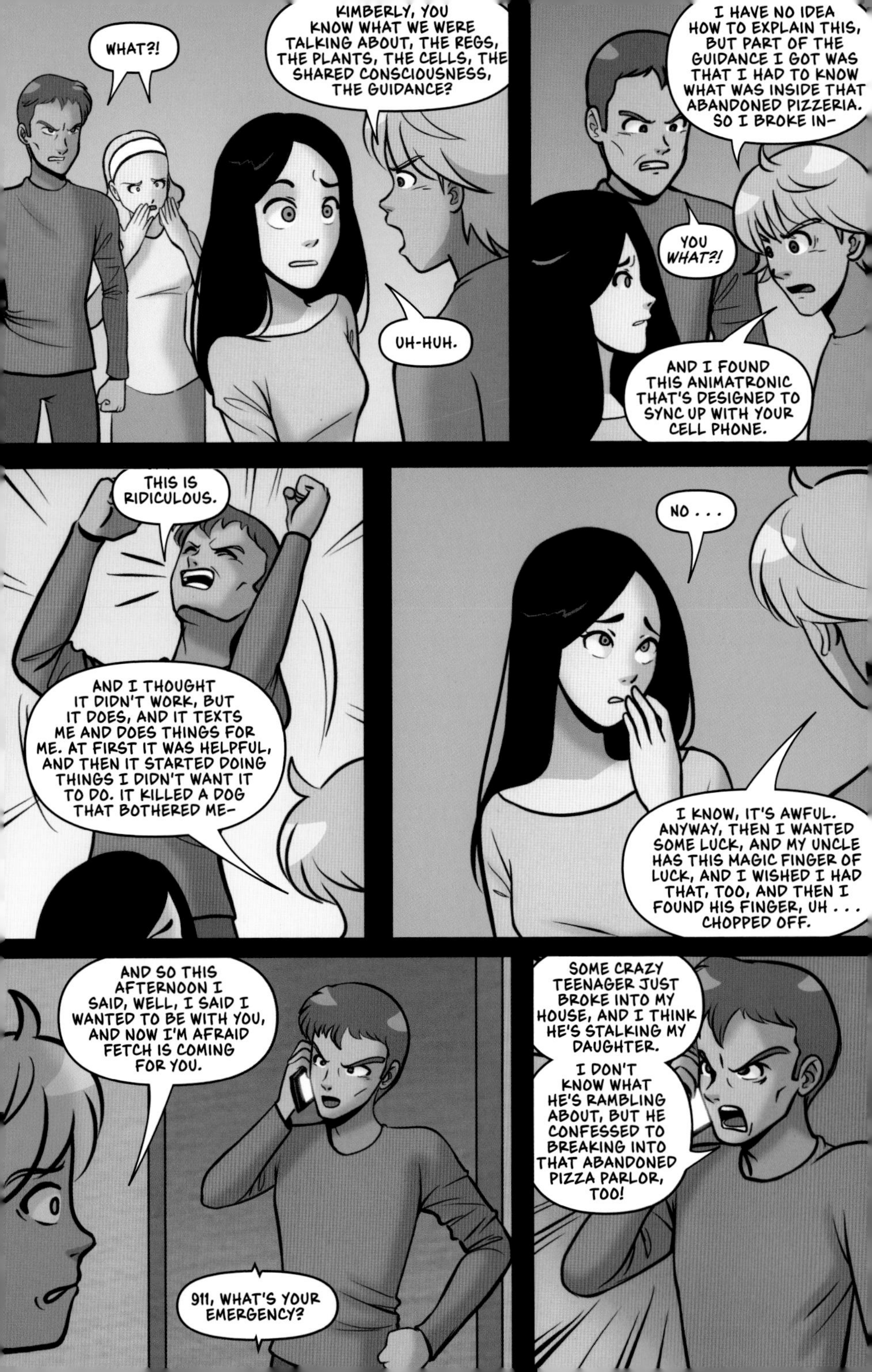
WHAT?!
KIMBERLY, YOU KNOW WHAT WE WERE TALKING ABOUT, THE REGS, THE PLANTS, THE CELLS, THE SHARED CONSCIOUSNESS, THE GUIDANCE?
UH-HUH.
I HAVE NO IDEA HOW TO EXPLAIN THIS, BUT PART OF THE GUIDANCE I GOT WAS THAT I HAD TO KNOW WHAT WAS INSIDE THAT ABANDONED PIZZERIA. SO I BROKE IN–
YOU WHAT?!
AND I FOUND THIS ANIMATRONIC THAT'S DESIGNED TO SYNC UP WITH YOUR CELL PHONE.
THIS IS RIDICULOUS.
AND I THOUGHT IT DIDN'T WORK, BUT IT DOES, AND IT TEXTS ME AND DOES THINGS FOR ME. AT FIRST IT WAS HELPFUL, AND THEN IT STARTED DOING THINGS I DIDN'T WANT IT TO DO. IT KILLED A DOG THAT BOTHERED ME–
NO . . .
I KNOW, IT'S AWFUL. ANYWAY, THEN I WANTED SOME LUCK, AND MY UNCLE HAS THIS MAGIC FINGER OF LUCK, AND I WISHED I HAD THAT, TOO, AND THEN I FOUND HIS FINGER, UH . . . CHOPPED OFF.
AND SO THIS AFTERNOON I SAID, WELL, I SAID I WANTED TO BE WITH YOU, AND NOW I'M AFRAID FETCH IS COMING FOR YOU.
911, WHAT'S YOUR EMERGENCY?
SOME CRAZY TEENAGER JUST BROKE INTO MY HOUSE, AND I THINK HE'S STALKING MY DAUGHTER.
I DON'T KNOW WHAT HE'S RAMBLING ABOUT, BUT HE CONFESSED TO BREAKING INTO THAT ABANDONED PIZZA PARLOR, TOO!

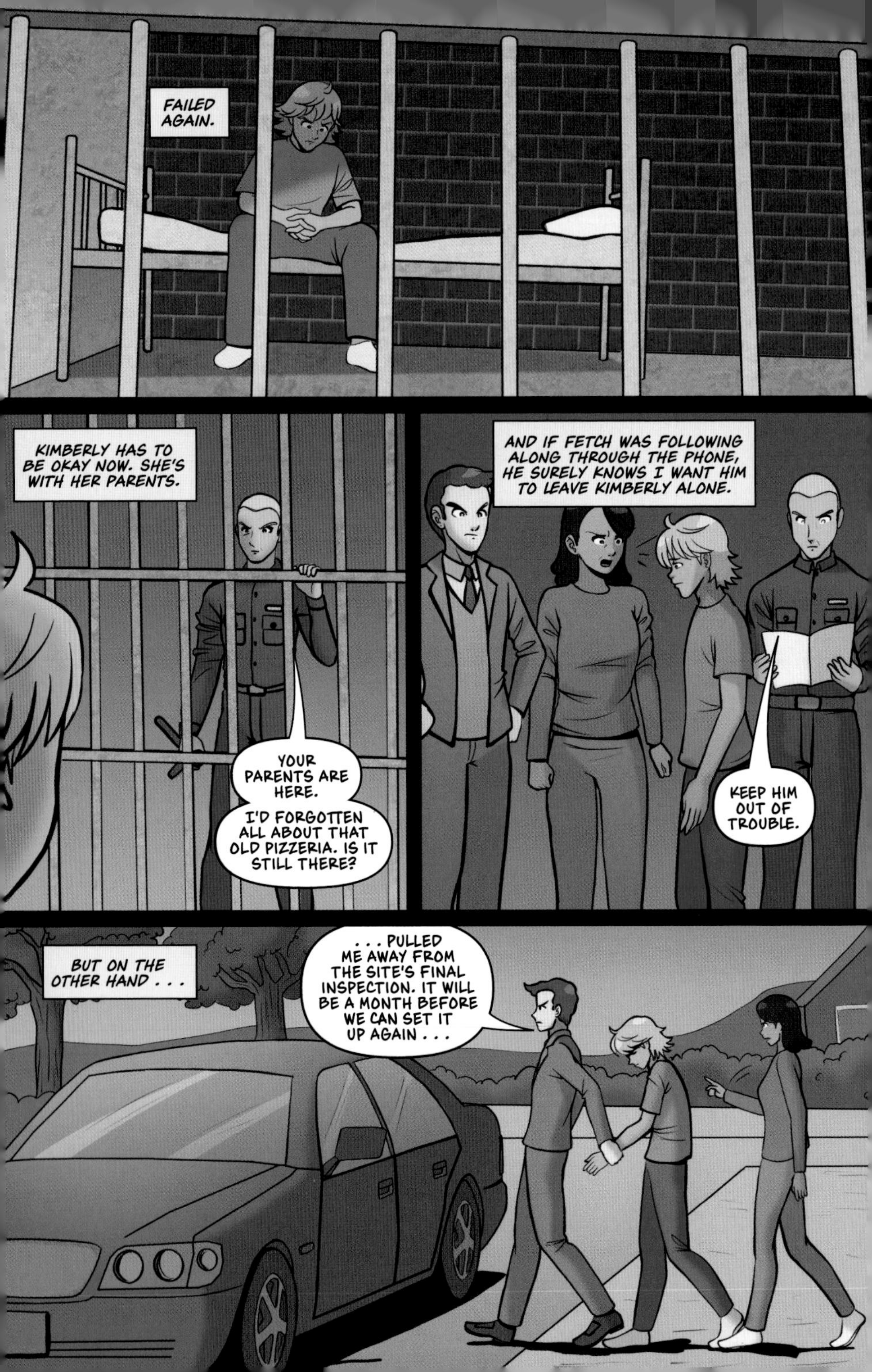
FAILED AGAIN.
KIMBERLY HAS TO BE OKAY NOW. SHE'S WITH HER PARENTS.
YOUR PARENTS ARE HERE.
I'D FORGOTTEN ALL ABOUT THAT OLD PIZZERIA. IS IT STILL THERE?
AND IF FETCH WAS FOLLOWING ALONG THROUGH THE PHONE, HE SURELY KNOWS I WANT HIM TO LEAVE KIMBERLY ALONE.
KEEP HIM OUT OF TROUBLE.
BUT ON THE OTHER HAND . . .
. . . PULLED ME AWAY FROM THE SITE'S FINAL INSPECTION. IT WILL BE A MONTH BEFORE WE CAN SET IT UP AGAIN . . .

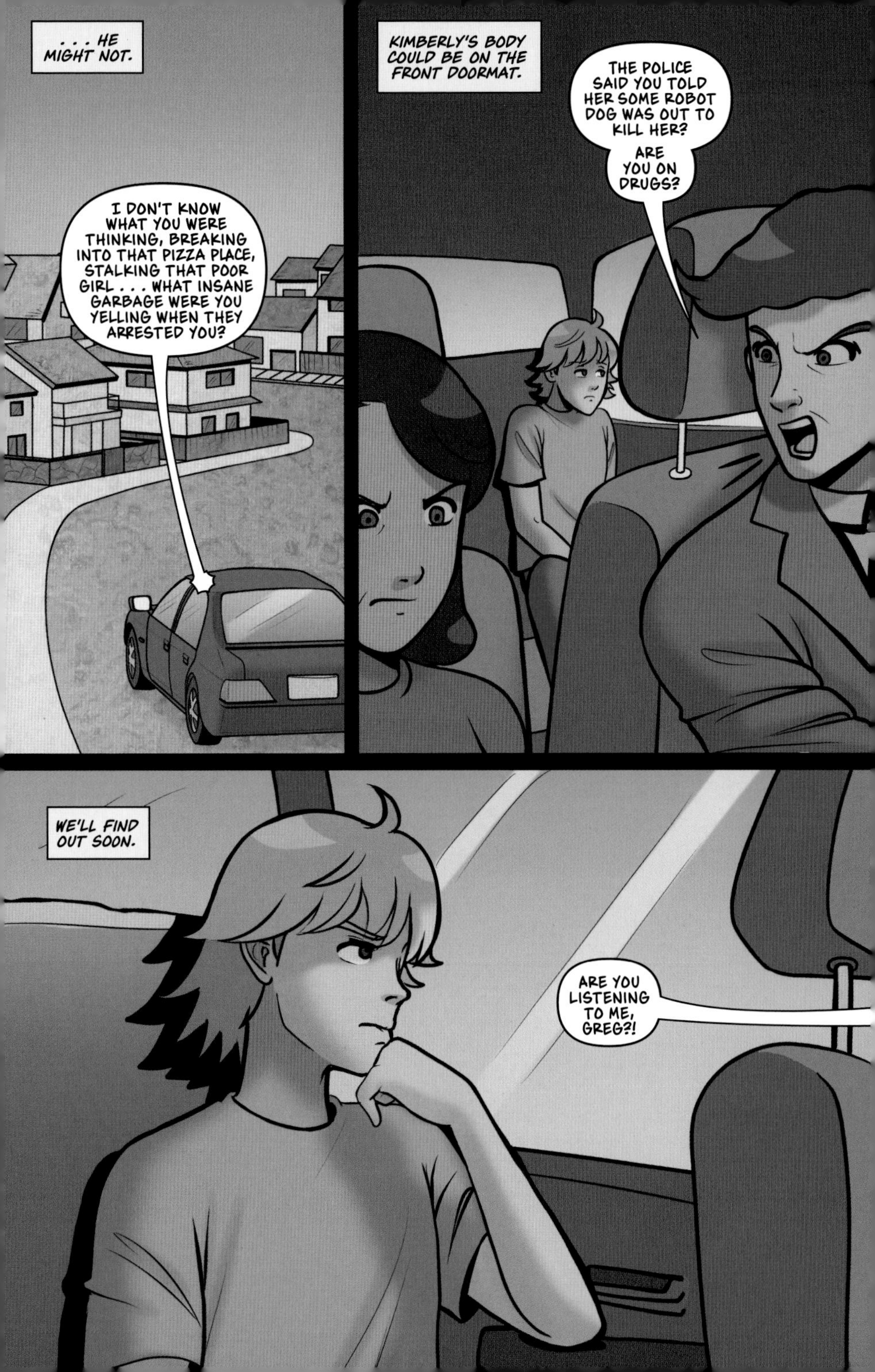
. . . HE MIGHT NOT.
I DON'T KNOW WHAT YOU WERE THINKING, BREAKING INTO THAT PIZZA PLACE, STALKING THAT POOR GIRL . . . WHAT INSANE GARBAGE WERE YOU YELLING WHEN THEY ARRESTED YOU?
KIMBERLY'S BODY COULD BE ON THE FRONT DOORMAT.
THE POLICE SAID YOU TOLD HER SOME ROBOT DOG WAS OUT TO KILL HER?
ARE YOU ON DRUGS?
WE'LL FIND OUT SOON.
ARE YOU LISTENING TO ME, GREG?!

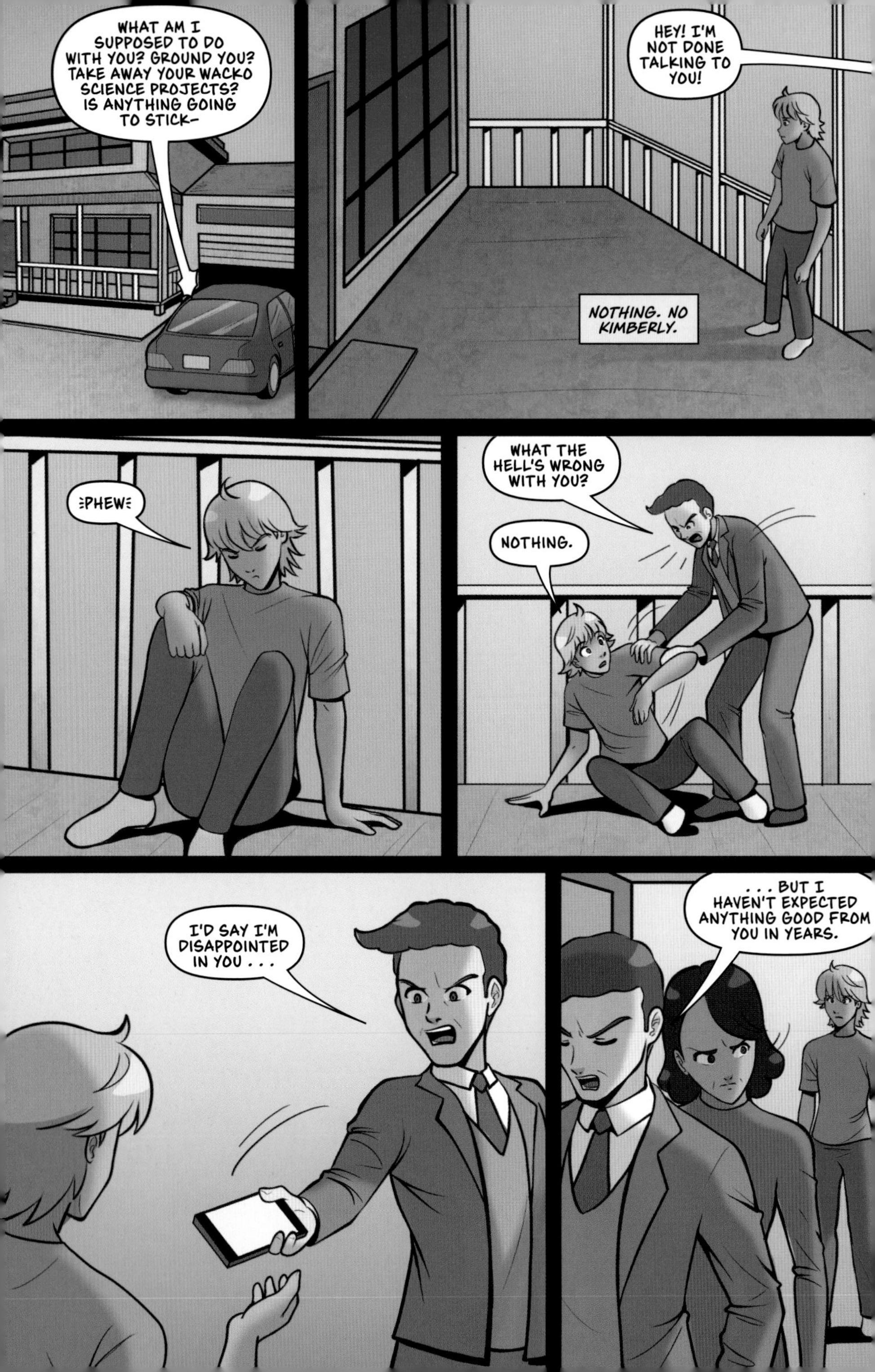
WHAT AM I SUPPOSED TO DO WITH YOU? GROUND YOU? TAKE AWAY YOUR WACKO SCIENCE PROJECTS? IS ANYTHING GOING TO STICK–
HEY! I'M NOT DONE TALKING TO YOU!
NOTHING. NO KIMBERLY.
PHEW
WHAT THE HELL'S WRONG WITH YOU?
NOTHING.
I'D SAY I'M DISAPPOINTED IN YOU . . .
. . . BUT I HAVEN'T EXPECTED ANYTHING GOOD FROM YOU IN YEARS.

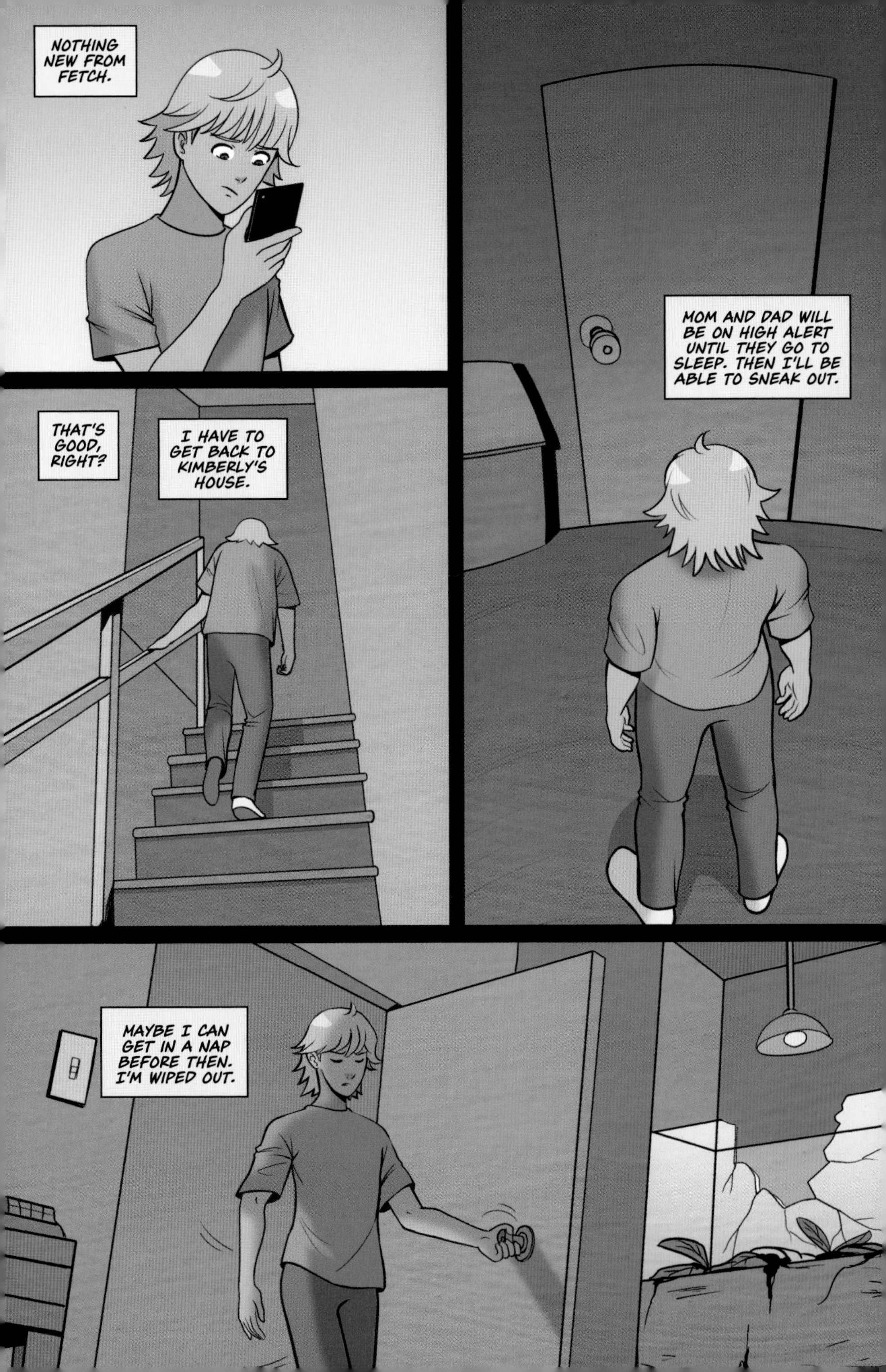
NOTHING NEW FROM FETCH.
THAT'S GOOD, RIGHT?
I HAVE TO GET BACK TO KIMBERLY'S HOUSE.
MOM AND DAD WILL BE ON HIGH ALERT UNTIL THEY GO TO SLEEP. THEN I'LL BE ABLE TO SNEAK OUT.
MAYBE I CAN GET IN A NAP BEFORE THEN. I'M WIPED OUT.

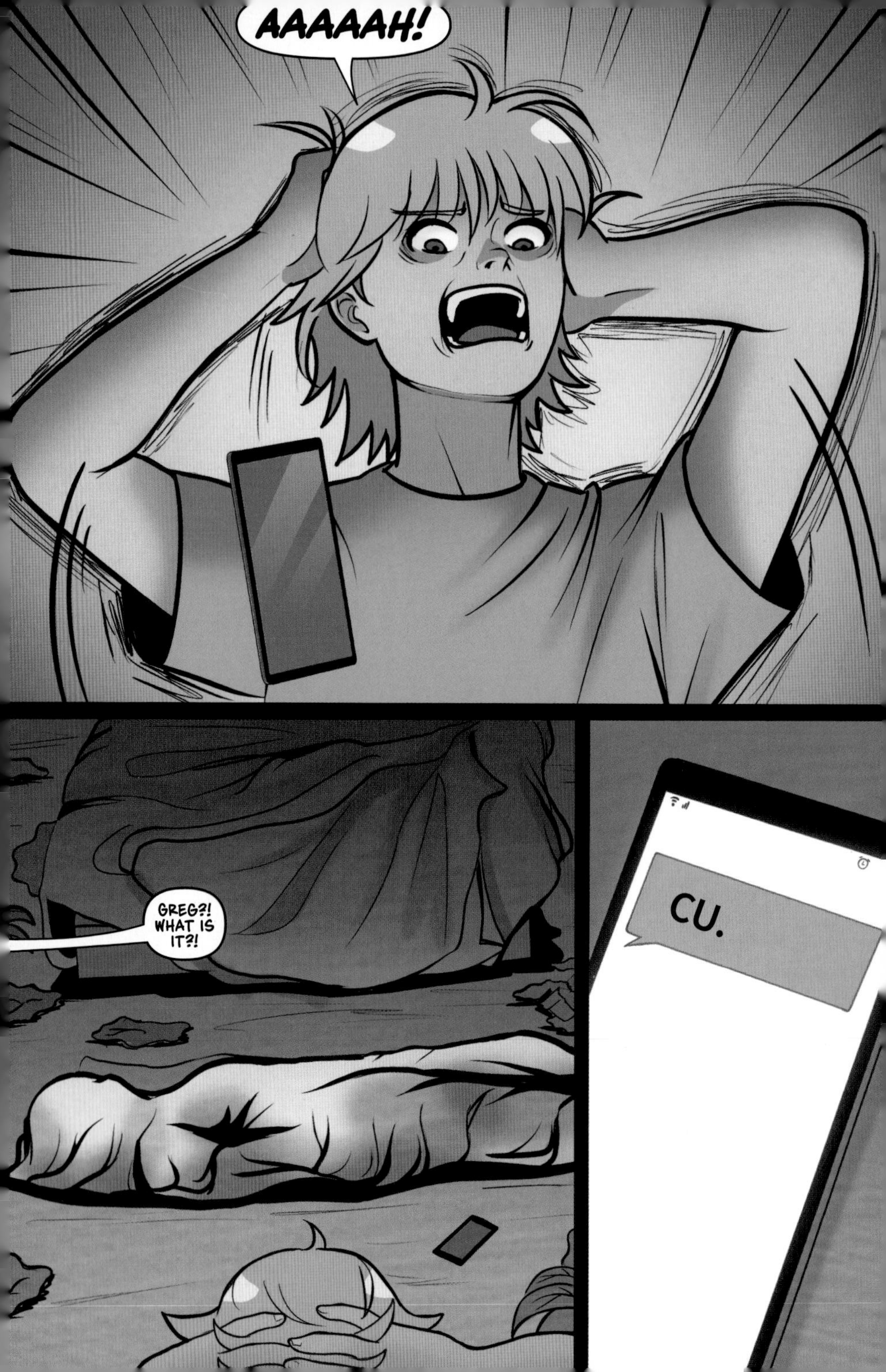
AAAAAH!
GREG?! WHAT IS IT?!
CU.

ROOM FOR ONE MORE

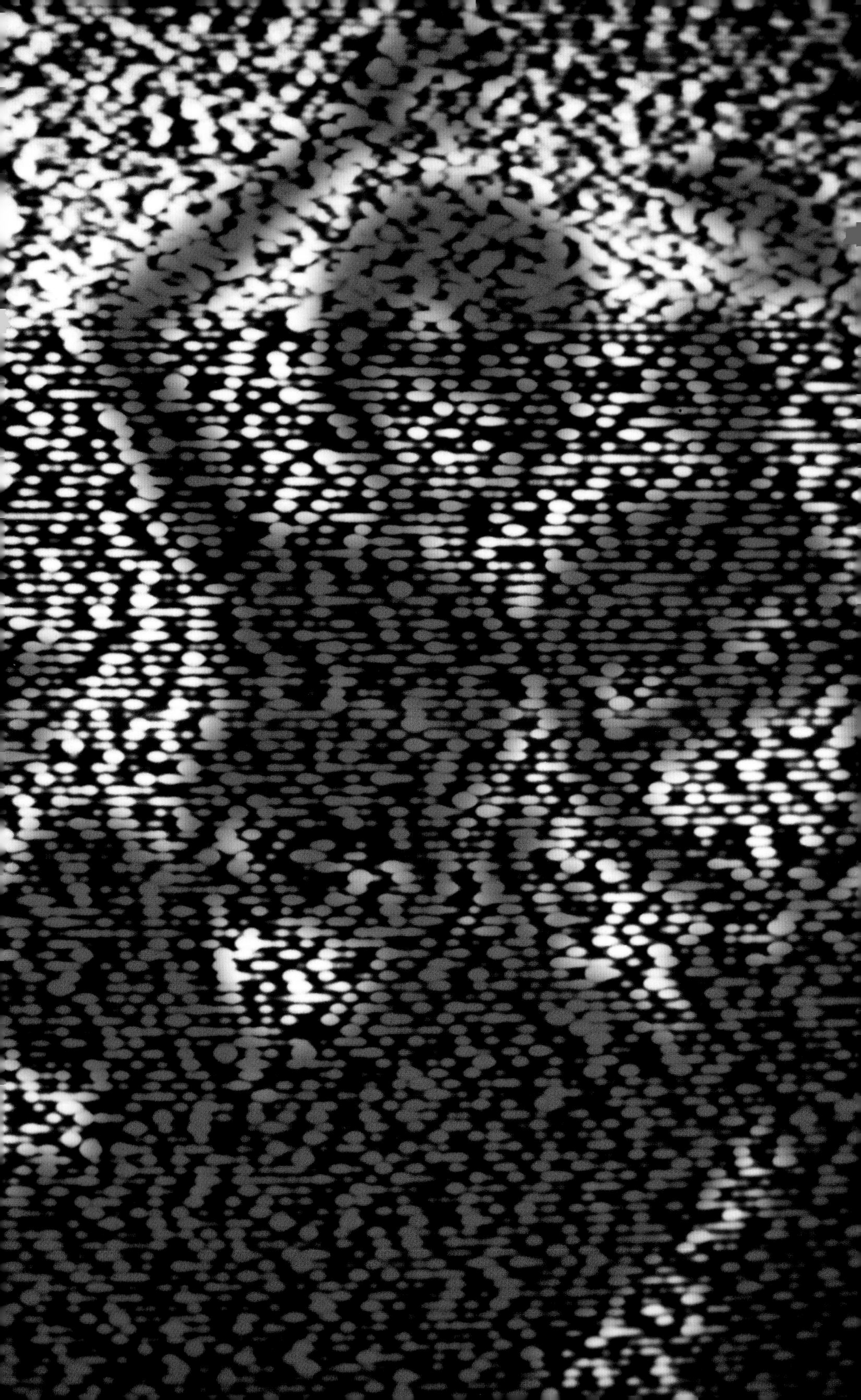

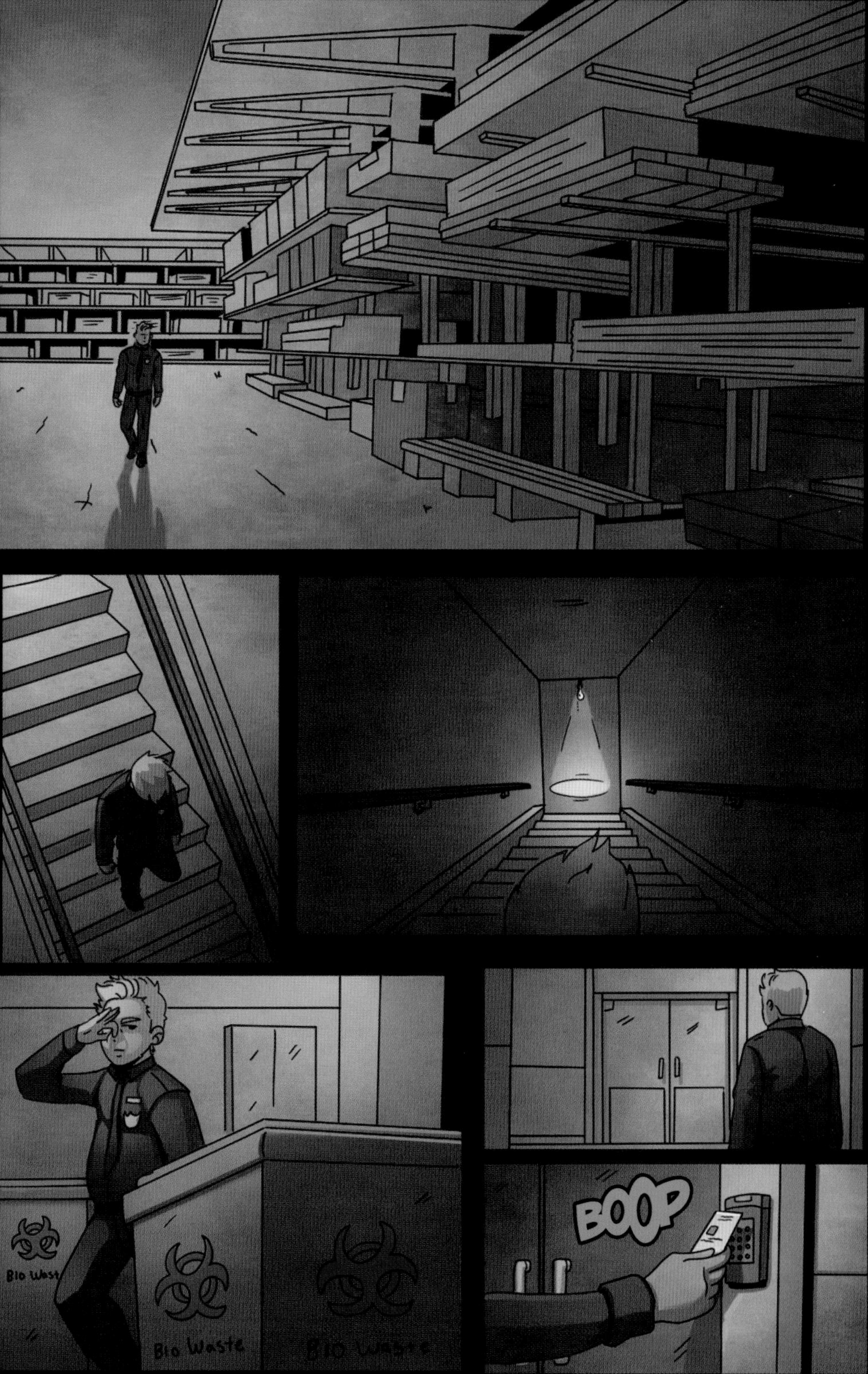
Bio Wast
Bio Waste
BIO Waste
BOOP

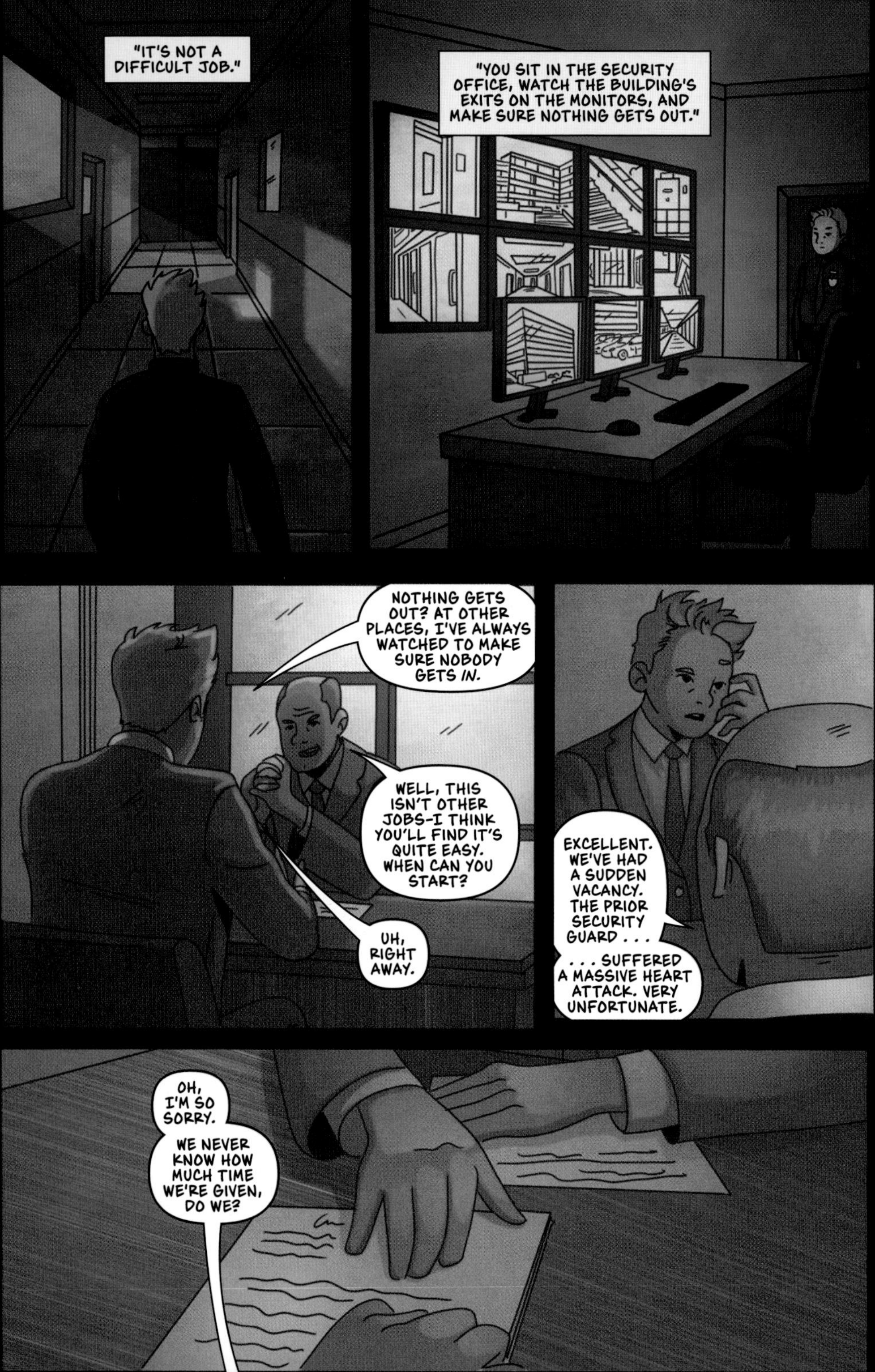
"IT'S NOT A DIFFICULT JOB."
"YOU SIT IN THE SECURITY OFFICE, WATCH THE BUILDING'S EXITS ON THE MONITORS, AND MAKE SURE NOTHING GETS OUT."
NOTHING GETS OUT? AT OTHER PLACES, I'VE ALWAYS WATCHED TO MAKE SURE NOBODY GETS *IN*.
WELL, THIS ISN'T OTHER JOBS–I THINK YOU'LL FIND IT'S QUITE EASY. WHEN CAN YOU START?
UH, RIGHT AWAY.
EXCELLENT. WE'VE HAD A SUDDEN VACANCY. THE PRIOR SECURITY GUARD . . .
. . . SUFFERED A MASSIVE HEART ATTACK. VERY UNFORTUNATE.
OH, I'M SO SORRY.
WE NEVER KNOW HOW MUCH TIME WE'RE GIVEN, DO WE?

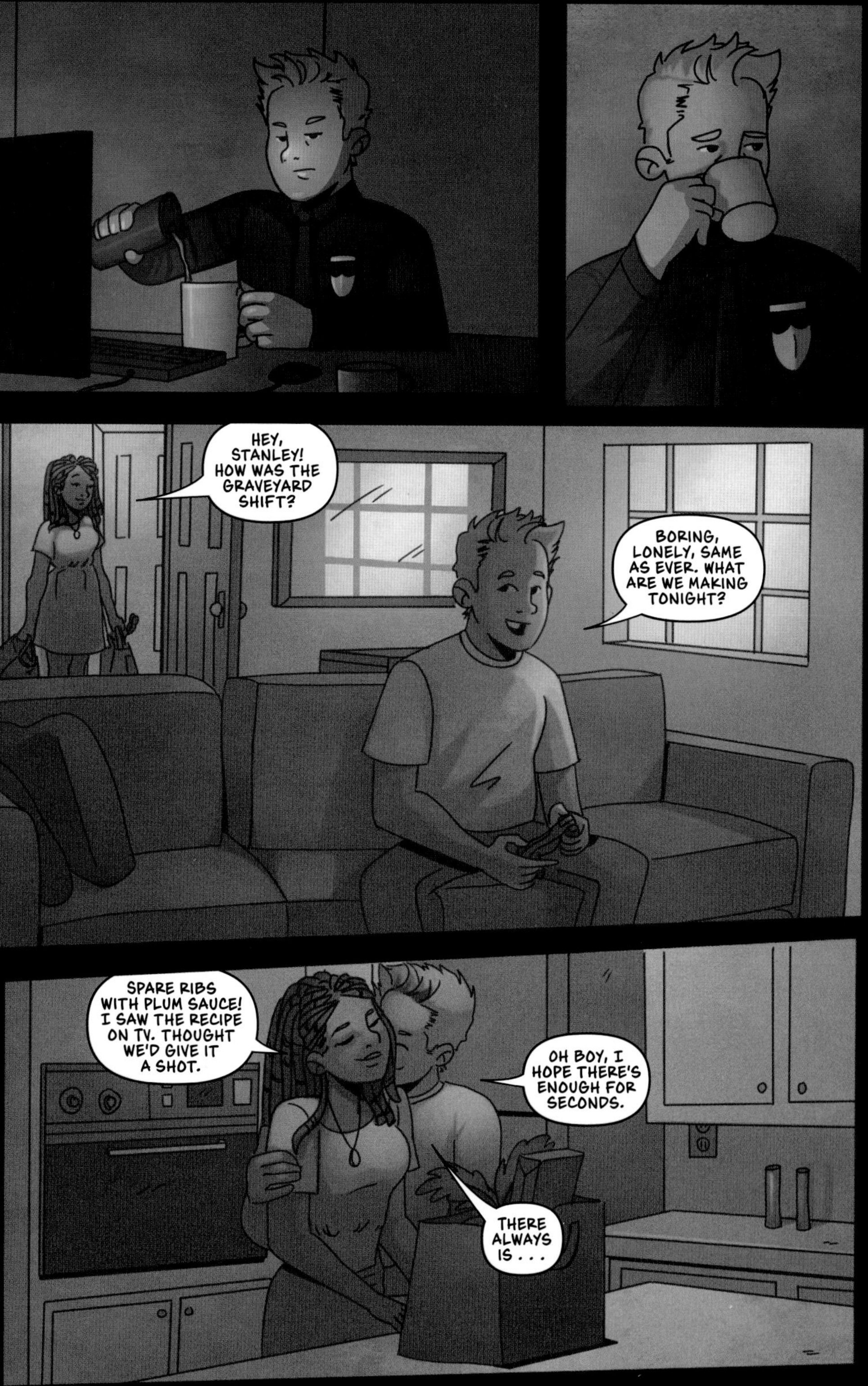
HEY, STANLEY! HOW WAS THE GRAVEYARD SHIFT?
BORING, LONELY, SAME AS EVER. WHAT ARE WE MAKING TONIGHT?
SPARE RIBS WITH PLUM SAUCE! I SAW THE RECIPE ON TV. THOUGHT WE'D GIVE IT A SHOT.
OH BOY, I HOPE THERE'S ENOUGH FOR SECONDS.
THERE ALWAYS IS . . .

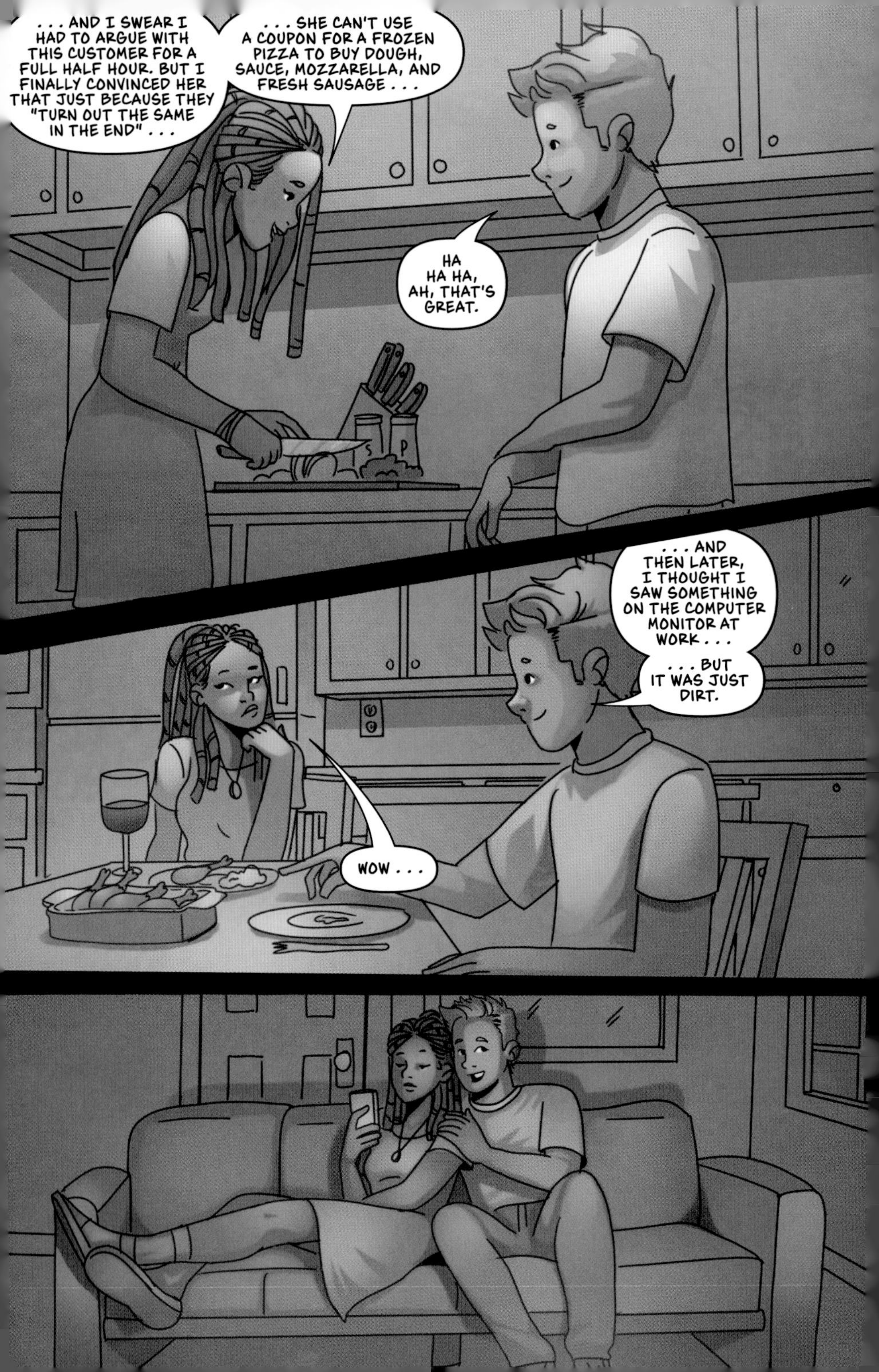
. . . AND I SWEAR I HAD TO ARGUE WITH THIS CUSTOMER FOR A FULL HALF HOUR. BUT I FINALLY CONVINCED HER THAT JUST BECAUSE THEY "TURN OUT THE SAME IN THE END" . . .
. . . SHE CAN'T USE A COUPON FOR A FROZEN PIZZA TO BUY DOUGH, SAUCE, MOZZARELLA, AND FRESH SAUSAGE . . .
HA HA HA, AH, THAT'S GREAT.
. . . AND THEN LATER, I THOUGHT I SAW SOMETHING ON THE COMPUTER MONITOR AT WORK . . .
. . . BUT IT WAS JUST DIRT.
WOW . . .

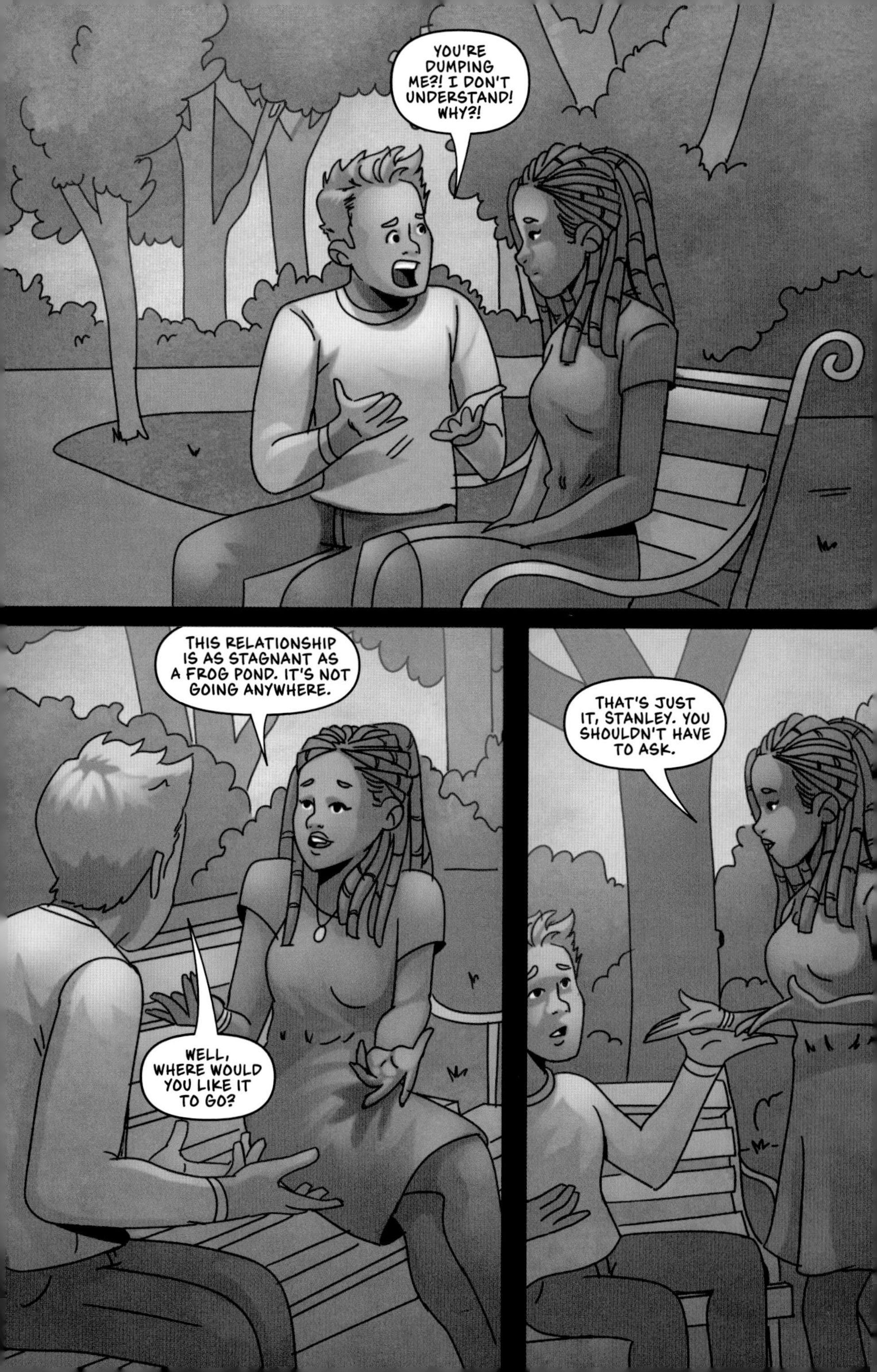
YOU'RE DUMPING ME?! I DON'T UNDERSTAND! WHY?!
THIS RELATIONSHIP IS AS STAGNANT AS A FROG POND. IT'S NOT GOING ANYWHERE.
WELL, WHERE WOULD YOU LIKE IT TO GO?
THAT'S JUST IT, STANLEY. YOU SHOULDN'T HAVE TO ASK.

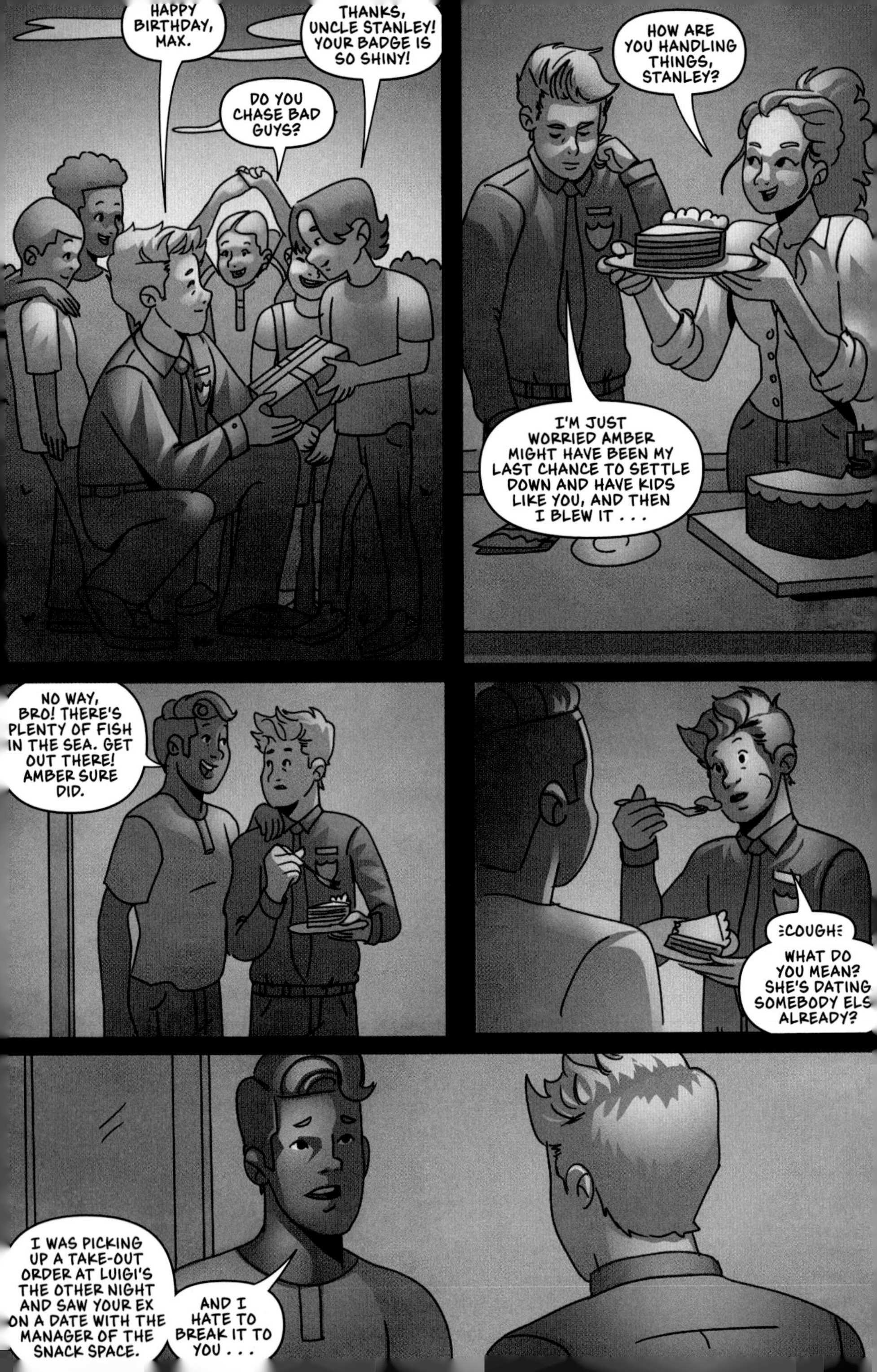
HAPPY BIRTHDAY, MAX.
THANKS, UNCLE STANLEY! YOUR BADGE IS SO SHINY!
DO YOU CHASE BAD GUYS?
HOW ARE YOU HANDLING THINGS, STANLEY?
I'M JUST WORRIED AMBER MIGHT HAVE BEEN MY LAST CHANCE TO SETTLE DOWN AND HAVE KIDS LIKE YOU, AND THEN I BLEW IT . . .
NO WAY, BRO! THERE'S PLENTY OF FISH IN THE SEA. GET OUT THERE! AMBER SURE DID.
COUGH
WHAT DO YOU MEAN? SHE'S DATING SOMEBODY ELS ALREADY?
I WAS PICKING UP A TAKE-OUT ORDER AT LUIGI'S THE OTHER NIGHT AND SAW YOUR EX ON A DATE WITH THE MANAGER OF THE SNACK SPACE.
AND I HATE TO BREAK IT TO YOU . . .

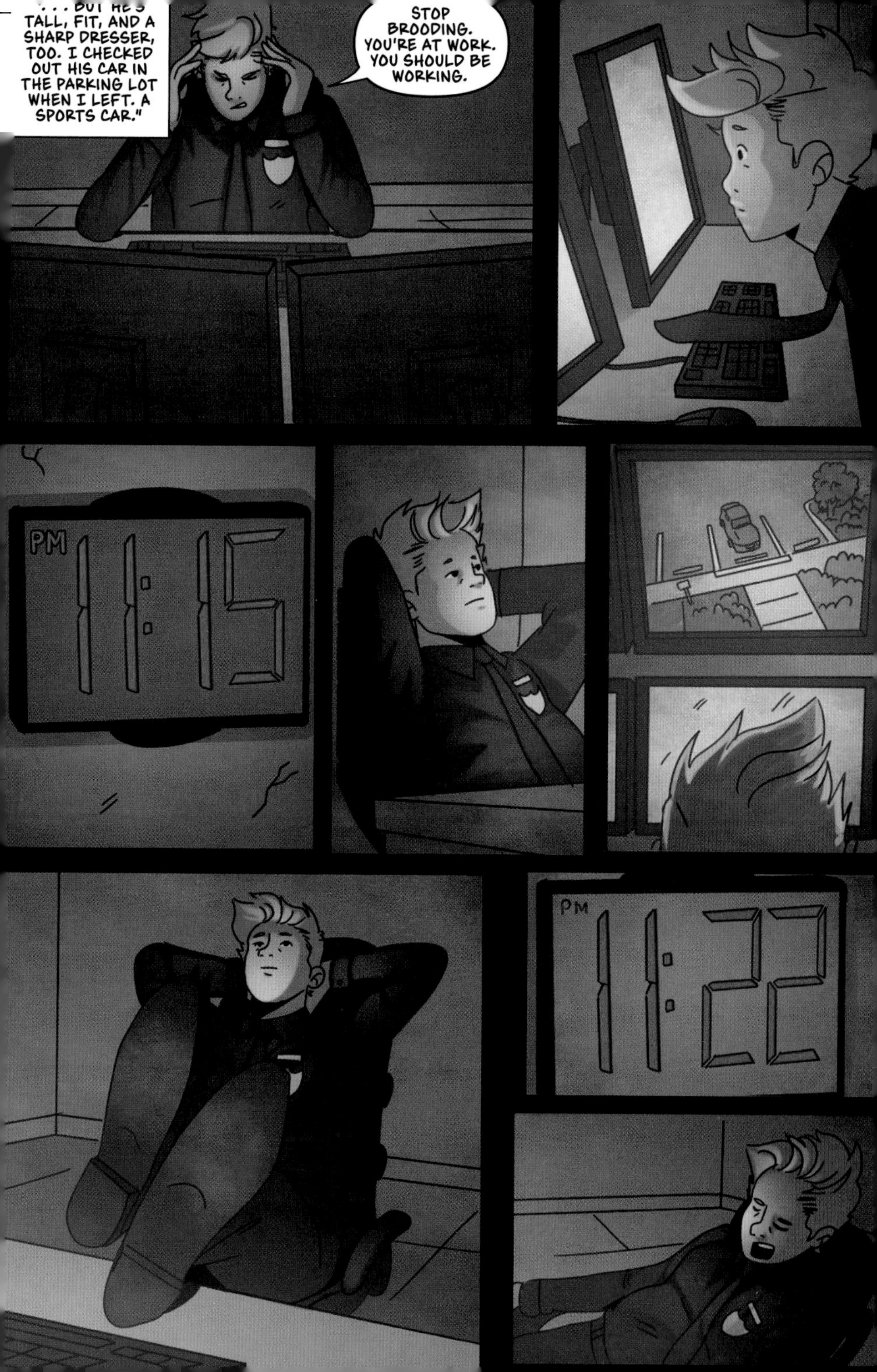
". . . BUT HE'S TALL, FIT, AND A SHARP DRESSER, TOO. I CHECKED OUT HIS CAR IN THE PARKING LOT WHEN I LEFT. A SPORTS CAR."
STOP BROODING. YOU'RE AT WORK. YOU SHOULD BE WORKING.
PM 11:15
PM 11:22

MOTION SENSOR ACTIVATED
MOTI SENSO ACTIVA
MOTION SENSOR ACTIVATED
SECURITY OFFICE VENT
BEEP BEEP BEEP BEEP BEEP BEEP BEEP
BEEP BEEP BEEP BEEP BEEP BEEP
BEEP BEE—

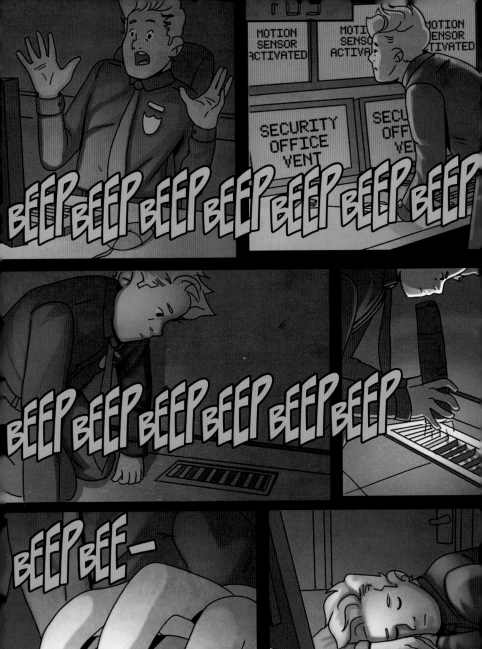

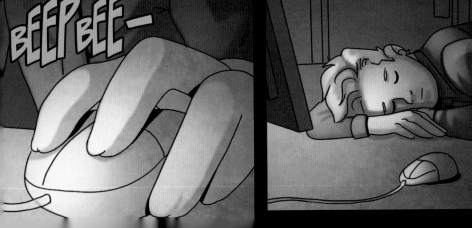

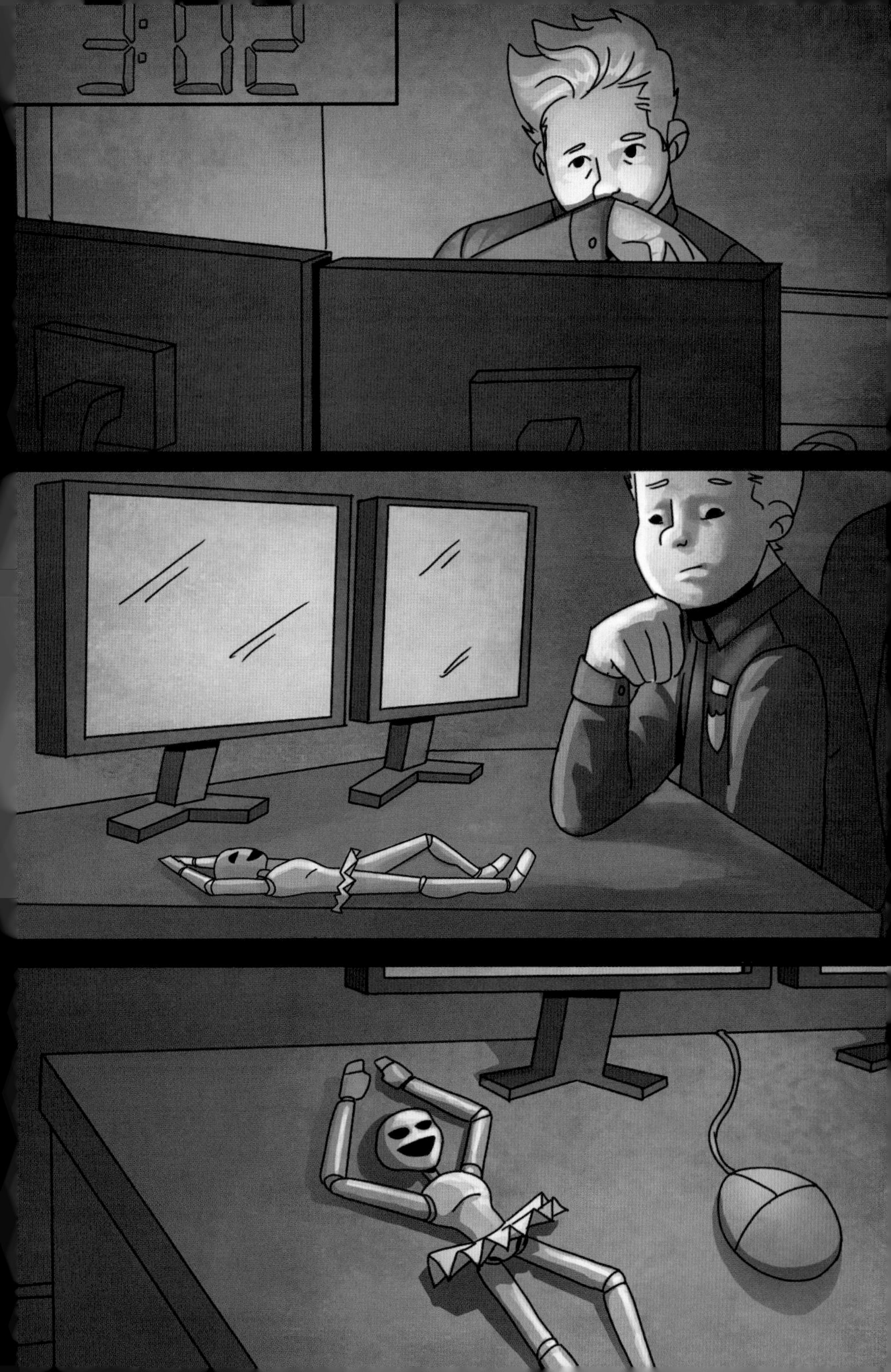
3:02

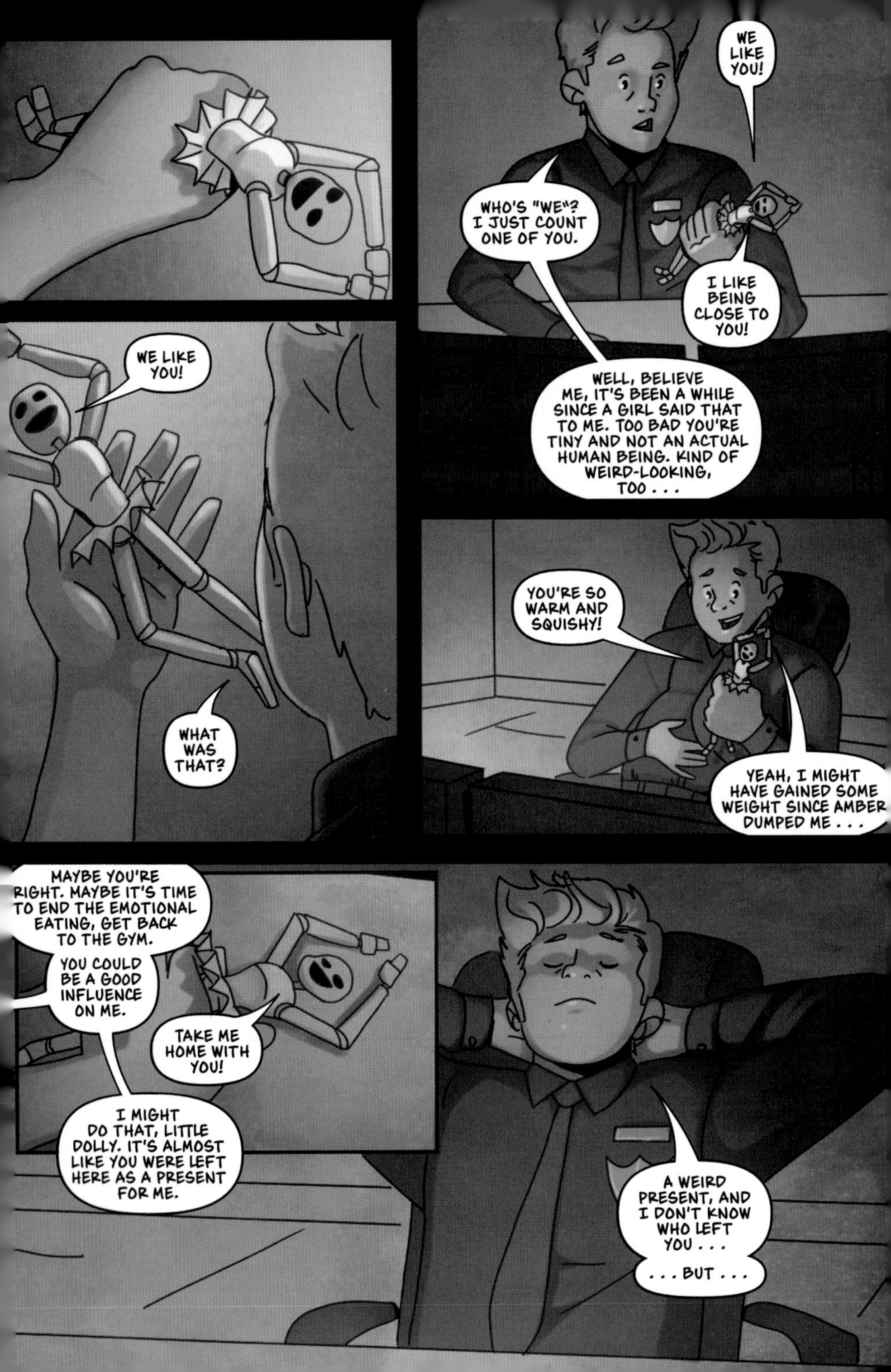
WE LIKE YOU!
WHO'S "WE"? I JUST COUNT ONE OF YOU.
I LIKE BEING CLOSE TO YOU!
WELL, BELIEVE ME, IT'S BEEN A WHILE SINCE A GIRL SAID THAT TO ME. TOO BAD YOU'RE TINY AND NOT AN ACTUAL HUMAN BEING. KIND OF WEIRD-LOOKING, TOO . . .
WE LIKE YOU!
WHAT WAS THAT?
YOU'RE SO WARM AND SQUISHY!
YEAH, I MIGHT HAVE GAINED SOME WEIGHT SINCE AMBER DUMPED ME . . .
MAYBE YOU'RE RIGHT. MAYBE IT'S TIME TO END THE EMOTIONAL EATING, GET BACK TO THE GYM.
YOU COULD BE A GOOD INFLUENCE ON ME.
TAKE ME HOME WITH YOU!
I MIGHT DO THAT, LITTLE DOLLY. IT'S ALMOST LIKE YOU WERE LEFT HERE AS A PRESENT FOR ME.
A WEIRD PRESENT, AND I DON'T KNOW WHO LEFT YOU . . .
. . . BUT . . .

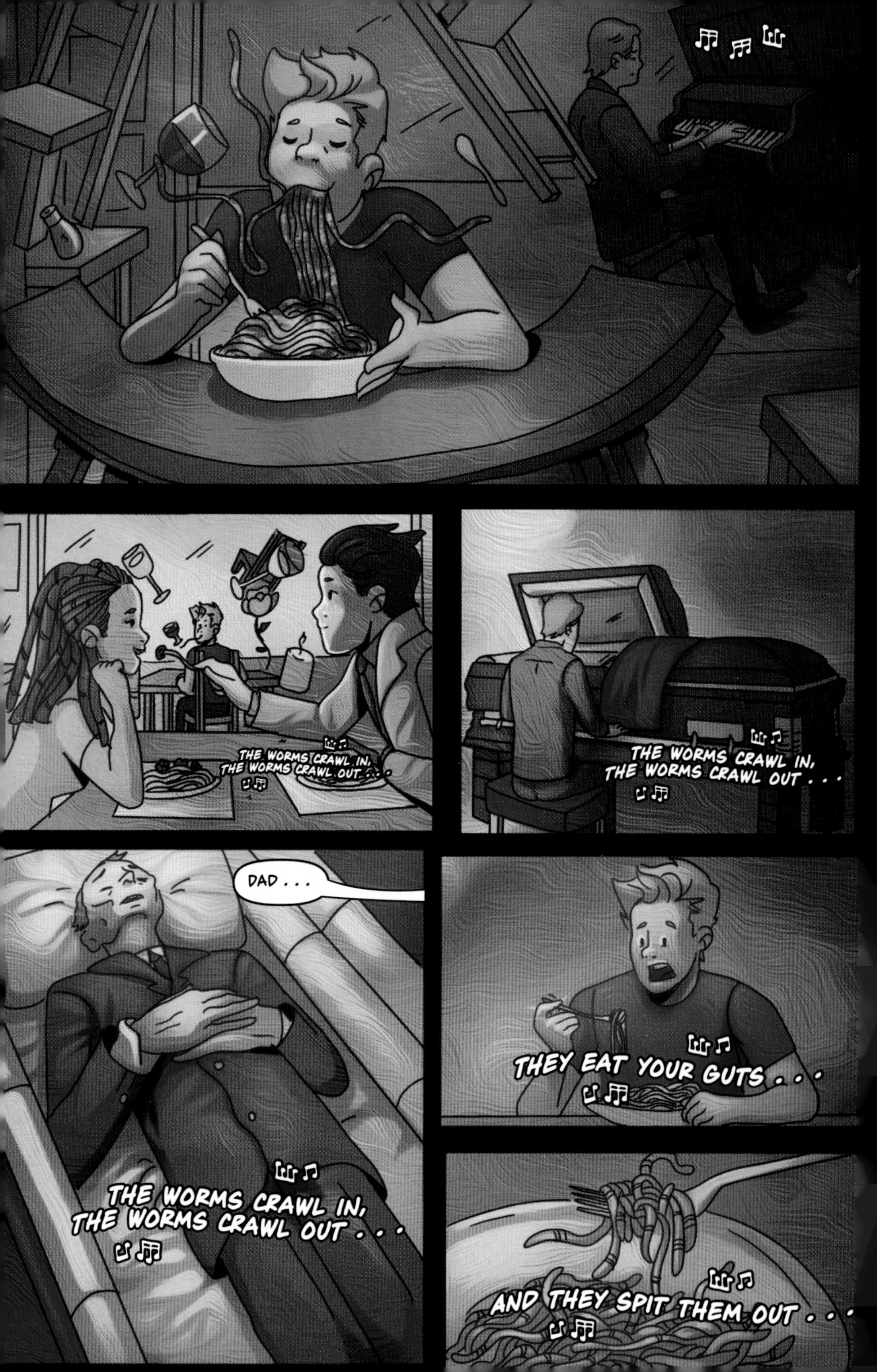
THE WORMS CRAWL IN,
THE WORMS CRAWL OUT . . .
THE WORMS CRAWL IN,
THE WORMS CRAWL OUT . . .
DAD . . .
THE WORMS CRAWL IN,
THE WORMS CRAWL OUT . . .
THEY EAT YOUR GUTS . . .
AND THEY SPIT THEM OUT . . .

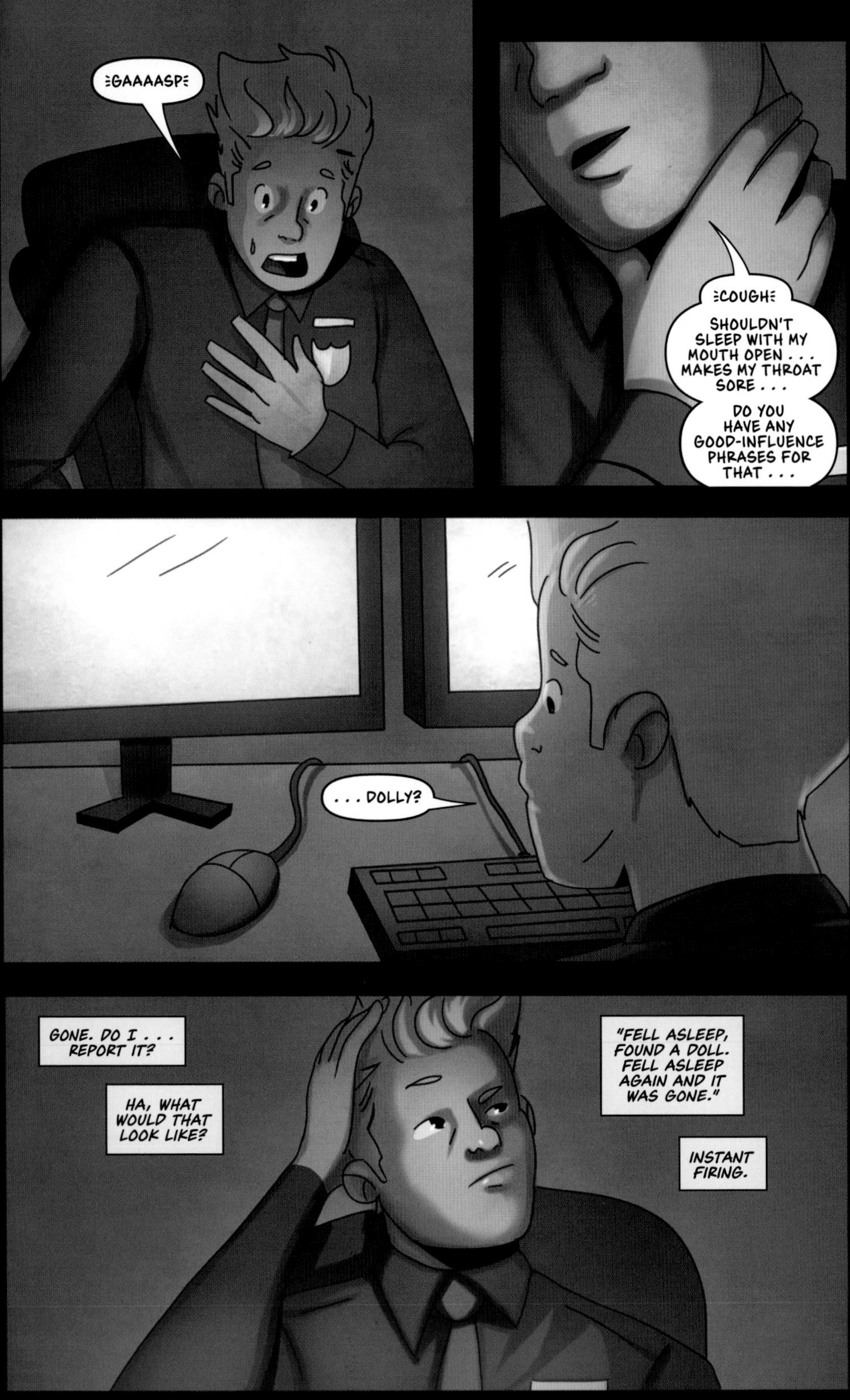

GAAAASP
COUGH
SHOULDN'T SLEEP WITH MY MOUTH OPEN . . . MAKES MY THROAT SORE . . .
DO YOU HAVE ANY GOOD-INFLUENCE PHRASES FOR THAT . . .
. . . DOLLY?
GONE. DO I . . . REPORT IT?
HA, WHAT WOULD THAT LOOK LIKE?
"FELL ASLEEP, FOUND A DOLL. FELL ASLEEP AGAIN AND IT WAS GONE."
INSTANT FIRING.

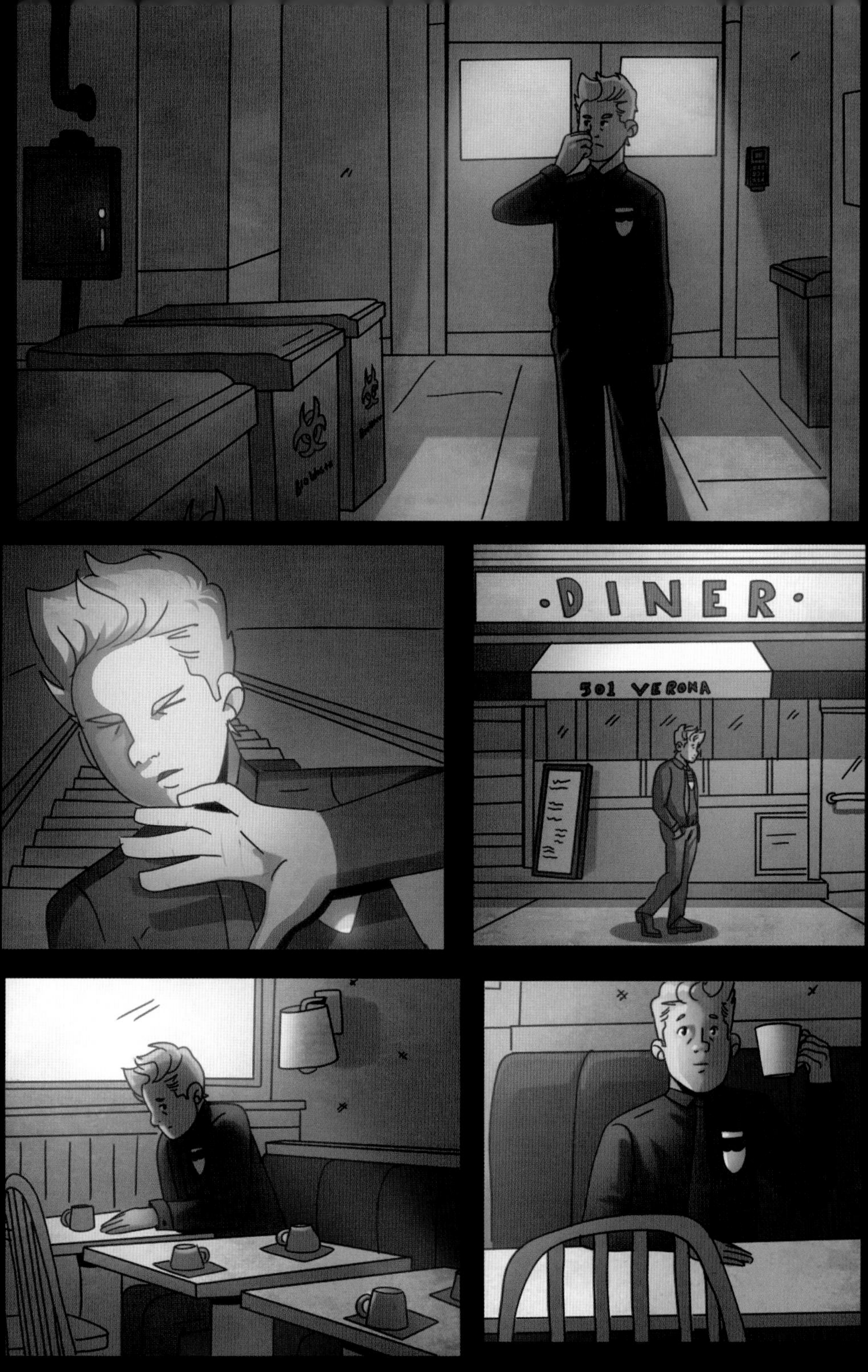
·DINER·
501 VERONA

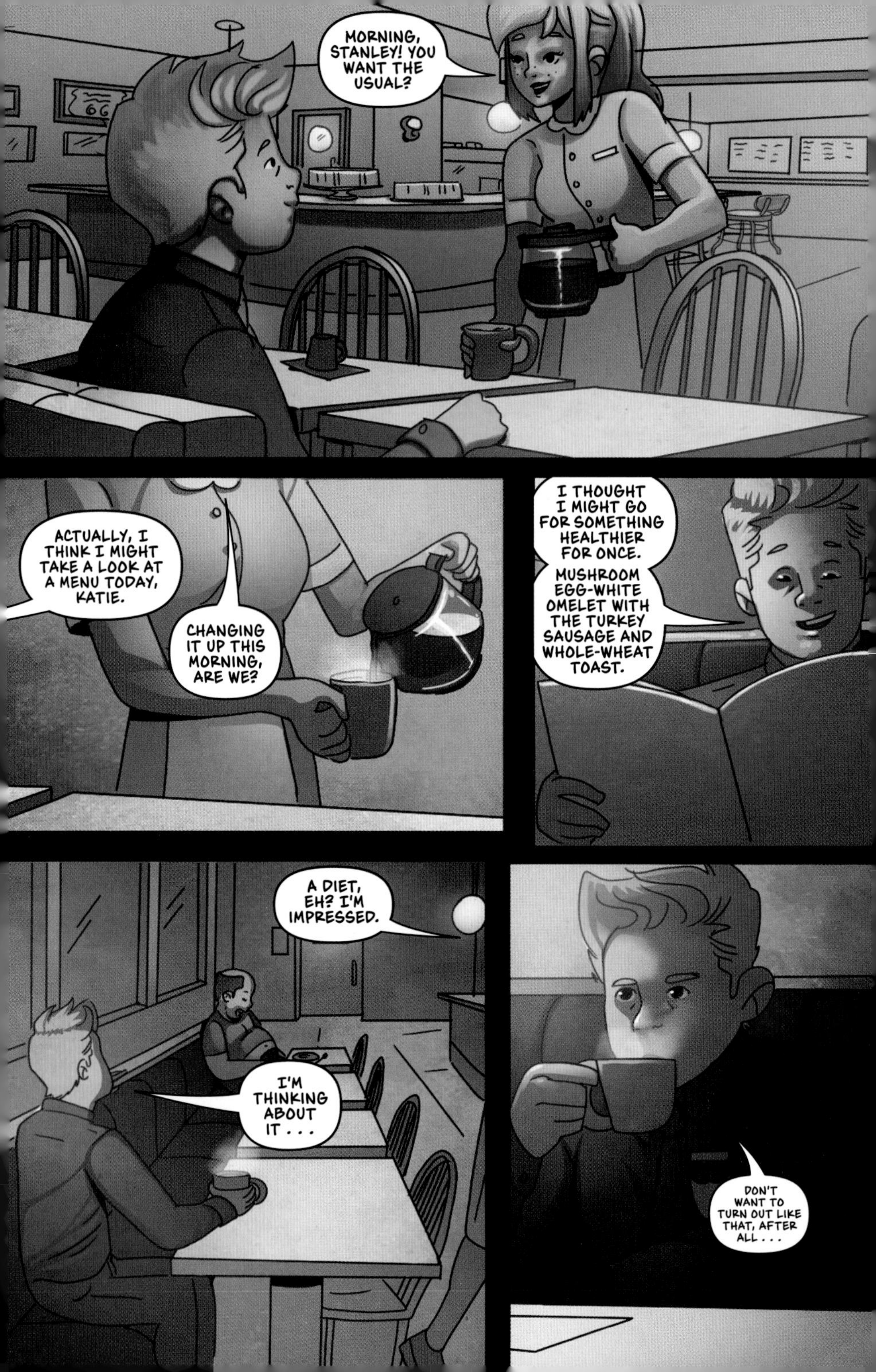
MORNING, STANLEY! YOU WANT THE USUAL?
ACTUALLY, I THINK I MIGHT TAKE A LOOK AT A MENU TODAY, KATIE.
CHANGING IT UP THIS MORNING, ARE WE?
I THOUGHT I MIGHT GO FOR SOMETHING HEALTHIER FOR ONCE.
MUSHROOM EGG-WHITE OMELET WITH THE TURKEY SAUSAGE AND WHOLE-WHEAT TOAST.
A DIET, EH? I'M IMPRESSED.
I'M THINKING ABOUT IT . . .
DON'T WANT TO TURN OUT LIKE THAT, AFTER ALL . . .

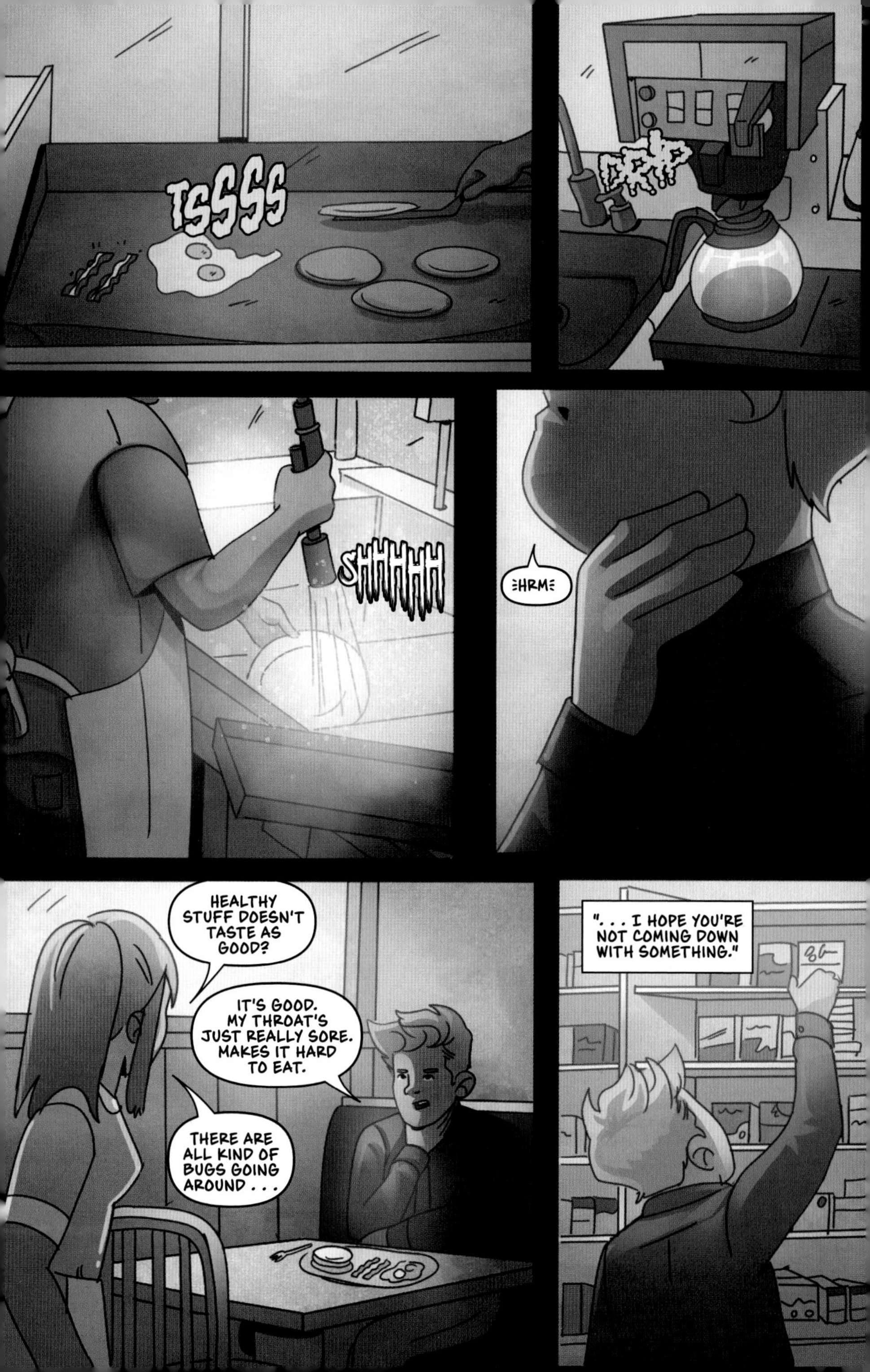
TSSSS
DRIP
SHHHHH
HRM
HEALTHY STUFF DOESN'T TASTE AS GOOD?
IT'S GOOD. MY THROAT'S JUST REALLY SORE. MAKES IT HARD TO EAT.
THERE ARE ALL KIND OF BUGS GOING AROUND . . .
". . . I HOPE YOU'RE NOT COMING DOWN WITH SOMETHING."

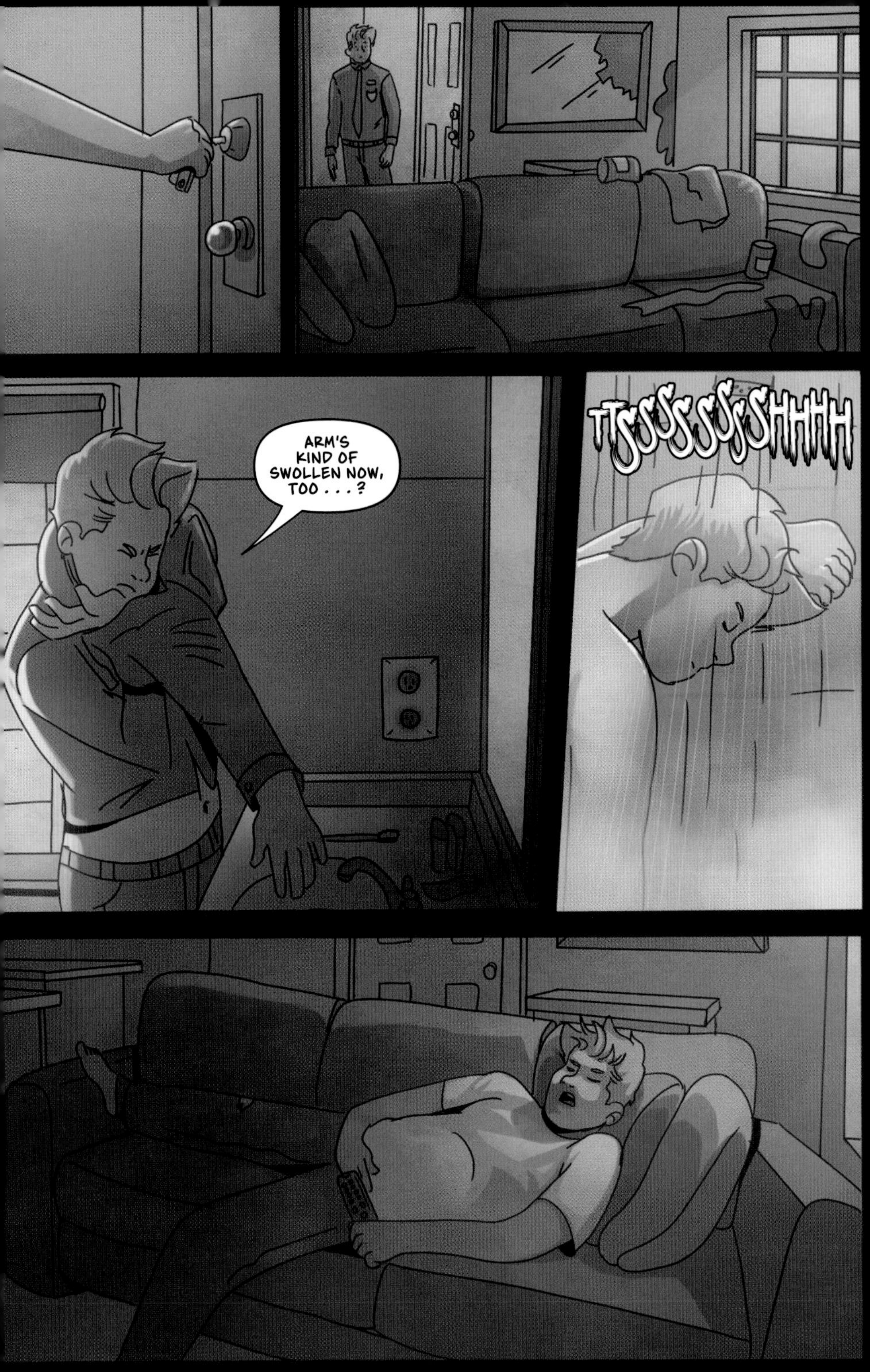
ARM'S KIND OF SWOLLEN NOW, TOO . . . ?
TTSSSSSSSSHHHH

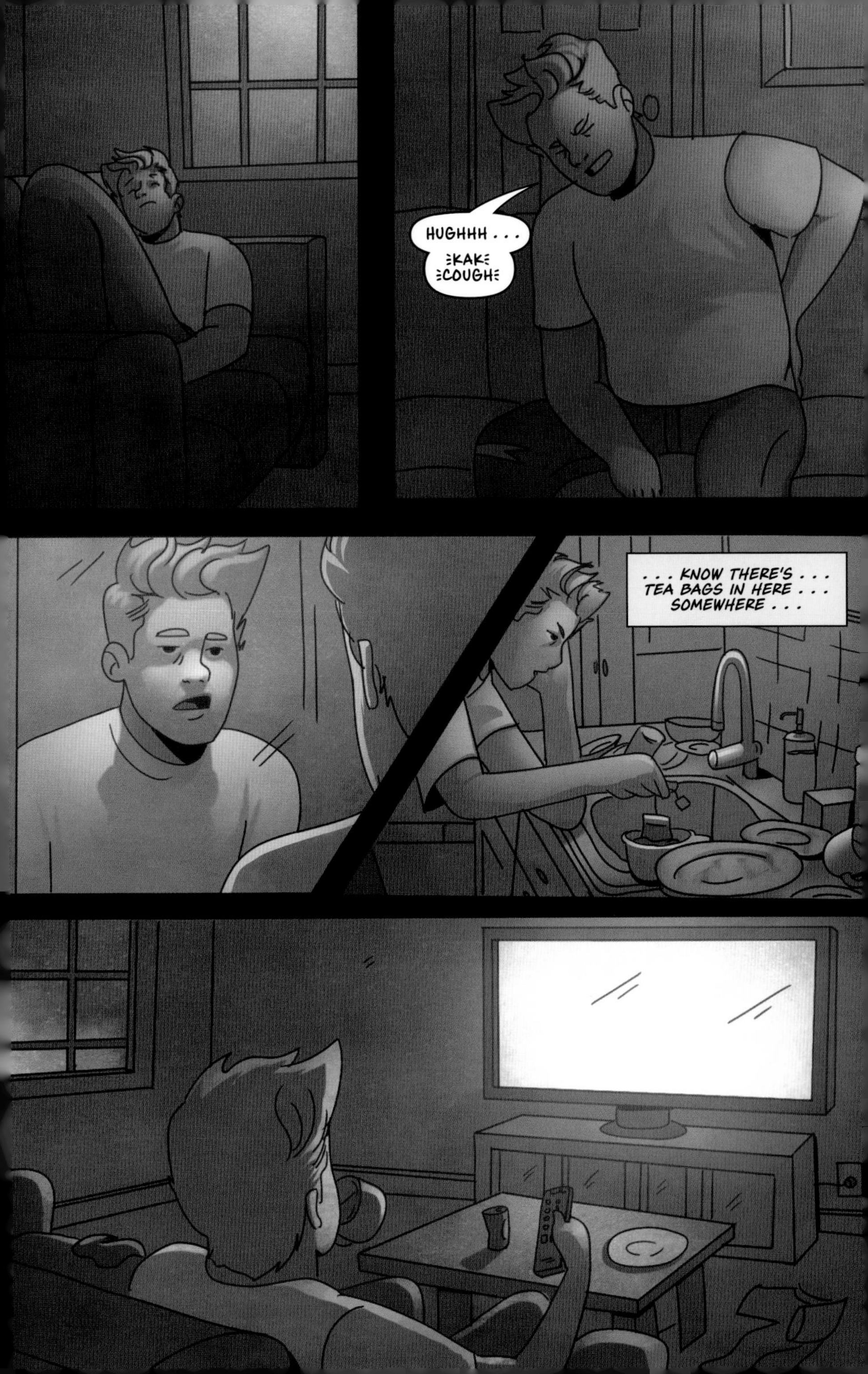
HUGHHH . . .
KAK COUGH
. . . KNOW THERE'S . . . TEA BAGS IN HERE . . . SOMEWHERE . . .

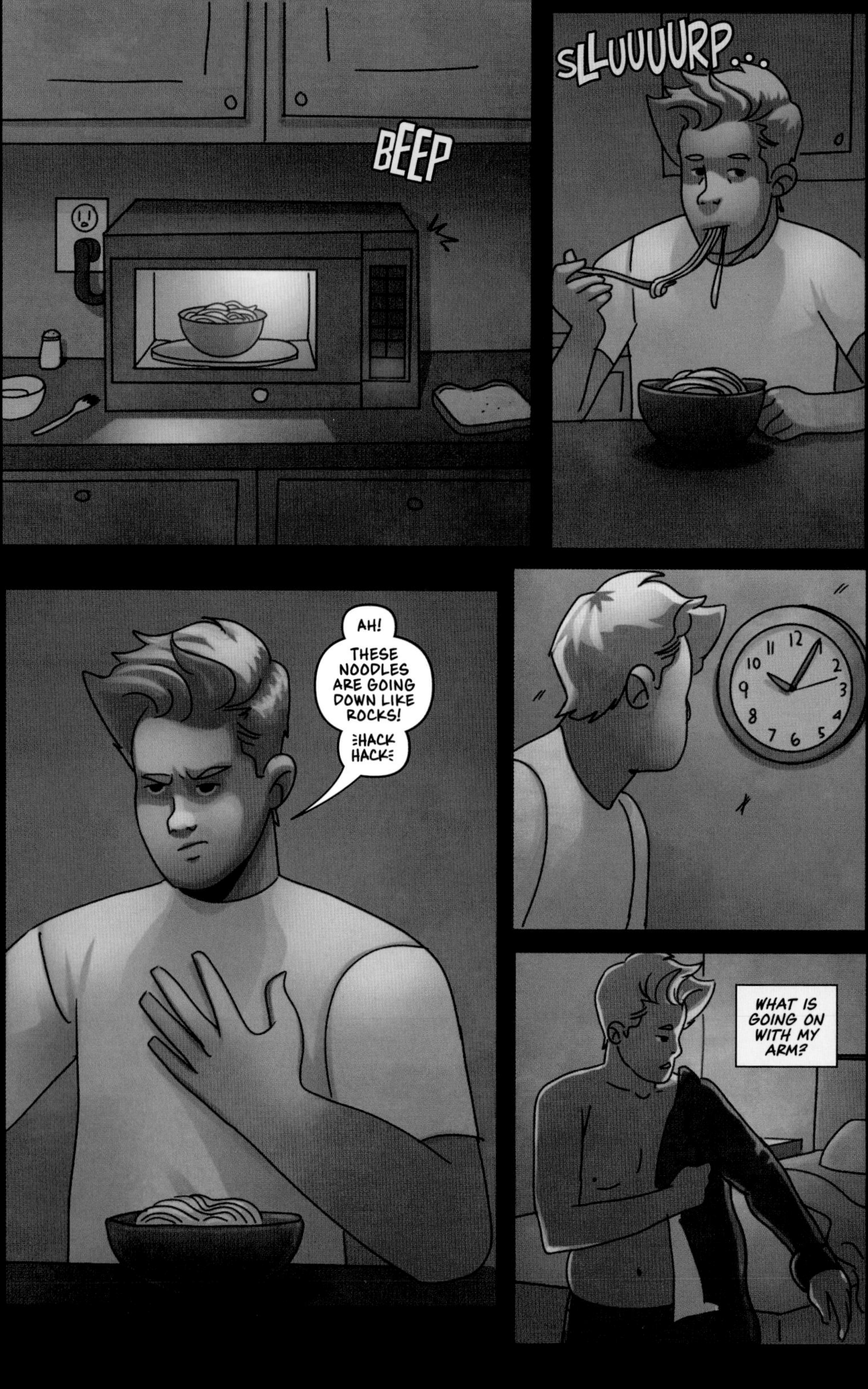
BEEP
SLLUUUURP...
AH!
THESE NOODLES ARE GOING DOWN LIKE ROCKS!
HACK HACK
WHAT IS GOING ON WITH MY ARM?

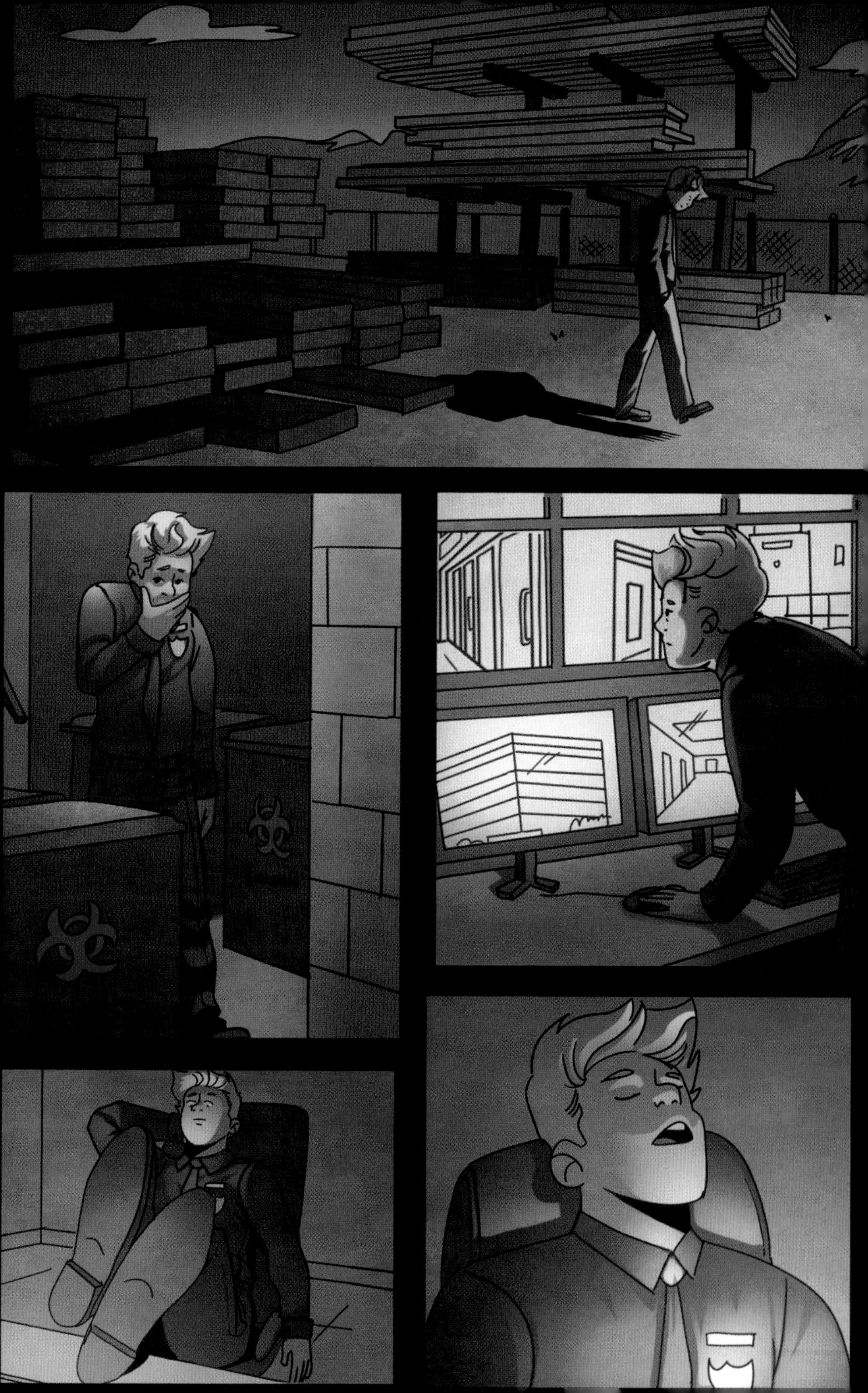

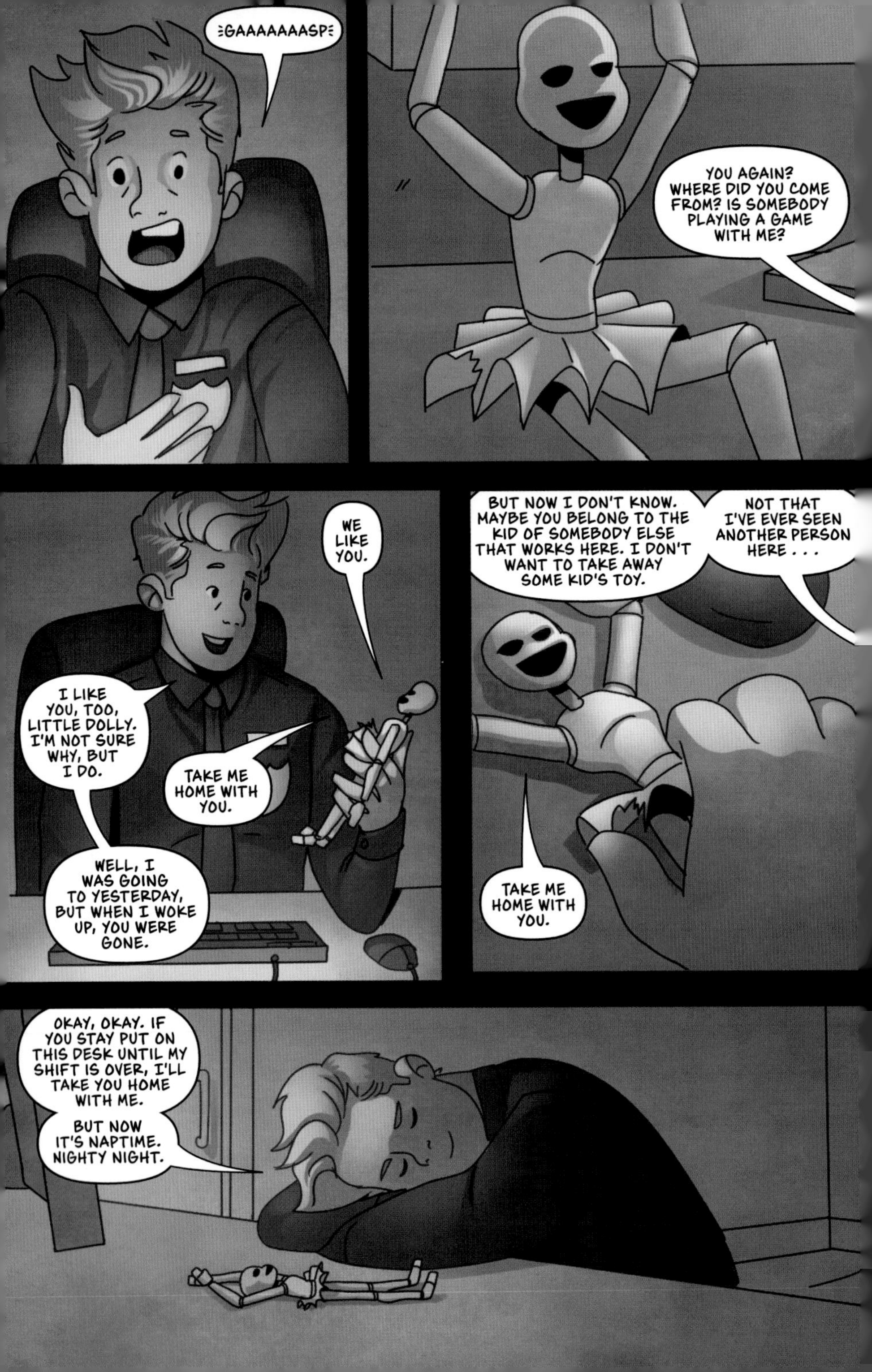
GAAAAAAASP
YOU AGAIN? WHERE DID YOU COME FROM? IS SOMEBODY PLAYING A GAME WITH ME?
WE LIKE YOU.
I LIKE YOU, TOO, LITTLE DOLLY. I'M NOT SURE WHY, BUT I DO.
TAKE ME HOME WITH YOU.
WELL, I WAS GOING TO YESTERDAY, BUT WHEN I WOKE UP, YOU WERE GONE.
BUT NOW I DON'T KNOW. MAYBE YOU BELONG TO THE KID OF SOMEBODY ELSE THAT WORKS HERE. I DON'T WANT TO TAKE AWAY SOME KID'S TOY.
NOT THAT I'VE EVER SEEN ANOTHER PERSON HERE . . .
TAKE ME HOME WITH YOU.
OKAY, OKAY. IF YOU STAY PUT ON THIS DESK UNTIL MY SHIFT IS OVER, I'LL TAKE YOU HOME WITH ME.
BUT NOW IT'S NAPTIME. NIGHTY NIGHT.

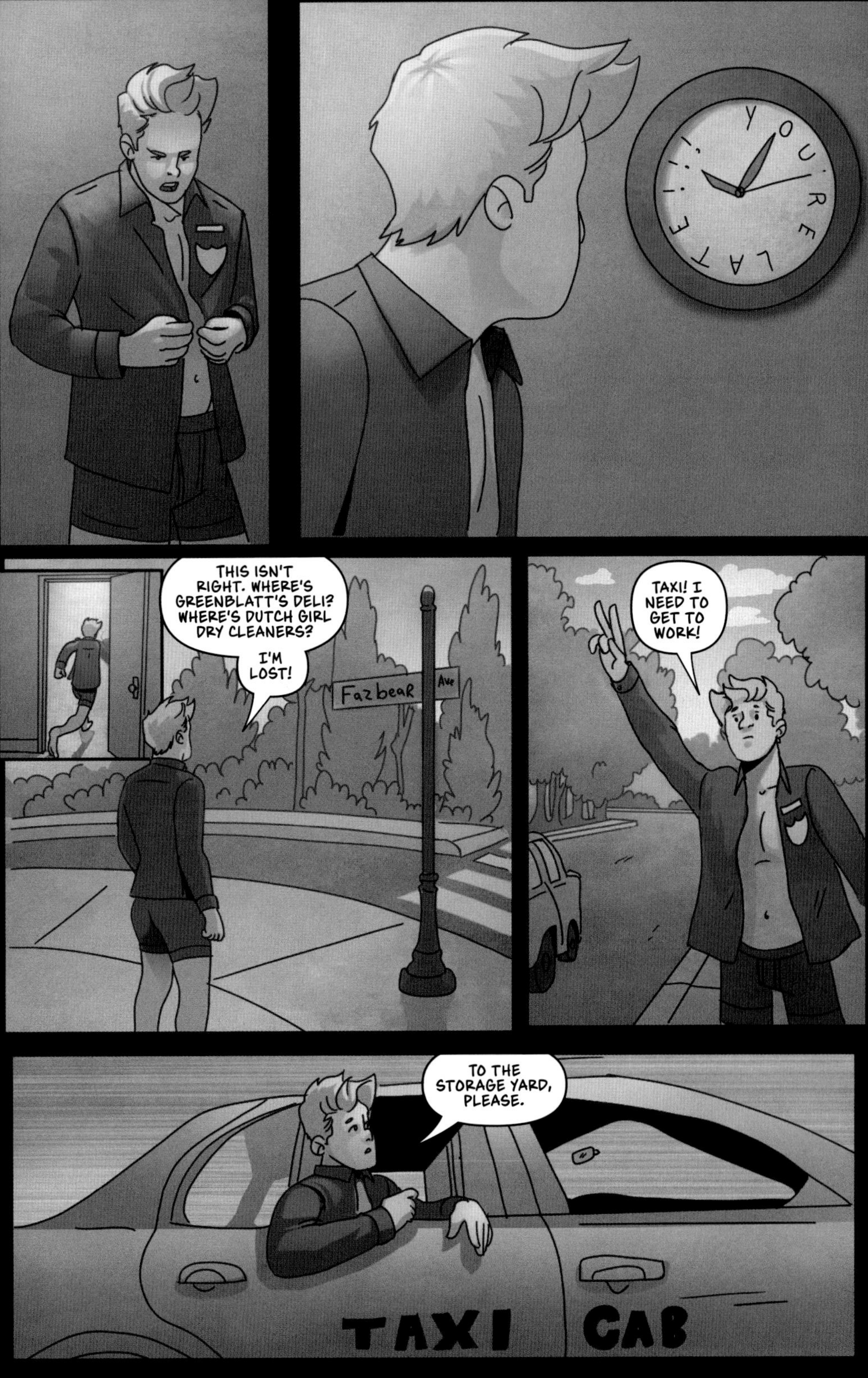

YOU'RE LATE!!!
THIS ISN'T RIGHT. WHERE'S GREENBLATT'S DELI? WHERE'S DUTCH GIRL DRY CLEANERS?
I'M LOST!
Fazbear Ave
TAXI! I NEED TO GET TO WORK!
TO THE STORAGE YARD, PLEASE.
TAXI CAB

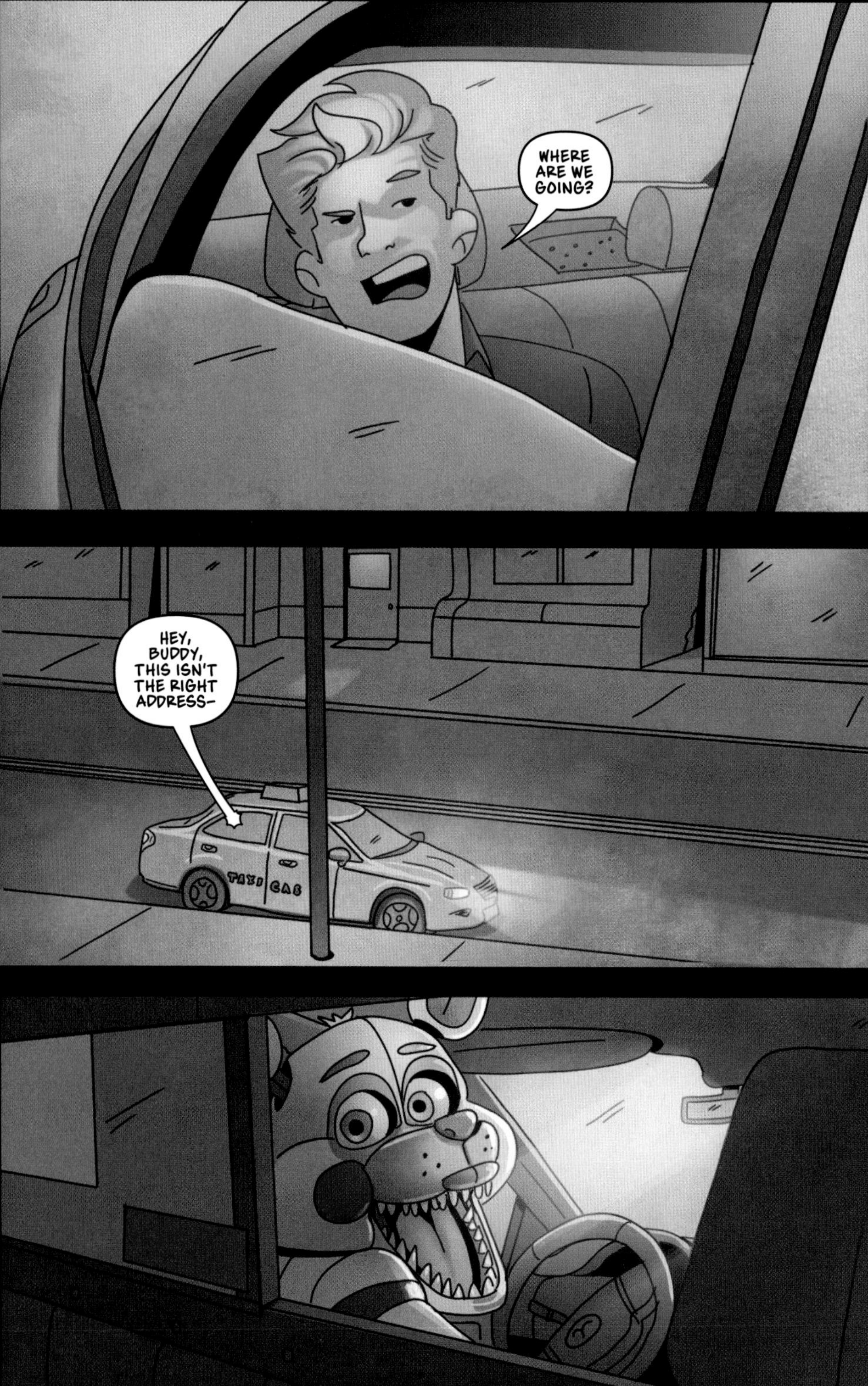
WHERE ARE WE GOING?
HEY, BUDDY, THIS ISN'T THE RIGHT ADDRESS-
TAXI CAB

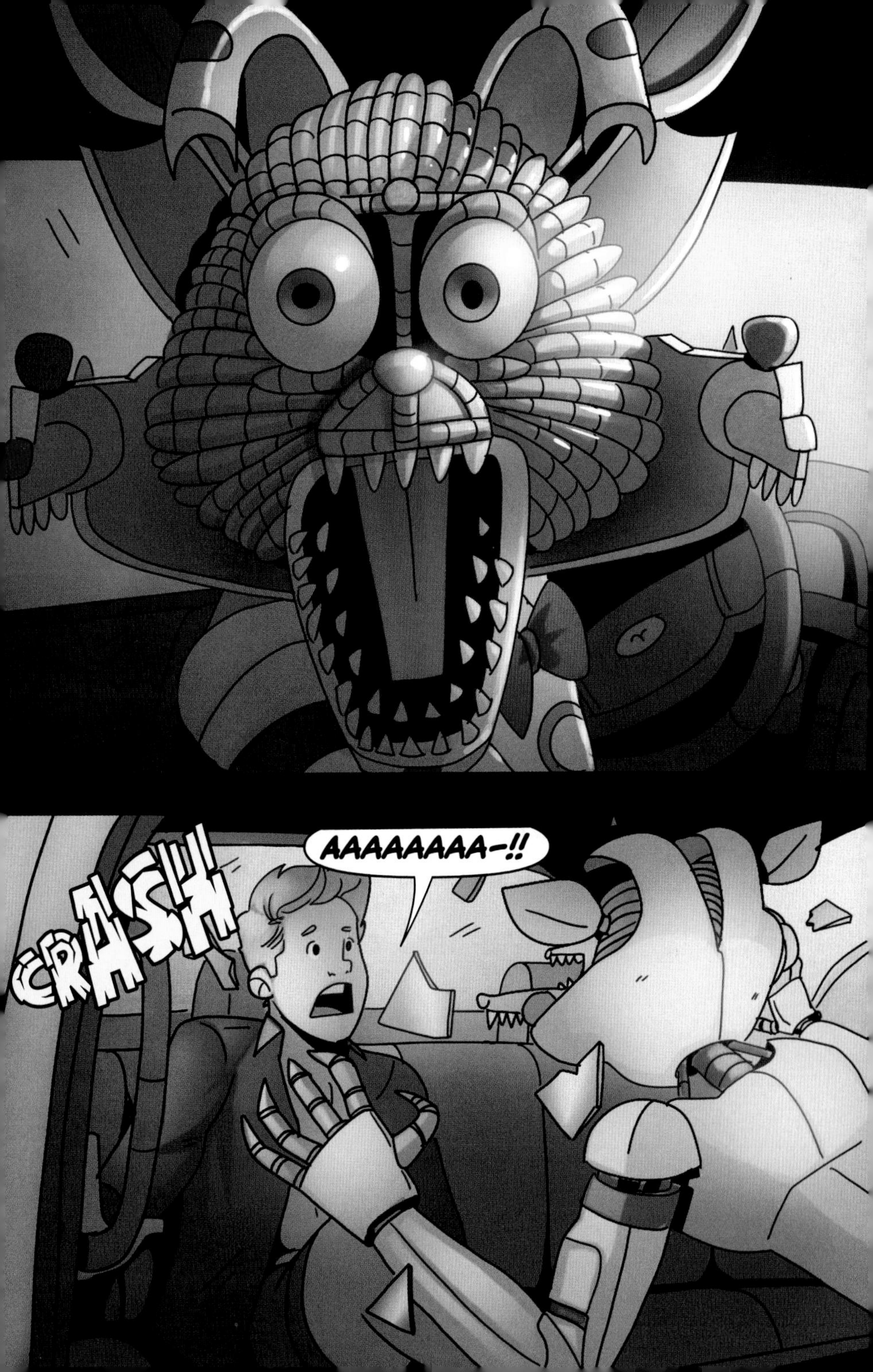
CRASH
AAAAAAAA-!!

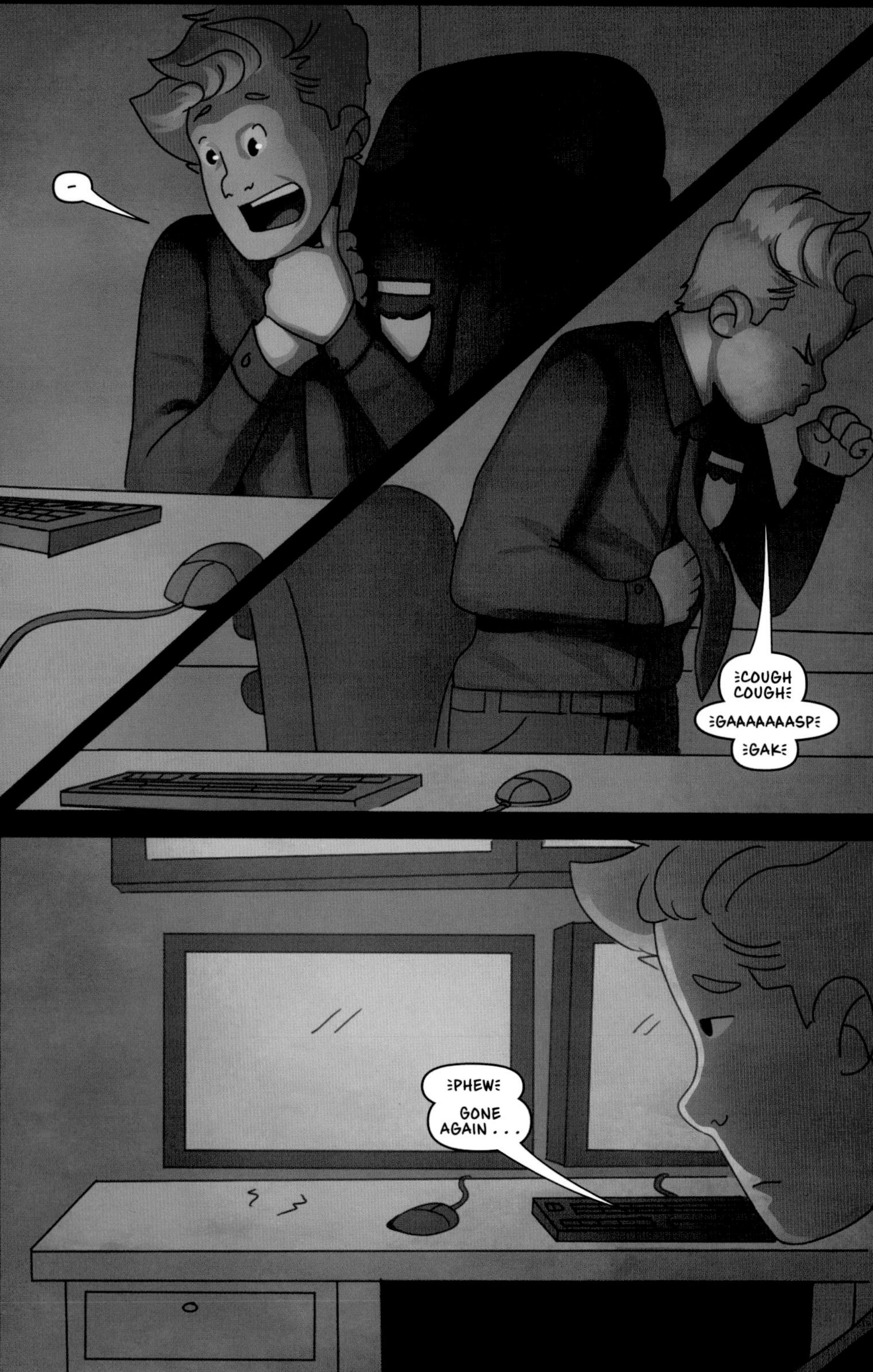

–
COUGH COUGH
GAAAAAAASP
GAK
PHEW
GONE AGAIN . . .

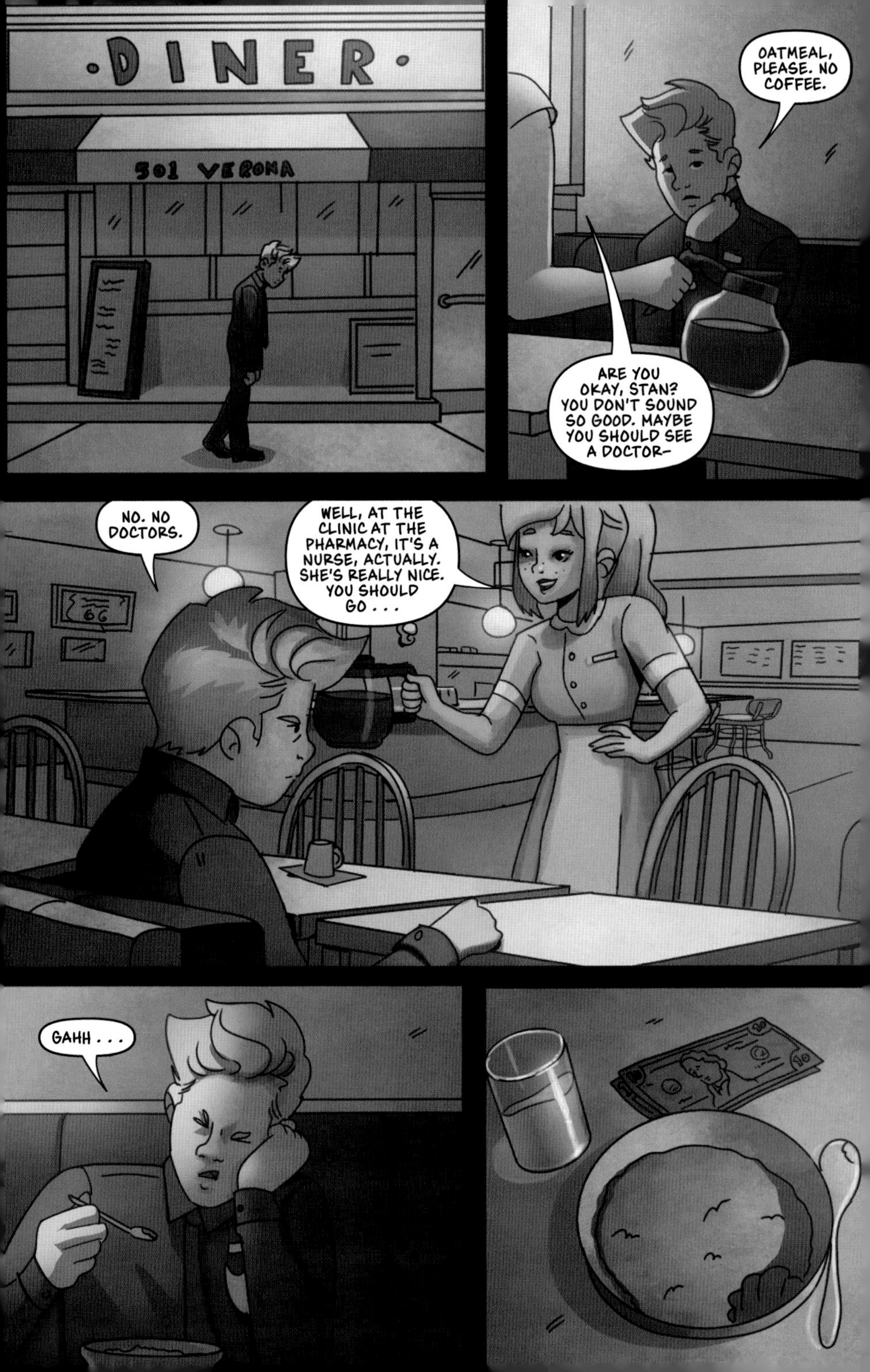
DINER
501 VERONA
OATMEAL, PLEASE. NO COFFEE.
ARE YOU OKAY, STAN? YOU DON'T SOUND SO GOOD. MAYBE YOU SHOULD SEE A DOCTOR-
NO. NO DOCTORS.
WELL, AT THE CLINIC AT THE PHARMACY, IT'S A NURSE, ACTUALLY. SHE'S REALLY NICE. YOU SHOULD GO . . .
GAHH . . .

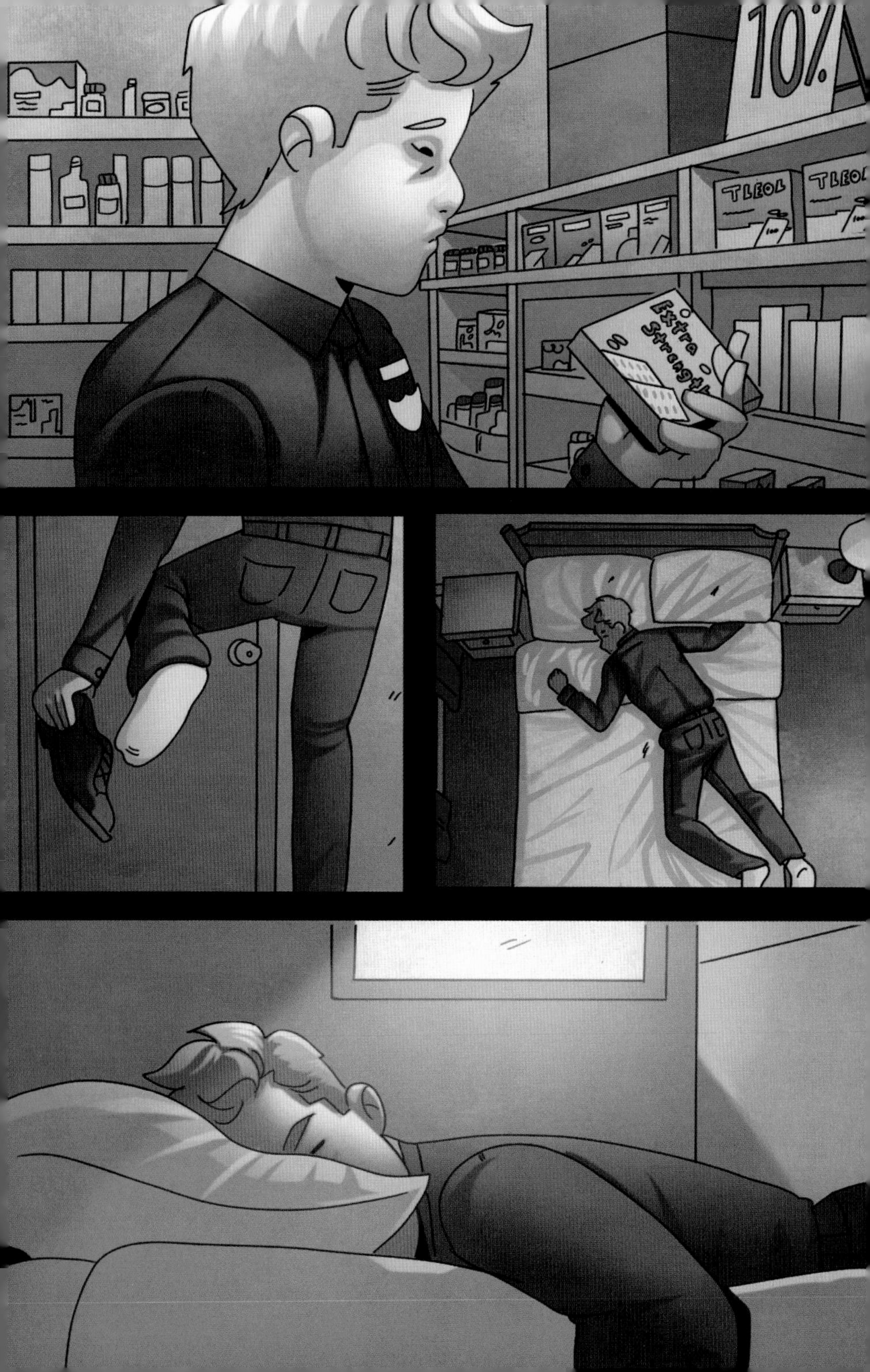
10%
TLEOL
TLEOL
Extra Strength

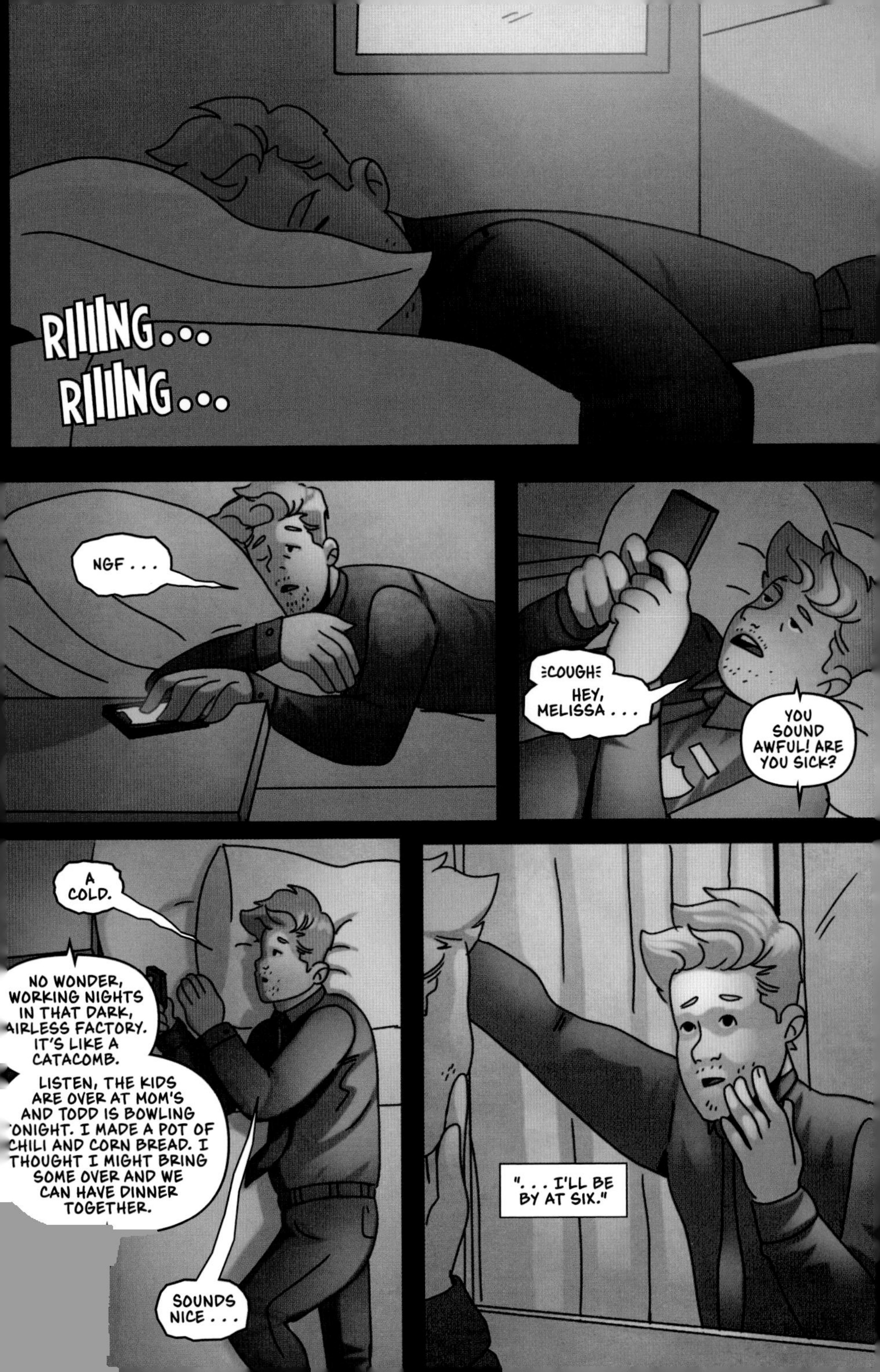
RIIIING...
RIIIING...
NGF . . .
≡COUGH≡ HEY, MELISSA . . .
YOU SOUND AWFUL! ARE YOU SICK?
A COLD.
NO WONDER, WORKING NIGHTS IN THAT DARK, AIRLESS FACTORY. IT'S LIKE A CATACOMB.
LISTEN, THE KIDS ARE OVER AT MOM'S AND TODD IS BOWLING TONIGHT. I MADE A POT OF CHILI AND CORN BREAD. I THOUGHT I MIGHT BRING SOME OVER AND WE CAN HAVE DINNER TOGETHER.
SOUNDS NICE . . .
". . . I'LL BE BY AT SIX."

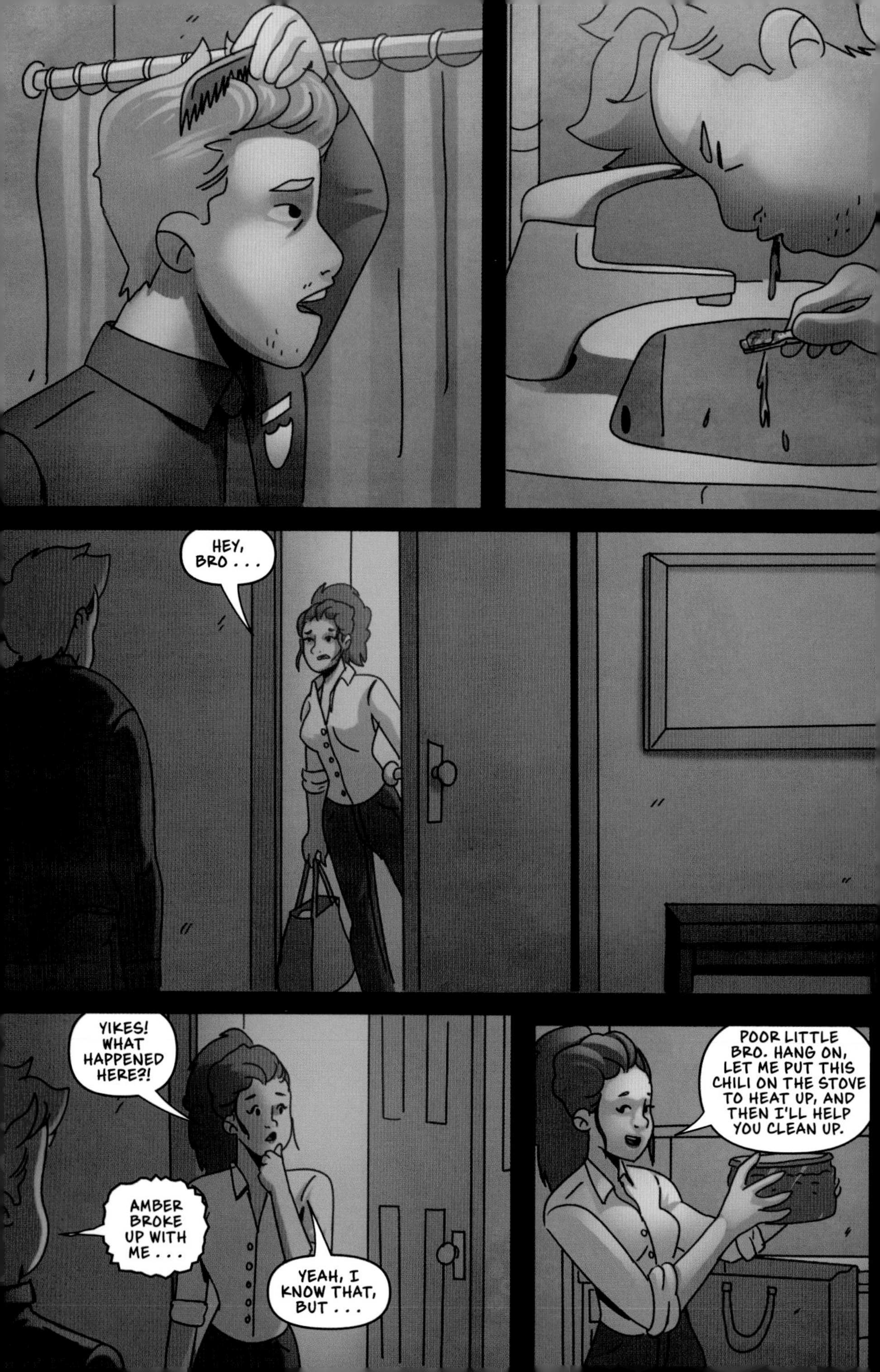
HEY, BRO . . .
YIKES! WHAT HAPPENED HERE?!
AMBER BROKE UP WITH ME . . .
YEAH, I KNOW THAT, BUT . . .
POOR LITTLE BRO. HANG ON, LET ME PUT THIS CHILI ON THE STOVE TO HEAT UP, AND THEN I'LL HELP YOU CLEAN UP.

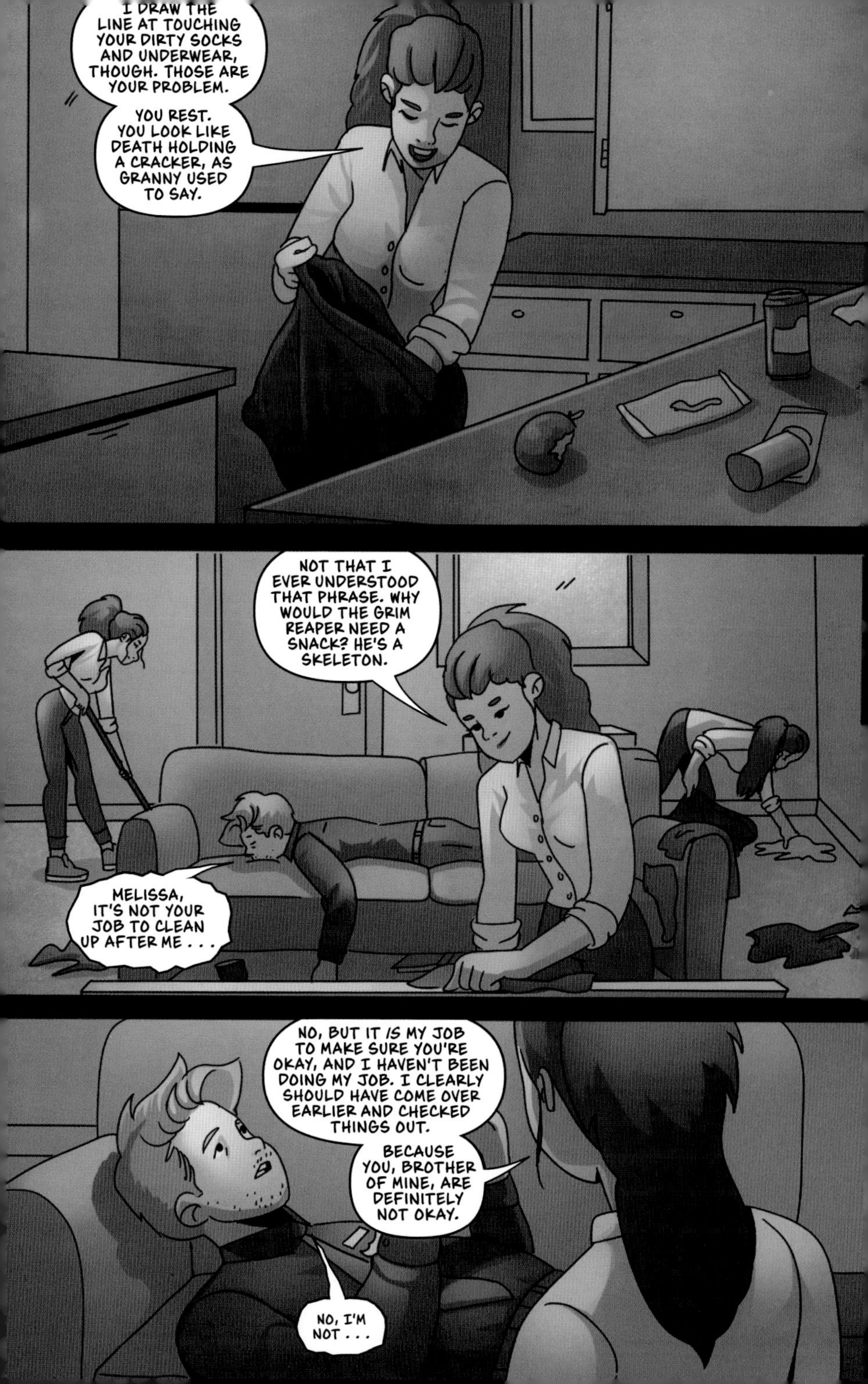
I DRAW THE LINE AT TOUCHING YOUR DIRTY SOCKS AND UNDERWEAR, THOUGH. THOSE ARE YOUR PROBLEM.
YOU REST. YOU LOOK LIKE DEATH HOLDING A CRACKER, AS GRANNY USED TO SAY.
NOT THAT I EVER UNDERSTOOD THAT PHRASE. WHY WOULD THE GRIM REAPER NEED A SNACK? HE'S A SKELETON.
MELISSA, IT'S NOT YOUR JOB TO CLEAN UP AFTER ME . . .
NO, BUT IT *IS* MY JOB TO MAKE SURE YOU'RE OKAY, AND I HAVEN'T BEEN DOING MY JOB. I CLEARLY SHOULD HAVE COME OVER EARLIER AND CHECKED THINGS OUT.
BECAUSE YOU, BROTHER OF MINE, ARE DEFINITELY NOT OKAY.
NO, I'M NOT . . .

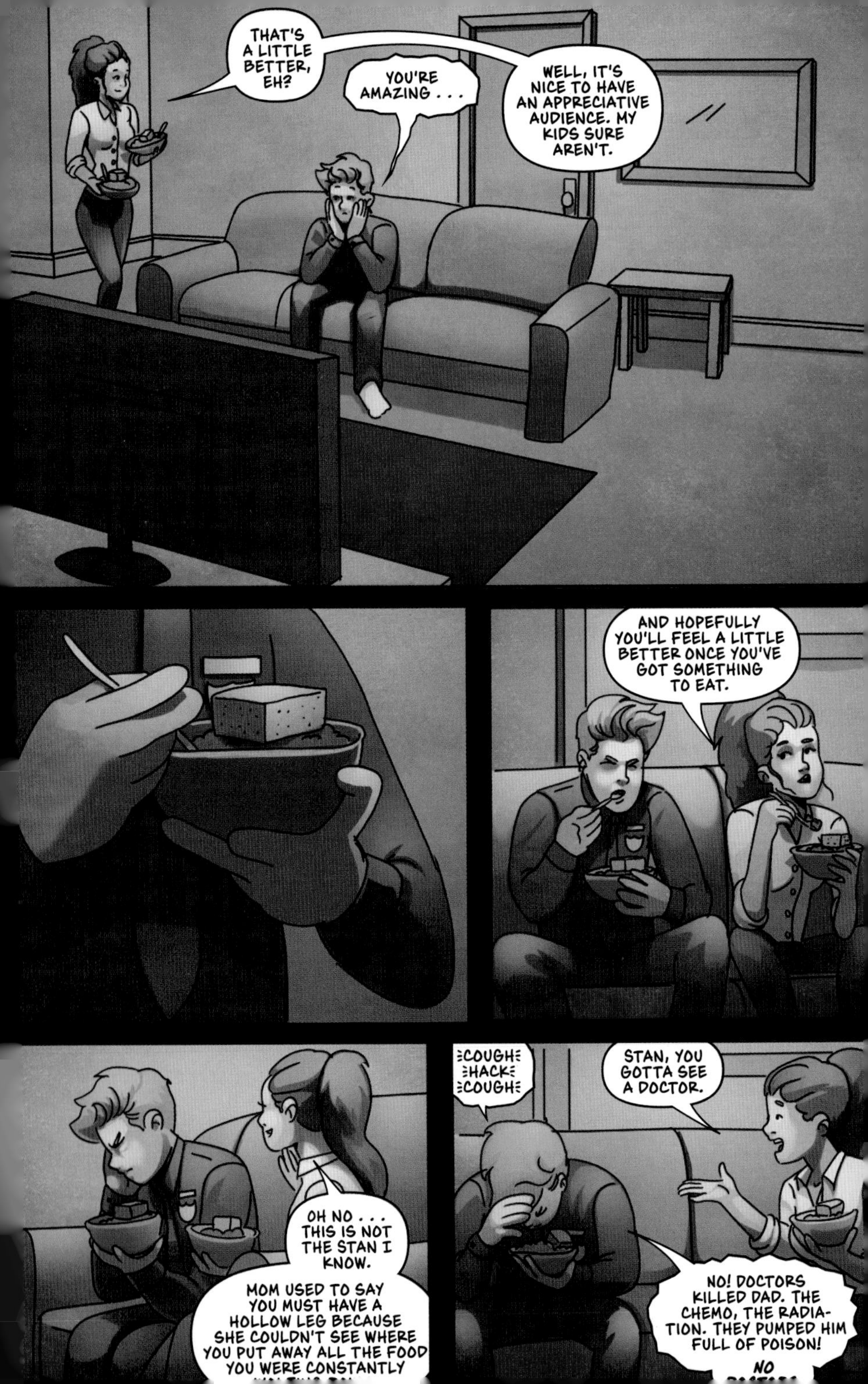
THAT'S A LITTLE BETTER, EH?
YOU'RE AMAZING . . .
WELL, IT'S NICE TO HAVE AN APPRECIATIVE AUDIENCE. MY KIDS SURE AREN'T.
AND HOPEFULLY YOU'LL FEEL A LITTLE BETTER ONCE YOU'VE GOT SOMETHING TO EAT.
OH NO . . . THIS IS NOT THE STAN I KNOW.
MOM USED TO SAY YOU MUST HAVE A HOLLOW LEG BECAUSE SHE COULDN'T SEE WHERE YOU PUT AWAY ALL THE FOOD YOU WERE CONSTANTLY
COUGH HACK COUGH
STAN, YOU GOTTA SEE A DOCTOR.
NO! DOCTORS KILLED DAD. THE CHEMO, THE RADIA-TION. THEY PUMPED HIM FULL OF POISON!
NO

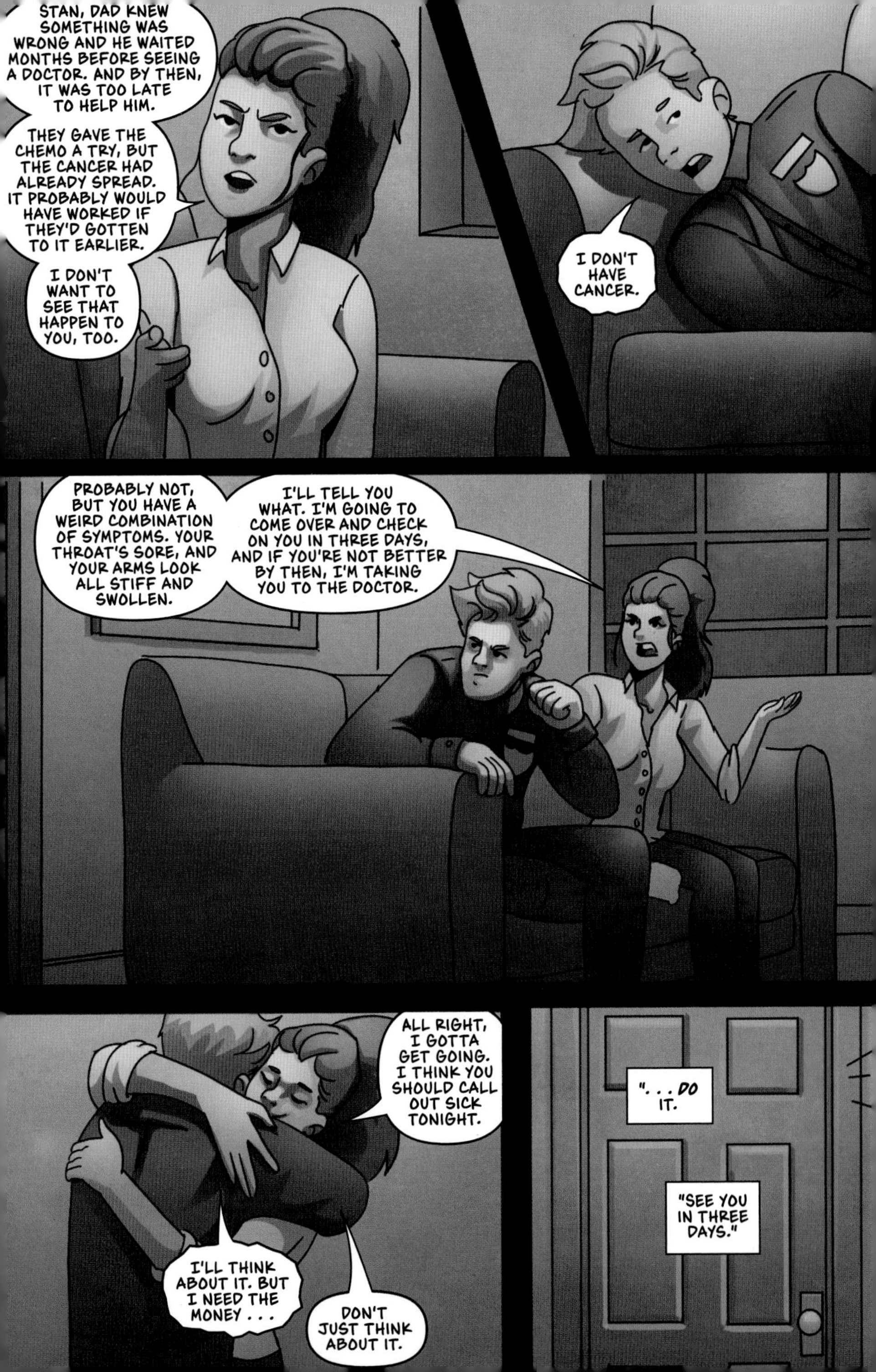
STAN, DAD KNEW SOMETHING WAS WRONG AND HE WAITED MONTHS BEFORE SEEING A DOCTOR. AND BY THEN, IT WAS TOO LATE TO HELP HIM.
THEY GAVE THE CHEMO A TRY, BUT THE CANCER HAD ALREADY SPREAD. IT PROBABLY WOULD HAVE WORKED IF THEY'D GOTTEN TO IT EARLIER.
I DON'T WANT TO SEE THAT HAPPEN TO YOU, TOO.
I DON'T HAVE CANCER.
PROBABLY NOT, BUT YOU HAVE A WEIRD COMBINATION OF SYMPTOMS. YOUR THROAT'S SORE, AND YOUR ARMS LOOK ALL STIFF AND SWOLLEN.
I'LL TELL YOU WHAT. I'M GOING TO COME OVER AND CHECK ON YOU IN THREE DAYS, AND IF YOU'RE NOT BETTER BY THEN, I'M TAKING YOU TO THE DOCTOR.
ALL RIGHT, I GOTTA GET GOING. I THINK YOU SHOULD CALL OUT SICK TONIGHT.
I'LL THINK ABOUT IT. BUT I NEED THE MONEY . . .
DON'T JUST THINK ABOUT IT.
". . . *DO* IT.
"SEE YOU IN THREE DAYS."

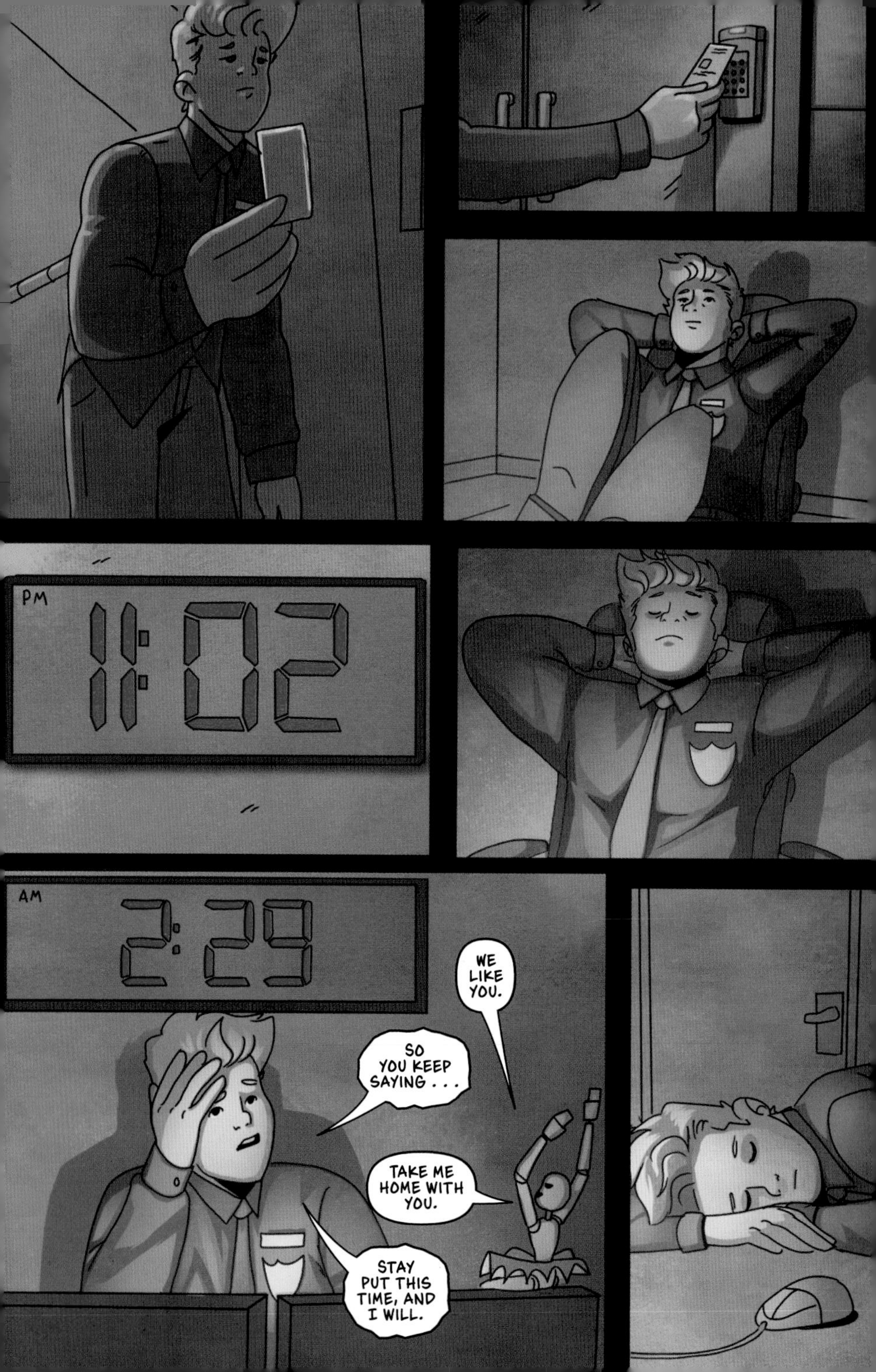
PM
11:02
AM
2:29
WE LIKE YOU.
SO YOU KEEP SAYING . . .
TAKE ME HOME WITH YOU.
STAY PUT THIS TIME, AND I WILL.

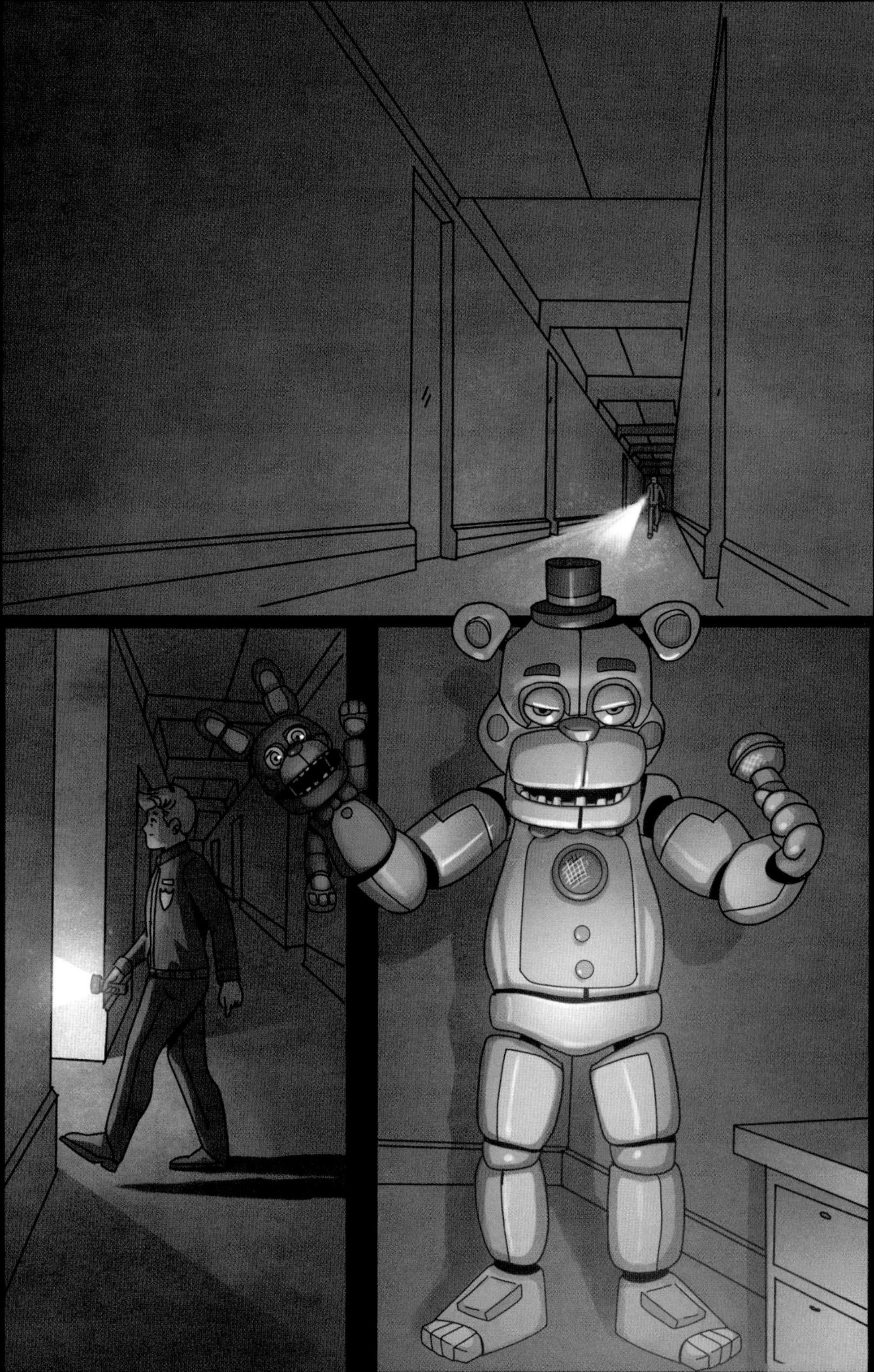

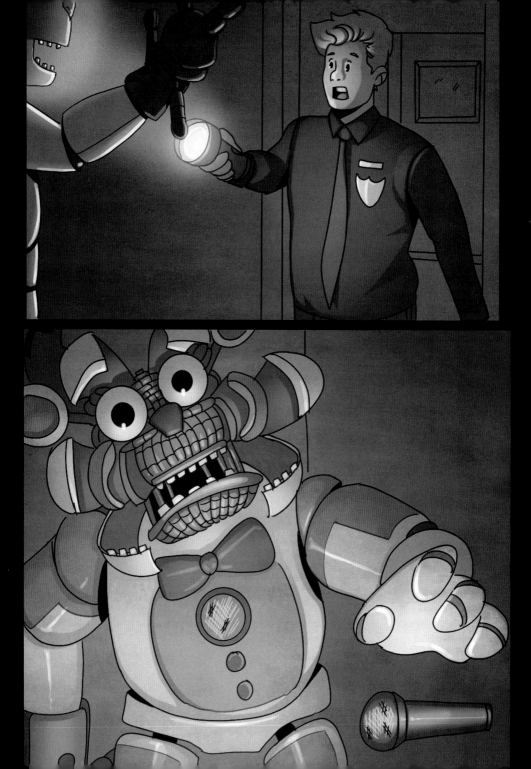

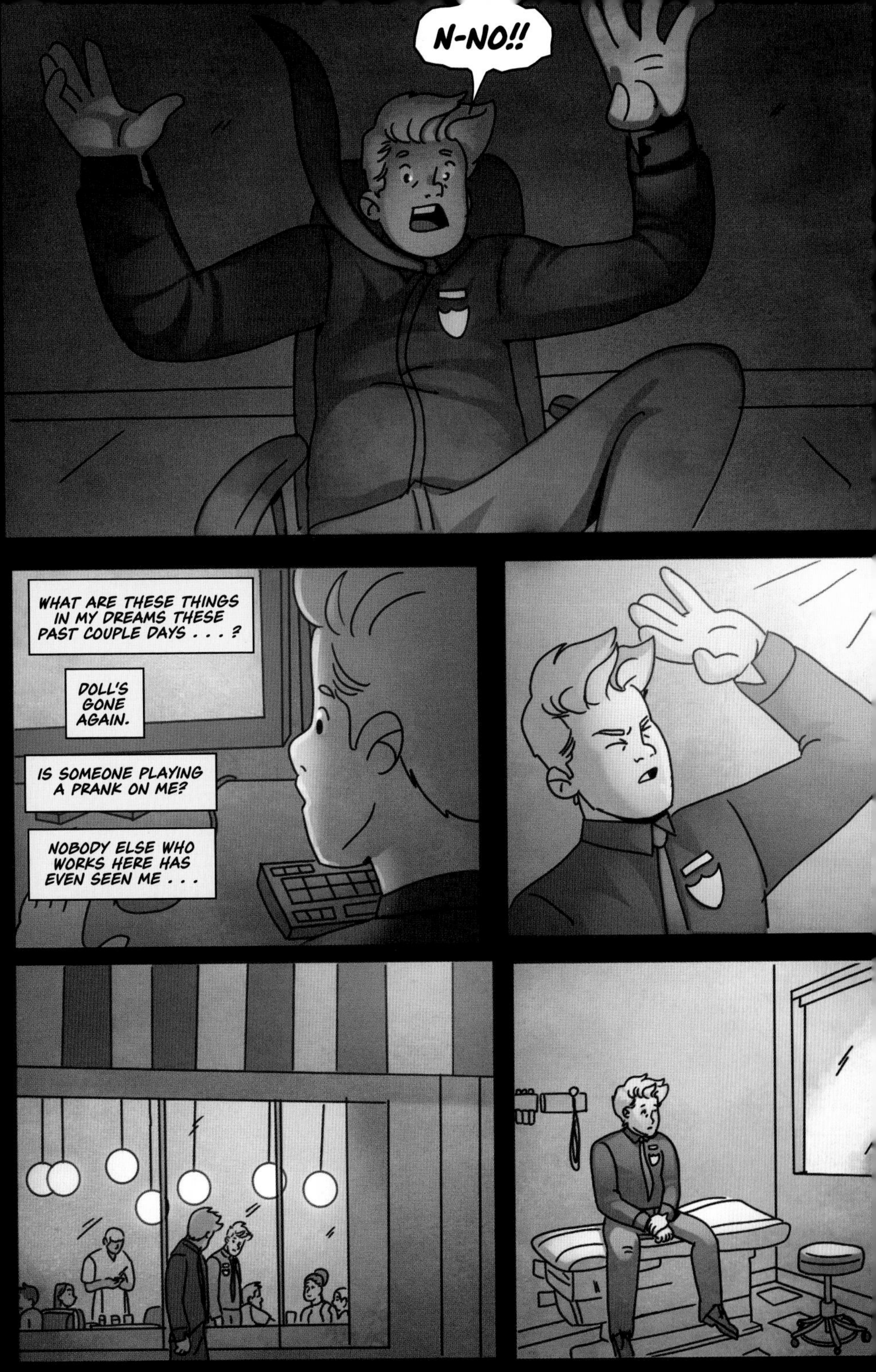

N-NO!!
WHAT ARE THESE THINGS IN MY DREAMS THESE PAST COUPLE DAYS . . . ?
DOLL'S GONE AGAIN.
IS SOMEONE PLAYING A PRANK ON ME?
NOBODY ELSE WHO WORKS HERE HAS EVEN SEEN ME . . .

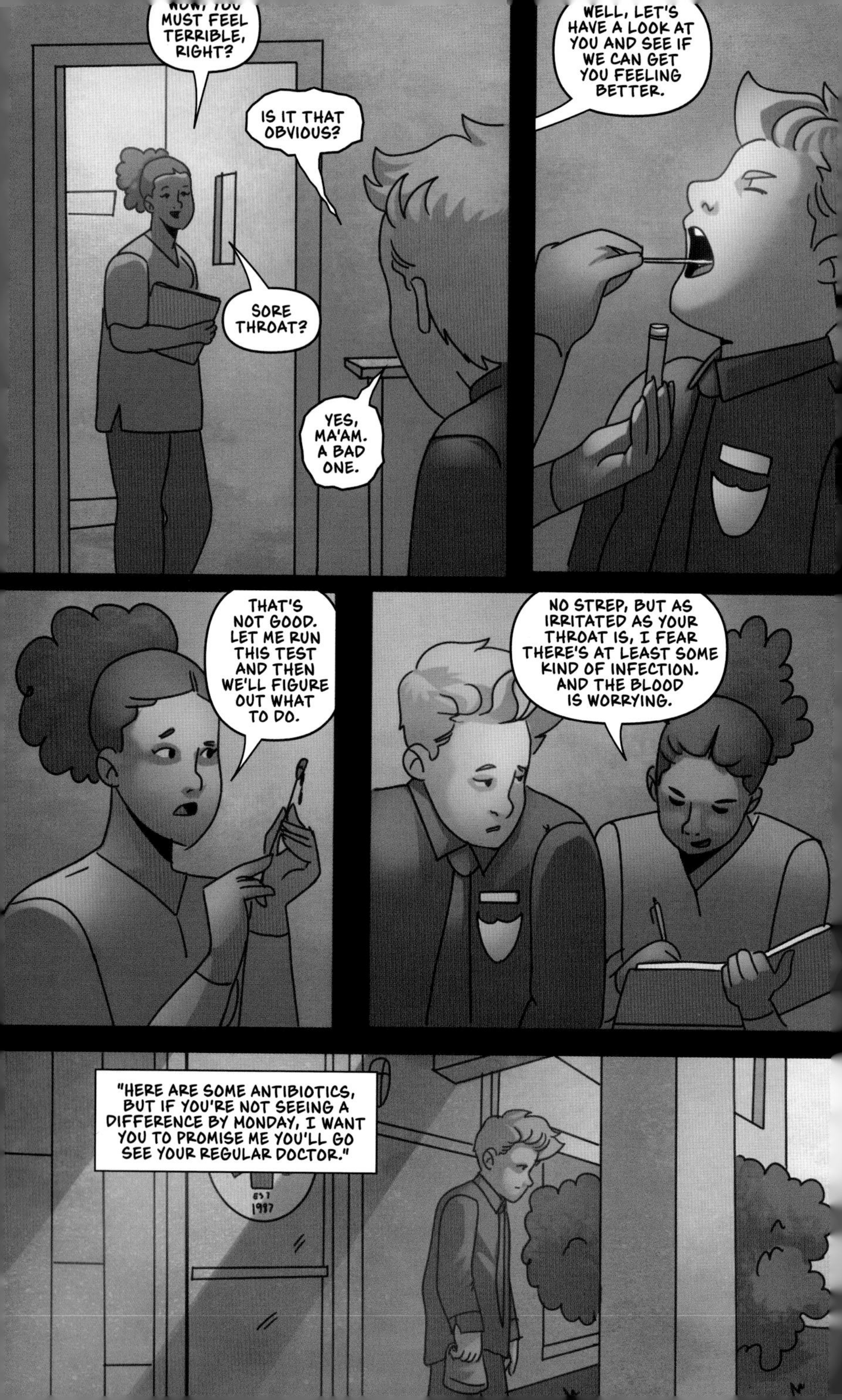

MUST FEEL TERRIBLE, RIGHT?
IS IT THAT OBVIOUS?
SORE THROAT?
YES, MA'AM. A BAD ONE.
WELL, LET'S HAVE A LOOK AT YOU AND SEE IF WE CAN GET YOU FEELING BETTER.
THAT'S NOT GOOD. LET ME RUN THIS TEST AND THEN WE'LL FIGURE OUT WHAT TO DO.
NO STREP, BUT AS IRRITATED AS YOUR THROAT IS, I FEAR THERE'S AT LEAST SOME KIND OF INFECTION. AND THE BLOOD IS WORRYING.
"HERE ARE SOME ANTIBIOTICS, BUT IF YOU'RE NOT SEEING A DIFFERENCE BY MONDAY, I WANT YOU TO PROMISE ME YOU'LL GO SEE YOUR REGULAR DOCTOR."
EST 1987

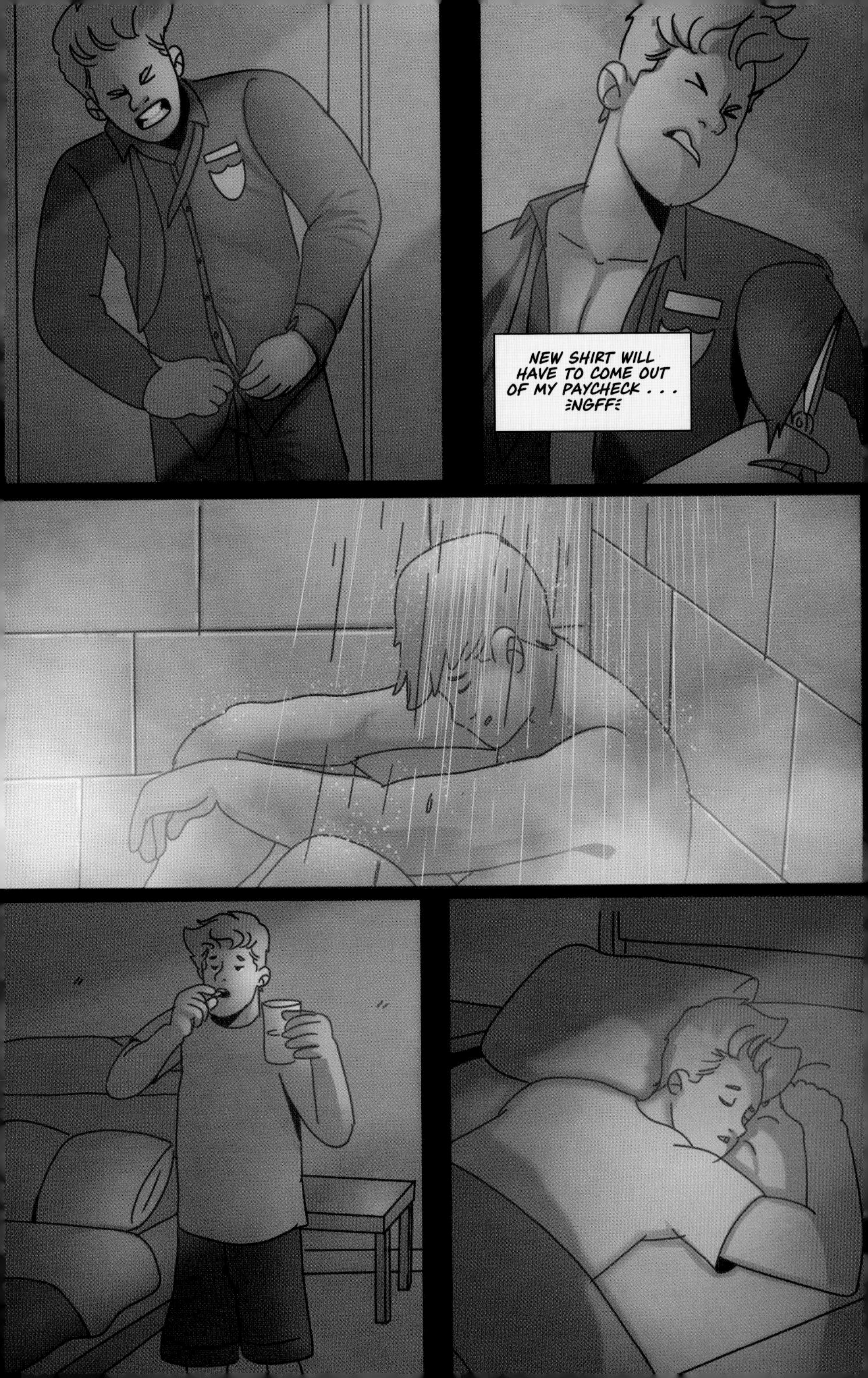
NEW SHIRT WILL HAVE TO COME OUT OF MY PAYCHECK . . .
NGFF

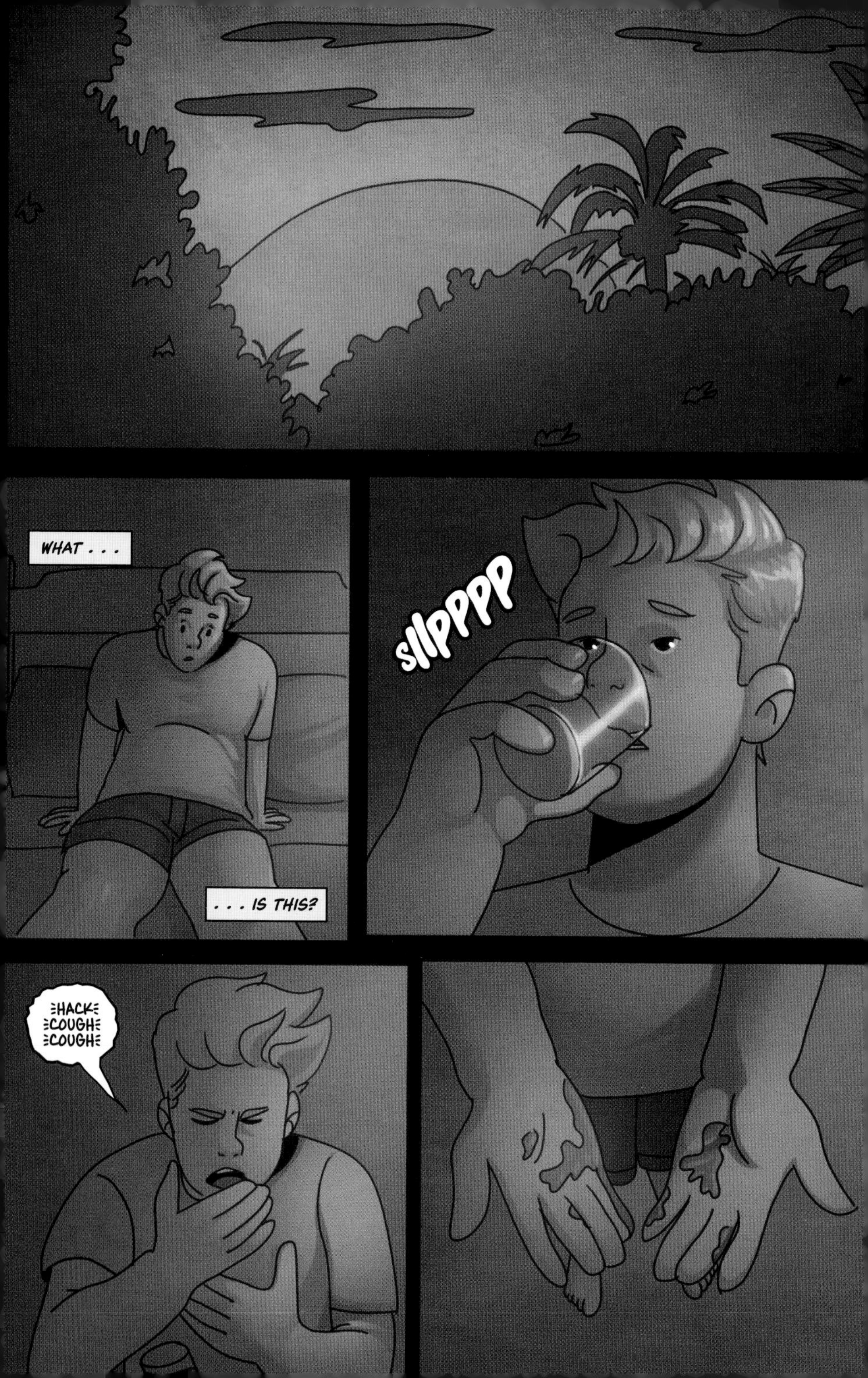
WHAT . . .
. . . IS THIS?
sllPPPP
HACK
COUGH
COUGH

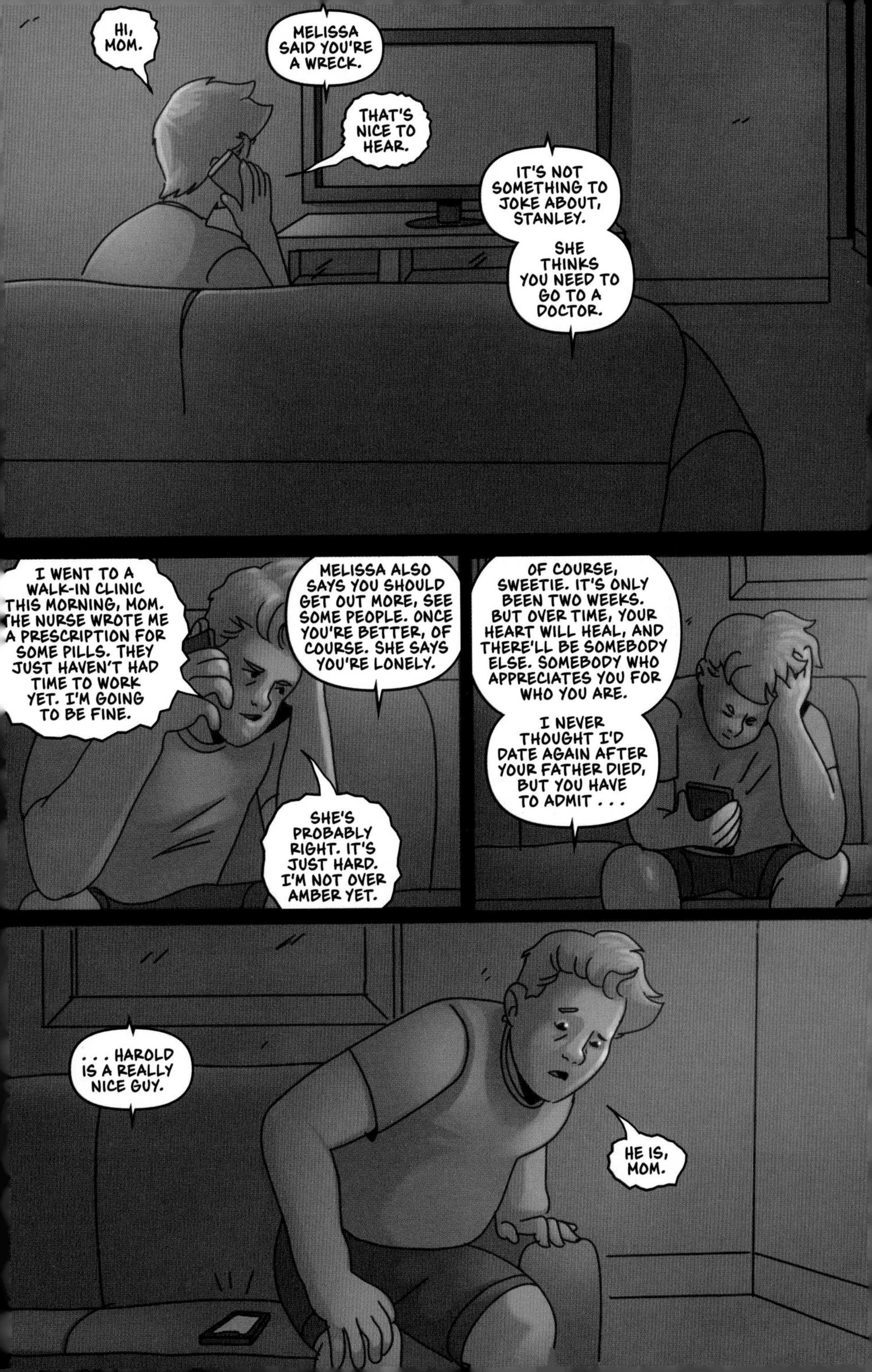
HI, MOM.
MELISSA SAID YOU'RE A WRECK.
THAT'S NICE TO HEAR.
IT'S NOT SOMETHING TO JOKE ABOUT, STANLEY.
SHE THINKS YOU NEED TO GO TO A DOCTOR.
I WENT TO A WALK-IN CLINIC THIS MORNING, MOM. THE NURSE WROTE ME A PRESCRIPTION FOR SOME PILLS. THEY JUST HAVEN'T HAD TIME TO WORK YET. I'M GOING TO BE FINE.
MELISSA ALSO SAYS YOU SHOULD GET OUT MORE, SEE SOME PEOPLE. ONCE YOU'RE BETTER, OF COURSE. SHE SAYS YOU'RE LONELY.
SHE'S PROBABLY RIGHT. IT'S JUST HARD. I'M NOT OVER AMBER YET.
OF COURSE, SWEETIE. IT'S ONLY BEEN TWO WEEKS. BUT OVER TIME, YOUR HEART WILL HEAL, AND THERE'LL BE SOMEBODY ELSE. SOMEBODY WHO APPRECIATES YOU FOR WHO YOU ARE.
I NEVER THOUGHT I'D DATE AGAIN AFTER YOUR FATHER DIED, BUT YOU HAVE TO ADMIT . . .
. . . HAROLD IS A REALLY NICE GUY.
HE IS, MOM.

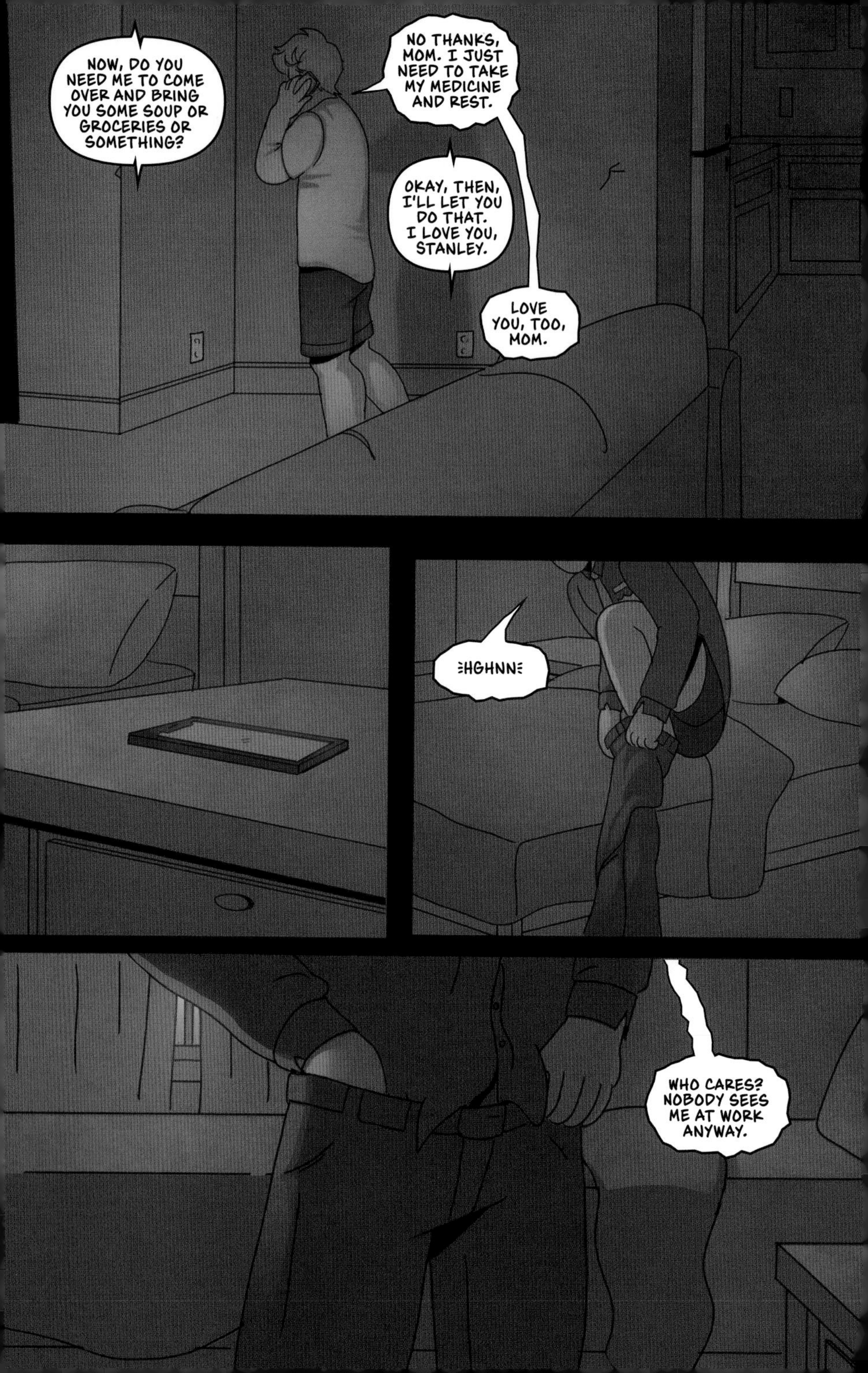
NOW, DO YOU NEED ME TO COME OVER AND BRING YOU SOME SOUP OR GROCERIES OR SOMETHING?
NO THANKS, MOM. I JUST NEED TO TAKE MY MEDICINE AND REST.
OKAY, THEN, I'LL LET YOU DO THAT. I LOVE YOU, STANLEY.
LOVE YOU, TOO, MOM.
HGHNN
WHO CARES? NOBODY SEES ME AT WORK ANYWAY.

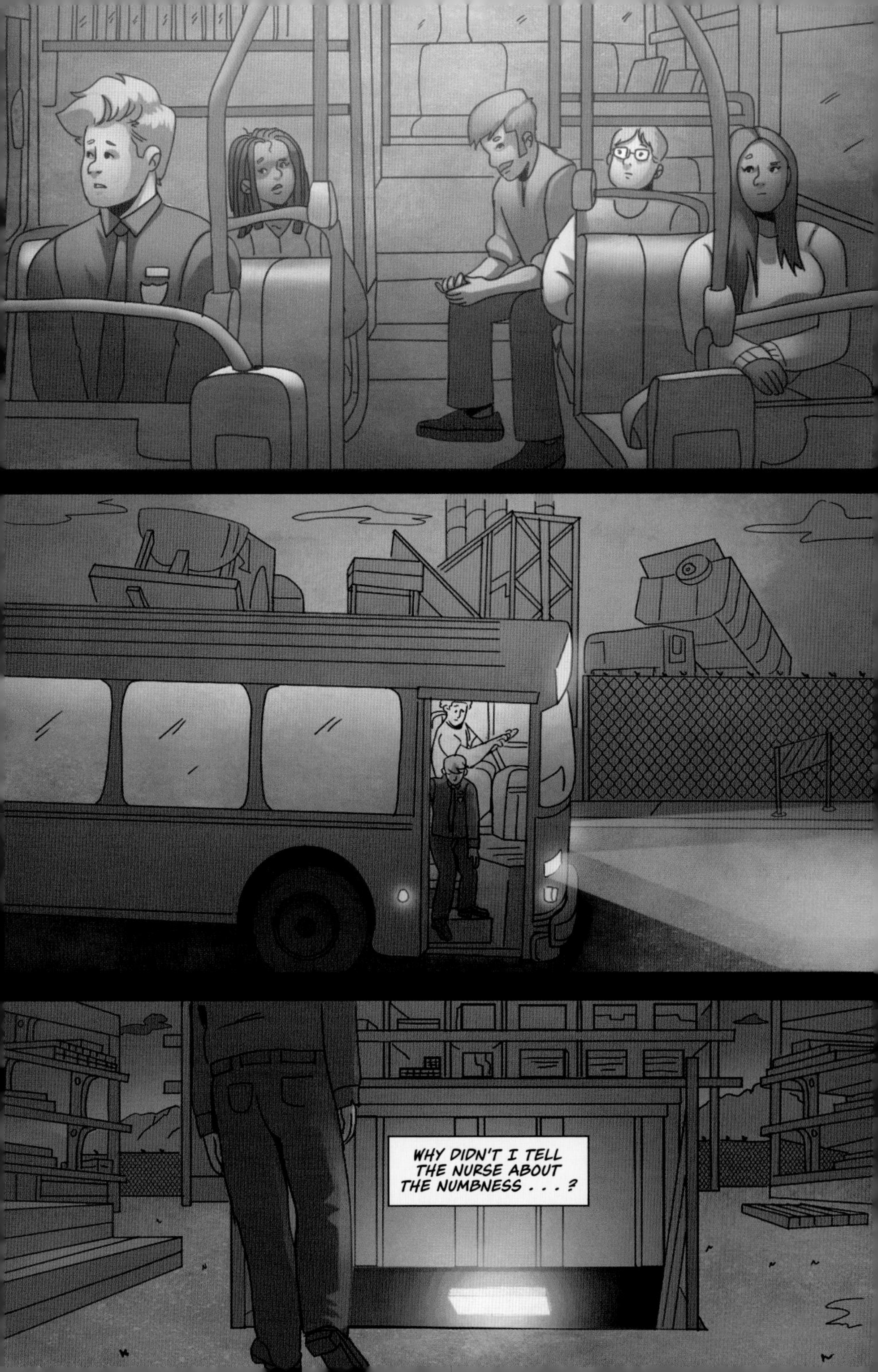
WHY DIDN'T I TELL THE NURSE ABOUT THE NUMBNESS . . . ?

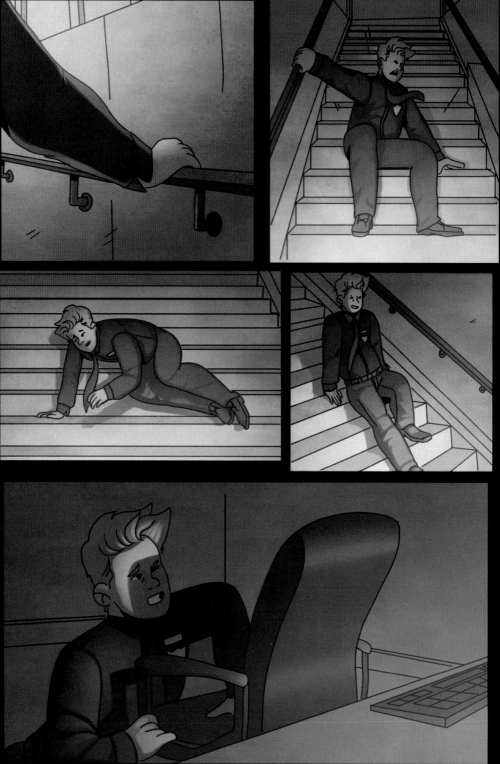

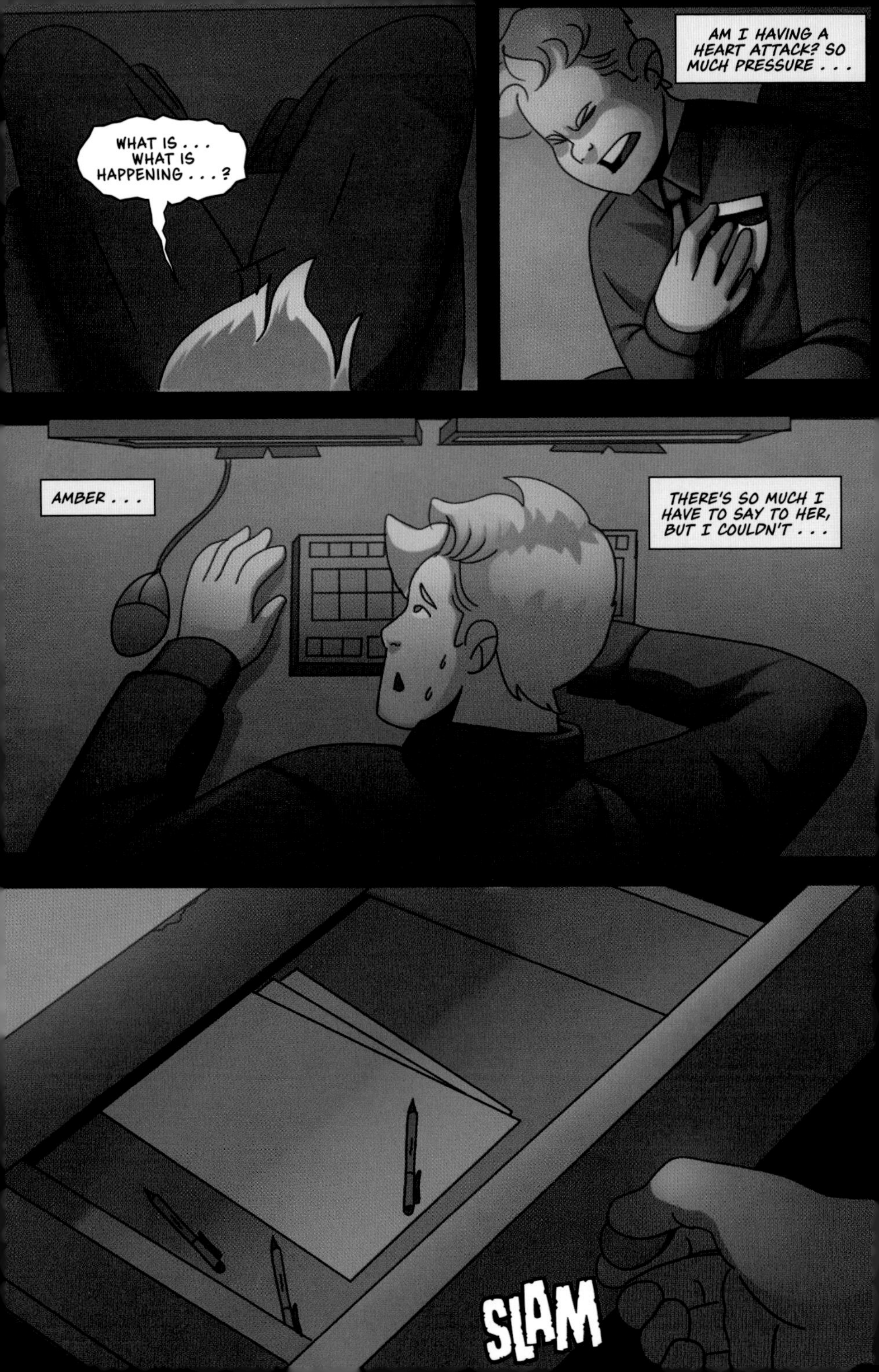
WHAT IS . . . WHAT IS HAPPENING . . . ?
AM I HAVING A HEART ATTACK? SO MUCH PRESSURE . . .
AMBER . . .
THERE'S SO MUCH I HAVE TO SAY TO HER, BUT I COULDN'T . . .
SLAM

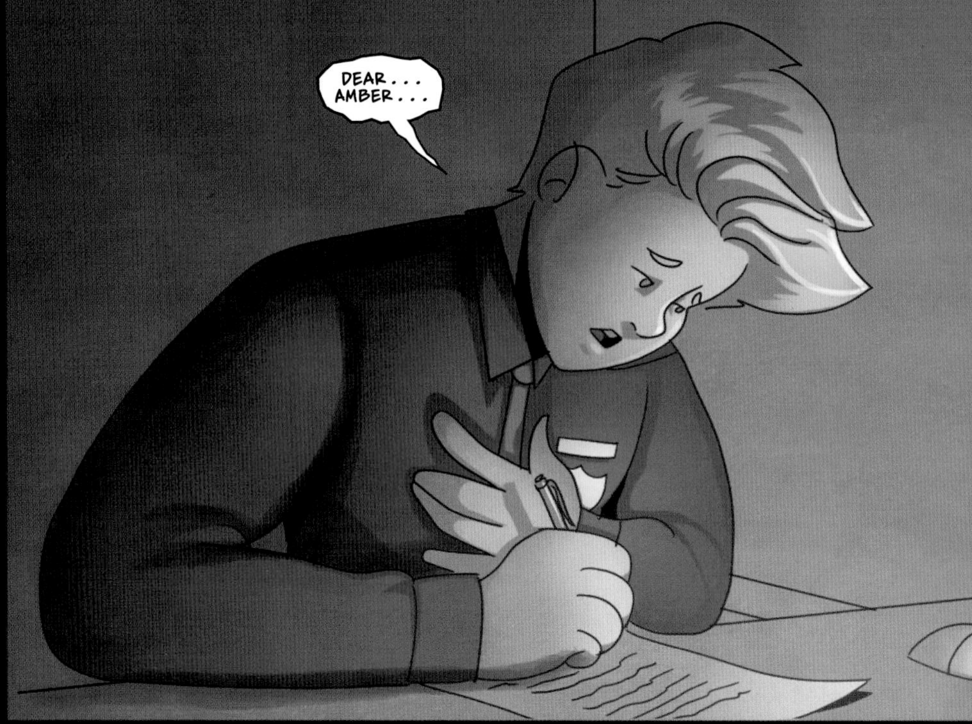
DEAR . . . AMBER . . .

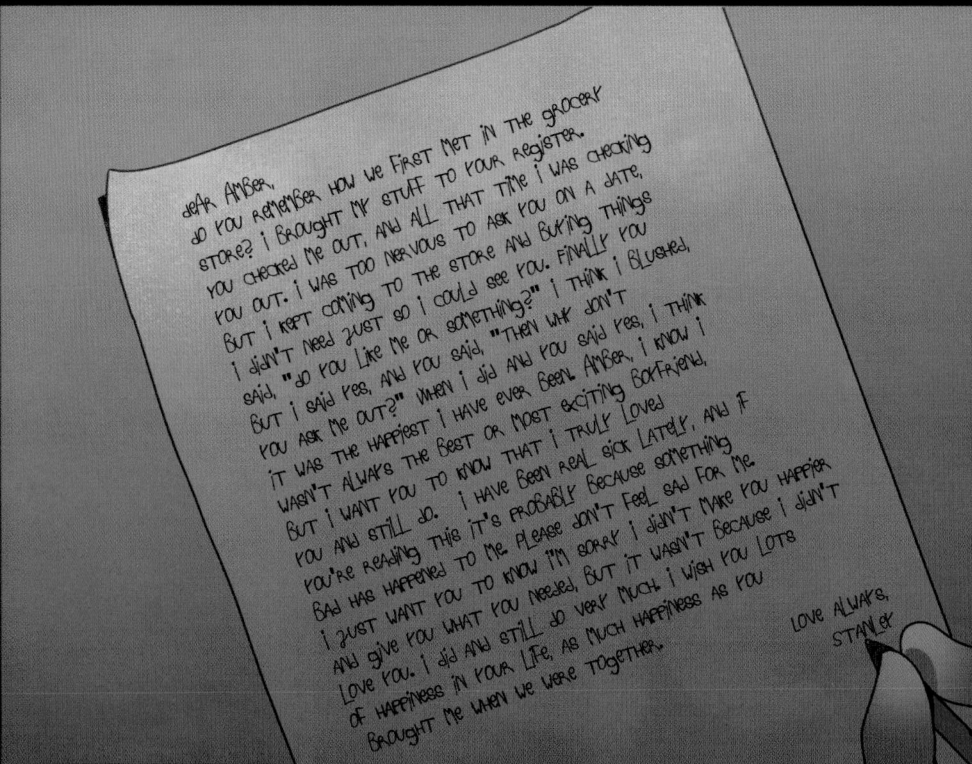
DEAR AMBER,
DO YOU REMEMBER HOW WE FIRST MET IN THE GROCERY
STORE? i BROUGHT MY STUFF TO YOUR REGISTER.
YOU CHECKED ME OUT, AND ALL THAT TIME i WAS CHECKING
YOU OUT. i WAS TOO NERVOUS TO ASK YOU ON A DATE,
BUT i KEPT COMING TO THE STORE AND BUYING THINGS
i DIDN'T NEED JUST SO i COULD SEE YOU. FINALLY YOU
SAID, "DO YOU LIKE ME OR SOMETHING?" i THINK i BLUSHED,
BUT i SAID YES, AND YOU SAID, "THEN WHY DON'T
YOU ASK ME OUT?" WHEN i DID AND YOU SAID YES, i THINK
iT WAS THE HAPPIEST i HAVE EVER BEEN. AMBER, i KNOW i
WASN'T ALWAYS THE BEST OR MOST EXCITING BOYFRIEND,
BUT i WANT YOU TO KNOW THAT i TRULY LOVED
YOU AND STILL DO. i HAVE BEEN REAL SICK LATELY, AND iF
YOU'RE READING THIS iT'S PROBABLY BECAUSE SOMETHING
BAD HAS HAPPENED TO ME. PLEASE DON'T FEEL SAD FOR ME.
i JUST WANT YOU TO KNOW i'M SORRY i DIDN'T MAKE YOU HAPPIER
AND GIVE YOU WHAT YOU NEEDED, BUT iT WASN'T BECAUSE i DIDN'T
LOVE YOU. i DID AND STILL DO VERY MUCH. i WISH YOU LOTS
OF HAPPINESS iN YOUR LIFE, AS MUCH HAPPINESS AS YOU
BROUGHT ME WHEN WE WERE TOGETHER.
LOVE ALWAYS,
STANLEY

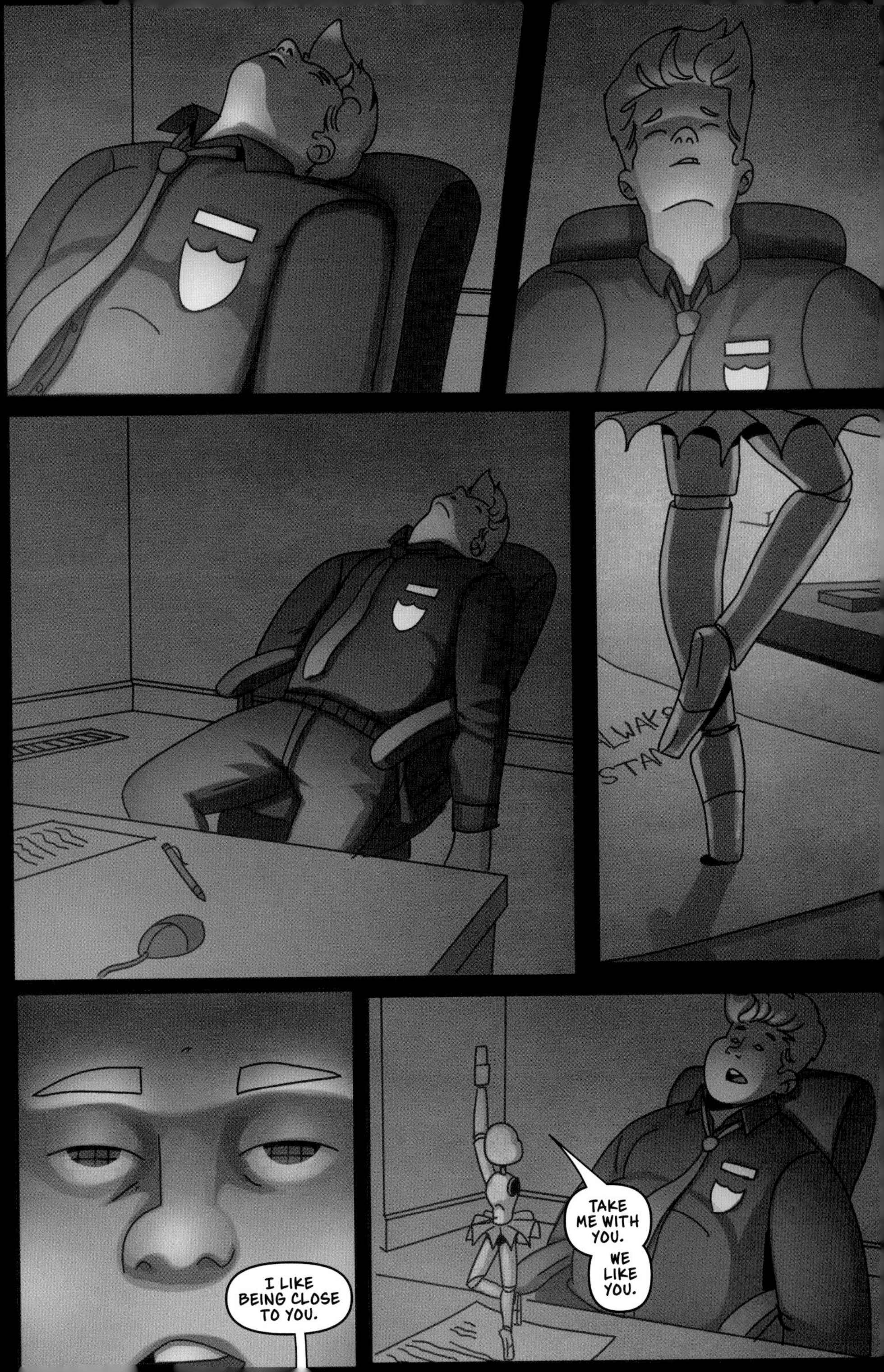
I LIKE BEING CLOSE TO YOU.
TAKE ME WITH YOU.
WE LIKE YOU.

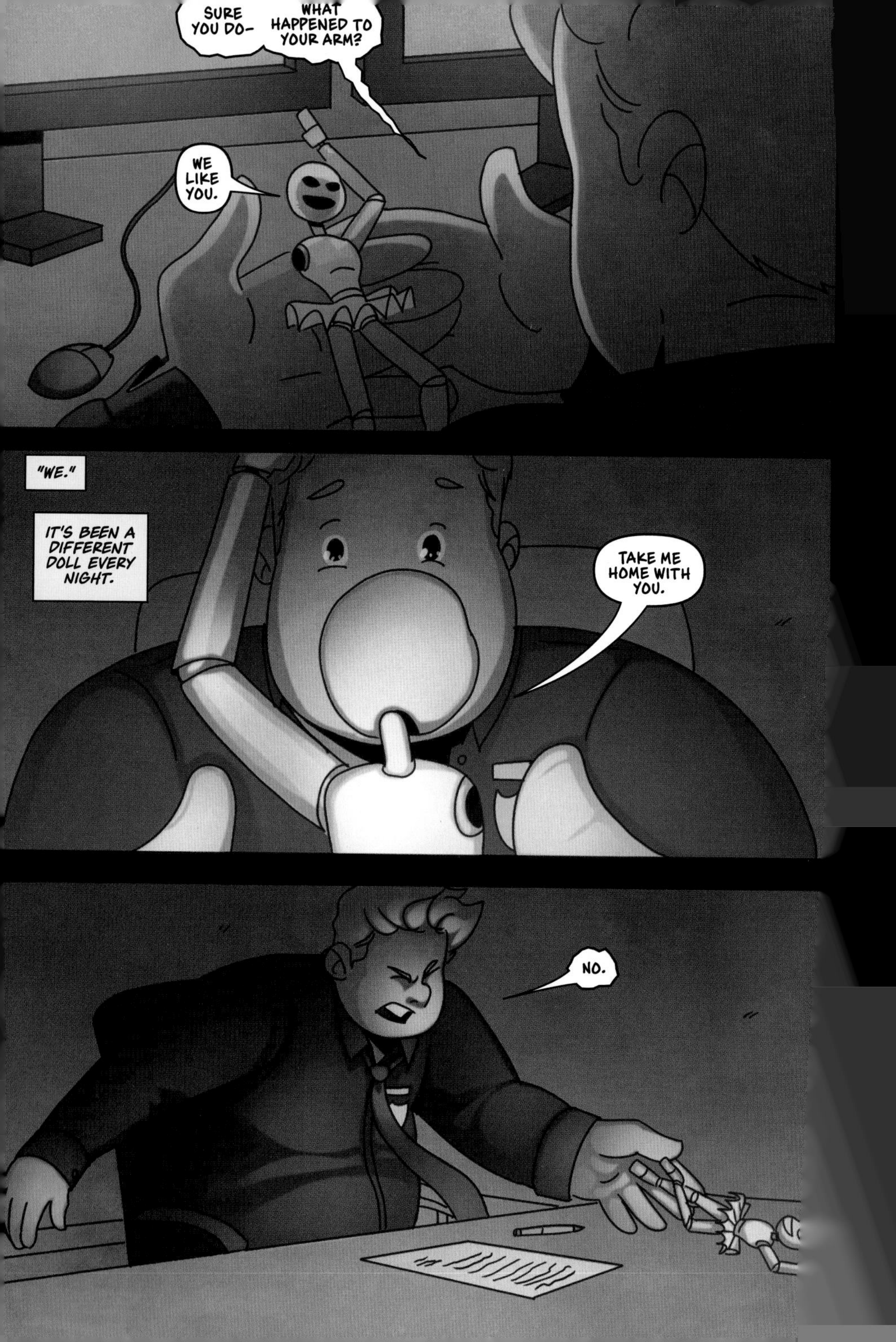
SURE YOU DO-
WHAT HAPPENED TO YOUR ARM?
WE LIKE YOU.
"WE."
IT'S BEEN A DIFFERENT DOLL EVERY NIGHT.
TAKE ME HOME WITH YOU.
NO.

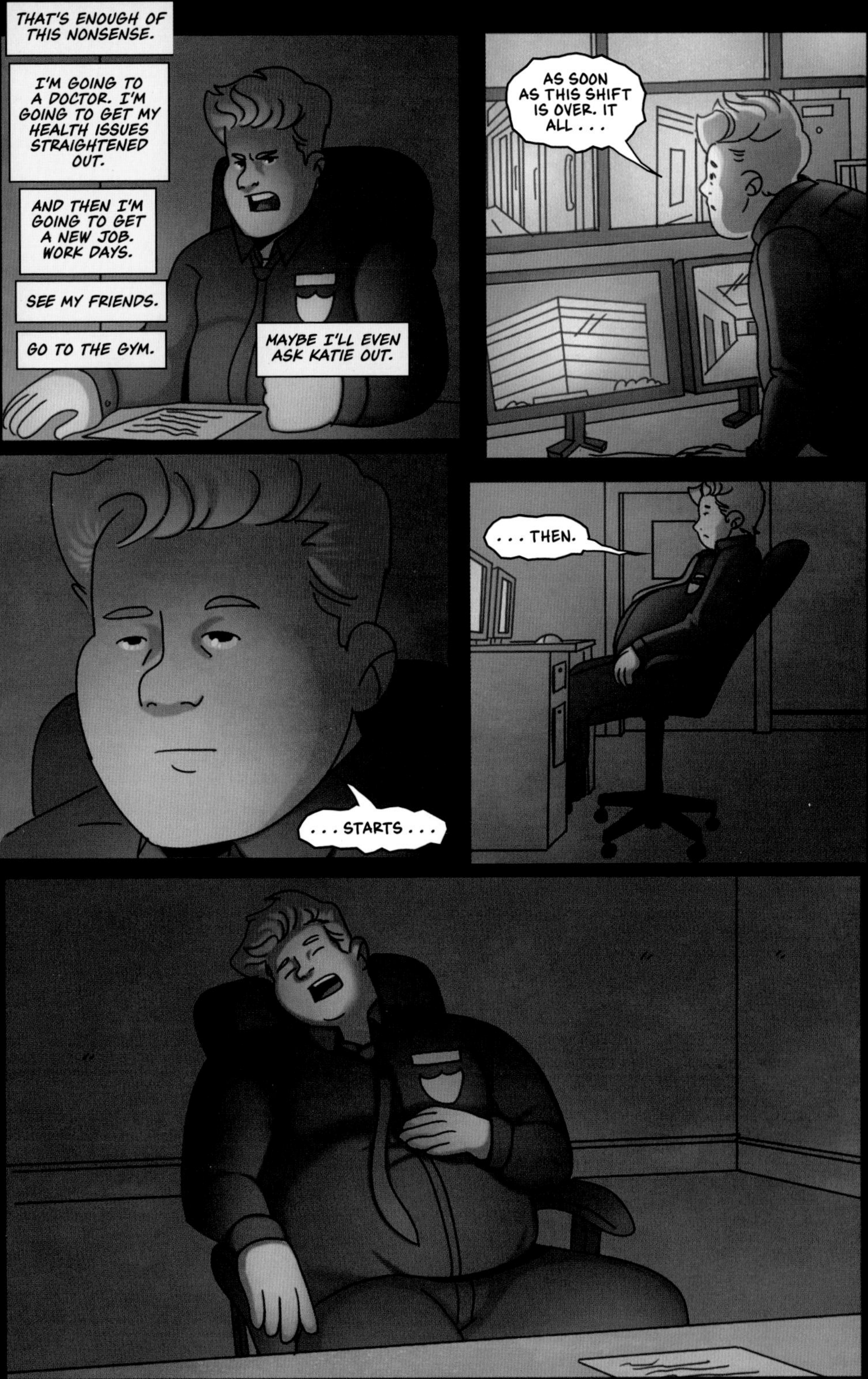
THAT'S ENOUGH OF THIS NONSENSE.
I'M GOING TO A DOCTOR. I'M GOING TO GET MY HEALTH ISSUES STRAIGHTENED OUT.
AND THEN I'M GOING TO GET A NEW JOB. WORK DAYS.
SEE MY FRIENDS.
GO TO THE GYM.
MAYBE I'LL EVEN ASK KATIE OUT.
AS SOON AS THIS SHIFT IS OVER. IT ALL . . .
. . . STARTS . . .
. . . THEN.

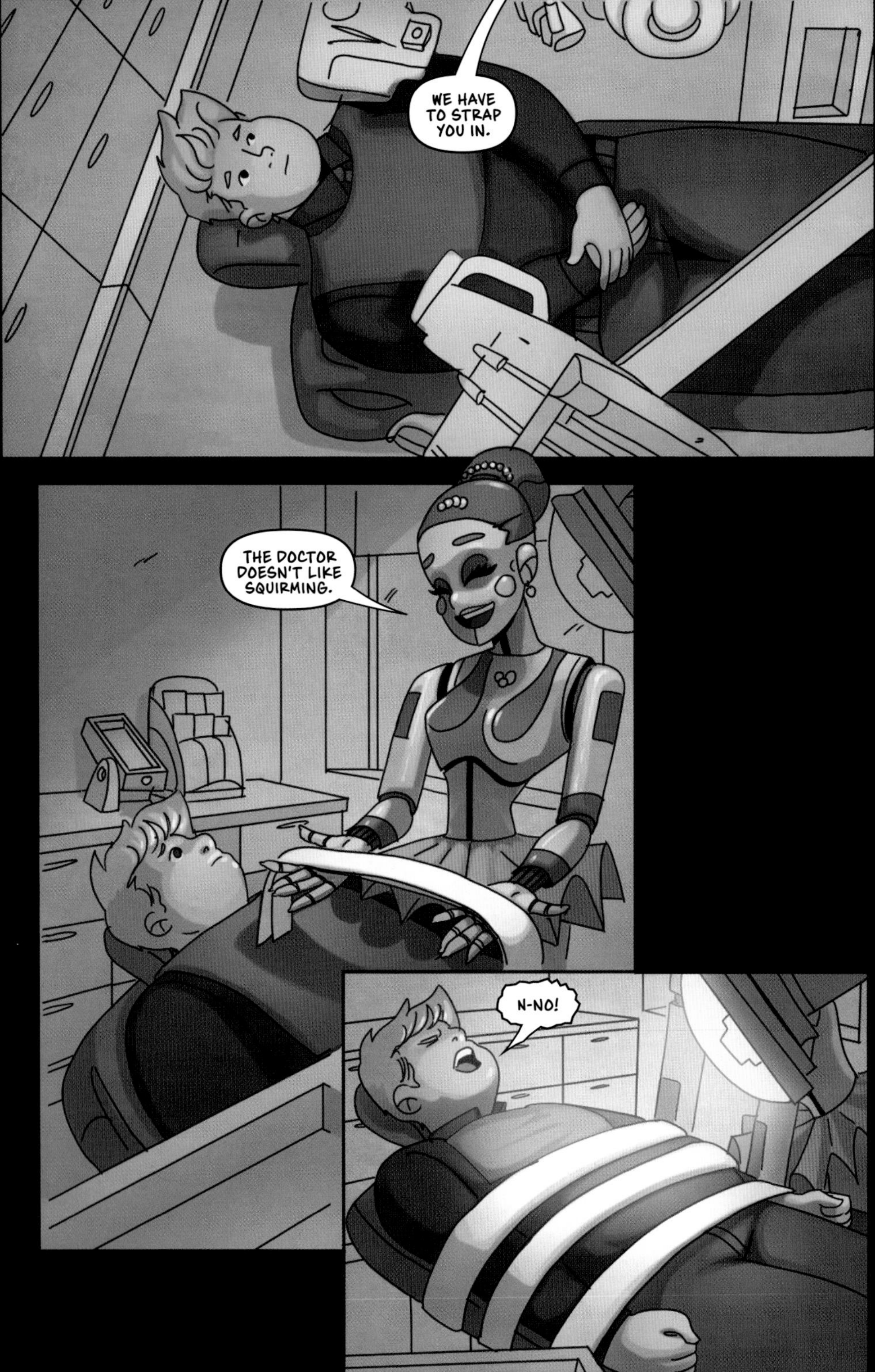
WE HAVE TO STRAP YOU IN.
THE DOCTOR DOESN'T LIKE SQUIRMING.
N-NO!

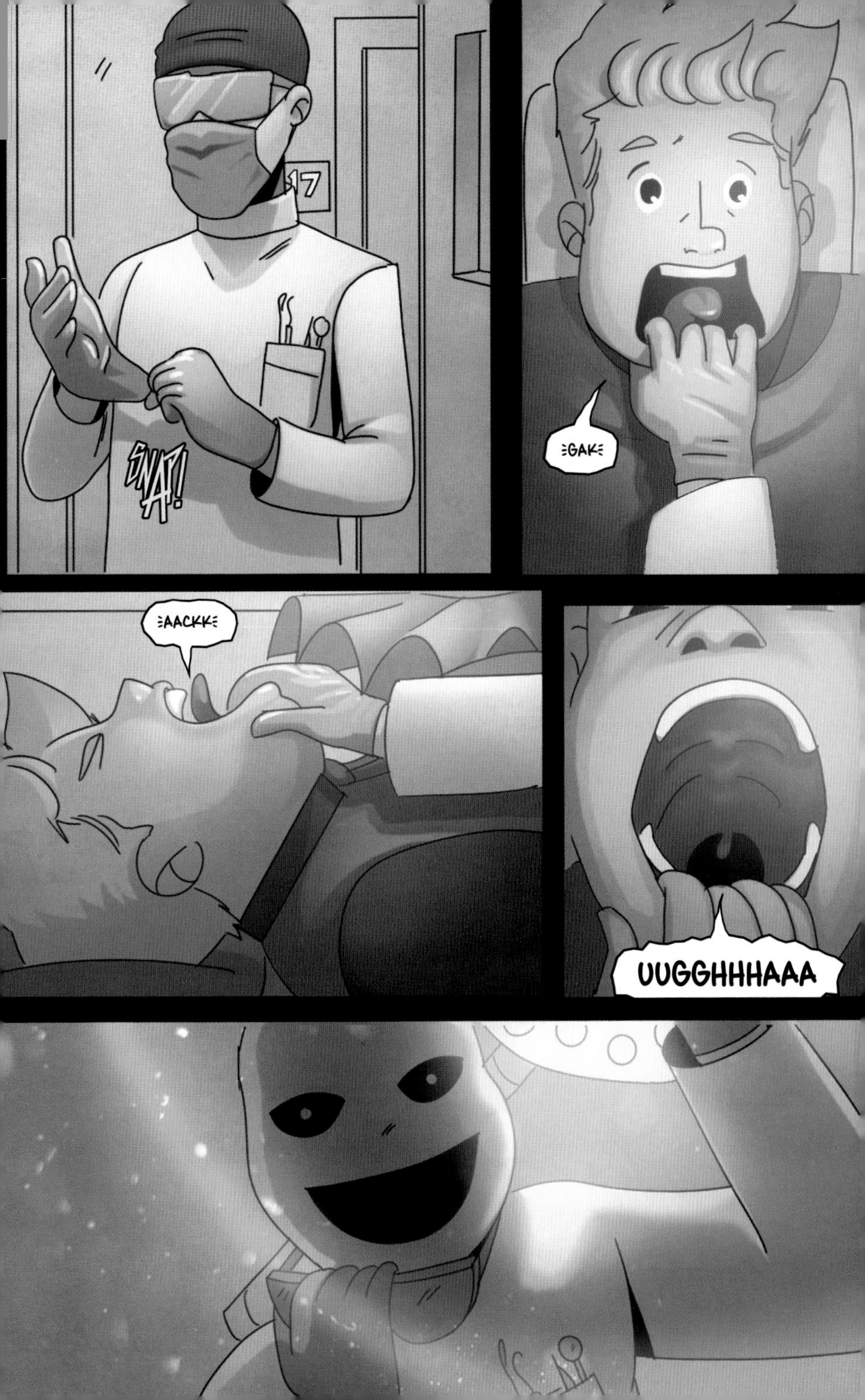
SNAP!
GAK
AACKK
UUGGHHHAAA

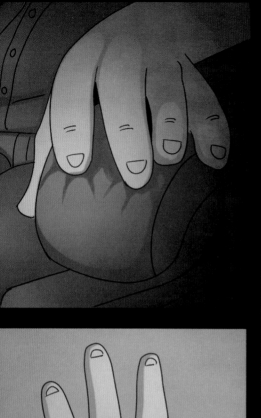

AH!

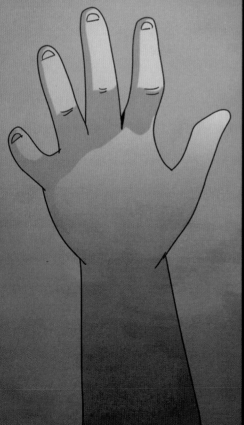

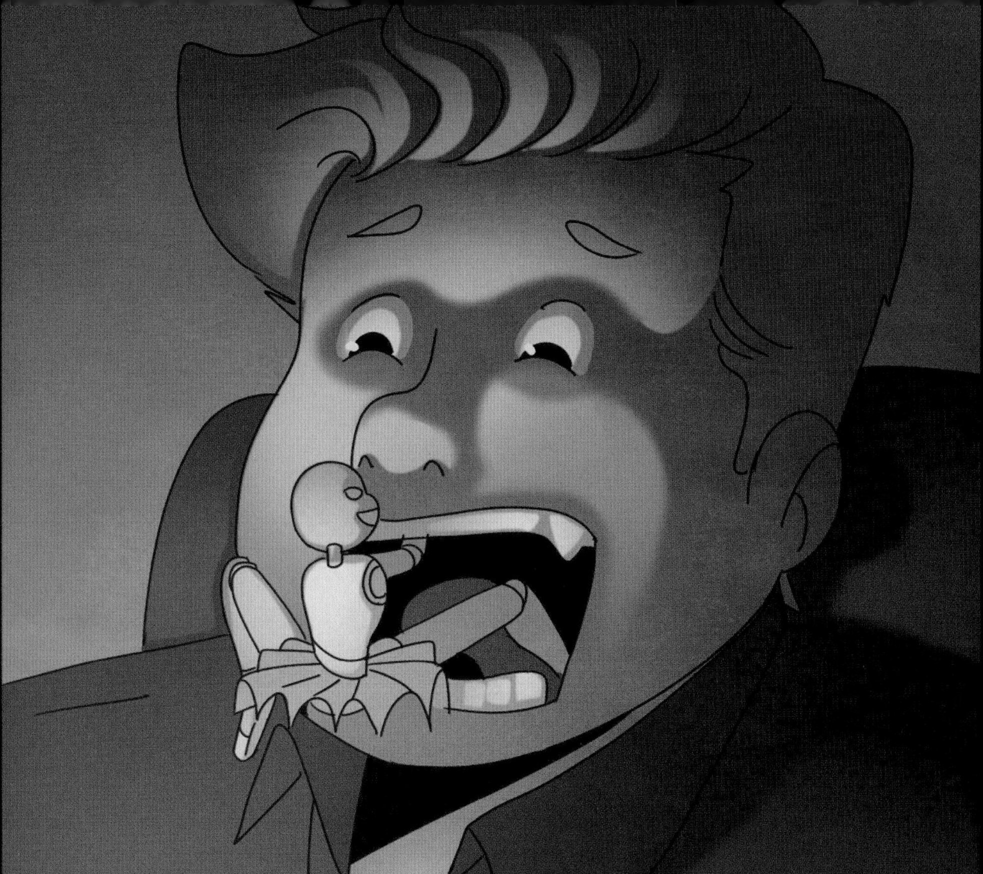

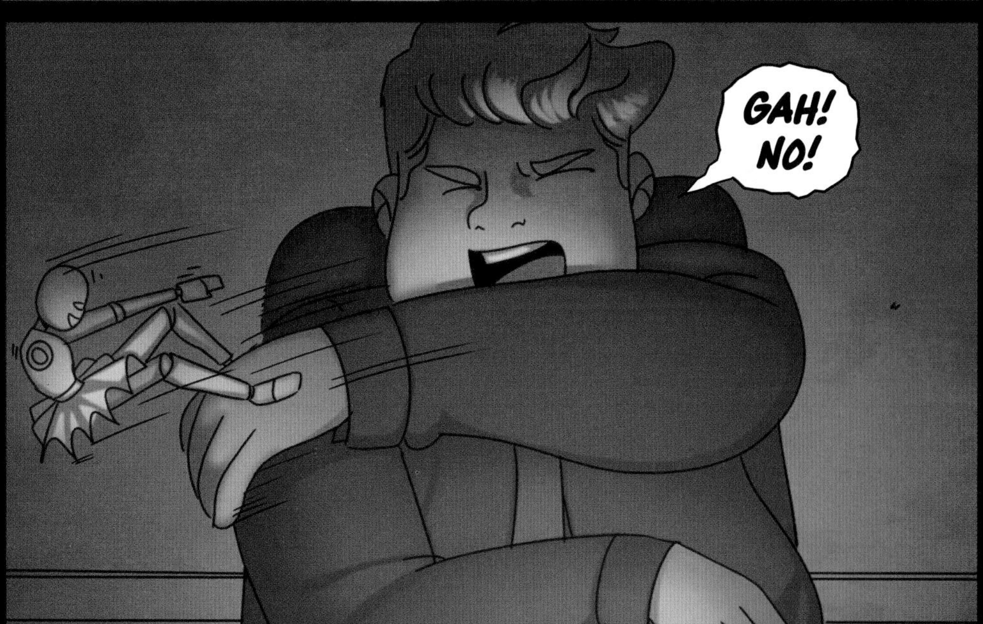
GAH! NO!

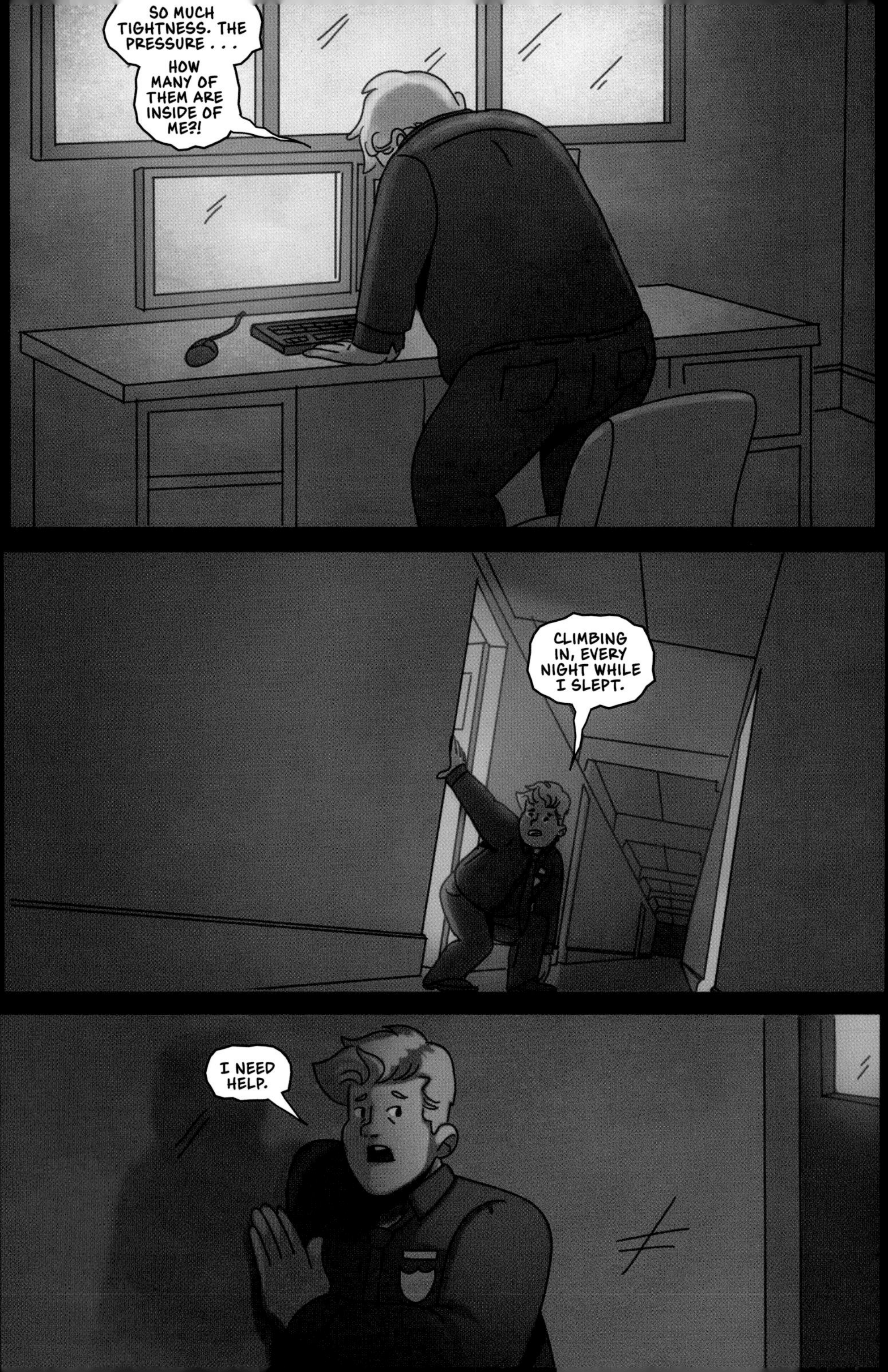
SO MUCH TIGHTNESS. THE PRESSURE . . .
HOW MANY OF THEM ARE INSIDE OF ME?!
CLIMBING IN, EVERY NIGHT WHILE I SLEPT.
I NEED HELP.

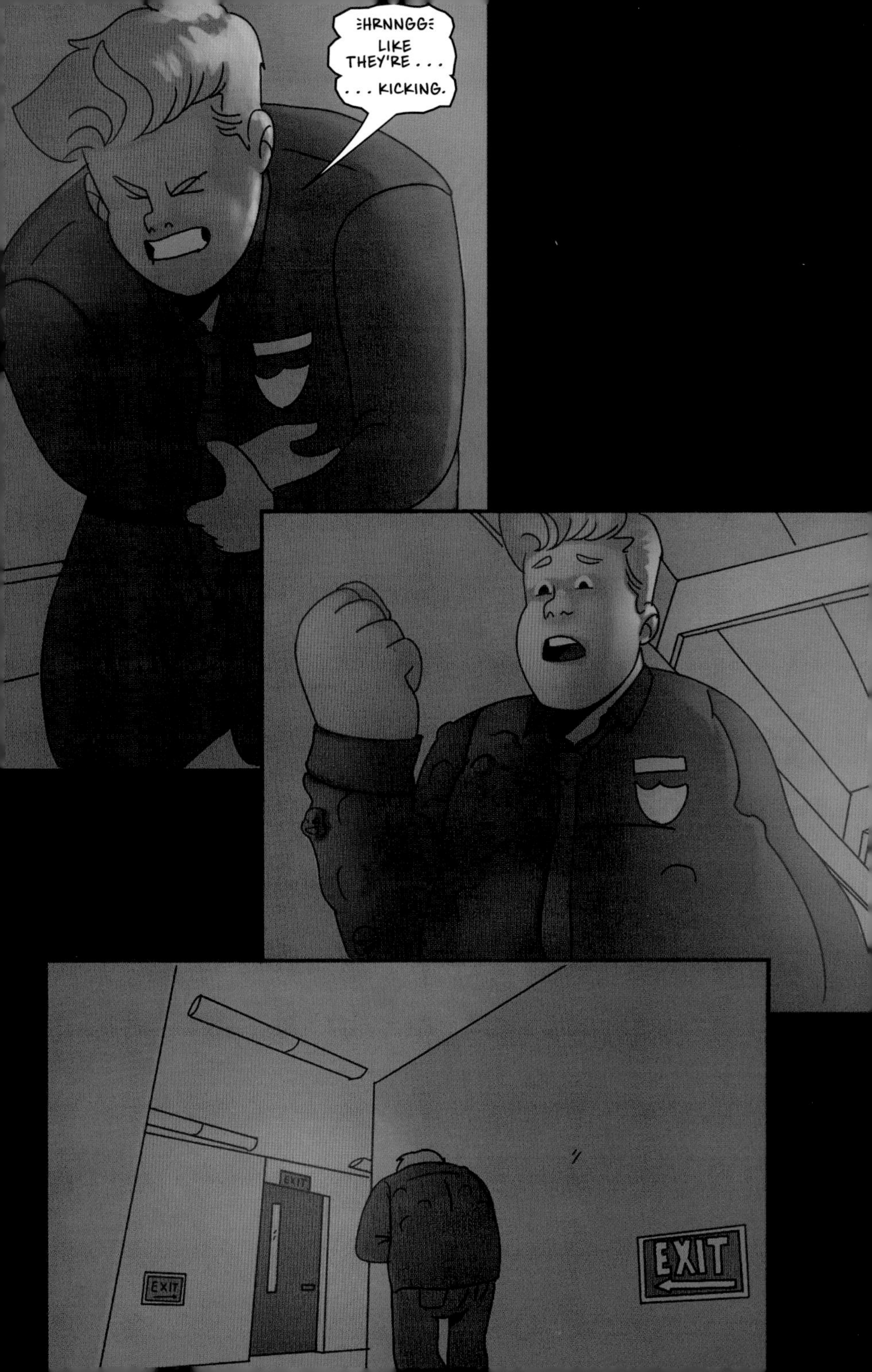
HRNNGG
LIKE THEY'RE . . .
. . . KICKING.
EXIT
EXIT
EXIT

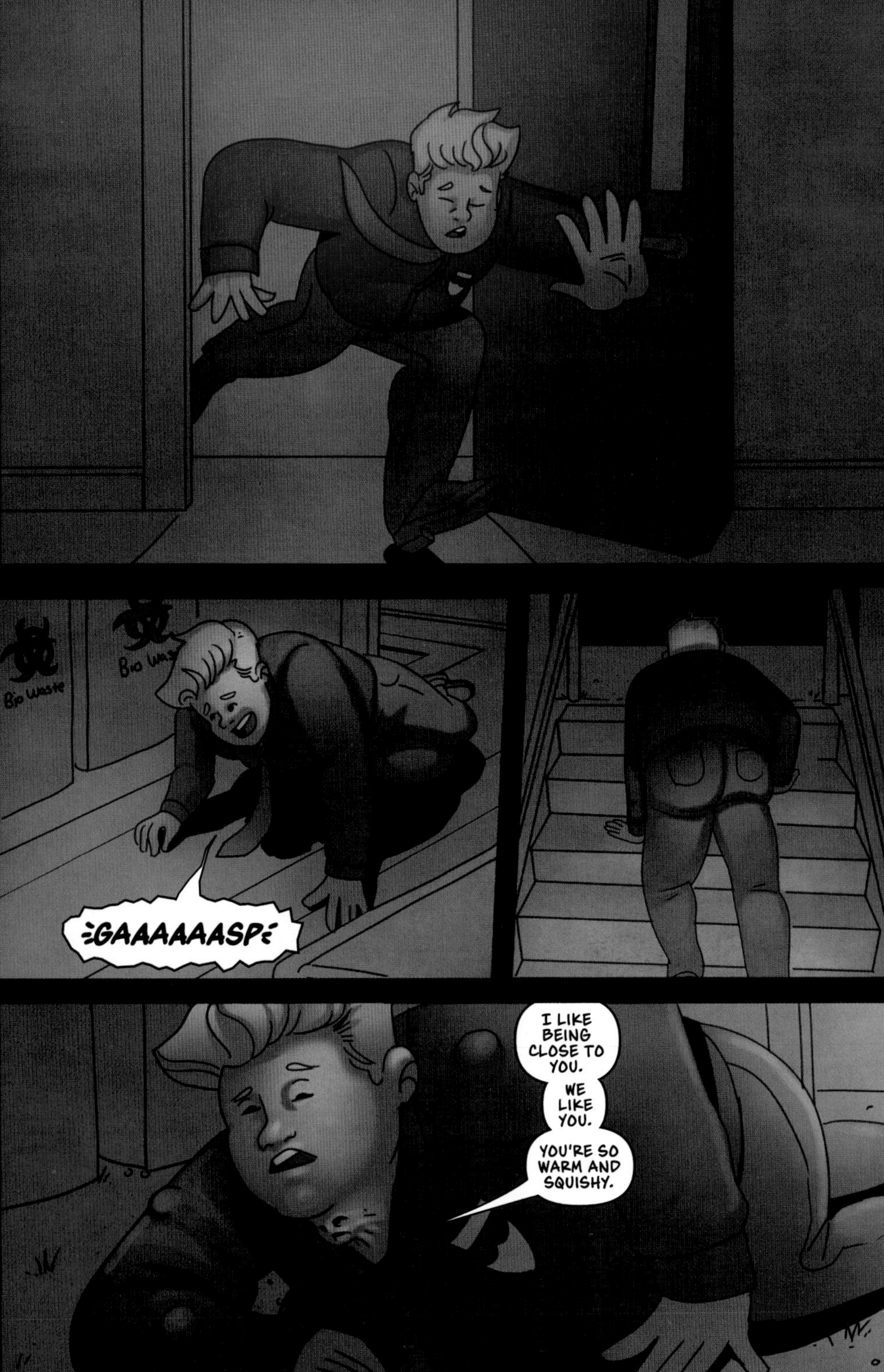

Bio Waste
Bio Waste
GAAAAAASP
I LIKE BEING CLOSE TO YOU.
WE LIKE YOU.
YOU'RE SO WARM AND SQUISHY.

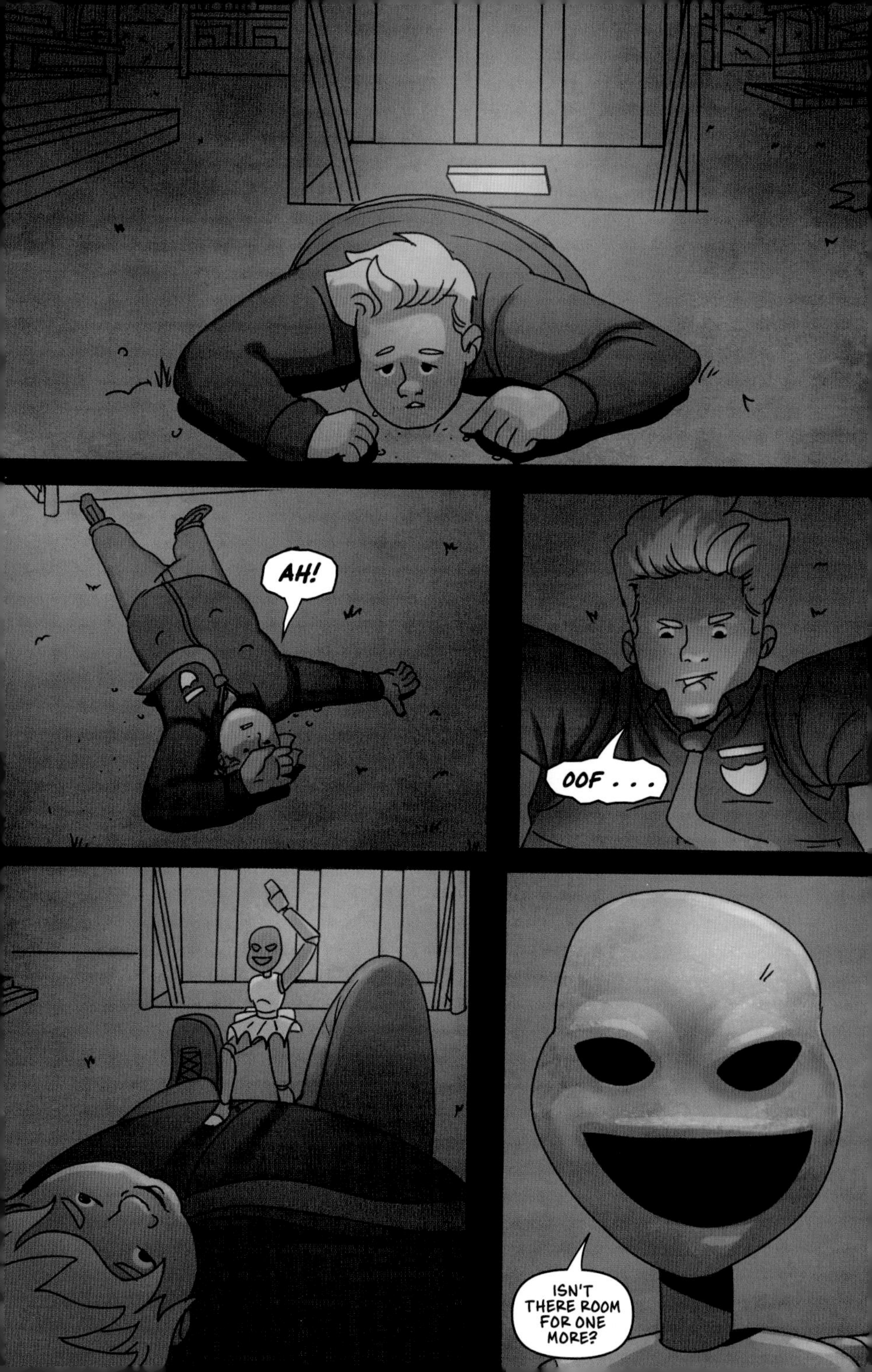
AH!
OOF . . .
ISN'T THERE ROOM FOR ONE MORE?

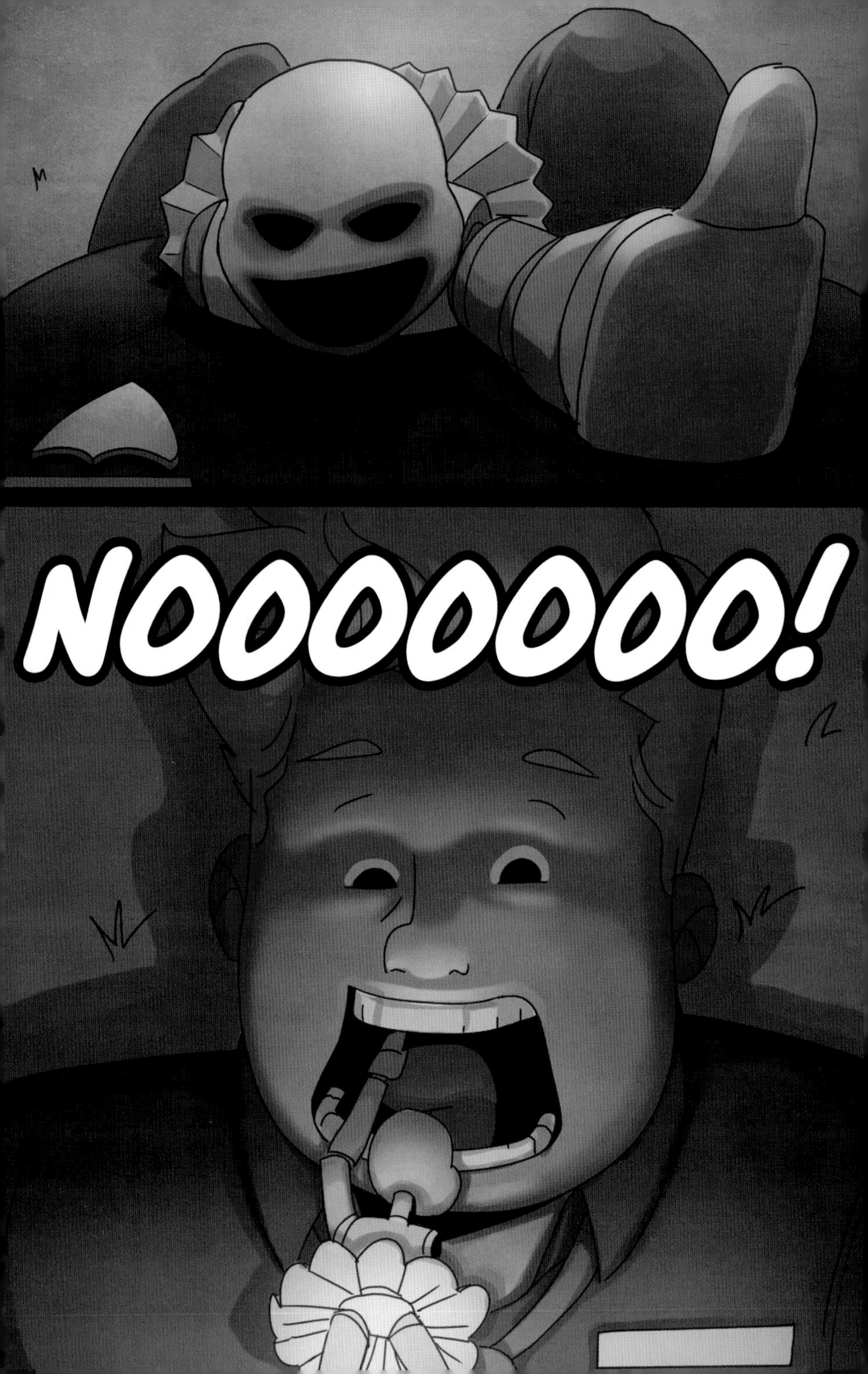
NOOOOOOO!

THE NEW KID

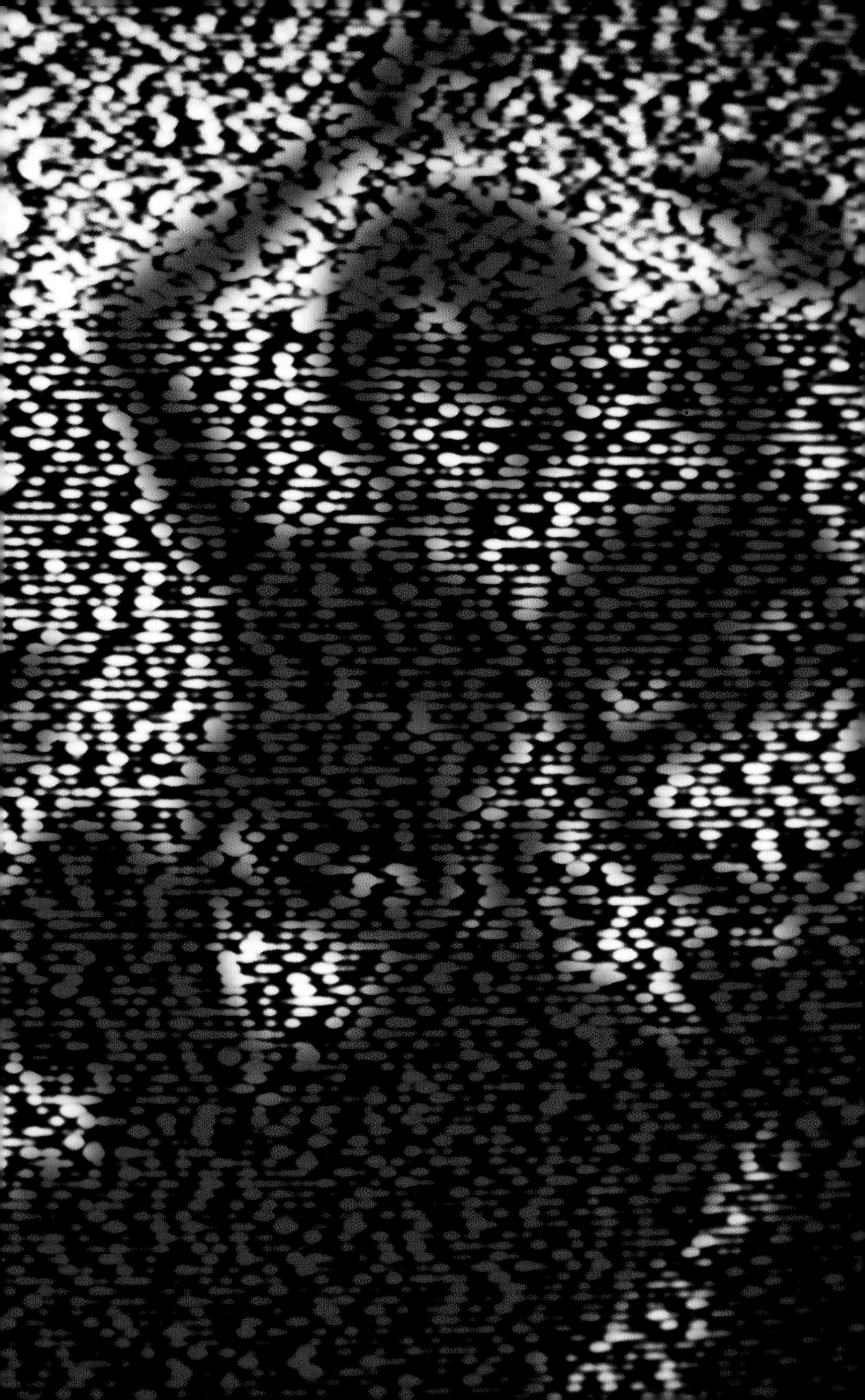

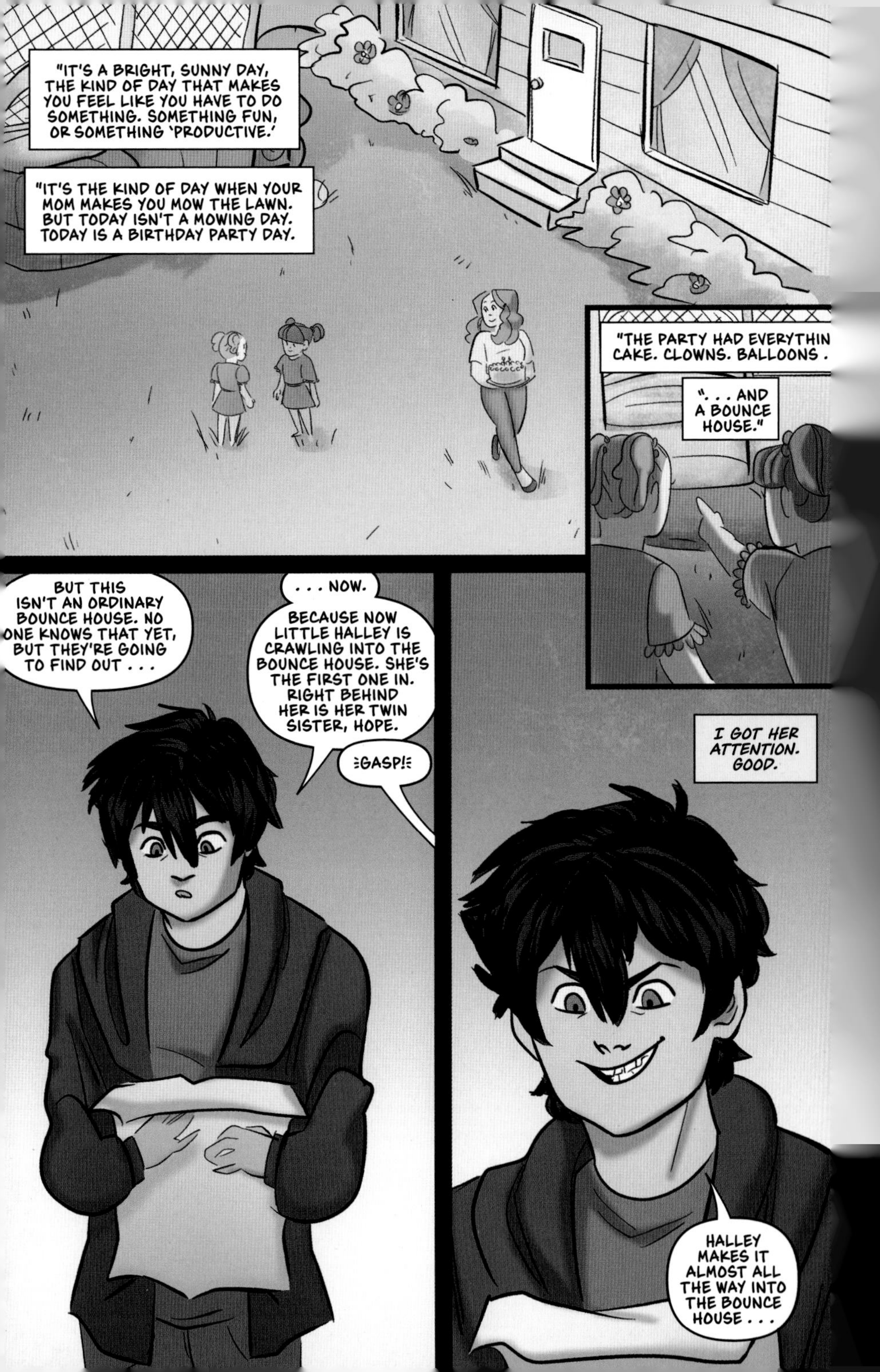
"IT'S A BRIGHT, SUNNY DAY, THE KIND OF DAY THAT MAKES YOU FEEL LIKE YOU HAVE TO DO SOMETHING. SOMETHING FUN, OR SOMETHING 'PRODUCTIVE.'
"IT'S THE KIND OF DAY WHEN YOUR MOM MAKES YOU MOW THE LAWN. BUT TODAY ISN'T A MOWING DAY. TODAY IS A BIRTHDAY PARTY DAY.
"THE PARTY HAD EVERYTHIN CAKE. CLOWNS. BALLOONS .
". . . AND A BOUNCE HOUSE."
BUT THIS ISN'T AN ORDINARY BOUNCE HOUSE. NO ONE KNOWS THAT YET, BUT THEY'RE GOING TO FIND OUT . . .
. . . NOW.
BECAUSE NOW LITTLE HALLEY IS CRAWLING INTO THE BOUNCE HOUSE. SHE'S THE FIRST ONE IN. RIGHT BEHIND HER IS HER TWIN SISTER, HOPE.
GASP!
I GOT HER ATTENTION. GOOD.
HALLEY MAKES IT ALMOST ALL THE WAY INTO THE BOUNCE HOUSE . . .

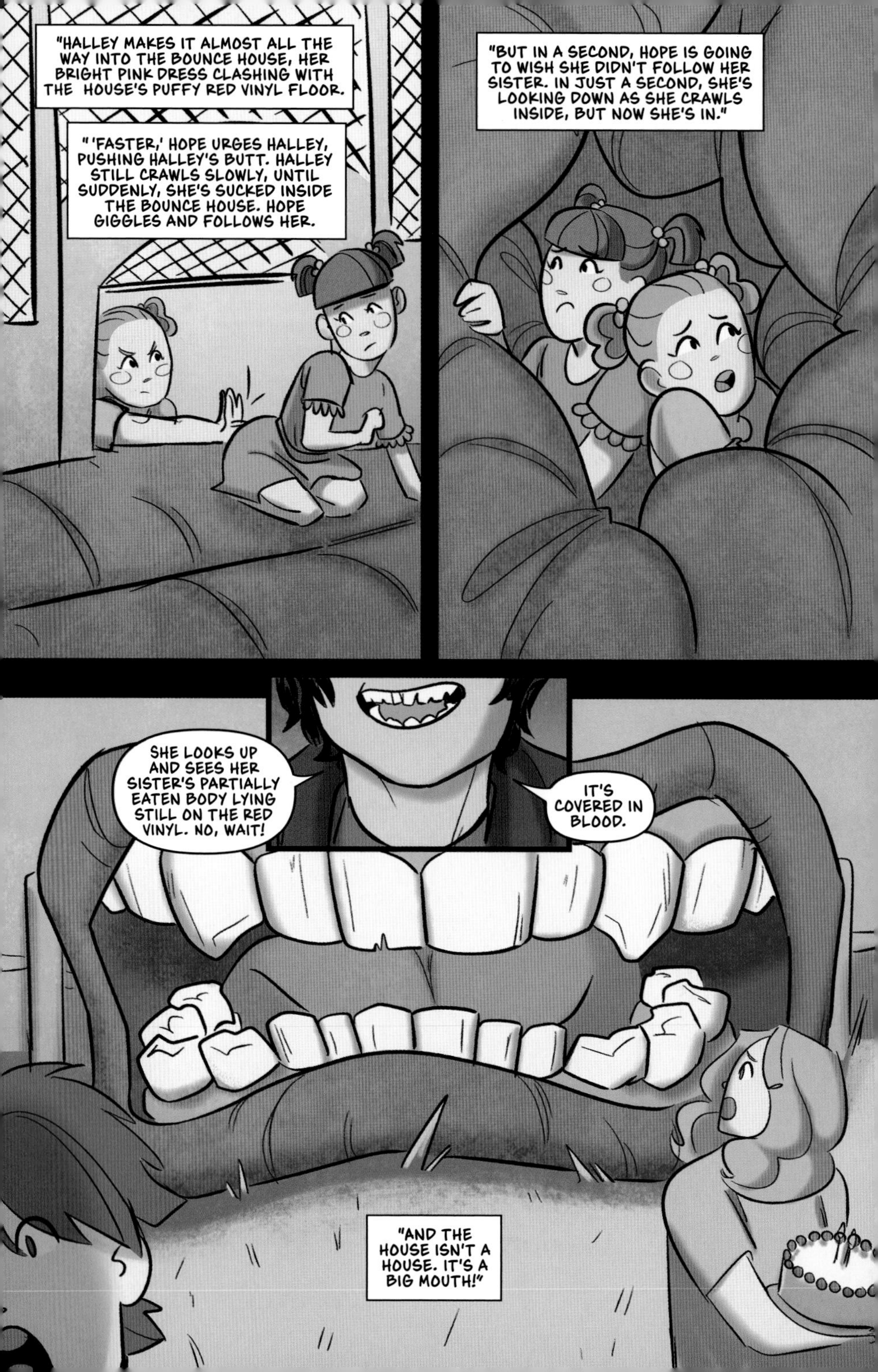
"HALLEY MAKES IT ALMOST ALL THE WAY INTO THE BOUNCE HOUSE, HER BRIGHT PINK DRESS CLASHING WITH THE HOUSE'S PUFFY RED VINYL FLOOR.
" 'FASTER,' HOPE URGES HALLEY, PUSHING HALLEY'S BUTT. HALLEY STILL CRAWLS SLOWLY, UNTIL SUDDENLY, SHE'S SUCKED INSIDE THE BOUNCE HOUSE. HOPE GIGGLES AND FOLLOWS HER.
"BUT IN A SECOND, HOPE IS GOING TO WISH SHE DIDN'T FOLLOW HER SISTER. IN JUST A SECOND, SHE'S LOOKING DOWN AS SHE CRAWLS INSIDE, BUT NOW SHE'S IN."
SHE LOOKS UP AND SEES HER SISTER'S PARTIALLY EATEN BODY LYING STILL ON THE RED VINYL. NO, WAIT!
IT'S COVERED IN BLOOD.
"AND THE HOUSE ISN'T A HOUSE. IT'S A BIG MOUTH!"

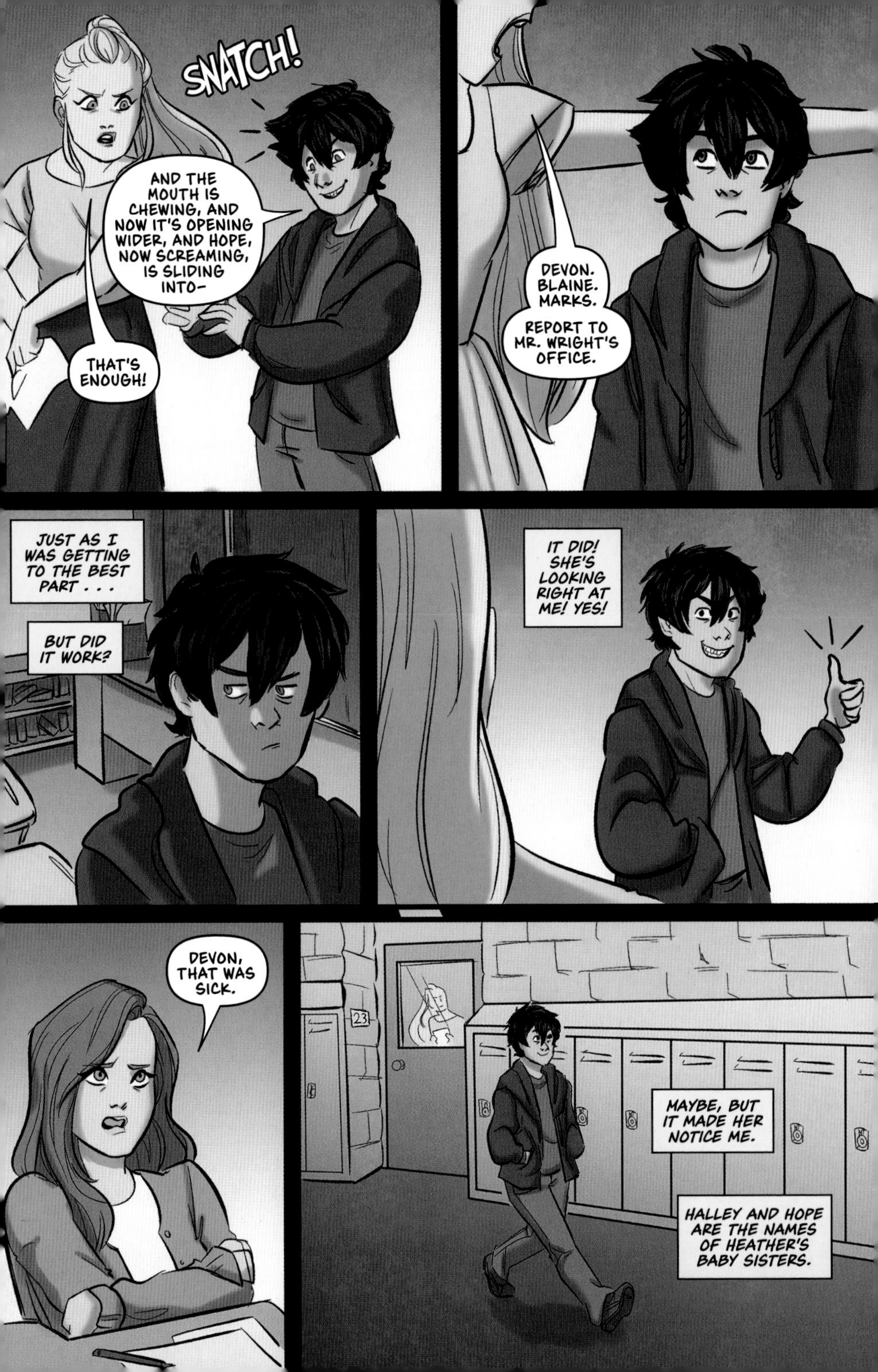
SNATCH!
AND THE MOUTH IS CHEWING, AND NOW IT'S OPENING WIDER, AND HOPE, NOW SCREAMING, IS SLIDING INTO–
THAT'S ENOUGH!
DEVON. BLAINE. MARKS.
REPORT TO MR. WRIGHT'S OFFICE.
JUST AS I WAS GETTING TO THE BEST PART . . .
BUT DID IT WORK?
IT DID! SHE'S LOOKING RIGHT AT ME! YES!
DEVON, THAT WAS SICK.
23
MAYBE, BUT IT MADE HER NOTICE ME.
HALLEY AND HOPE ARE THE NAMES OF HEATHER'S BABY SISTERS.

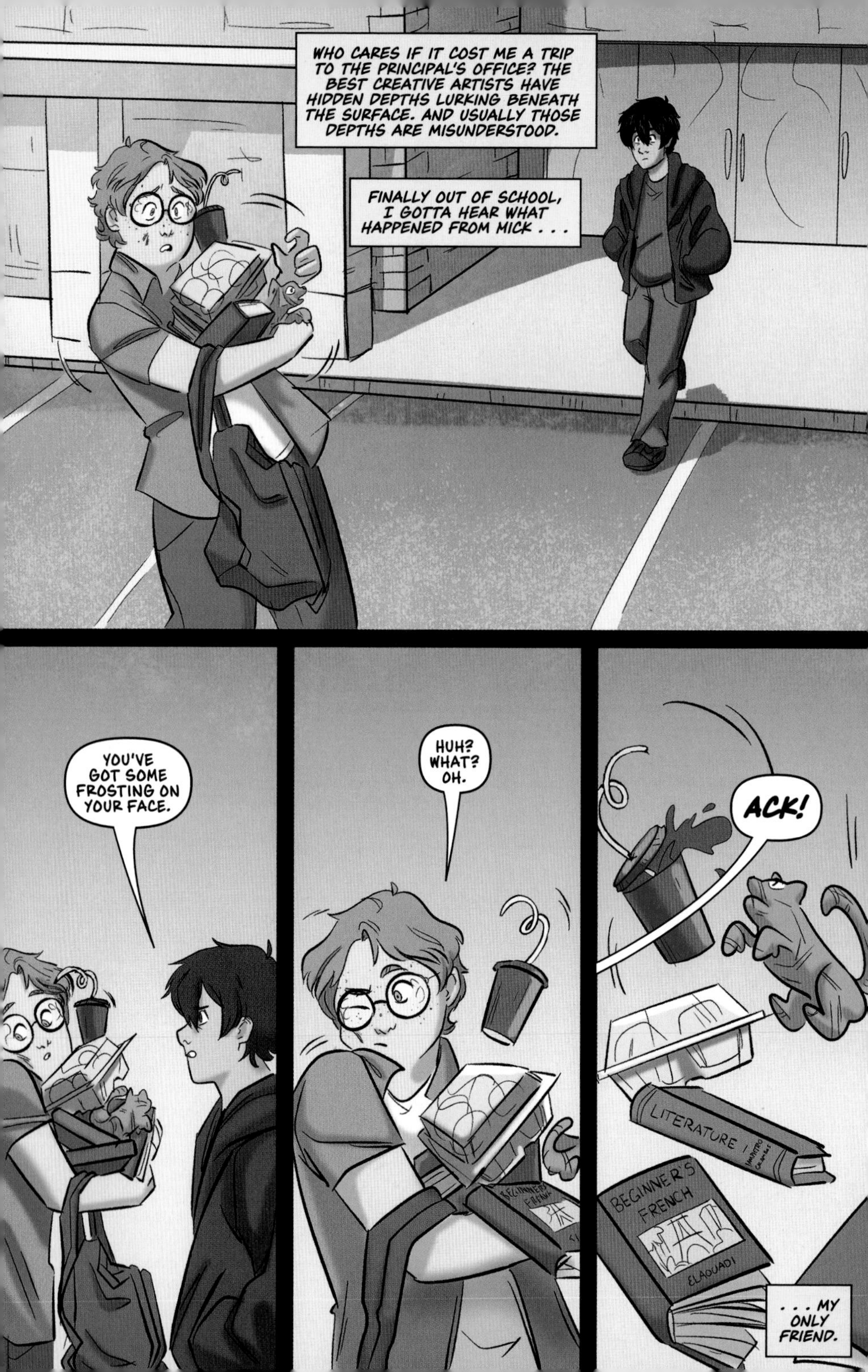
WHO CARES IF IT COST ME A TRIP TO THE PRINCIPAL'S OFFICE? THE BEST CREATIVE ARTISTS HAVE HIDDEN DEPTHS LURKING BENEATH THE SURFACE. AND USUALLY THOSE DEPTHS ARE MISUNDERSTOOD.
FINALLY OUT OF SCHOOL, I GOTTA HEAR WHAT HAPPENED FROM MICK . . .
YOU'VE GOT SOME FROSTING ON YOUR FACE.
HUH? WHAT? OH.
ACK!
LITERATURE I
BEGINNER'S FRENCH
ELAOUADI
. . . MY ONLY FRIEND.

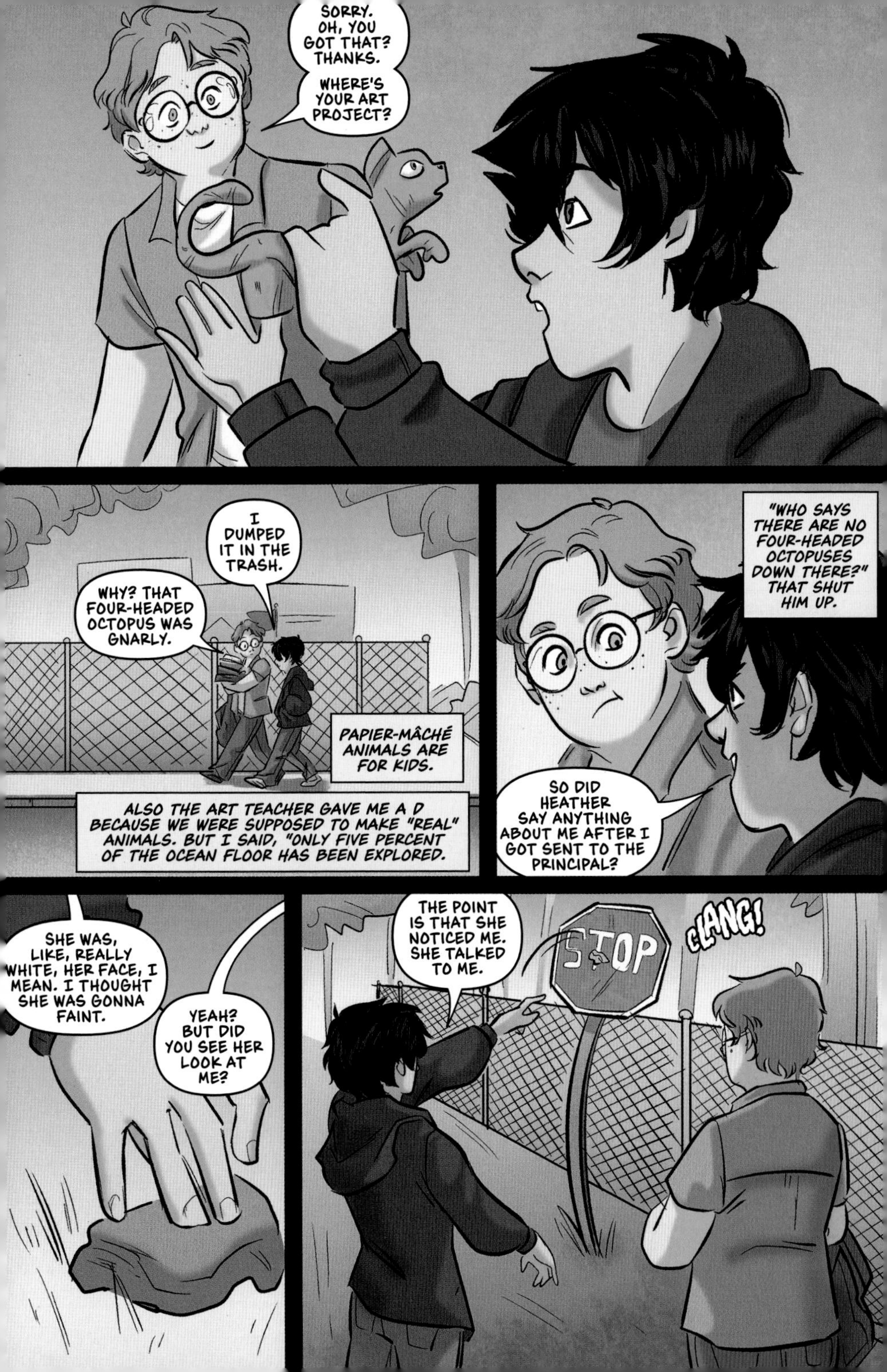
SORRY. OH, YOU GOT THAT? THANKS.
WHERE'S YOUR ART PROJECT?
I DUMPED IT IN THE TRASH.
WHY? THAT FOUR-HEADED OCTOPUS WAS GNARLY.
PAPIER-MÂCHÉ ANIMALS ARE FOR KIDS.
ALSO THE ART TEACHER GAVE ME A D BECAUSE WE WERE SUPPOSED TO MAKE "REAL" ANIMALS. BUT I SAID, "ONLY FIVE PERCENT OF THE OCEAN FLOOR HAS BEEN EXPLORED.
"WHO SAYS THERE ARE NO FOUR-HEADED OCTOPUSES DOWN THERE?" THAT SHUT HIM UP.
SO DID HEATHER SAY ANYTHING ABOUT ME AFTER I GOT SENT TO THE PRINCIPAL?
SHE WAS, LIKE, REALLY WHITE, HER FACE, I MEAN. I THOUGHT SHE WAS GONNA FAINT.
YEAH? BUT DID YOU SEE HER LOOK AT ME?
THE POINT IS THAT SHE NOTICED ME. SHE TALKED TO ME.
STOP
CLANG!

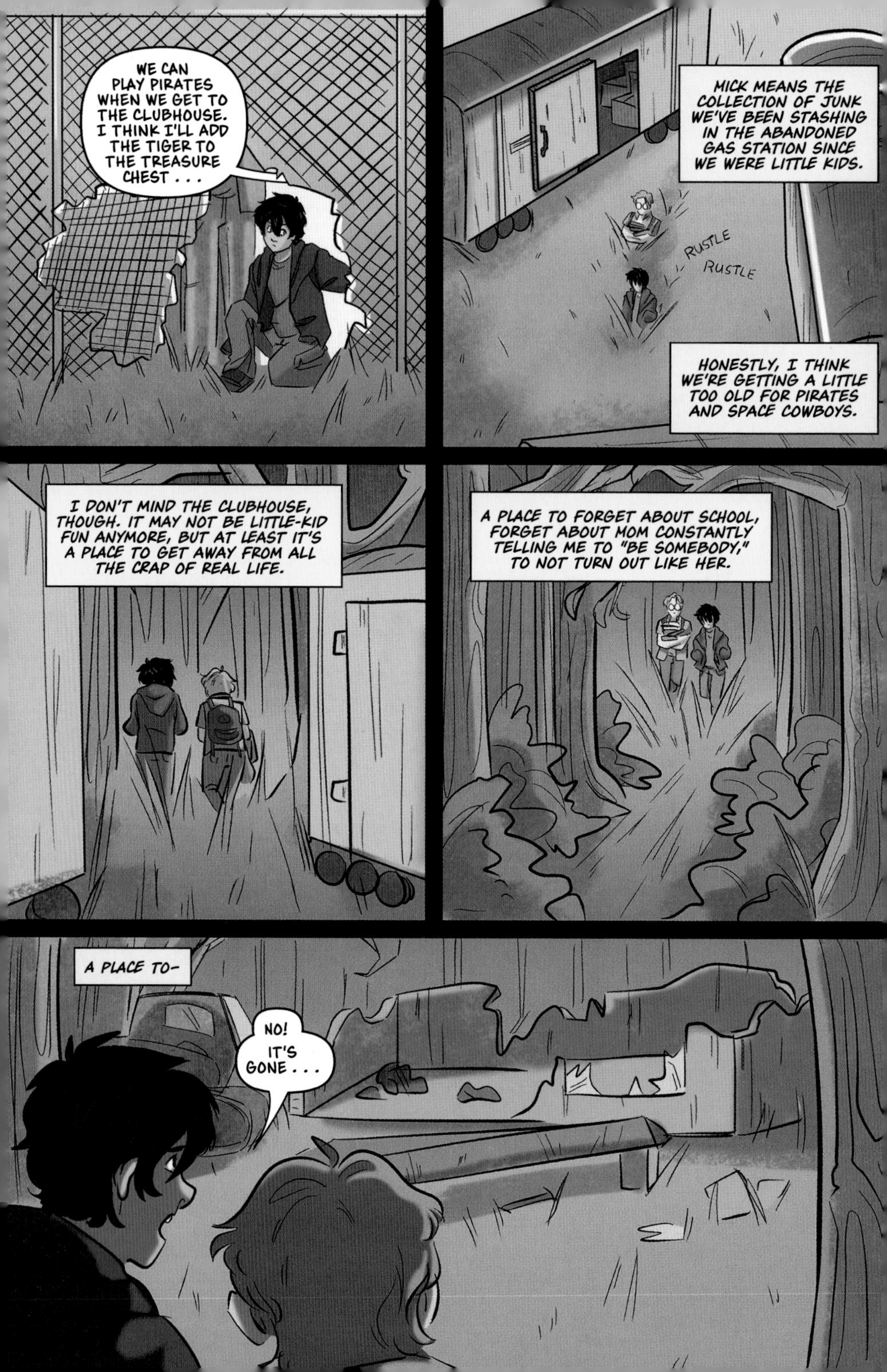
WE CAN PLAY PIRATES WHEN WE GET TO THE CLUBHOUSE. I THINK I'LL ADD THE TIGER TO THE TREASURE CHEST . . .
MICK MEANS THE COLLECTION OF JUNK WE'VE BEEN STASHING IN THE ABANDONED GAS STATION SINCE WE WERE LITTLE KIDS.
RUSTLE
RUSTLE
HONESTLY, I THINK WE'RE GETTING A LITTLE TOO OLD FOR PIRATES AND SPACE COWBOYS.
I DON'T MIND THE CLUBHOUSE, THOUGH. IT MAY NOT BE LITTLE-KID FUN ANYMORE, BUT AT LEAST IT'S A PLACE TO GET AWAY FROM ALL THE CRAP OF REAL LIFE.
A PLACE TO FORGET ABOUT SCHOOL, FORGET ABOUT MOM CONSTANTLY TELLING ME TO "BE SOMEBODY," TO NOT TURN OUT LIKE HER.
A PLACE TO-
NO! IT'S GONE . . .

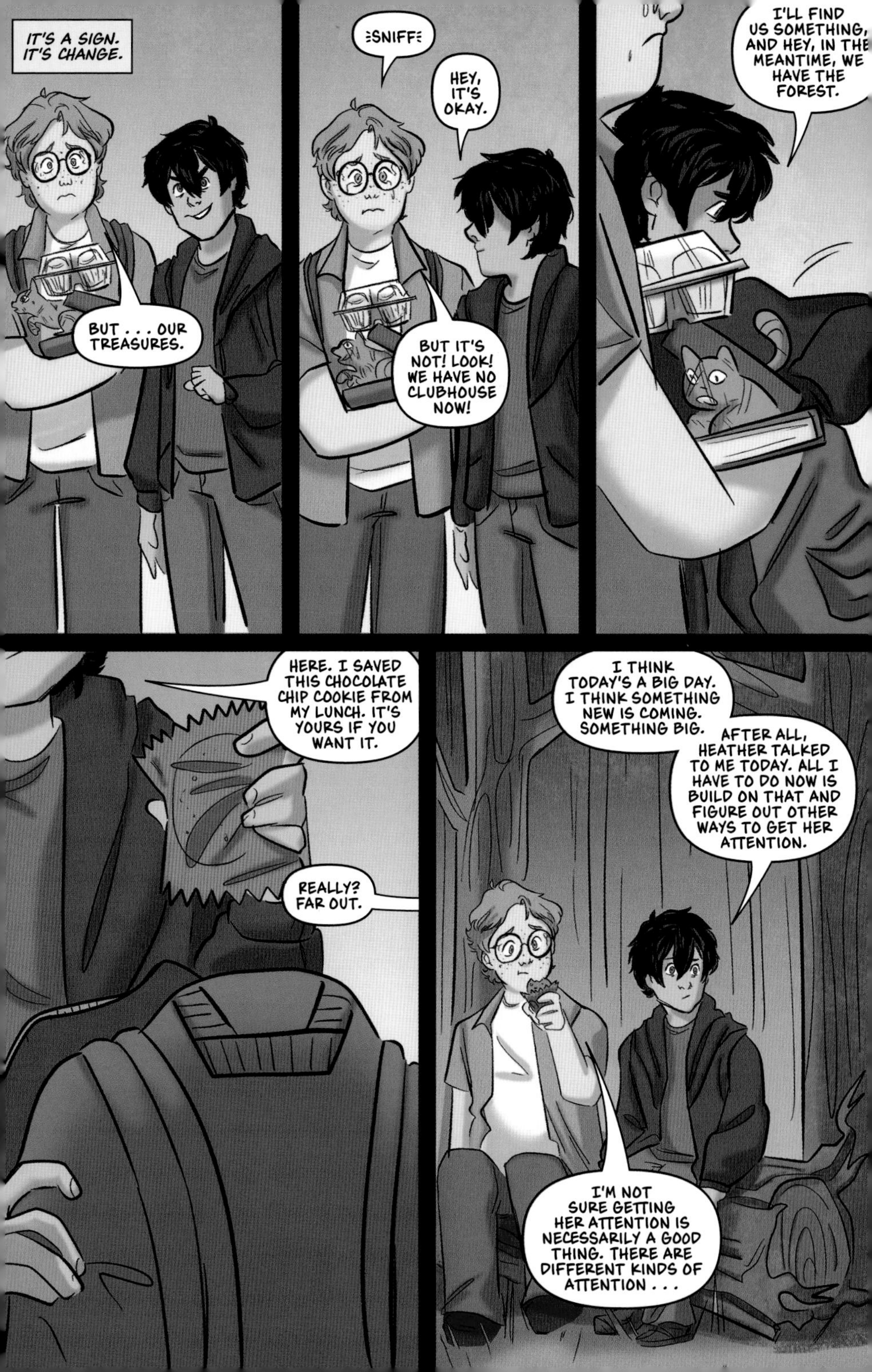
IT'S A SIGN. IT'S CHANGE.
BUT . . . OUR TREASURES.
SNIFF
HEY, IT'S OKAY.
BUT IT'S NOT! LOOK! WE HAVE NO CLUBHOUSE NOW!
I'LL FIND US SOMETHING, AND HEY, IN THE MEANTIME, WE HAVE THE FOREST.
HERE. I SAVED THIS CHOCOLATE CHIP COOKIE FROM MY LUNCH. IT'S YOURS IF YOU WANT IT.
REALLY? FAR OUT.
I THINK TODAY'S A BIG DAY. I THINK SOMETHING NEW IS COMING. SOMETHING BIG.
AFTER ALL, HEATHER TALKED TO ME TODAY. ALL I HAVE TO DO NOW IS BUILD ON THAT AND FIGURE OUT OTHER WAYS TO GET HER ATTENTION.
I'M NOT SURE GETTING HER ATTENTION IS NECESSARILY A GOOD THING. THERE ARE DIFFERENT KINDS OF ATTENTION . . .

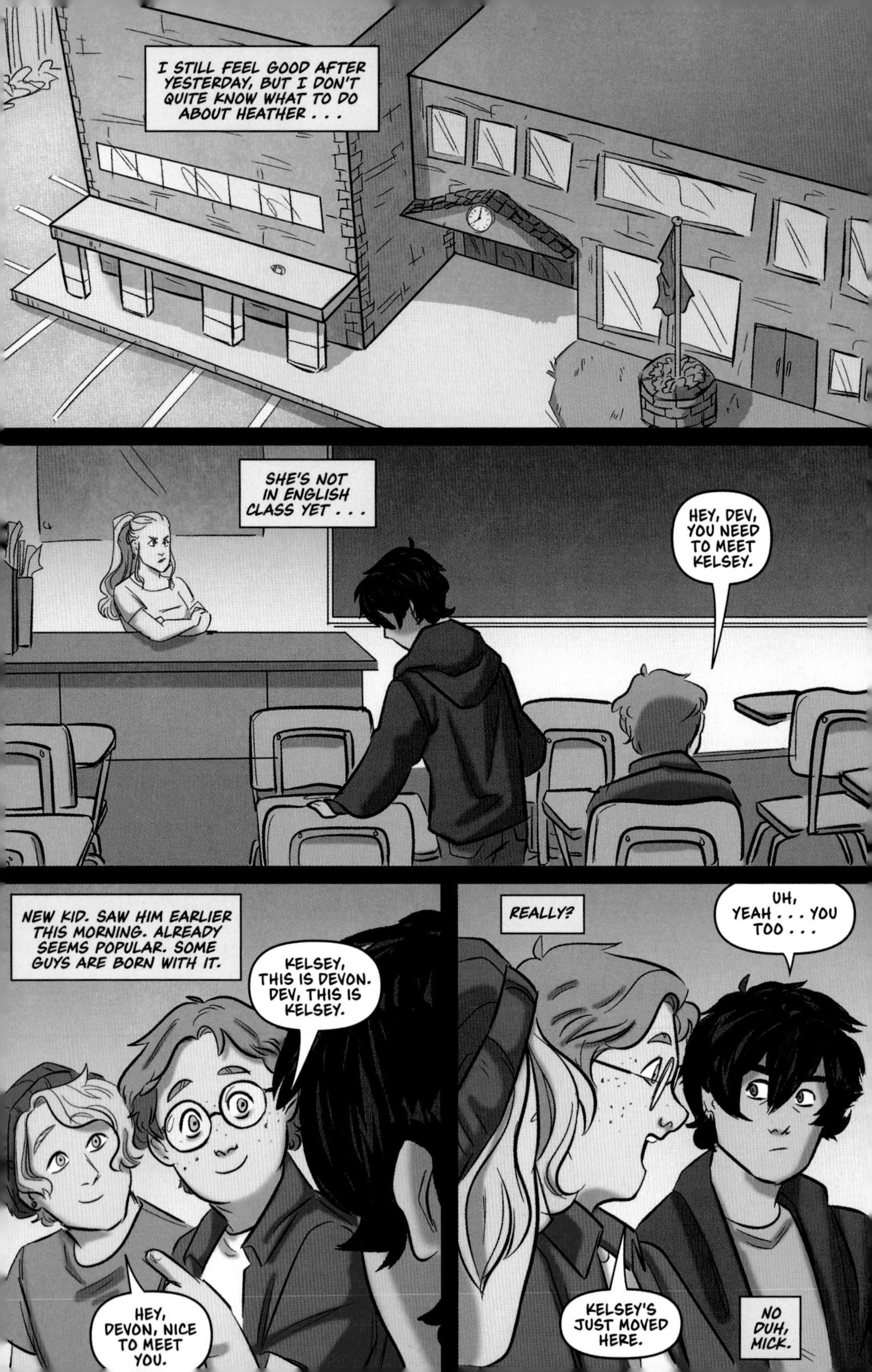
I STILL FEEL GOOD AFTER YESTERDAY, BUT I DON'T QUITE KNOW WHAT TO DO ABOUT HEATHER . . .
SHE'S NOT IN ENGLISH CLASS YET . . .
HEY, DEV, YOU NEED TO MEET KELSEY.
NEW KID. SAW HIM EARLIER THIS MORNING. ALREADY SEEMS POPULAR. SOME GUYS ARE BORN WITH IT.
KELSEY, THIS IS DEVON. DEV, THIS IS KELSEY.
HEY, DEVON, NICE TO MEET YOU.
REALLY?
UH, YEAH . . . YOU TOO . . .
KELSEY'S JUST MOVED HERE.
NO DUH, MICK.

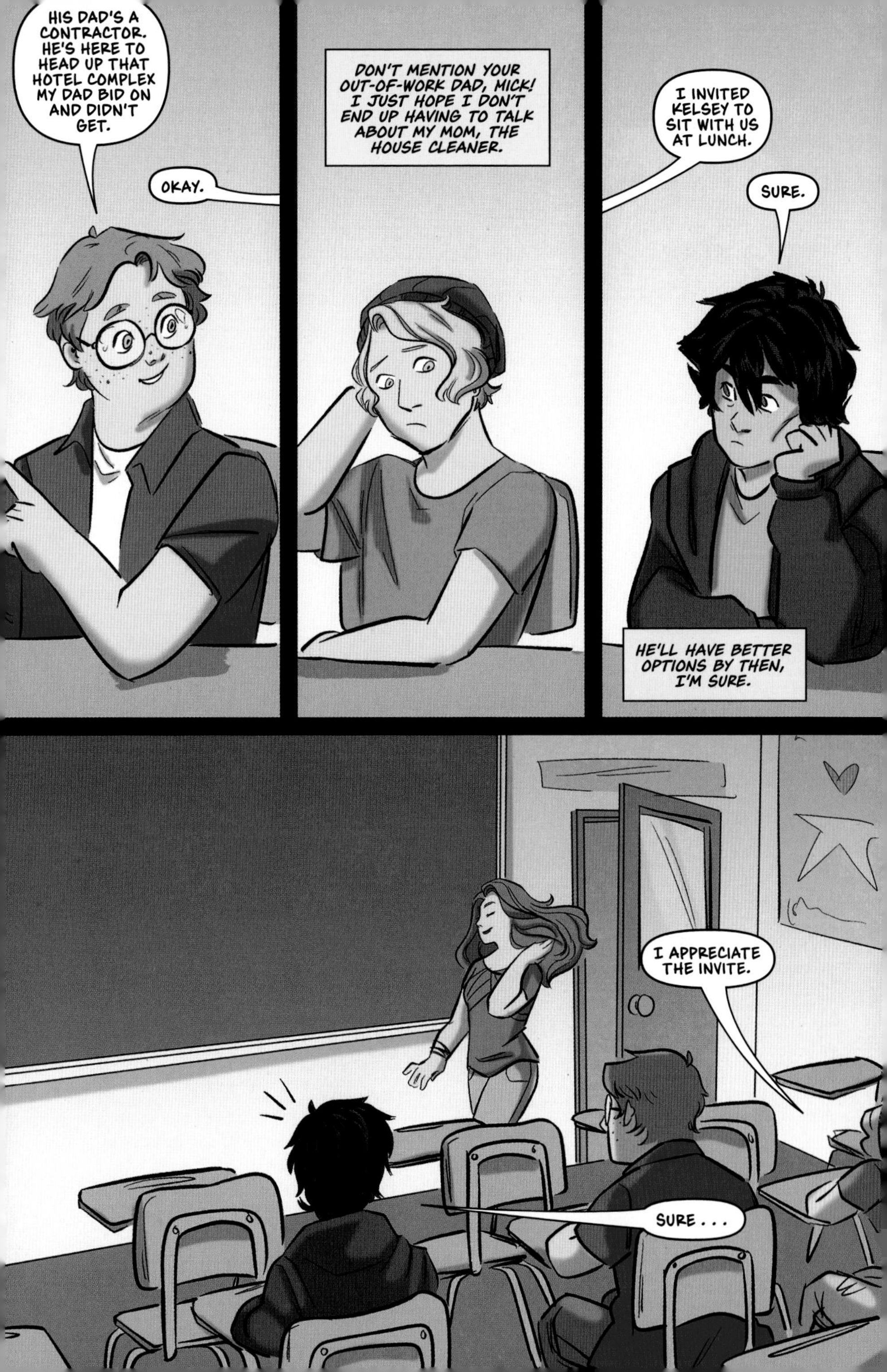
HIS DAD'S A CONTRACTOR. HE'S HERE TO HEAD UP THAT HOTEL COMPLEX MY DAD BID ON AND DIDN'T GET.
OKAY.
DON'T MENTION YOUR OUT-OF-WORK DAD, MICK! I JUST HOPE I DON'T END UP HAVING TO TALK ABOUT MY MOM, THE HOUSE CLEANER.
I INVITED KELSEY TO SIT WITH US AT LUNCH.
SURE.
HE'LL HAVE BETTER OPTIONS BY THEN, I'M SURE.
I APPRECIATE THE INVITE.
SURE . . .

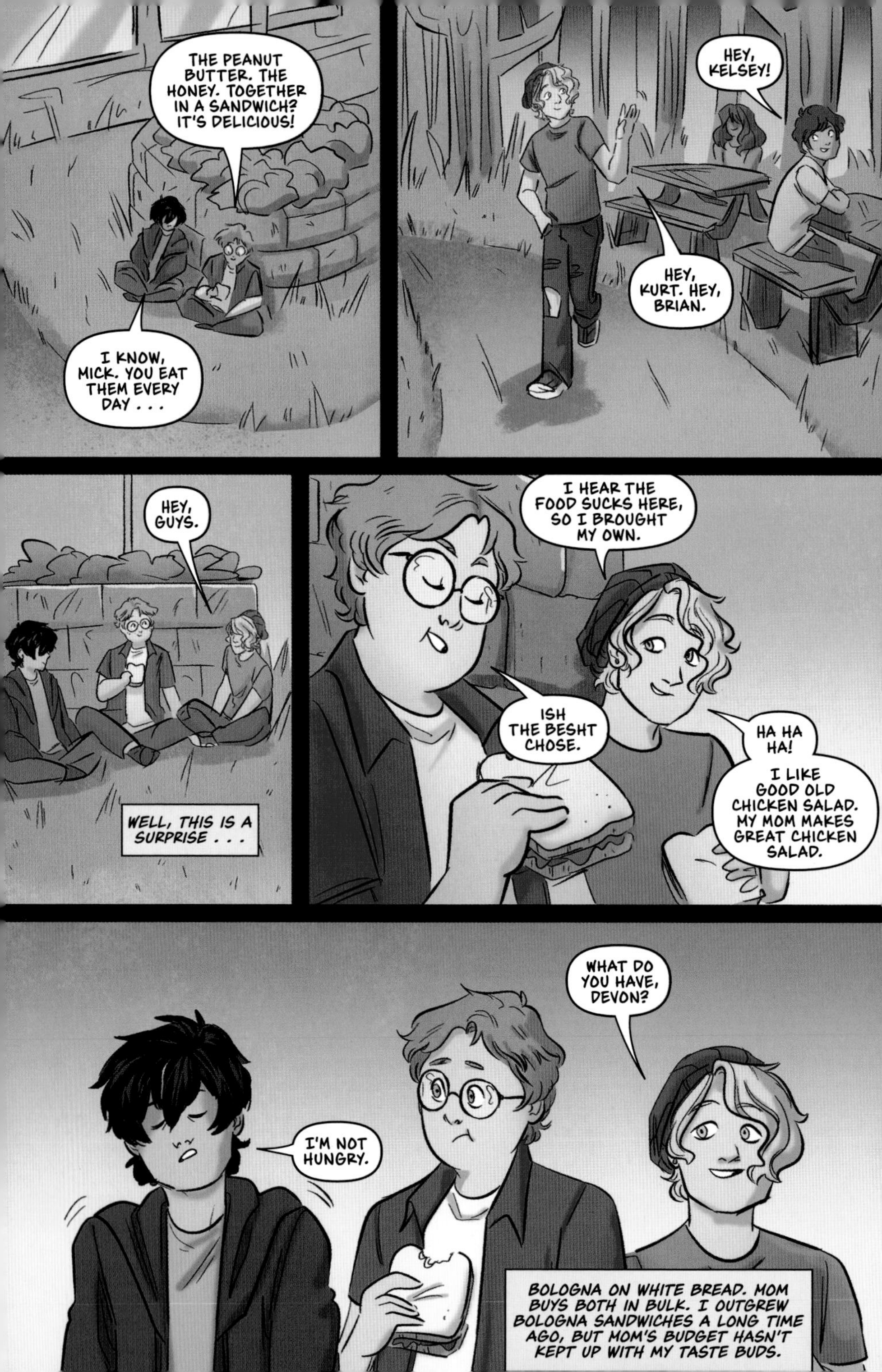
THE PEANUT BUTTER. THE HONEY. TOGETHER IN A SANDWICH? IT'S DELICIOUS!
I KNOW, MICK. YOU EAT THEM EVERY DAY . . .
HEY, KELSEY!
HEY, KURT. HEY, BRIAN.
HEY, GUYS.
WELL, THIS IS A SURPRISE . . .
I HEAR THE FOOD SUCKS HERE, SO I BROUGHT MY OWN.
ISH THE BESHT CHOSE.
HA HA HA!
I LIKE GOOD OLD CHICKEN SALAD. MY MOM MAKES GREAT CHICKEN SALAD.
WHAT DO YOU HAVE, DEVON?
I'M NOT HUNGRY.
BOLOGNA ON WHITE BREAD. MOM BUYS BOTH IN BULK. I OUTGREW BOLOGNA SANDWICHES A LONG TIME AGO, BUT MOM'S BUDGET HASN'T KEPT UP WITH MY TASTE BUDS.

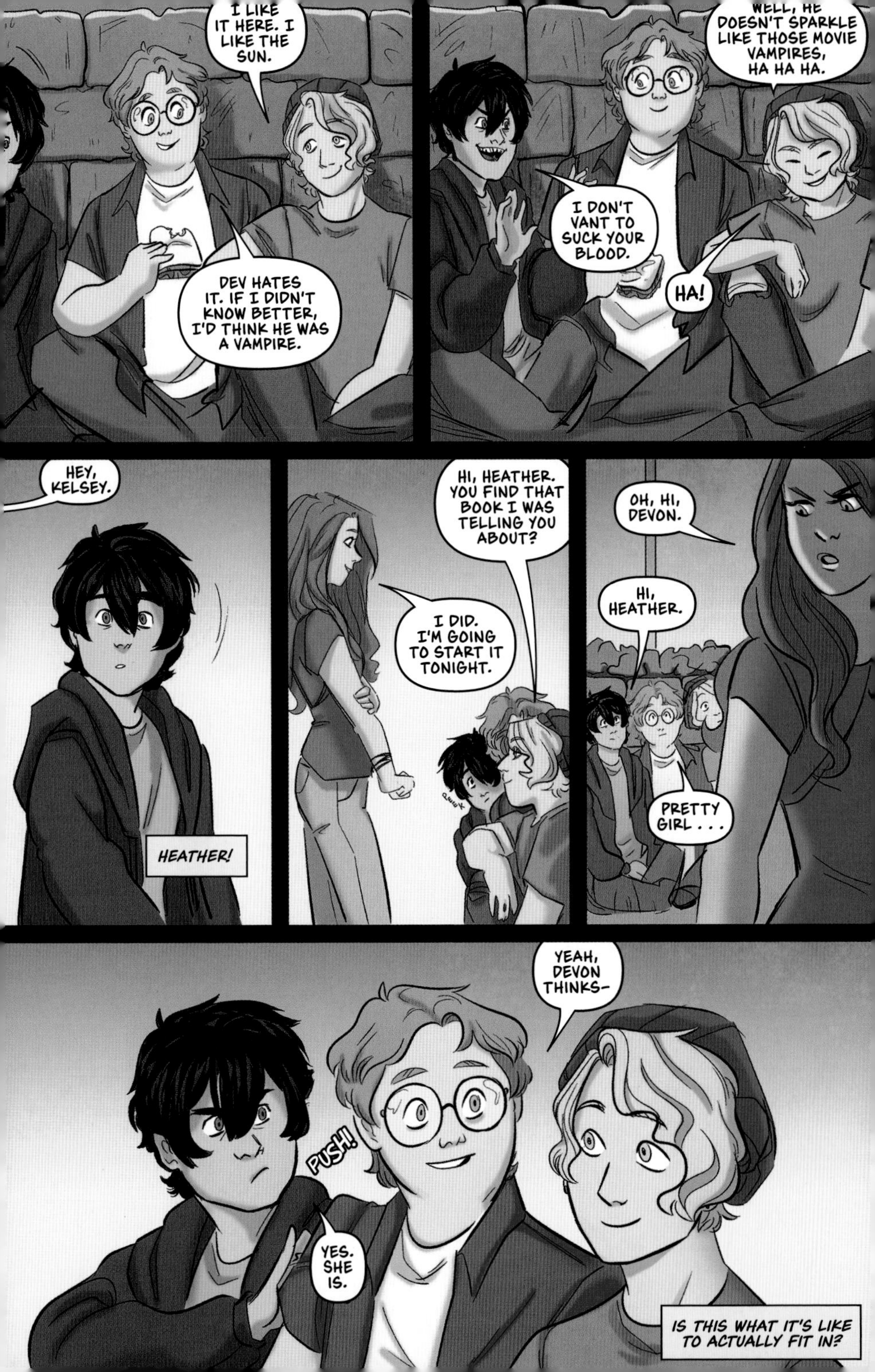

I LIKE IT HERE. I LIKE THE SUN.
DEV HATES IT. IF I DIDN'T KNOW BETTER, I'D THINK HE WAS A VAMPIRE.
WELL, HE DOESN'T SPARKLE LIKE THOSE MOVIE VAMPIRES, HA HA HA.
I DON'T VANT TO SUCK YOUR BLOOD.
HA!
HEY, KELSEY.
HEATHER!
HI, HEATHER. YOU FIND THAT BOOK I WAS TELLING YOU ABOUT?
I DID. I'M GOING TO START IT TONIGHT.
OH, HI, DEVON.
HI, HEATHER.
PRETTY GIRL . . .
YEAH, DEVON THINKS–
PUSH!
YES. SHE IS.
IS THIS WHAT IT'S LIKE TO ACTUALLY FIT IN?

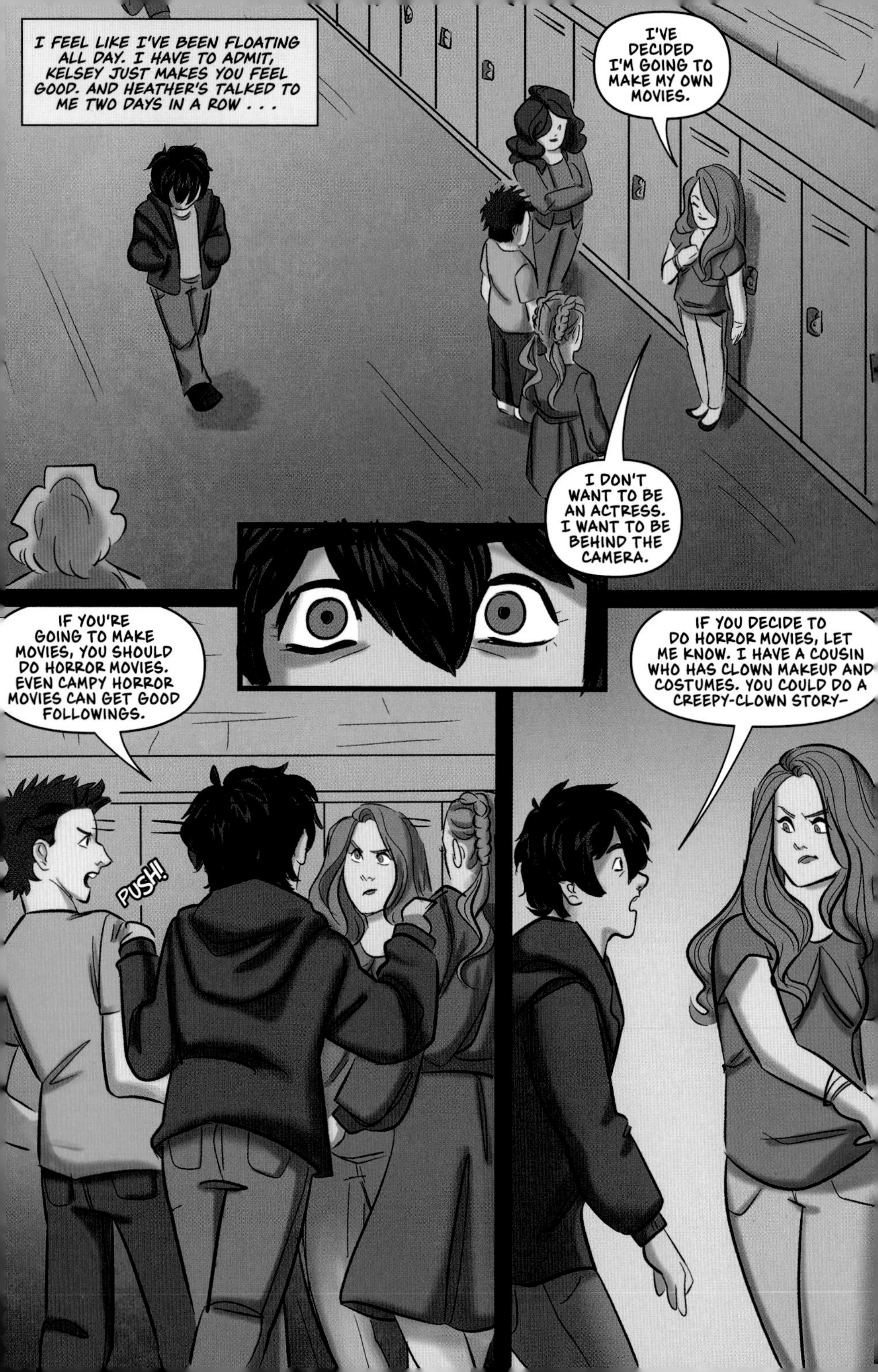
I FEEL LIKE I'VE BEEN FLOATING ALL DAY. I HAVE TO ADMIT, KELSEY JUST MAKES YOU FEEL GOOD. AND HEATHER'S TALKED TO ME TWO DAYS IN A ROW . . .
I'VE DECIDED I'M GOING TO MAKE MY OWN MOVIES.
I DON'T WANT TO BE AN ACTRESS. I WANT TO BE BEHIND THE CAMERA.
IF YOU'RE GOING TO MAKE MOVIES, YOU SHOULD DO HORROR MOVIES. EVEN CAMPY HORROR MOVIES CAN GET GOOD FOLLOWINGS.
PUSH!
IF YOU DECIDE TO DO HORROR MOVIES, LET ME KNOW. I HAVE A COUSIN WHO HAS CLOWN MAKEUP AND COSTUMES. YOU COULD DO A CREEPY-CLOWN STORY–

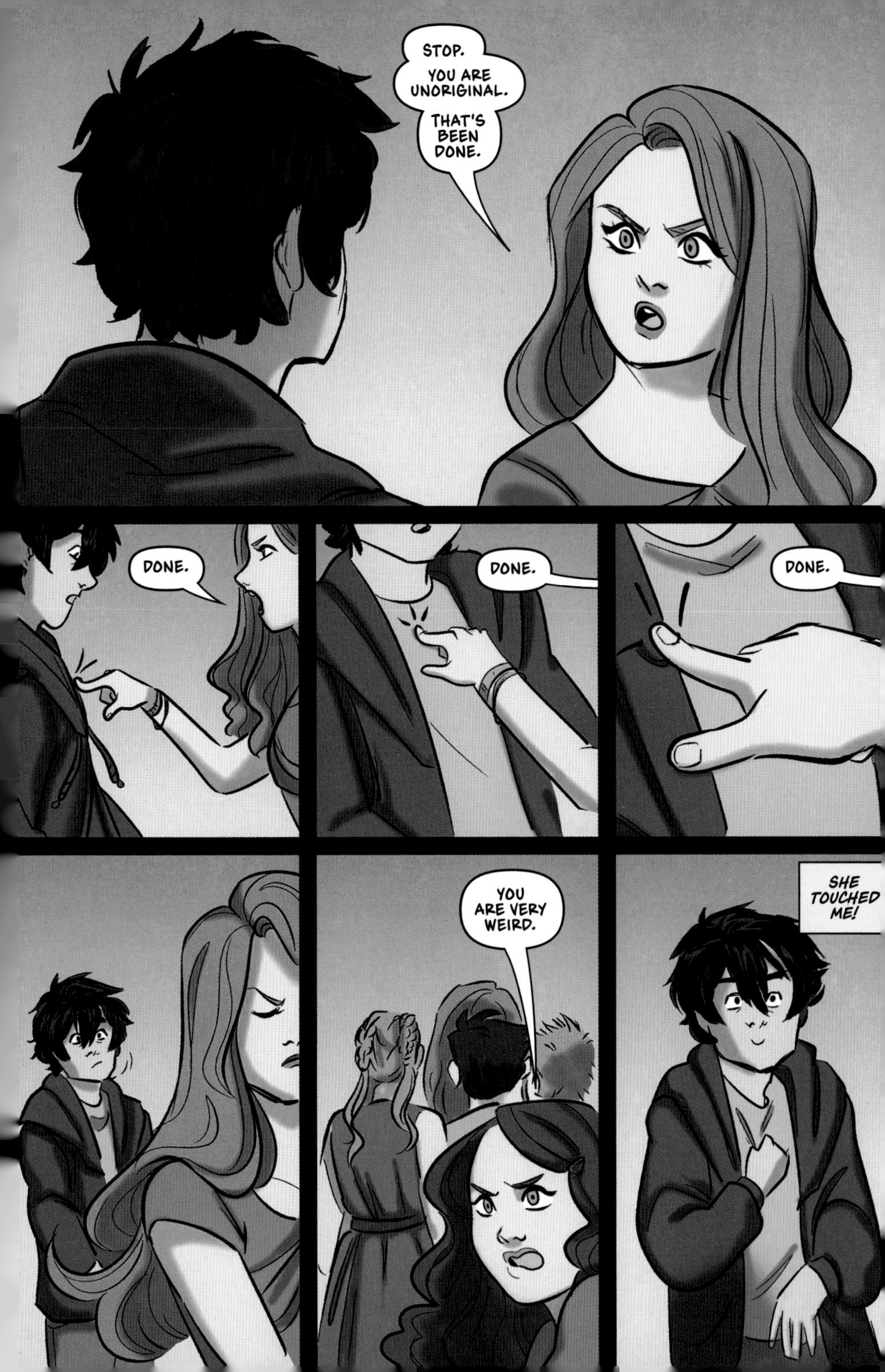
STOP.
YOU ARE UNORIGINAL.
THAT'S BEEN DONE.
DONE.
DONE.
DONE.
YOU ARE VERY WEIRD.
SHE TOUCHED ME!

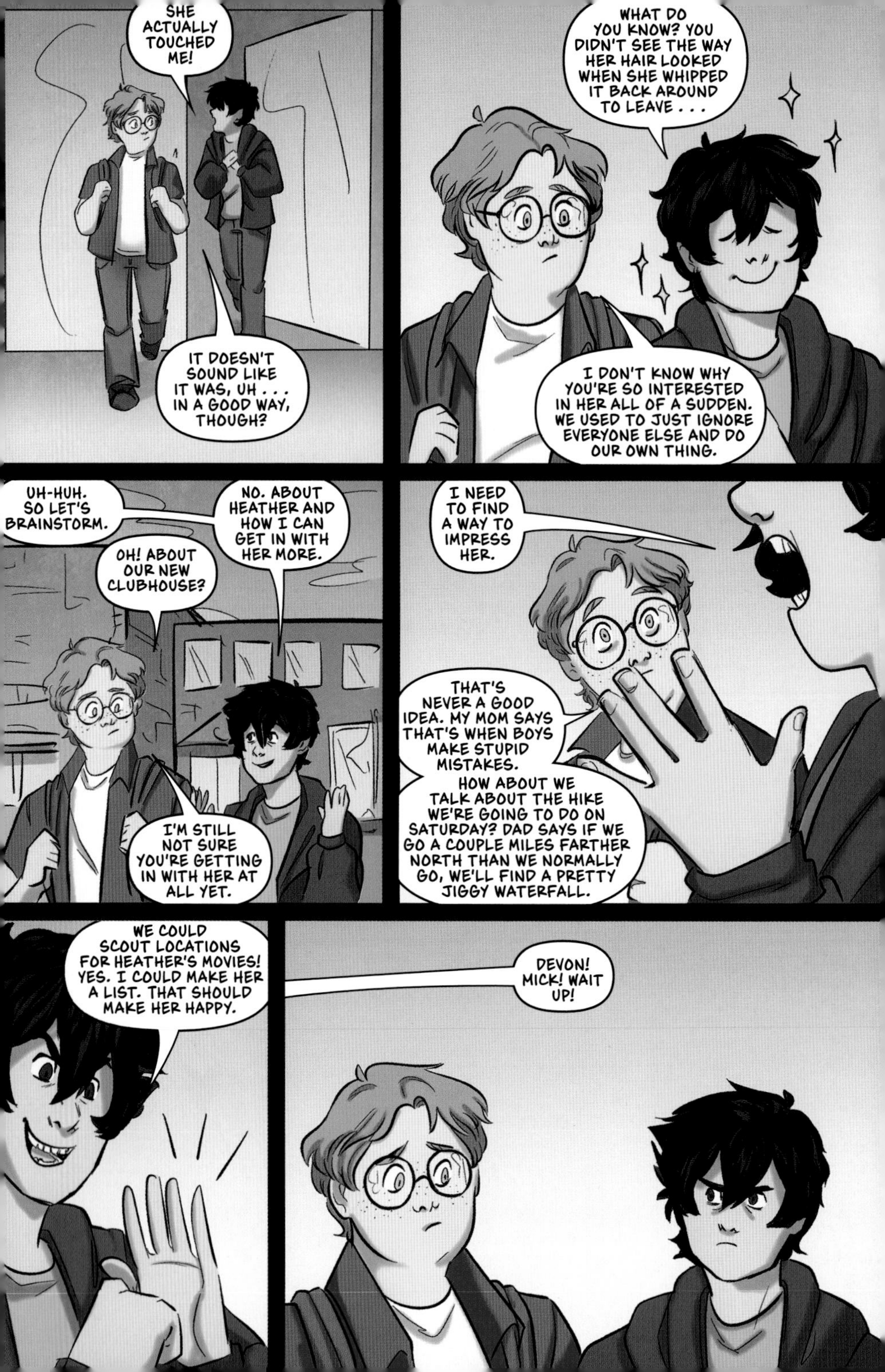
SHE ACTUALLY TOUCHED ME!
IT DOESN'T SOUND LIKE IT WAS, UH . . . IN A GOOD WAY, THOUGH?
WHAT DO YOU KNOW? YOU DIDN'T SEE THE WAY HER HAIR LOOKED WHEN SHE WHIPPED IT BACK AROUND TO LEAVE . . .
I DON'T KNOW WHY YOU'RE SO INTERESTED IN HER ALL OF A SUDDEN. WE USED TO JUST IGNORE EVERYONE ELSE AND DO OUR OWN THING.
UH-HUH. SO LET'S BRAINSTORM.
OH! ABOUT OUR NEW CLUBHOUSE?
NO. ABOUT HEATHER AND HOW I CAN GET IN WITH HER MORE.
I'M STILL NOT SURE YOU'RE GETTING IN WITH HER AT ALL YET.
I NEED TO FIND A WAY TO IMPRESS HER.
THAT'S NEVER A GOOD IDEA. MY MOM SAYS THAT'S WHEN BOYS MAKE STUPID MISTAKES.
HOW ABOUT WE TALK ABOUT THE HIKE WE'RE GOING TO DO ON SATURDAY? DAD SAYS IF WE GO A COUPLE MILES FARTHER NORTH THAN WE NORMALLY GO, WE'LL FIND A PRETTY JIGGY WATERFALL.
WE COULD SCOUT LOCATIONS FOR HEATHER'S MOVIES! YES. I COULD MAKE HER A LIST. THAT SHOULD MAKE HER HAPPY.
DEVON! MICK! WAIT UP!

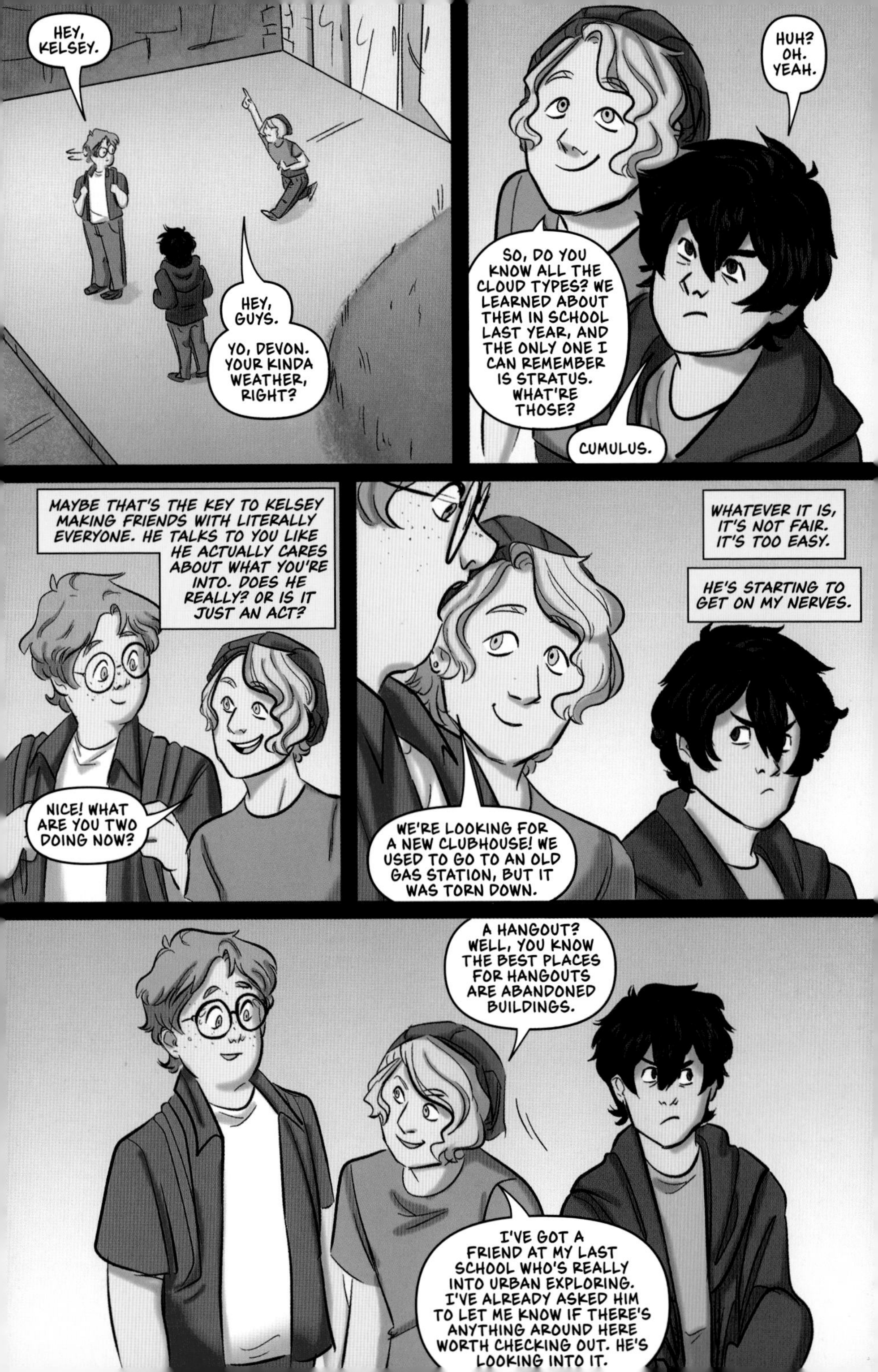
HEY, KELSEY.
HEY, GUYS.
YO, DEVON. YOUR KINDA WEATHER, RIGHT?
HUH? OH. YEAH.
SO, DO YOU KNOW ALL THE CLOUD TYPES? WE LEARNED ABOUT THEM IN SCHOOL LAST YEAR, AND THE ONLY ONE I CAN REMEMBER IS STRATUS. WHAT'RE THOSE?
CUMULUS.
MAYBE THAT'S THE KEY TO KELSEY MAKING FRIENDS WITH LITERALLY EVERYONE. HE TALKS TO YOU LIKE HE ACTUALLY CARES ABOUT WHAT YOU'RE INTO. DOES HE REALLY? OR IS IT JUST AN ACT?
NICE! WHAT ARE YOU TWO DOING NOW?
WE'RE LOOKING FOR A NEW CLUBHOUSE! WE USED TO GO TO AN OLD GAS STATION, BUT IT WAS TORN DOWN.
WHATEVER IT IS, IT'S NOT FAIR. IT'S TOO EASY.
HE'S STARTING TO GET ON MY NERVES.
A HANGOUT? WELL, YOU KNOW THE BEST PLACES FOR HANGOUTS ARE ABANDONED BUILDINGS.
I'VE GOT A FRIEND AT MY LAST SCHOOL WHO'S REALLY INTO URBAN EXPLORING. I'VE ALREADY ASKED HIM TO LET ME KNOW IF THERE'S ANYTHING AROUND HERE WORTH CHECKING OUT. HE'S LOOKING INTO IT.

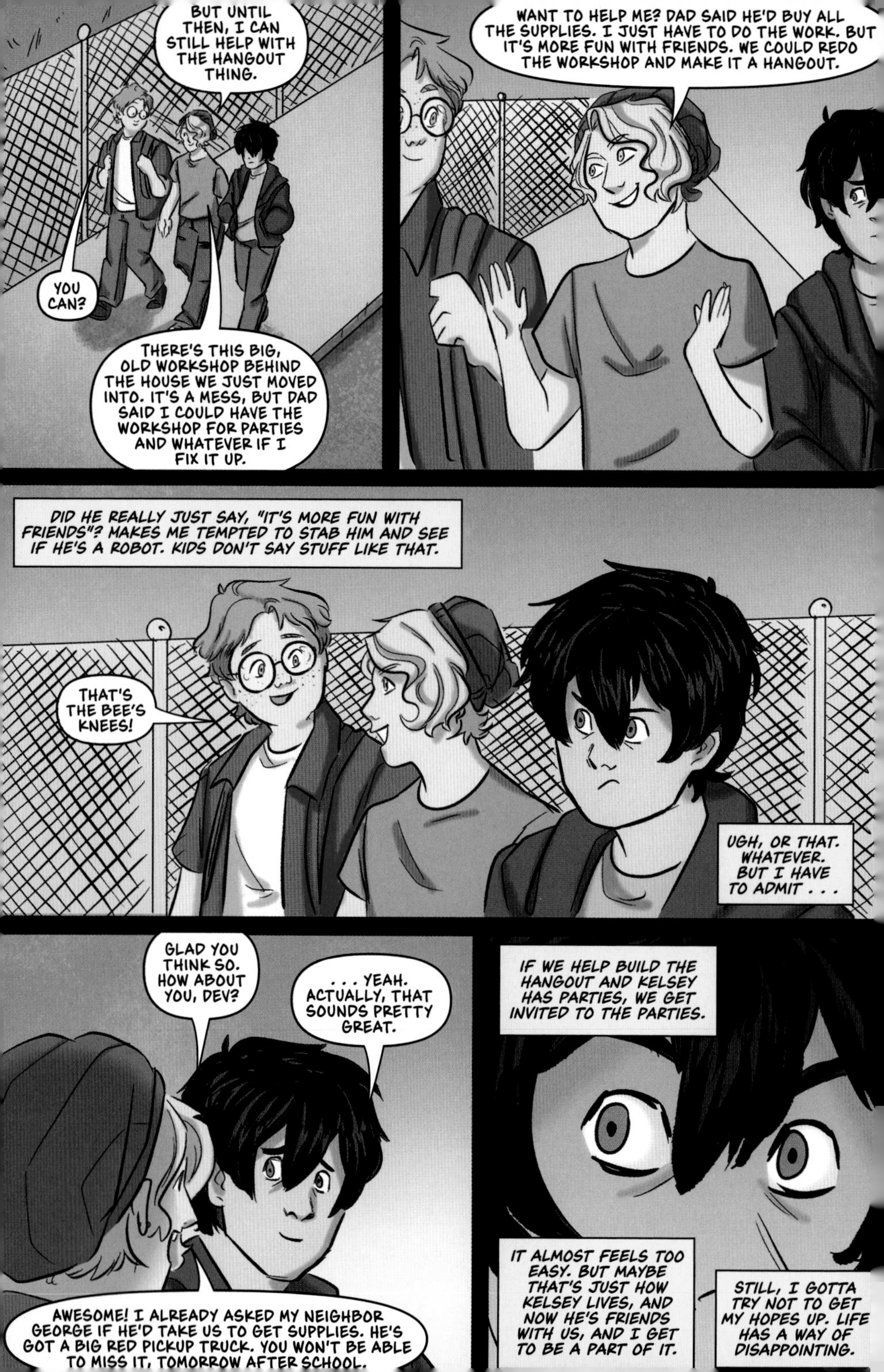
BUT UNTIL THEN, I CAN STILL HELP WITH THE HANGOUT THING.
YOU CAN?
THERE'S THIS BIG, OLD WORKSHOP BEHIND THE HOUSE WE JUST MOVED INTO. IT'S A MESS, BUT DAD SAID I COULD HAVE THE WORKSHOP FOR PARTIES AND WHATEVER IF I FIX IT UP.
WANT TO HELP ME? DAD SAID HE'D BUY ALL THE SUPPLIES. I JUST HAVE TO DO THE WORK. BUT IT'S MORE FUN WITH FRIENDS. WE COULD REDO THE WORKSHOP AND MAKE IT A HANGOUT.
DID HE REALLY JUST SAY, "IT'S MORE FUN WITH FRIENDS"? MAKES ME TEMPTED TO STAB HIM AND SEE IF HE'S A ROBOT. KIDS DON'T SAY STUFF LIKE THAT.
THAT'S THE BEE'S KNEES!
UGH, OR THAT. WHATEVER. BUT I HAVE TO ADMIT . . .
GLAD YOU THINK SO. HOW ABOUT YOU, DEV?
. . . YEAH. ACTUALLY, THAT SOUNDS PRETTY GREAT.
AWESOME! I ALREADY ASKED MY NEIGHBOR GEORGE IF HE'D TAKE US TO GET SUPPLIES. HE'S GOT A BIG RED PICKUP TRUCK. YOU WON'T BE ABLE TO MISS IT, TOMORROW AFTER SCHOOL.
IF WE HELP BUILD THE HANGOUT AND KELSEY HAS PARTIES, WE GET INVITED TO THE PARTIES.
IT ALMOST FEELS TOO EASY. BUT MAYBE THAT'S JUST HOW KELSEY LIVES, AND NOW HE'S FRIENDS WITH US, AND I GET TO BE A PART OF IT.
STILL, I GOTTA TRY NOT TO GET MY HOPES UP. LIFE HAS A WAY OF DISAPPOINTING.

JUSTICE
TODAY, WE'RE TALKING ABOUT JUSTICE. THE CONCEPT IS GENERALLY DERIVED FROM MANY FIELDS OF STUDY. ETHICS, RATIONAL THOUGHT, THE LAW, RELIGION, AND JUST GENERAL IDEAS OF FAIRNESS.
UNDERLYING ALL OF THAT, THOUGH, IS USUALLY SOME KIND OF GUT FEELING. JUSTICE IS, IN MOST CASES, INTUITIVE. WE KNOW IT WHEN WE FEEL IT. SO, WHAT DOES IT MEAN TO YOU?
JUSTICE
JUSTICE BALANCES THE SCALES. IT REMOVES THE DOWNSIDE SO THE DOWNSIDE CAN'T OUTWEIGH THE UPSIDE.
OKAY, INTERESTING PERSPECTIVE. YES, HEATHER?
I THINK JUSTICE IS PAYBACK. LIKE, SOMEONE DISSES YOU, SO YOU HAVE TO DISS THEM BACK.
"PAYBACK" SEEMS A LITTLE VAGUE. PERHAPS IT'S TOO OPEN TO INTERPRETATION. WHAT IF PAYBACK GOES TOO FAR?
ACCIDENTS HAPPEN.
HA! HA! HA! HA! HA! HA! HA! HA! HA! HA! HA!
...

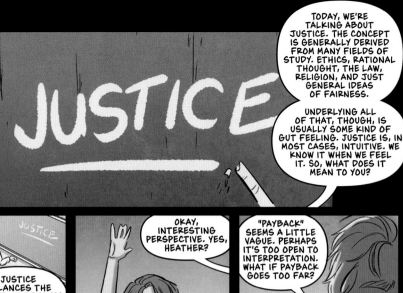

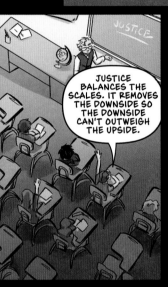

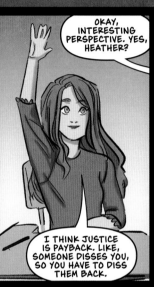

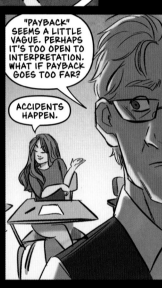

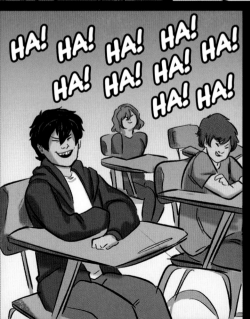

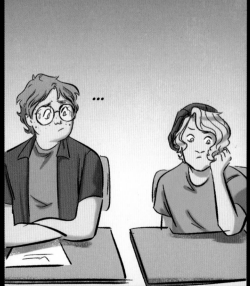

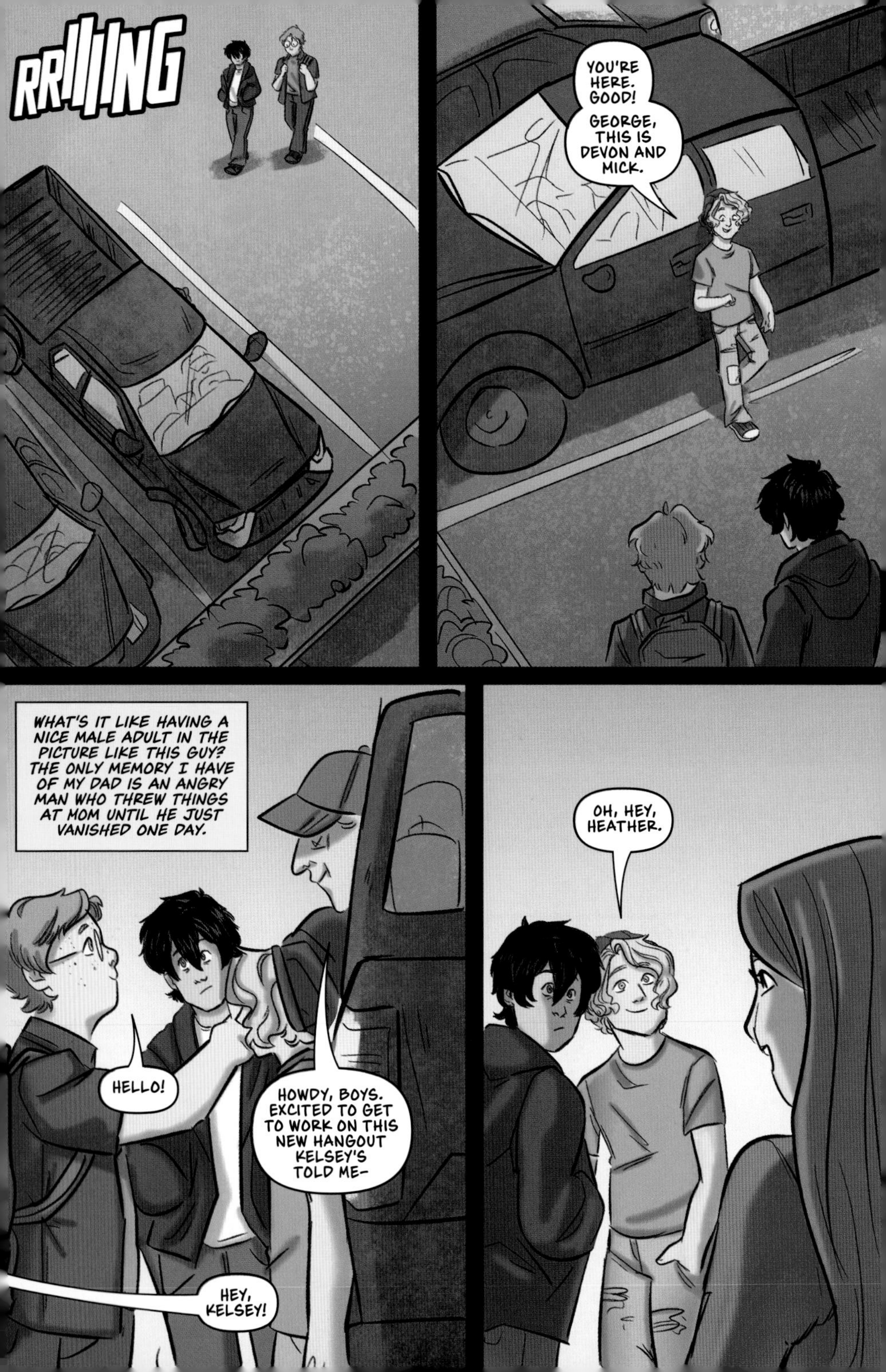
RRIIIIING
YOU'RE HERE. GOOD!
GEORGE, THIS IS DEVON AND MICK.
WHAT'S IT LIKE HAVING A NICE MALE ADULT IN THE PICTURE LIKE THIS GUY? THE ONLY MEMORY I HAVE OF MY DAD IS AN ANGRY MAN WHO THREW THINGS AT MOM UNTIL HE JUST VANISHED ONE DAY.
HELLO!
HOWDY, BOYS. EXCITED TO GET TO WORK ON THIS NEW HANGOUT KELSEY'S TOLD ME-
HEY, KELSEY!
OH, HEY, HEATHER.

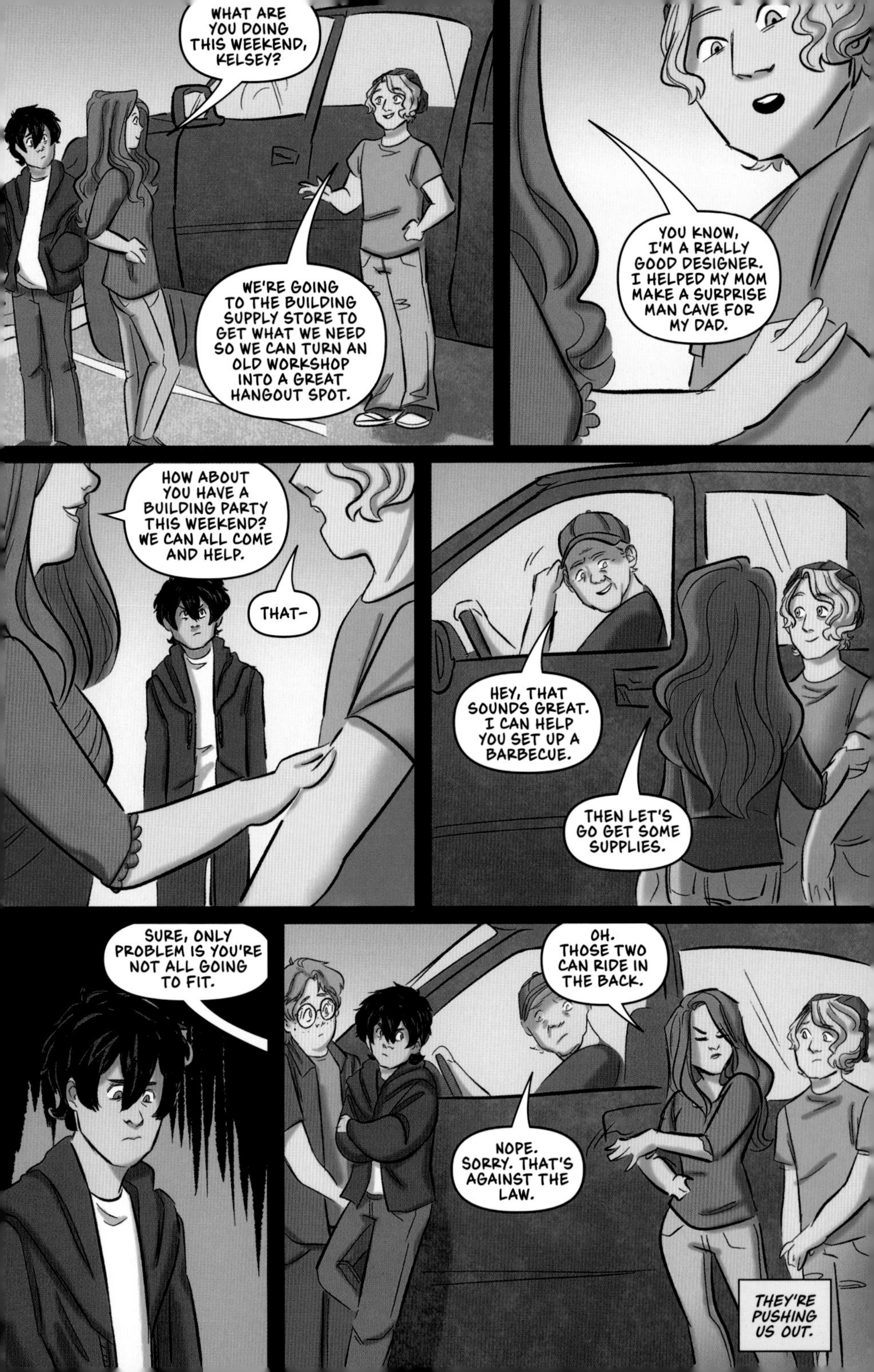
WHAT ARE YOU DOING THIS WEEKEND, KELSEY?
WE'RE GOING TO THE BUILDING SUPPLY STORE TO GET WHAT WE NEED SO WE CAN TURN AN OLD WORKSHOP INTO A GREAT HANGOUT SPOT.
YOU KNOW, I'M A REALLY GOOD DESIGNER. I HELPED MY MOM MAKE A SURPRISE MAN CAVE FOR MY DAD.
HOW ABOUT YOU HAVE A BUILDING PARTY THIS WEEKEND? WE CAN ALL COME AND HELP.
THAT-
HEY, THAT SOUNDS GREAT. I CAN HELP YOU SET UP A BARBECUE.
THEN LET'S GO GET SOME SUPPLIES.
SURE, ONLY PROBLEM IS YOU'RE NOT ALL GOING TO FIT.
OH. THOSE TWO CAN RIDE IN THE BACK.
NOPE. SORRY. THAT'S AGAINST THE LAW.
THEY'RE PUSHING US OUT.

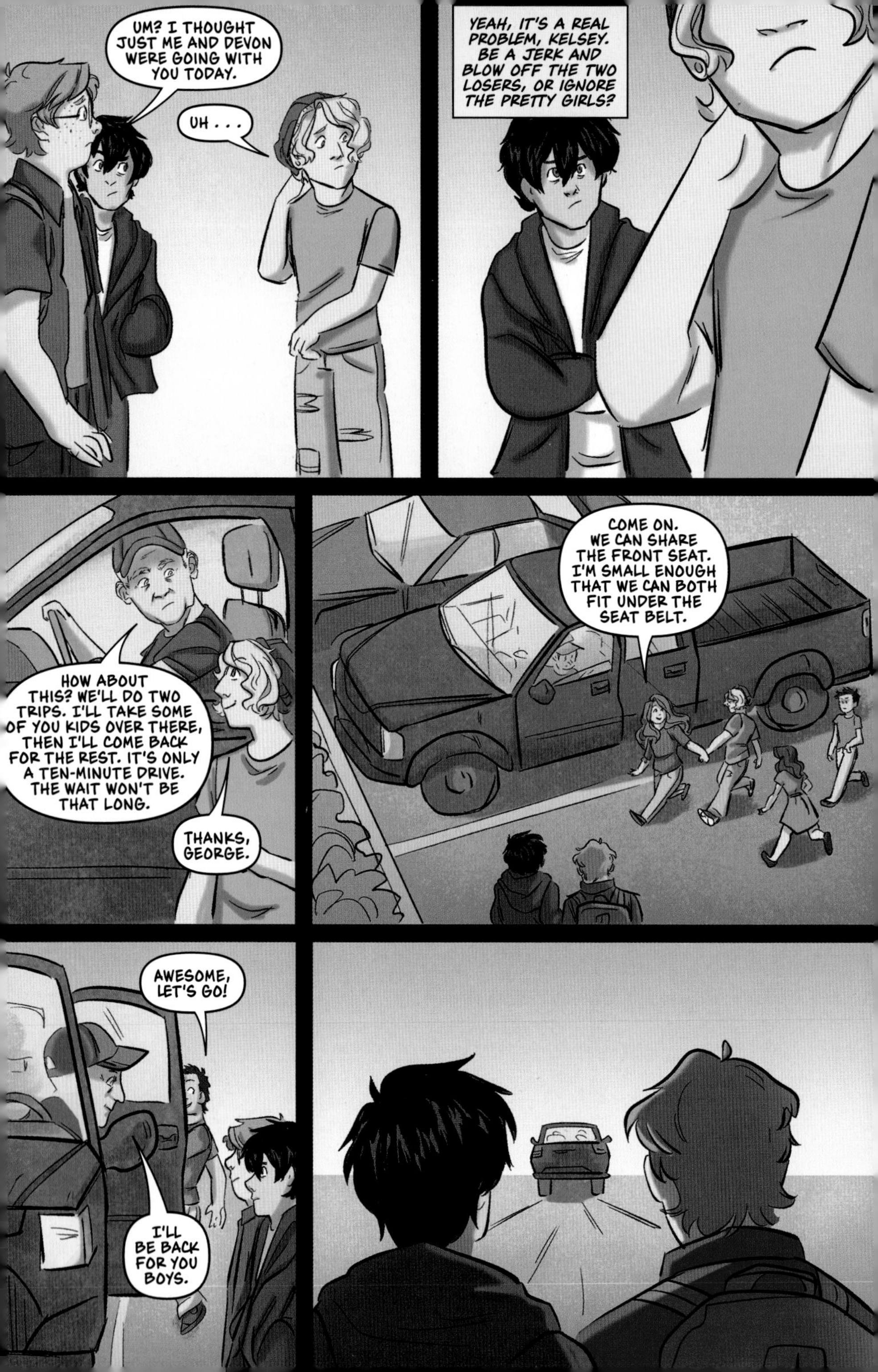
UM? I THOUGHT JUST ME AND DEVON WERE GOING WITH YOU TODAY.
UH . . .
YEAH, IT'S A REAL PROBLEM, KELSEY. BE A JERK AND BLOW OFF THE TWO LOSERS, OR IGNORE THE PRETTY GIRLS?
HOW ABOUT THIS? WE'LL DO TWO TRIPS. I'LL TAKE SOME OF YOU KIDS OVER THERE, THEN I'LL COME BACK FOR THE REST. IT'S ONLY A TEN-MINUTE DRIVE. THE WAIT WON'T BE THAT LONG.
THANKS, GEORGE.
COME ON. WE CAN SHARE THE FRONT SEAT. I'M SMALL ENOUGH THAT WE CAN BOTH FIT UNDER THE SEAT BELT.
AWESOME, LET'S GO!
I'LL BE BACK FOR YOU BOYS.

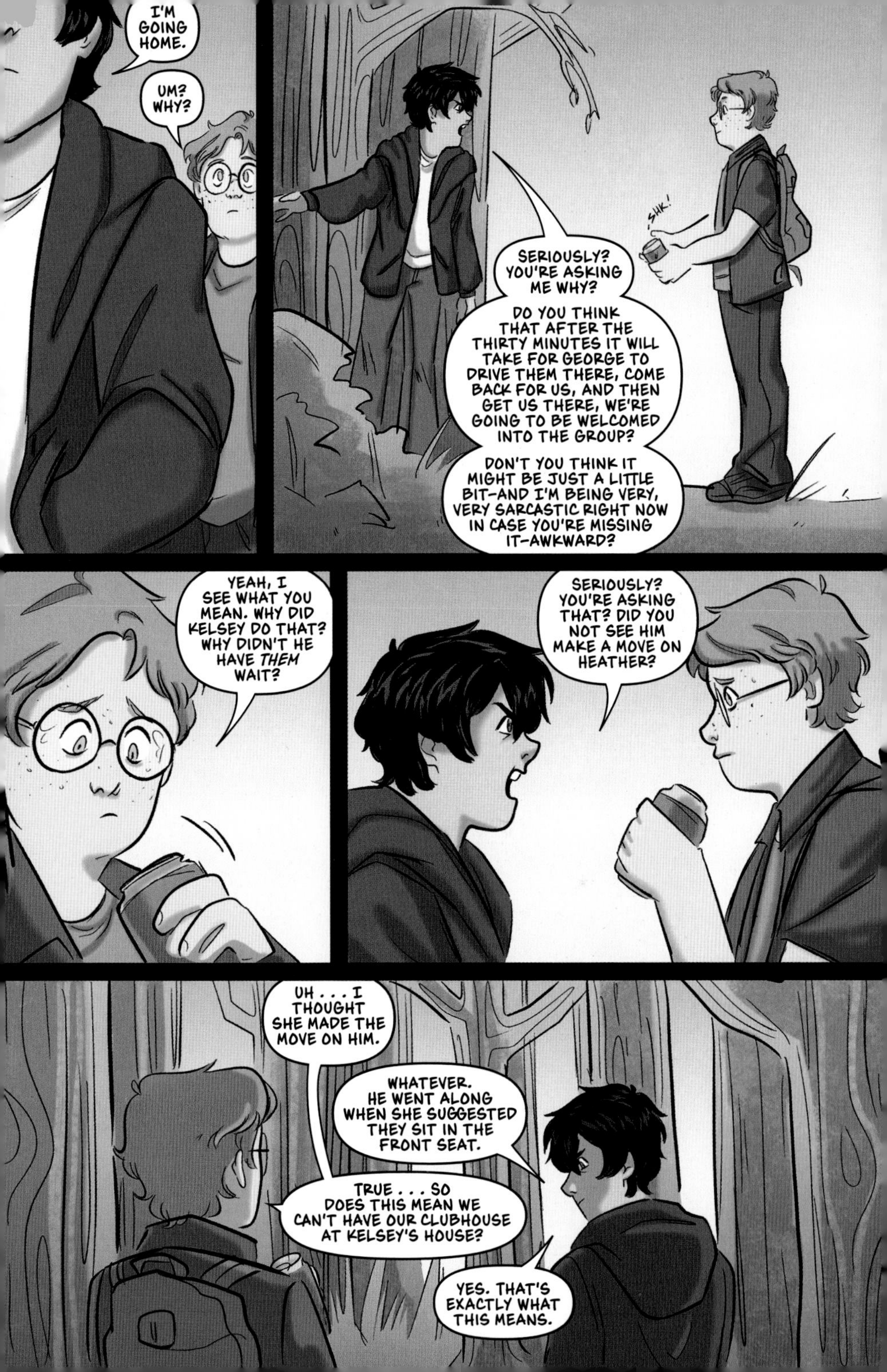
I'M GOING HOME.
UM? WHY?
SHK!
SERIOUSLY? YOU'RE ASKING ME WHY?
DO YOU THINK THAT AFTER THE THIRTY MINUTES IT WILL TAKE FOR GEORGE TO DRIVE THEM THERE, COME BACK FOR US, AND THEN GET US THERE, WE'RE GOING TO BE WELCOMED INTO THE GROUP?
DON'T YOU THINK IT MIGHT BE JUST A LITTLE BIT—AND I'M BEING VERY, VERY SARCASTIC RIGHT NOW IN CASE YOU'RE MISSING IT—AWKWARD?
YEAH, I SEE WHAT YOU MEAN. WHY DID KELSEY DO THAT? WHY DIDN'T HE HAVE *THEM* WAIT?
SERIOUSLY? YOU'RE ASKING THAT? DID YOU NOT SEE HIM MAKE A MOVE ON HEATHER?
UH . . . I THOUGHT SHE MADE THE MOVE ON HIM.
WHATEVER. HE WENT ALONG WHEN SHE SUGGESTED THEY SIT IN THE FRONT SEAT.
TRUE . . . SO DOES THIS MEAN WE CAN'T HAVE OUR CLUBHOUSE AT KELSEY'S HOUSE?
YES. THAT'S EXACTLY WHAT THIS MEANS.

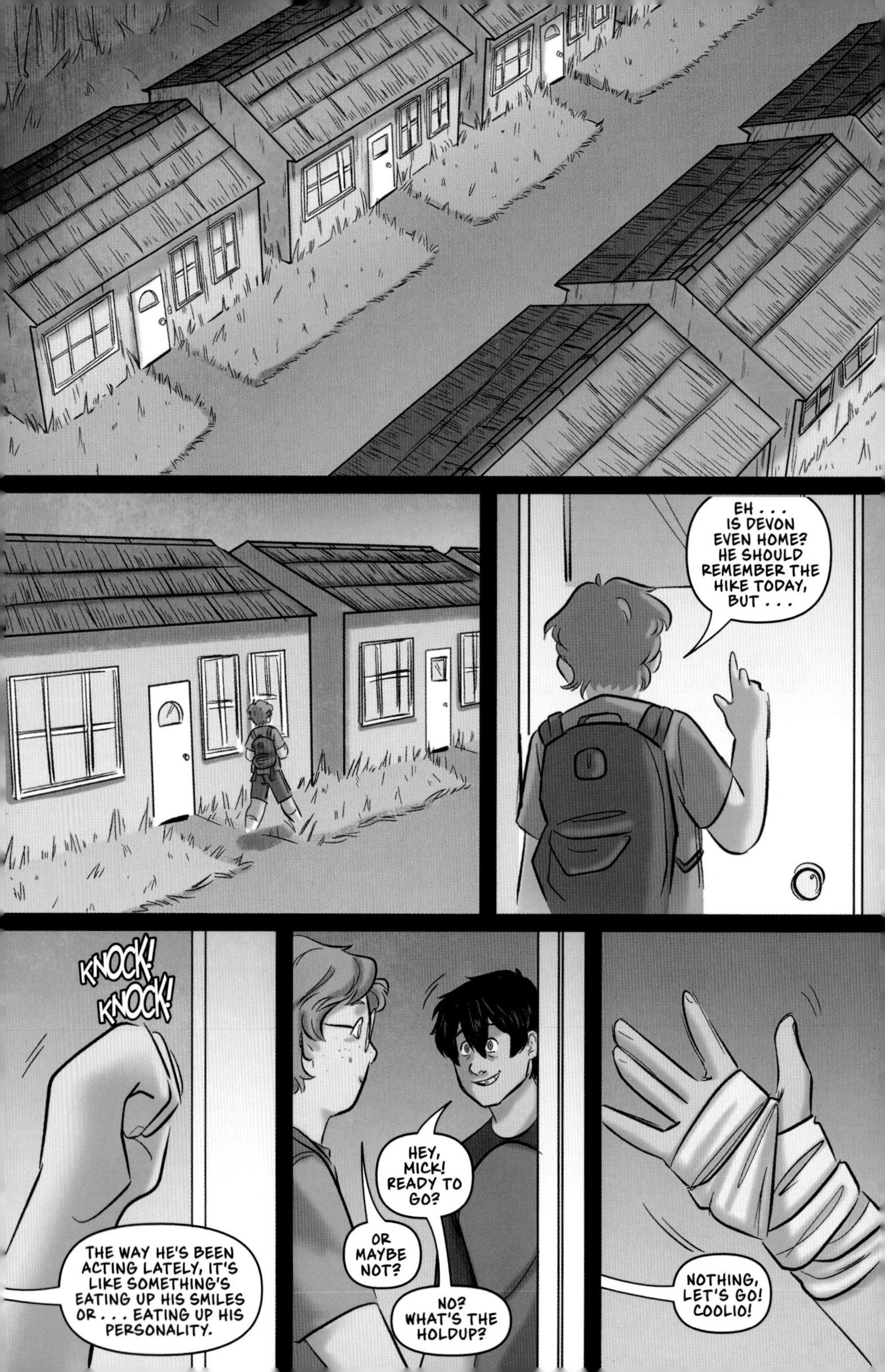
EH . . . IS DEVON EVEN HOME? HE SHOULD REMEMBER THE HIKE TODAY, BUT . . .
KNOCK! KNOCK!
THE WAY HE'S BEEN ACTING LATELY, IT'S LIKE SOMETHING'S EATING UP HIS SMILES OR . . . EATING UP HIS PERSONALITY.
HEY, MICK! READY TO GO?
OR MAYBE NOT?
NO? WHAT'S THE HOLDUP?
NOTHING, LET'S GO! COOLIO!

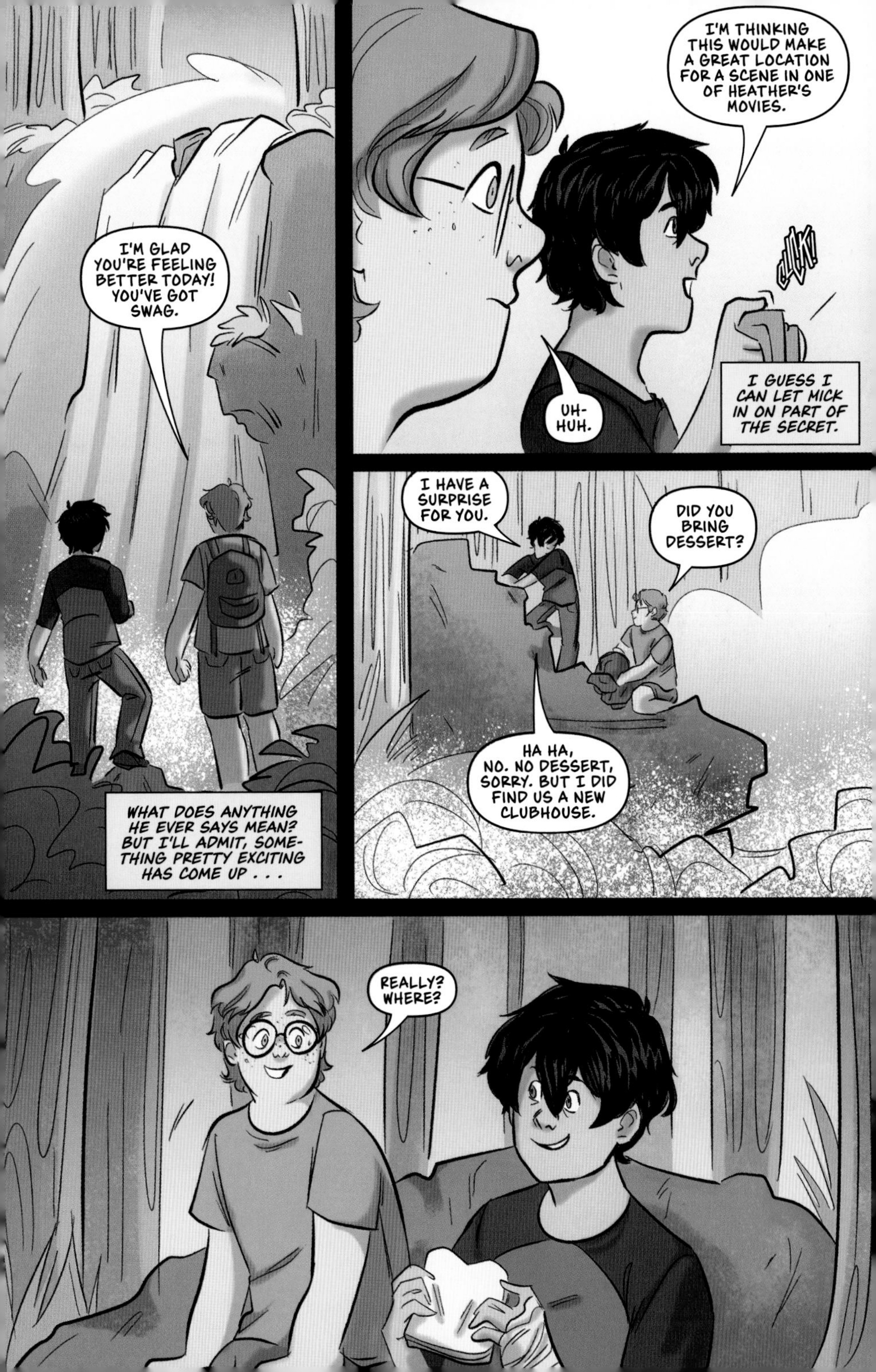
I'M GLAD YOU'RE FEELING BETTER TODAY! YOU'VE GOT SWAG.
WHAT DOES ANYTHING HE EVER SAYS MEAN? BUT I'LL ADMIT, SOME-THING PRETTY EXCITING HAS COME UP . . .
I'M THINKING THIS WOULD MAKE A GREAT LOCATION FOR A SCENE IN ONE OF HEATHER'S MOVIES.
CLIK!
UH-HUH.
I GUESS I CAN LET MICK IN ON PART OF THE SECRET.
I HAVE A SURPRISE FOR YOU.
DID YOU BRING DESSERT?
HA HA, NO. NO DESSERT, SORRY. BUT I DID FIND US A NEW CLUBHOUSE.
REALLY? WHERE?

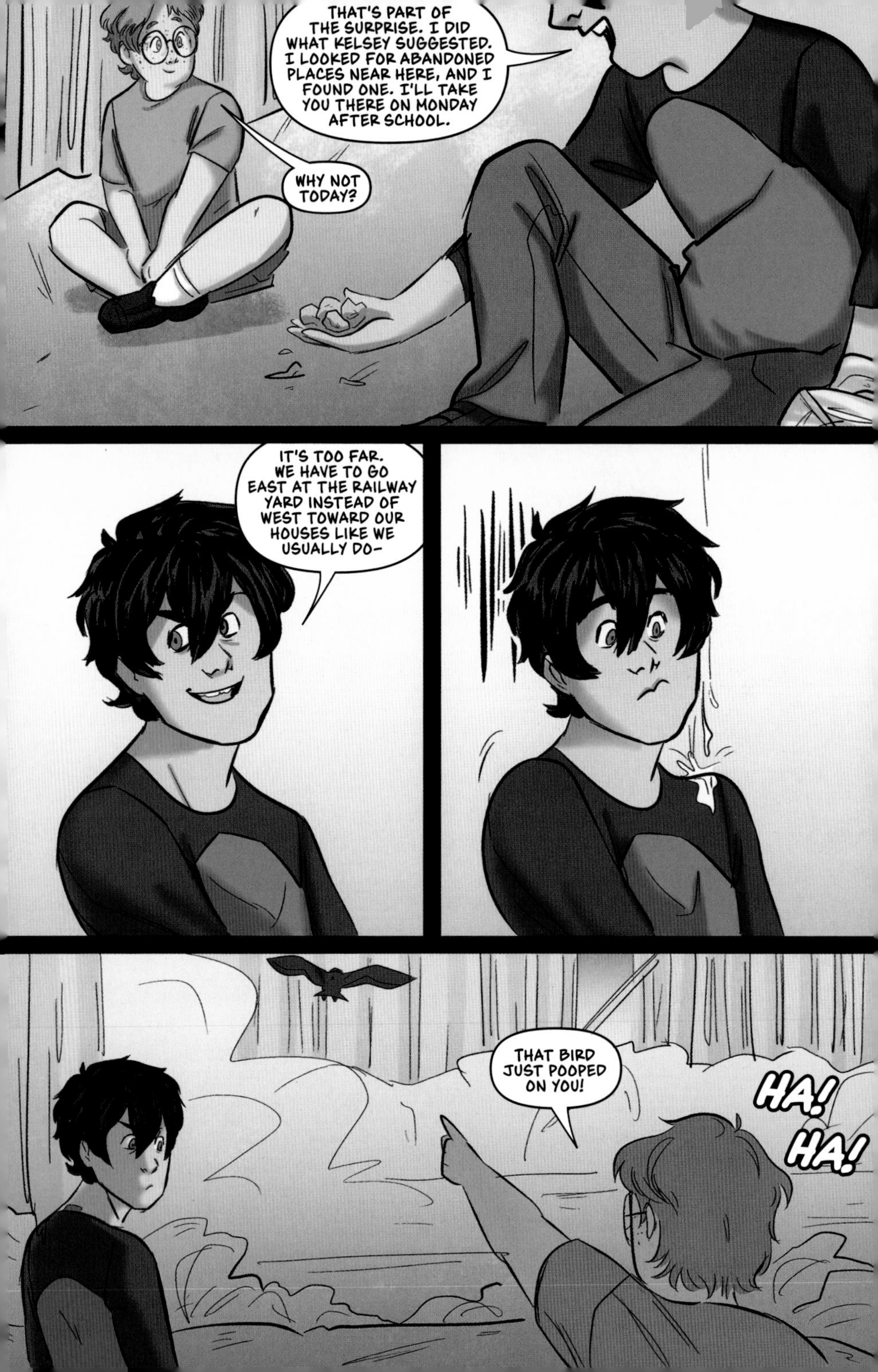
THAT'S PART OF THE SURPRISE. I DID WHAT KELSEY SUGGESTED. I LOOKED FOR ABANDONED PLACES NEAR HERE, AND I FOUND ONE. I'LL TAKE YOU THERE ON MONDAY AFTER SCHOOL.
WHY NOT TODAY?
IT'S TOO FAR. WE HAVE TO GO EAST AT THE RAILWAY YARD INSTEAD OF WEST TOWARD OUR HOUSES LIKE WE USUALLY DO–
THAT BIRD JUST POOPED ON YOU!
HA! HA!

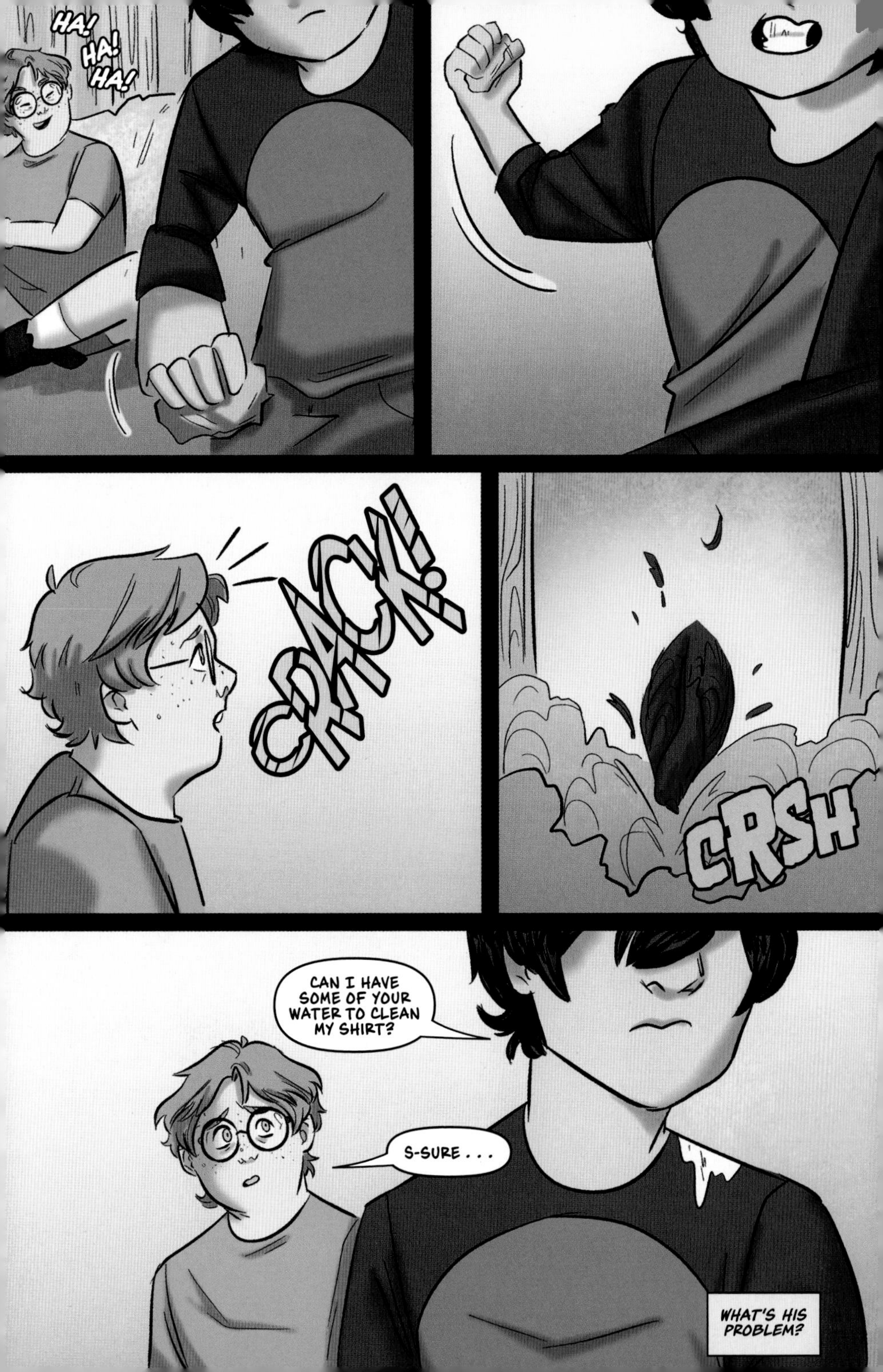
HA!
HA!
HA!
CRACK!
CRSH
CAN I HAVE SOME OF YOUR WATER TO CLEAN MY SHIRT?
S-SURE . . .
WHAT'S HIS PROBLEM?

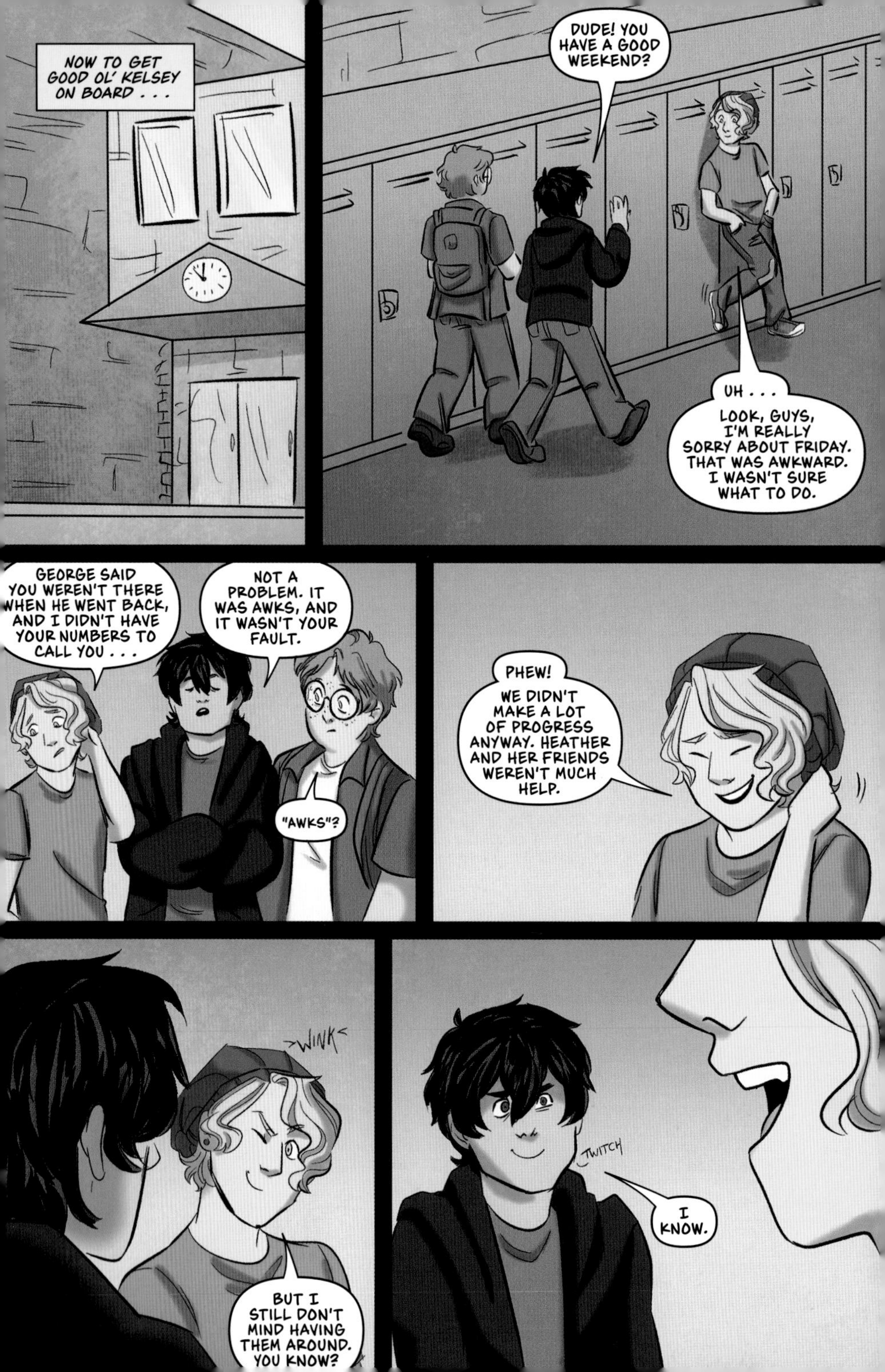
NOW TO GET GOOD OL' KELSEY ON BOARD . . .
DUDE! YOU HAVE A GOOD WEEKEND?
UH . . .
LOOK, GUYS, I'M REALLY SORRY ABOUT FRIDAY. THAT WAS AWKWARD. I WASN'T SURE WHAT TO DO.
GEORGE SAID YOU WEREN'T THERE WHEN HE WENT BACK, AND I DIDN'T HAVE YOUR NUMBERS TO CALL YOU . . .
NOT A PROBLEM. IT WAS AWKS, AND IT WASN'T YOUR FAULT.
"AWKS"?
PHEW!
WE DIDN'T MAKE A LOT OF PROGRESS ANYWAY. HEATHER AND HER FRIENDS WEREN'T MUCH HELP.
>WINK<
BUT I STILL DON'T MIND HAVING THEM AROUND. YOU KNOW?
TWITCH
I KNOW.

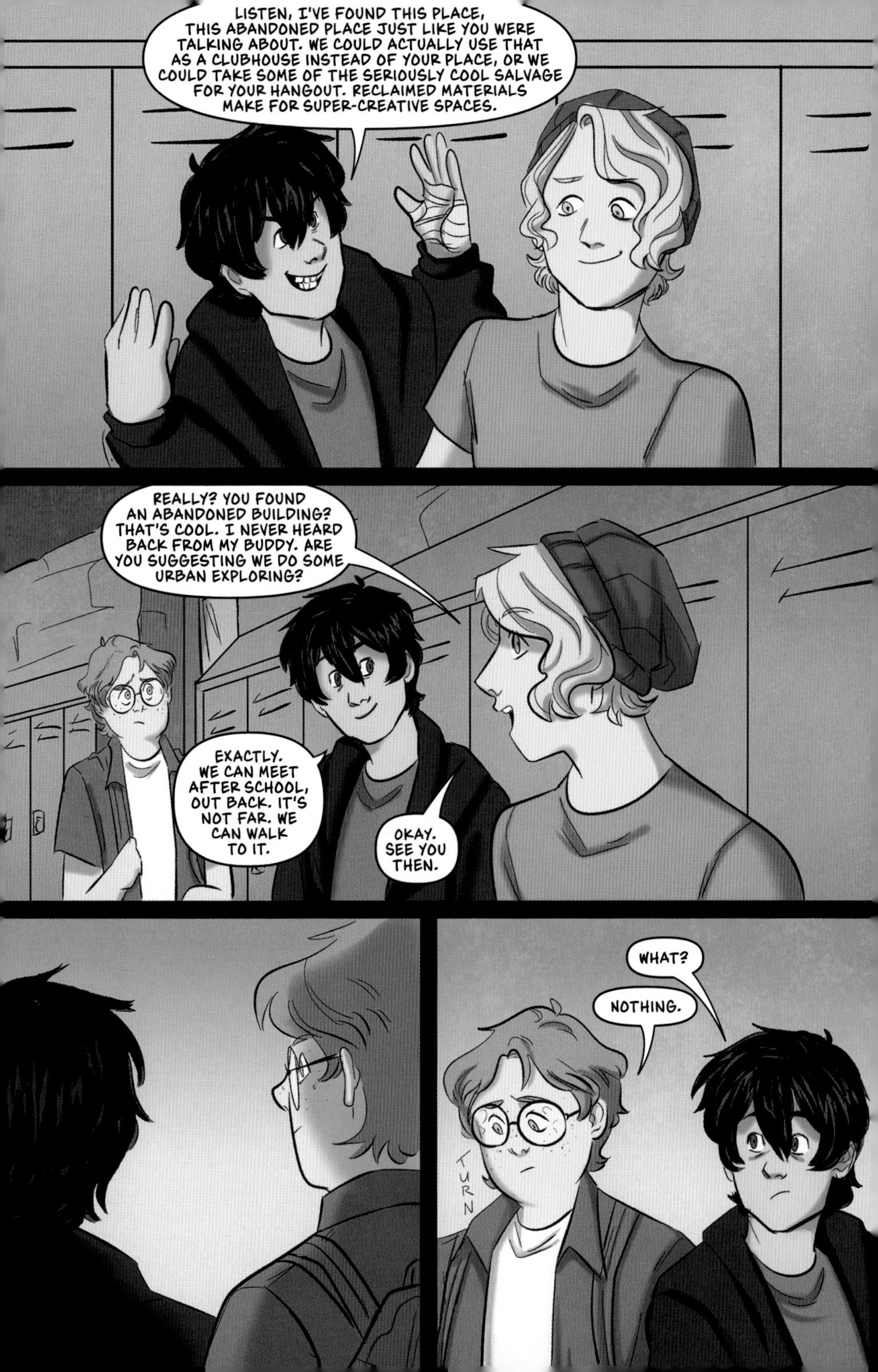
LISTEN, I'VE FOUND THIS PLACE, THIS ABANDONED PLACE JUST LIKE YOU WERE TALKING ABOUT. WE COULD ACTUALLY USE THAT AS A CLUBHOUSE INSTEAD OF YOUR PLACE, OR WE COULD TAKE SOME OF THE SERIOUSLY COOL SALVAGE FOR YOUR HANGOUT. RECLAIMED MATERIALS MAKE FOR SUPER-CREATIVE SPACES.
REALLY? YOU FOUND AN ABANDONED BUILDING? THAT'S COOL. I NEVER HEARD BACK FROM MY BUDDY. ARE YOU SUGGESTING WE DO SOME URBAN EXPLORING?
EXACTLY. WE CAN MEET AFTER SCHOOL, OUT BACK. IT'S NOT FAR. WE CAN WALK TO IT.
OKAY. SEE YOU THEN.
WHAT?
NOTHING.
TURN

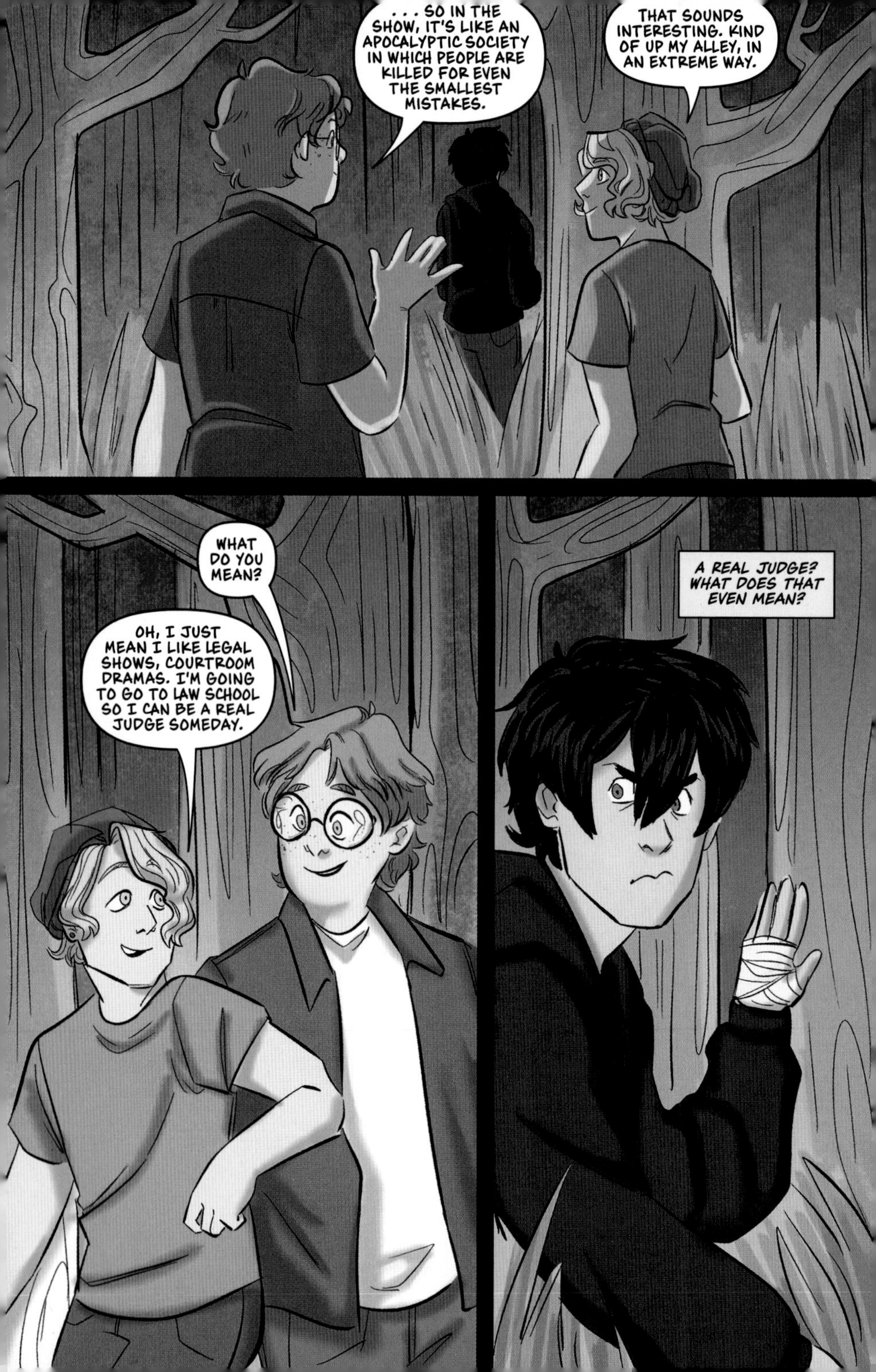
. . . SO IN THE SHOW, IT'S LIKE AN APOCALYPTIC SOCIETY IN WHICH PEOPLE ARE KILLED FOR EVEN THE SMALLEST MISTAKES.
THAT SOUNDS INTERESTING. KIND OF UP MY ALLEY, IN AN EXTREME WAY.
WHAT DO YOU MEAN?
OH, I JUST MEAN I LIKE LEGAL SHOWS, COURTROOM DRAMAS. I'M GOING TO GO TO LAW SCHOOL SO I CAN BE A REAL JUDGE SOMEDAY.
A REAL JUDGE? WHAT DOES THAT EVEN MEAN?

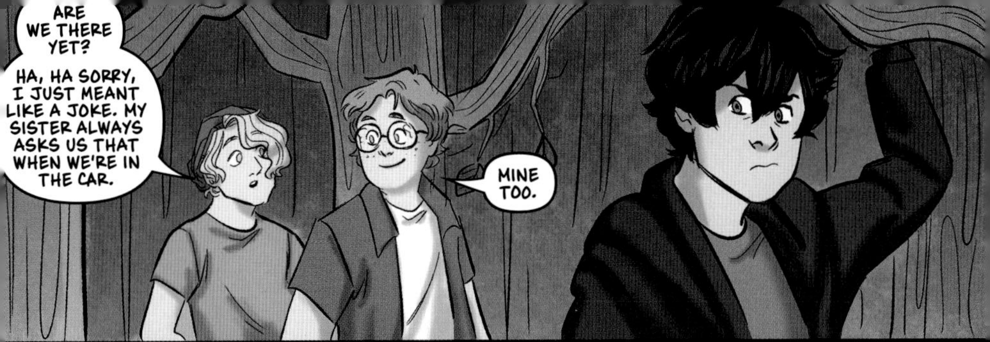
ARE WE THERE YET?
HA, HA SORRY, I JUST MEANT LIKE A JOKE. MY SISTER ALWAYS ASKS US THAT WHEN WE'RE IN THE CAR.
MINE TOO.

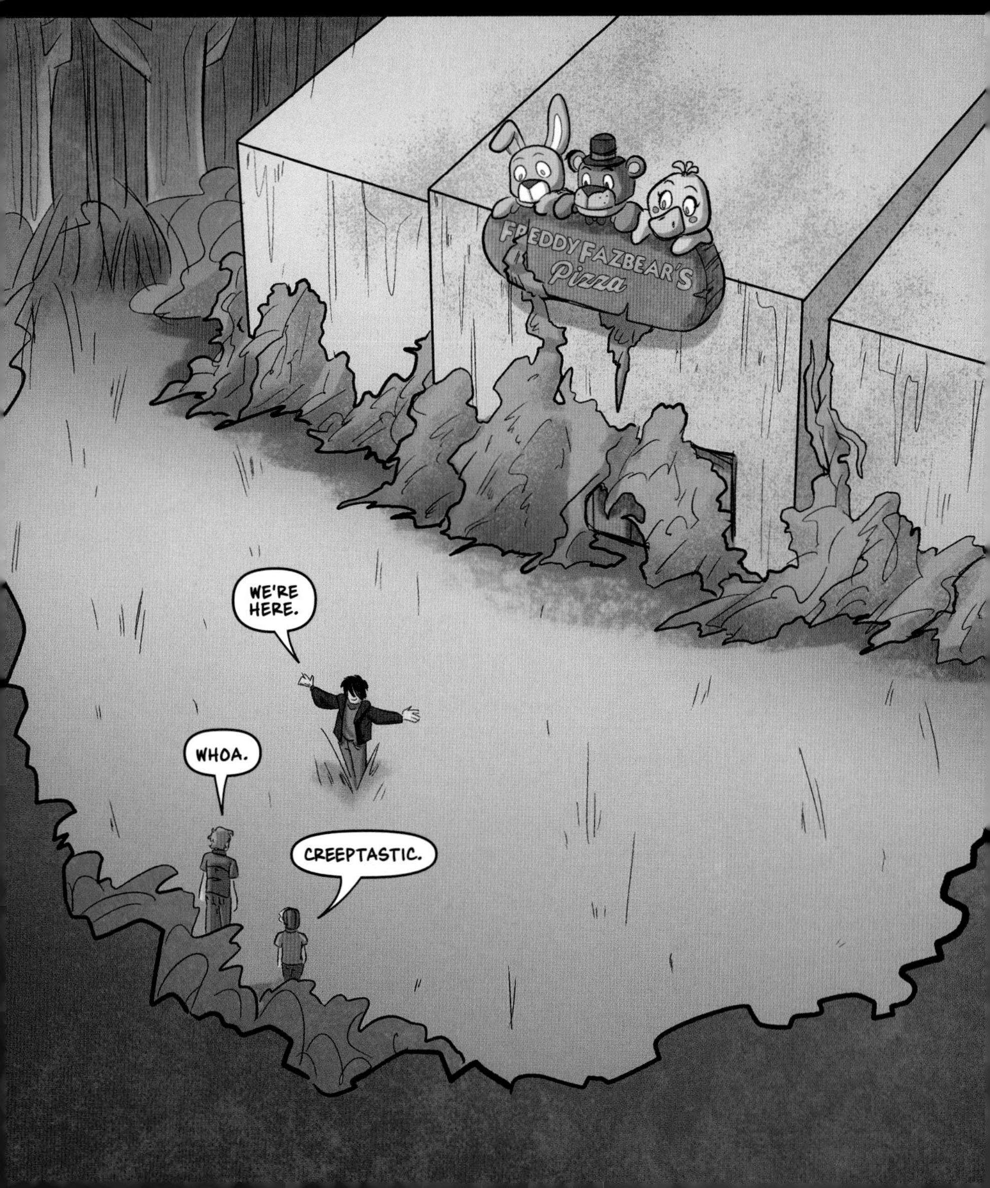
FREDDY FAZBEAR'S Pizza
WE'RE HERE.
WHOA.
CREEPTASTIC.

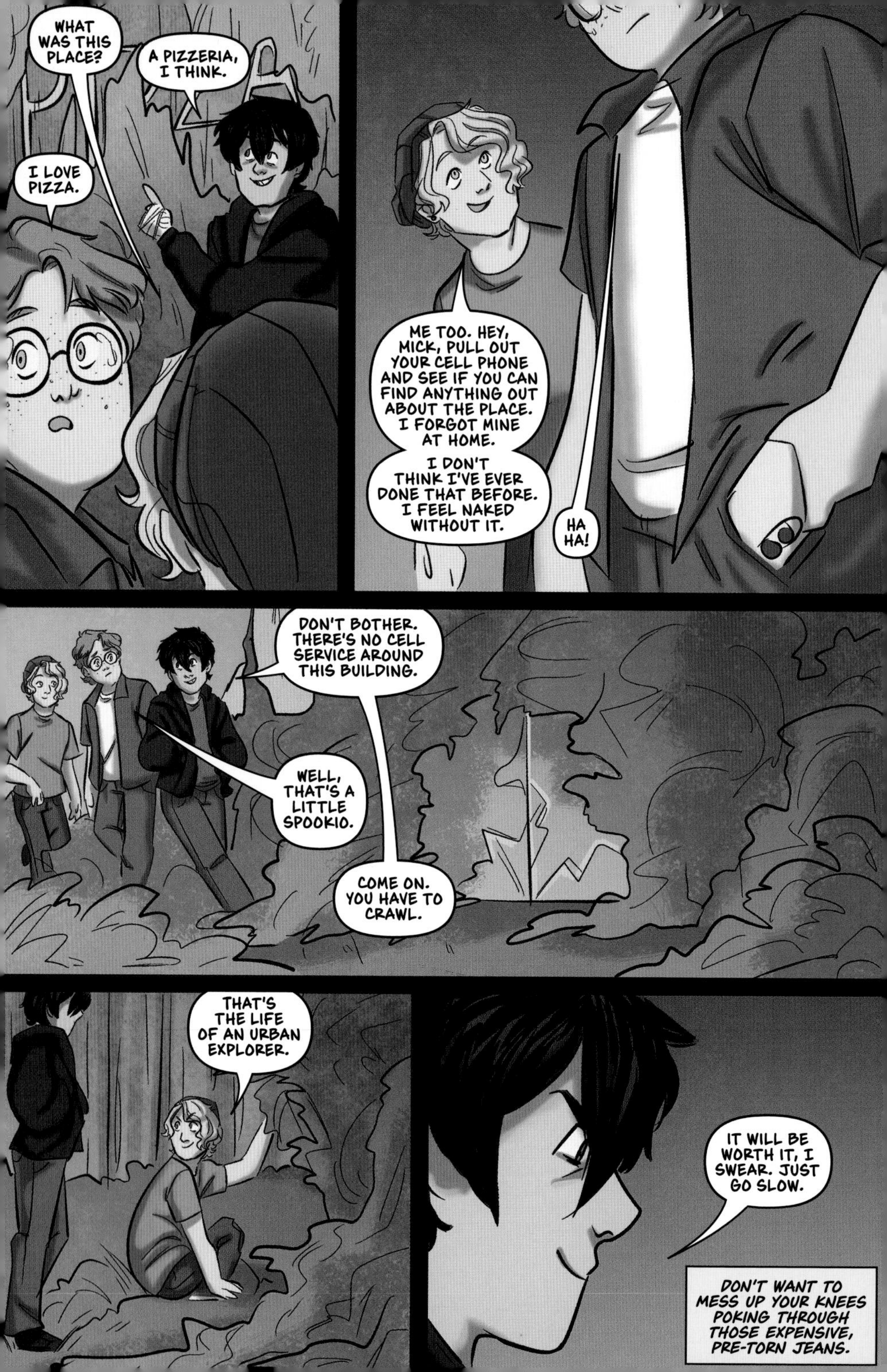

WHAT WAS THIS PLACE?
A PIZZERIA, I THINK.
I LOVE PIZZA.
ME TOO. HEY, MICK, PULL OUT YOUR CELL PHONE AND SEE IF YOU CAN FIND ANYTHING OUT ABOUT THE PLACE. I FORGOT MINE AT HOME.
I DON'T THINK I'VE EVER DONE THAT BEFORE. I FEEL NAKED WITHOUT IT.
HA HA!
DON'T BOTHER. THERE'S NO CELL SERVICE AROUND THIS BUILDING.
WELL, THAT'S A LITTLE SPOOKIO.
COME ON. YOU HAVE TO CRAWL.
THAT'S THE LIFE OF AN URBAN EXPLORER.
IT WILL BE WORTH IT, I SWEAR. JUST GO SLOW.
DON'T WANT TO MESS UP YOUR KNEES POKING THROUGH THOSE EXPENSIVE, PRE-TORN JEANS.

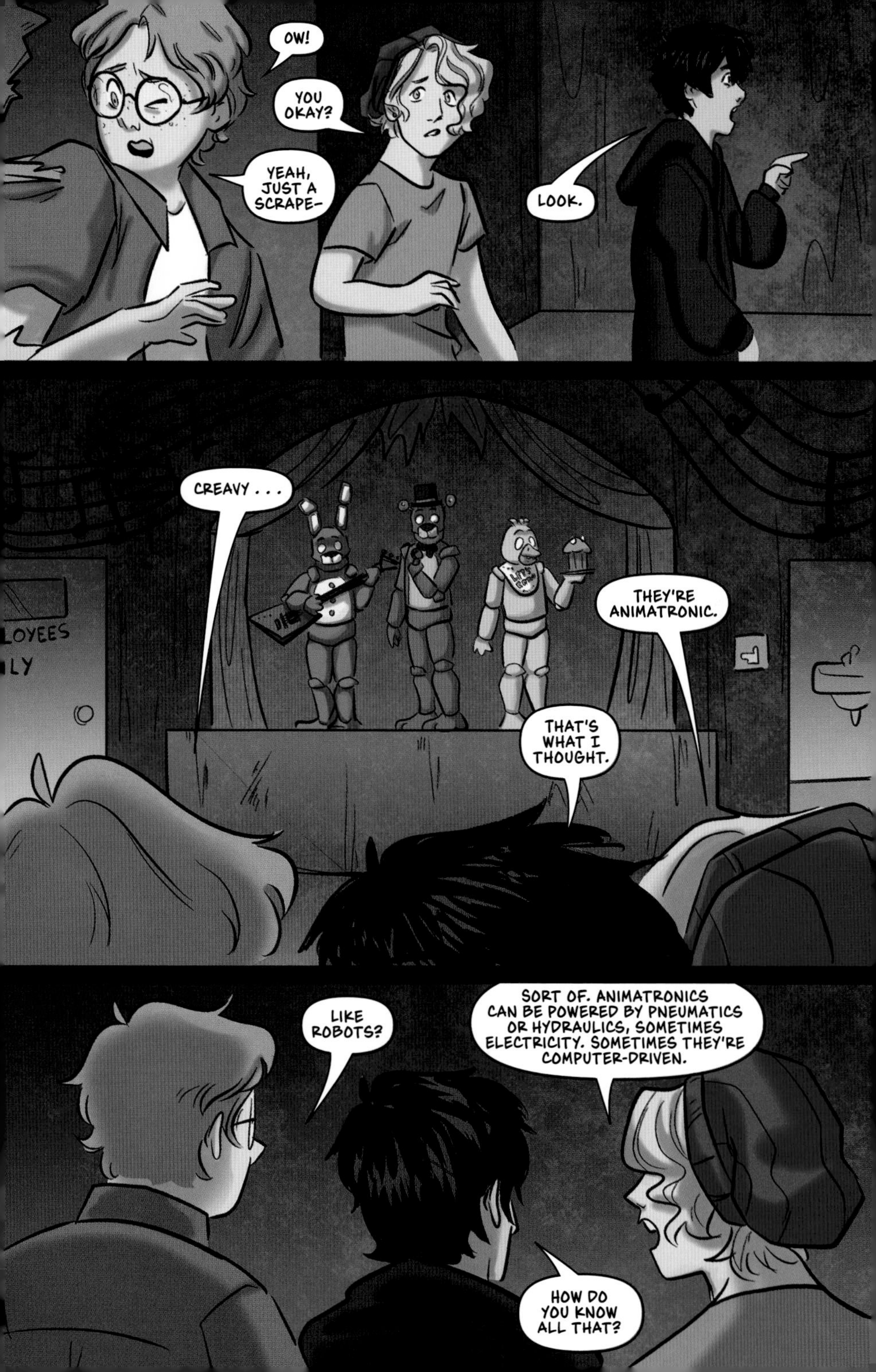
OW!
YOU OKAY?
YEAH, JUST A SCRAPE-
LOOK.
CREAVY . . .
THEY'RE ANIMATRONIC.
THAT'S WHAT I THOUGHT.
LIKE ROBOTS?
SORT OF. ANIMATRONICS CAN BE POWERED BY PNEUMATICS OR HYDRAULICS, SOMETIMES ELECTRICITY. SOMETIMES THEY'RE COMPUTER-DRIVEN.
HOW DO YOU KNOW ALL THAT?

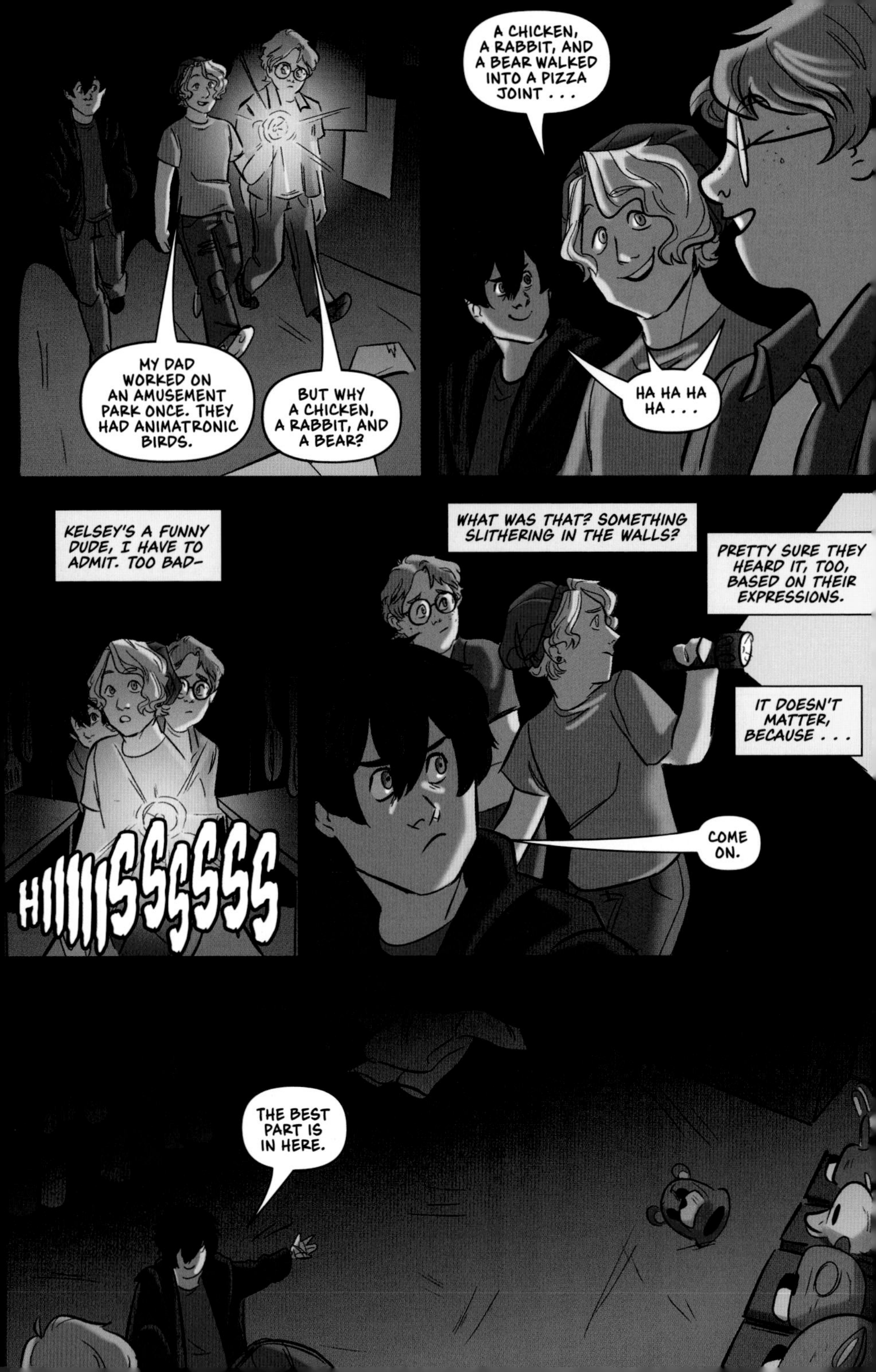
MY DAD WORKED ON AN AMUSEMENT PARK ONCE. THEY HAD ANIMATRONIC BIRDS.
BUT WHY A CHICKEN, A RABBIT, AND A BEAR?
A CHICKEN, A RABBIT, AND A BEAR WALKED INTO A PIZZA JOINT . . .
HA HA HA HA . . .
KELSEY'S A FUNNY DUDE, I HAVE TO ADMIT. TOO BAD-
HIIIIISSSSSS
WHAT WAS THAT? SOMETHING SLITHERING IN THE WALLS?
PRETTY SURE THEY HEARD IT, TOO, BASED ON THEIR EXPRESSIONS.
IT DOESN'T MATTER, BECAUSE . . .
COME ON.
THE BEST PART IS IN HERE.

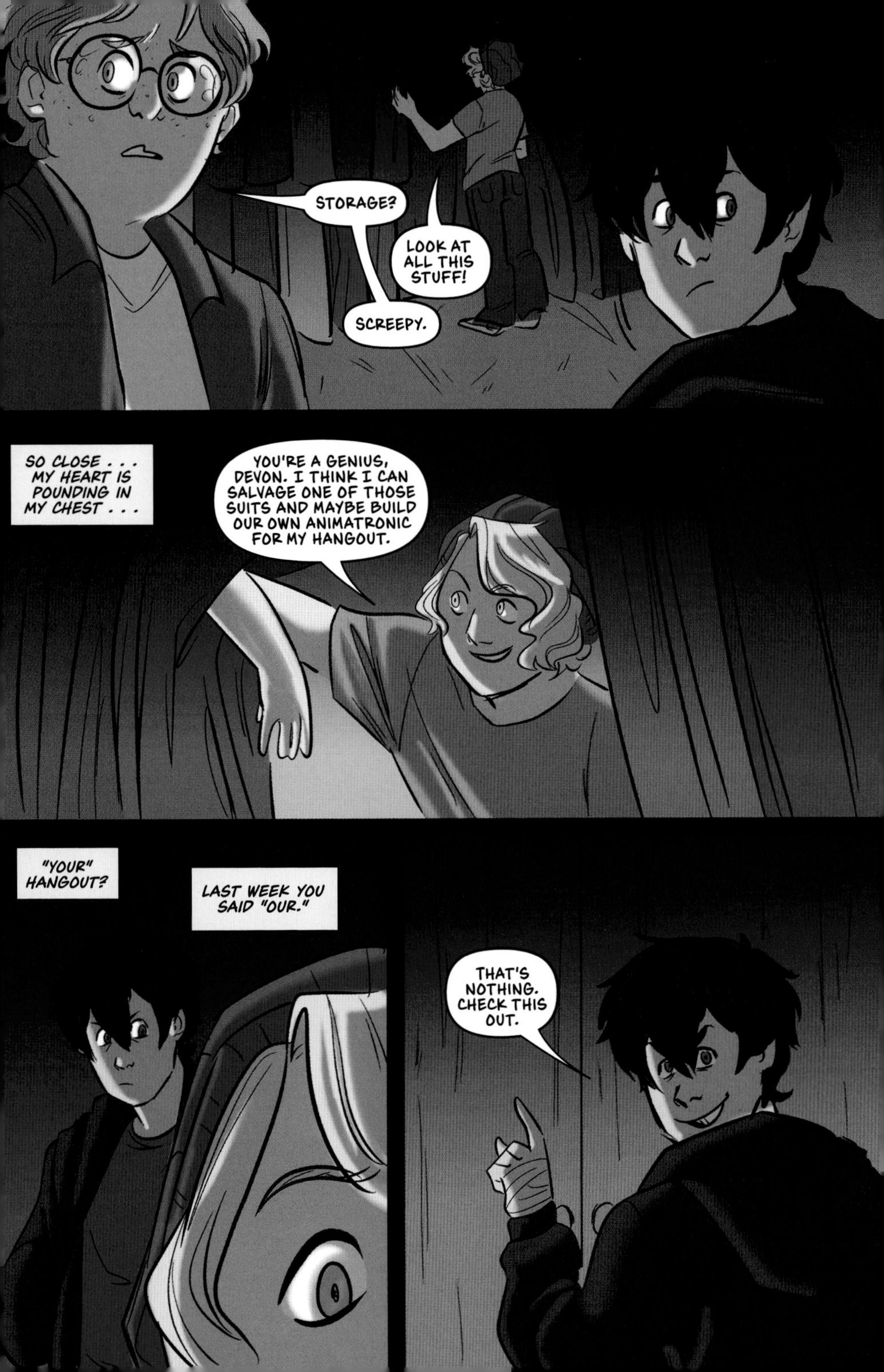
STORAGE?
SCREEPY.
LOOK AT ALL THIS STUFF!
SO CLOSE . . . MY HEART IS POUNDING IN MY CHEST . . .
YOU'RE A GENIUS, DEVON. I THINK I CAN SALVAGE ONE OF THOSE SUITS AND MAYBE BUILD OUR OWN ANIMATRONIC FOR MY HANGOUT.
"YOUR" HANGOUT?
LAST WEEK YOU SAID "OUR."
THAT'S NOTHING. CHECK THIS OUT.

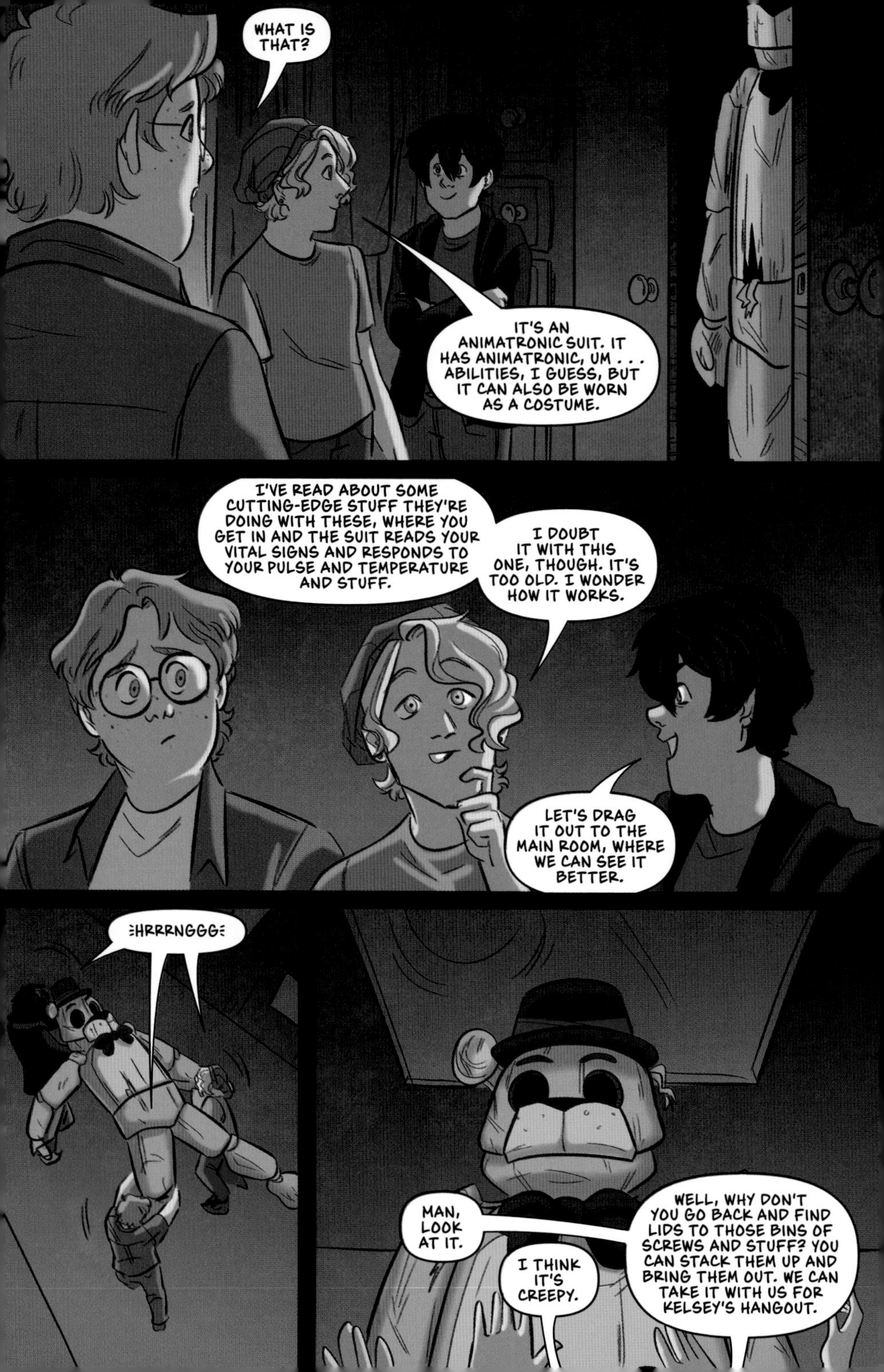
WHAT IS THAT?
IT'S AN ANIMATRONIC SUIT. IT HAS ANIMATRONIC, UM . . . ABILITIES, I GUESS, BUT IT CAN ALSO BE WORN AS A COSTUME.
I'VE READ ABOUT SOME CUTTING-EDGE STUFF THEY'RE DOING WITH THESE, WHERE YOU GET IN AND THE SUIT READS YOUR VITAL SIGNS AND RESPONDS TO YOUR PULSE AND TEMPERATURE AND STUFF.
I DOUBT IT WITH THIS ONE, THOUGH. IT'S TOO OLD. I WONDER HOW IT WORKS.
LET'S DRAG IT OUT TO THE MAIN ROOM, WHERE WE CAN SEE IT BETTER.
HRRRNGGG
MAN, LOOK AT IT.
I THINK IT'S CREEPY.
WELL, WHY DON'T YOU GO BACK AND FIND LIDS TO THOSE BINS OF SCREWS AND STUFF? YOU CAN STACK THEM UP AND BRING THEM OUT. WE CAN TAKE IT WITH US FOR KELSEY'S HANGOUT.

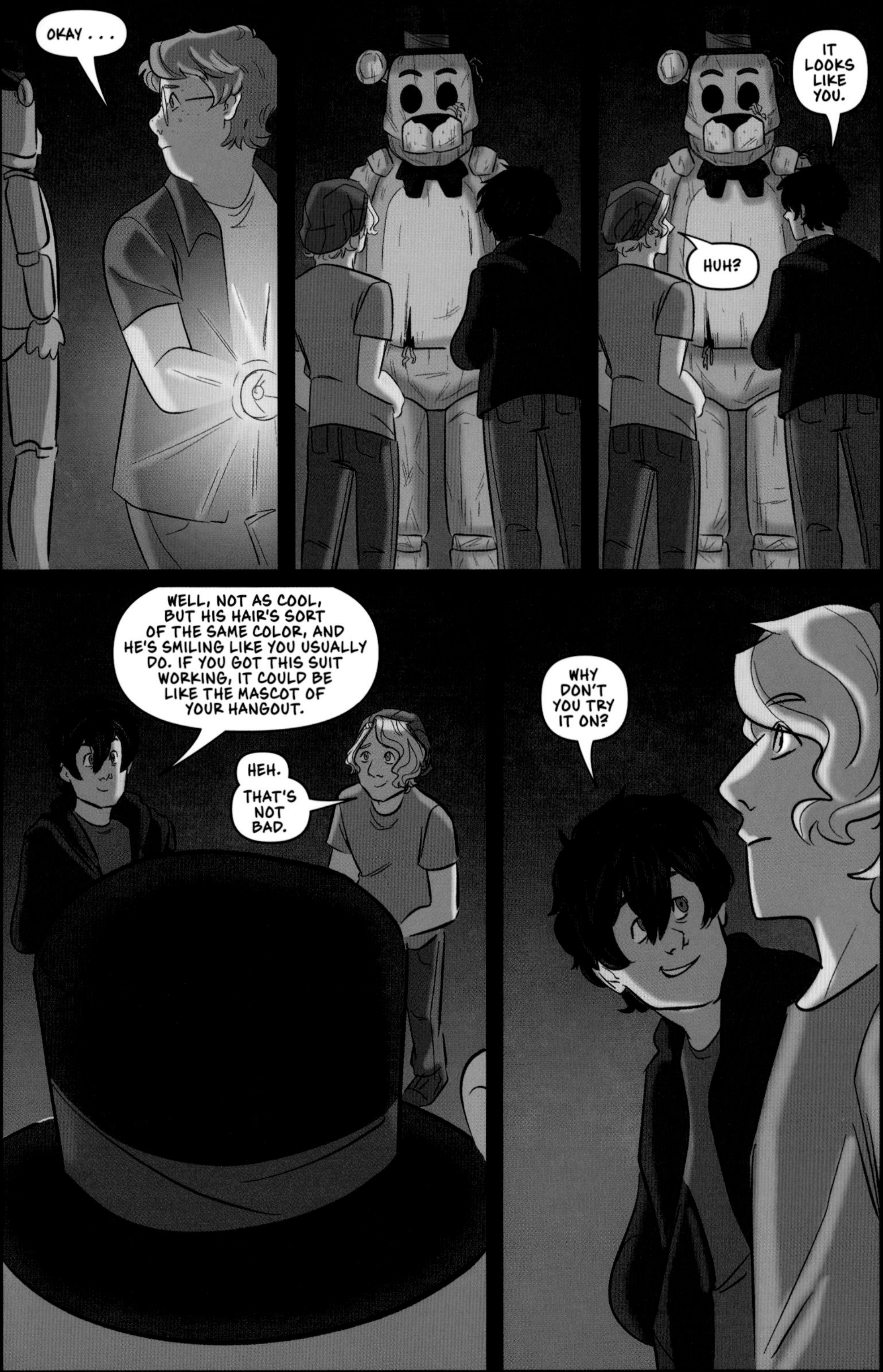
OKAY . . .
IT LOOKS LIKE YOU.
HUH?
WELL, NOT AS COOL, BUT HIS HAIR'S SORT OF THE SAME COLOR, AND HE'S SMILING LIKE YOU USUALLY DO. IF YOU GOT THIS SUIT WORKING, IT COULD BE LIKE THE MASCOT OF YOUR HANGOUT.
HEH.
THAT'S NOT BAD.
WHY DON'T YOU TRY IT ON?

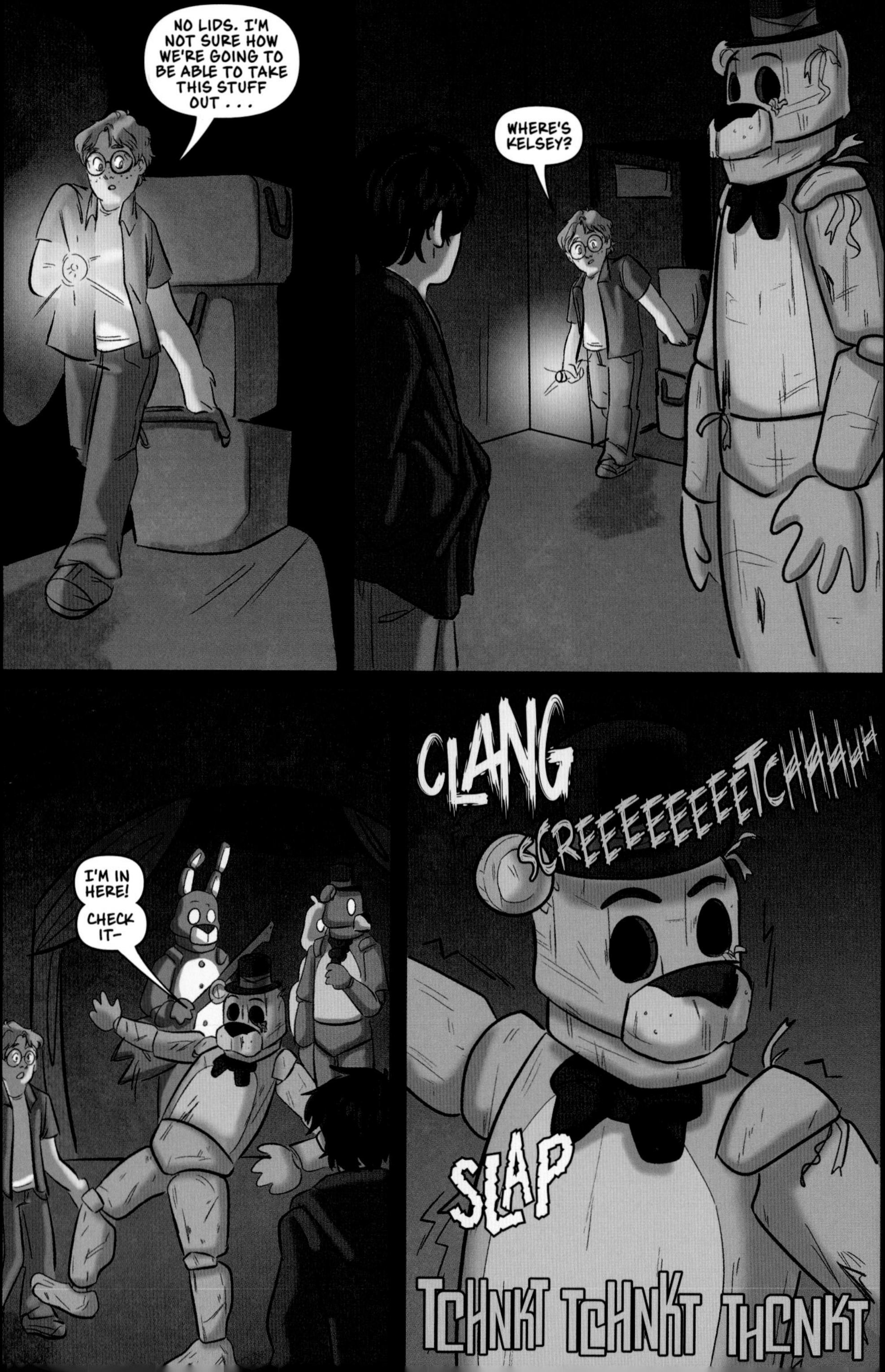
NO LIDS. I'M NOT SURE HOW WE'RE GOING TO BE ABLE TO TAKE THIS STUFF OUT . . .
WHERE'S KELSEY?
I'M IN HERE!
CHECK IT-
CLANG
SCREEEEEEEEETCHHHHH
SLAP
TCHNKT TCHNKT THCNKT

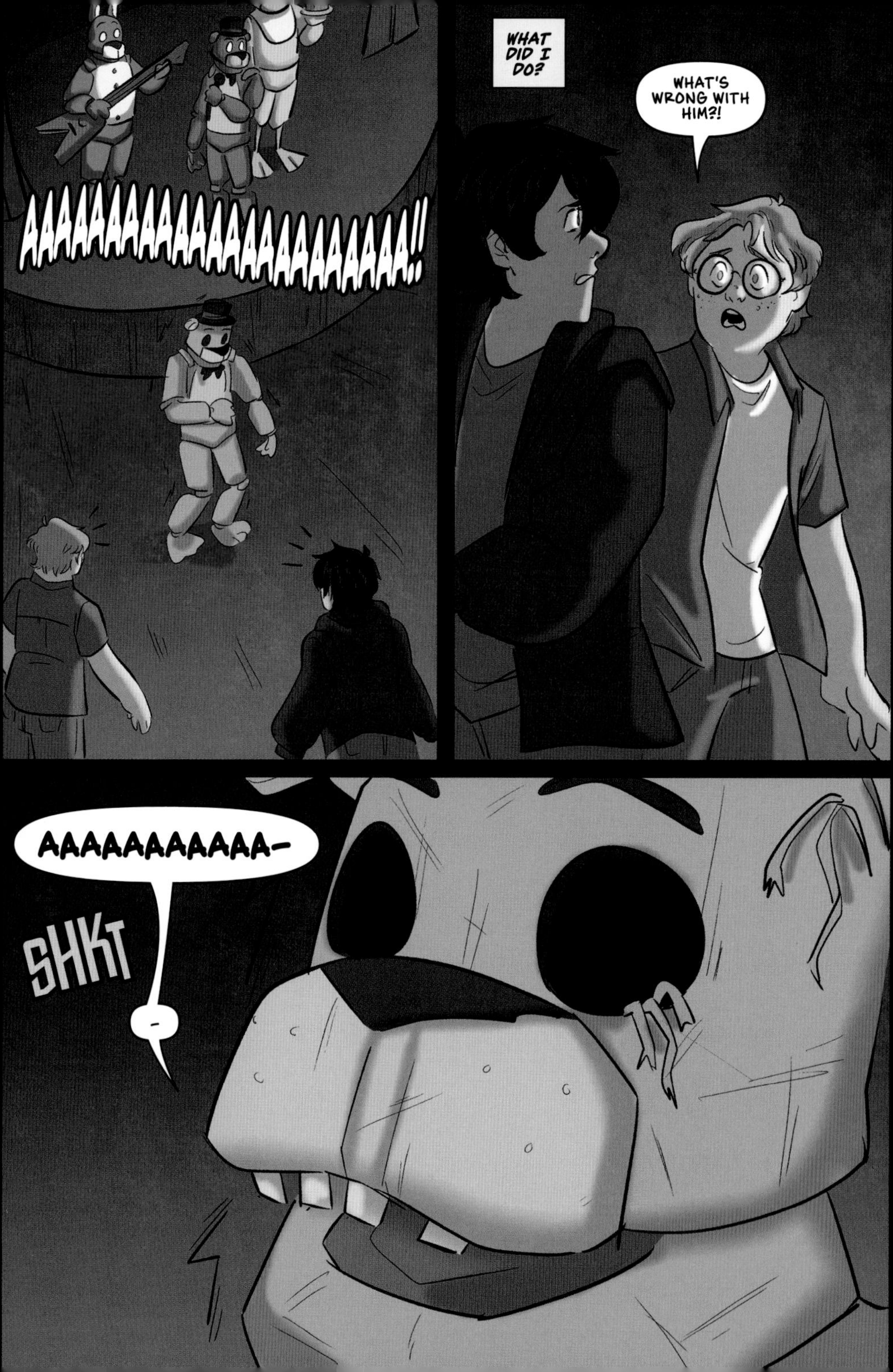
AAAAAAAAAAAAAAAAAAAAAA!!
WHAT DID I DO?
WHAT'S WRONG WITH HIM?!
AAAAAAAAAAA-
SHKT
-

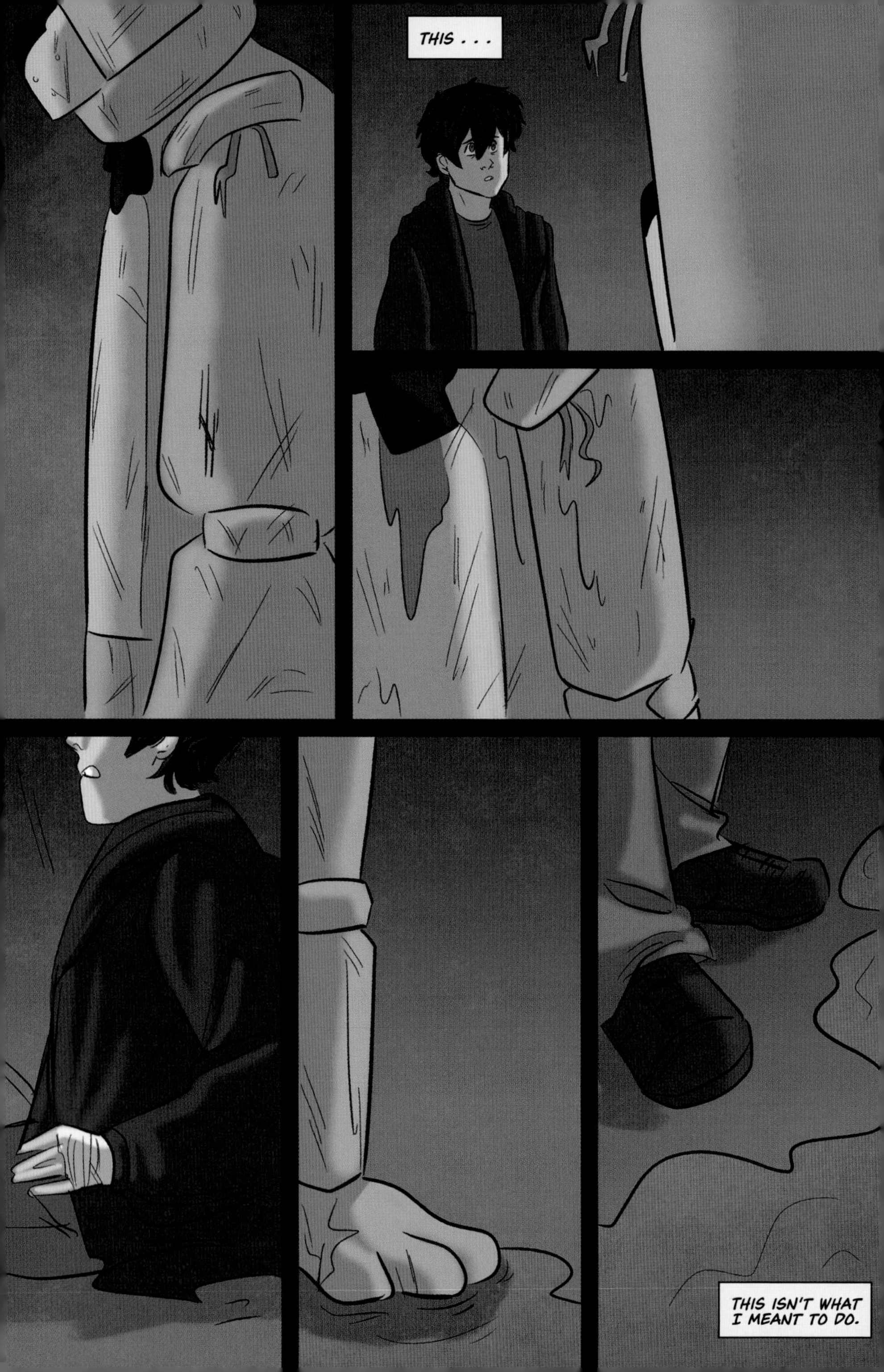
THIS . . .
THIS ISN'T WHAT I MEANT TO DO.

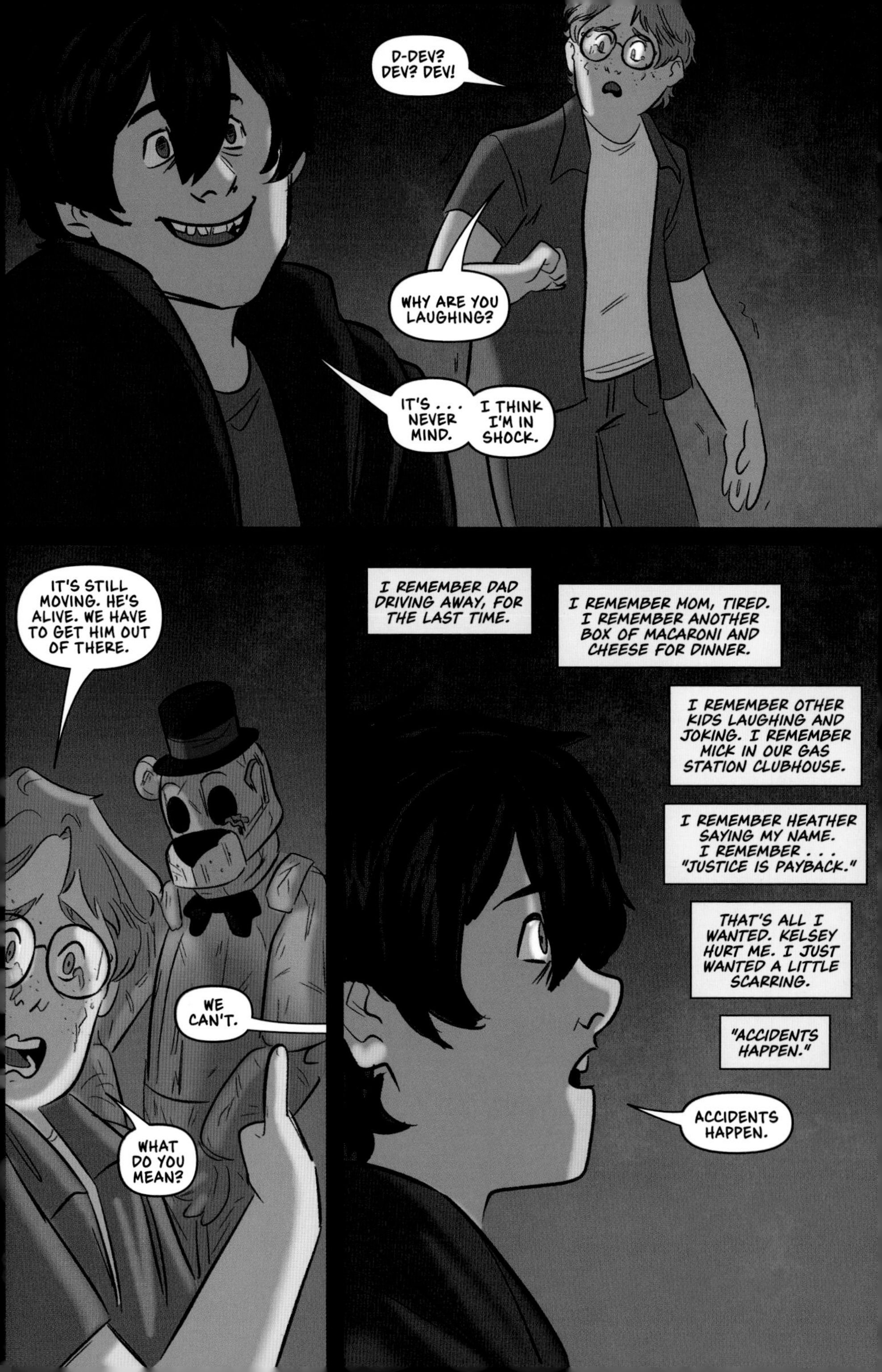
D-DEV? DEV? DEV!
WHY ARE YOU LAUGHING?
IT'S . . . NEVER MIND.
I THINK I'M IN SHOCK.
IT'S STILL MOVING. HE'S ALIVE. WE HAVE TO GET HIM OUT OF THERE.
WE CAN'T.
WHAT DO YOU MEAN?
I REMEMBER DAD DRIVING AWAY, FOR THE LAST TIME.
I REMEMBER MOM, TIRED. I REMEMBER ANOTHER BOX OF MACARONI AND CHEESE FOR DINNER.
I REMEMBER OTHER KIDS LAUGHING AND JOKING. I REMEMBER MICK IN OUR GAS STATION CLUBHOUSE.
I REMEMBER HEATHER SAYING MY NAME. I REMEMBER . . . "JUSTICE IS PAYBACK."
THAT'S ALL I WANTED. KELSEY HURT ME. I JUST WANTED A LITTLE SCARRING.
"ACCIDENTS HAPPEN."
ACCIDENTS HAPPEN.

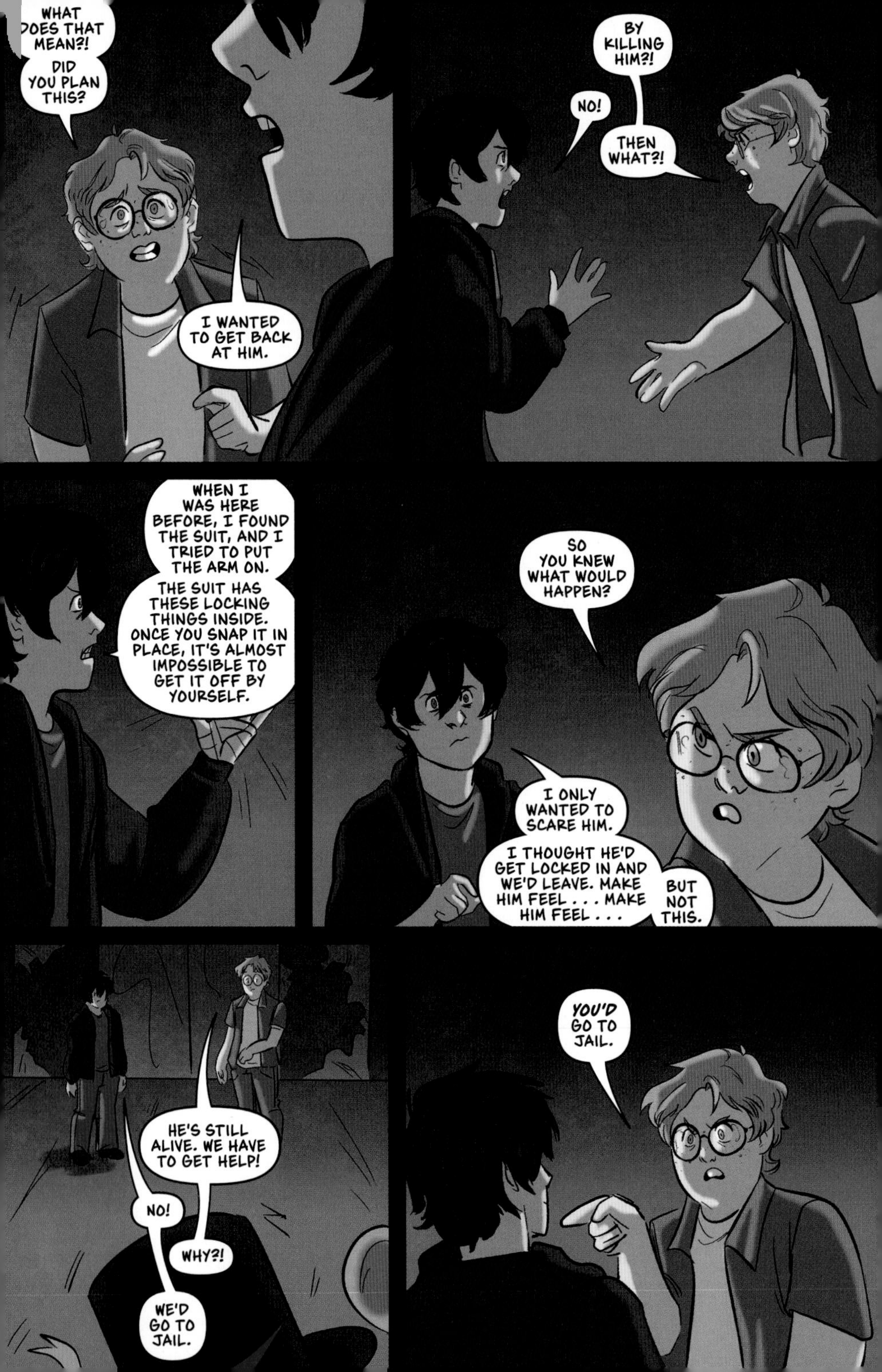
WHAT DOES THAT MEAN?!
DID YOU PLAN THIS?
I WANTED TO GET BACK AT HIM.
BY KILLING HIM?!
NO!
THEN WHAT?!
WHEN I WAS HERE BEFORE, I FOUND THE SUIT, AND I TRIED TO PUT THE ARM ON.
THE SUIT HAS THESE LOCKING THINGS INSIDE. ONCE YOU SNAP IT IN PLACE, IT'S ALMOST IMPOSSIBLE TO GET IT OFF BY YOURSELF.
SO YOU KNEW WHAT WOULD HAPPEN?
I ONLY WANTED TO SCARE HIM.
I THOUGHT HE'D GET LOCKED IN AND WE'D LEAVE. MAKE HIM FEEL . . . MAKE HIM FEEL . . .
BUT NOT THIS.
HE'S STILL ALIVE. WE HAVE TO GET HELP!
NO!
WHY?!
WE'D GO TO JAIL.
YOU'D GO TO JAIL.

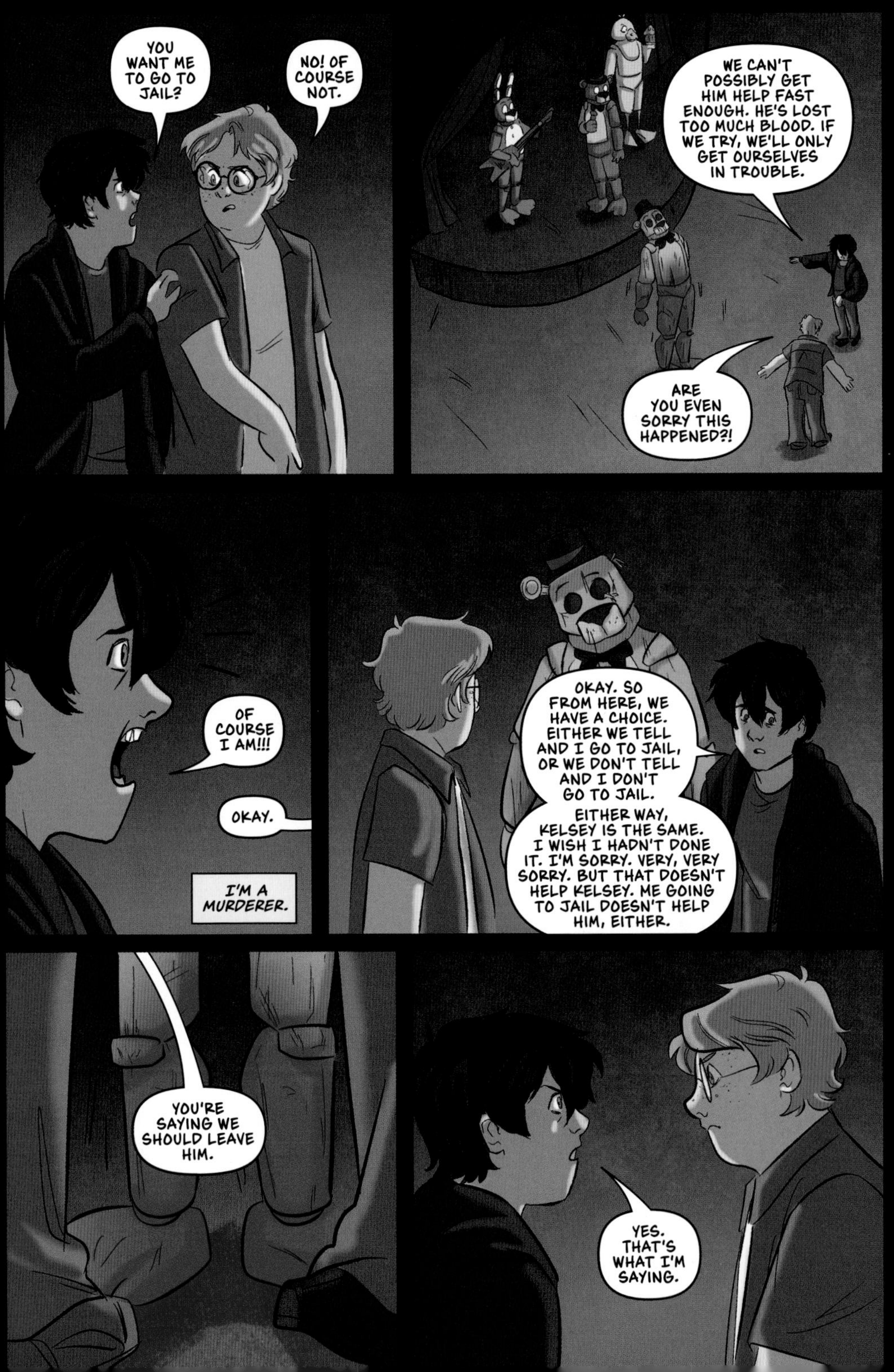
YOU WANT ME TO GO TO JAIL?
NO! OF COURSE NOT.
WE CAN'T POSSIBLY GET HIM HELP FAST ENOUGH. HE'S LOST TOO MUCH BLOOD. IF WE TRY, WE'LL ONLY GET OURSELVES IN TROUBLE.
ARE YOU EVEN SORRY THIS HAPPENED?!
OF COURSE I AM!!!
OKAY.
I'M A MURDERER.
OKAY. SO FROM HERE, WE HAVE A CHOICE. EITHER WE TELL AND I GO TO JAIL, OR WE DON'T TELL AND I DON'T GO TO JAIL.
EITHER WAY, KELSEY IS THE SAME. I WISH I HADN'T DONE IT. I'M SORRY. VERY, VERY SORRY. BUT THAT DOESN'T HELP KELSEY. ME GOING TO JAIL DOESN'T HELP HIM, EITHER.
YOU'RE SAYING WE SHOULD LEAVE HIM.
YES. THAT'S WHAT I'M SAYING.

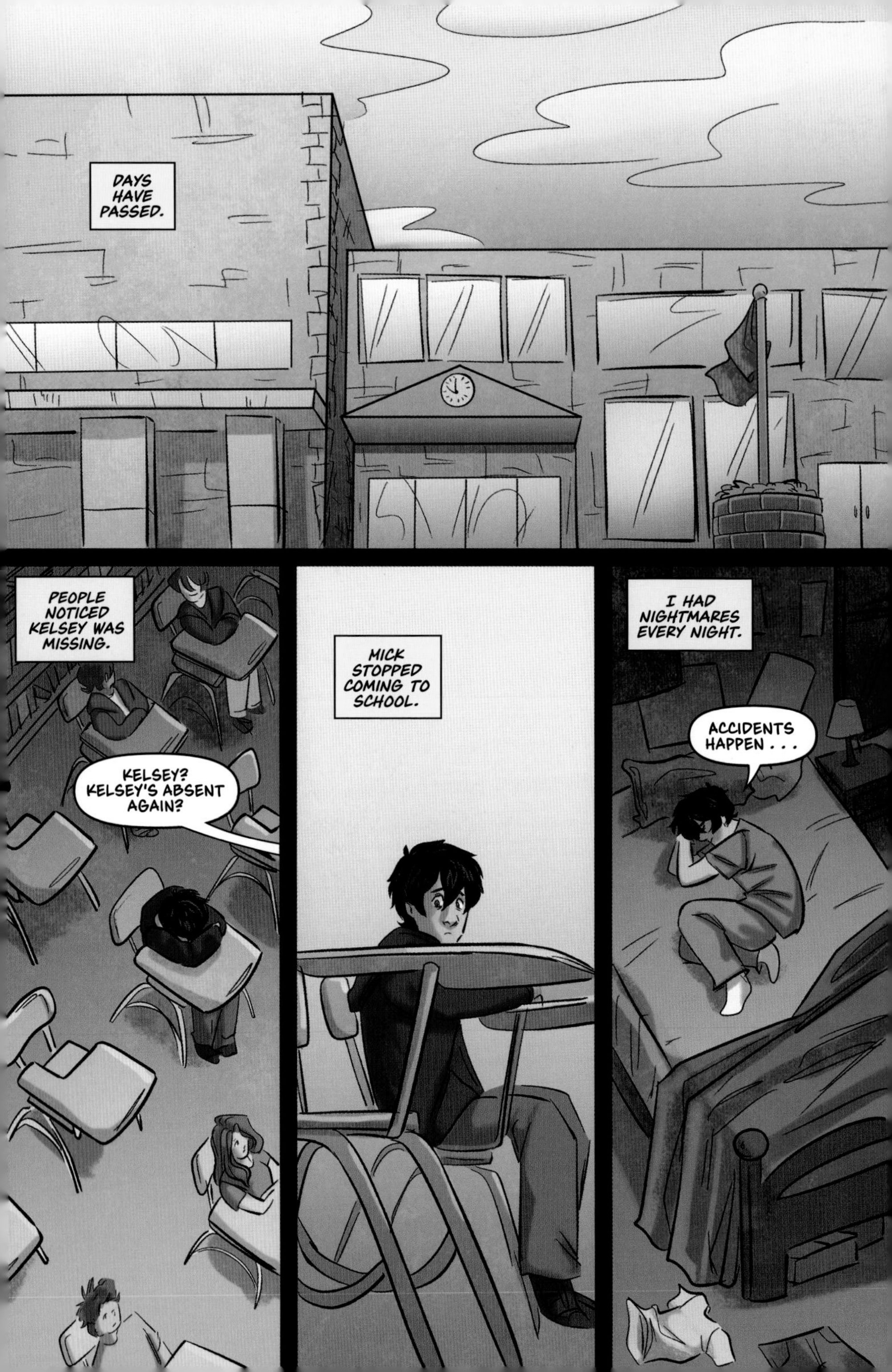
DAYS HAVE PASSED.
PEOPLE NOTICED KELSEY WAS MISSING.
KELSEY? KELSEY'S ABSENT AGAIN?
MICK STOPPED COMING TO SCHOOL.
I HAD NIGHTMARES EVERY NIGHT.
ACCIDENTS HAPPEN . . .

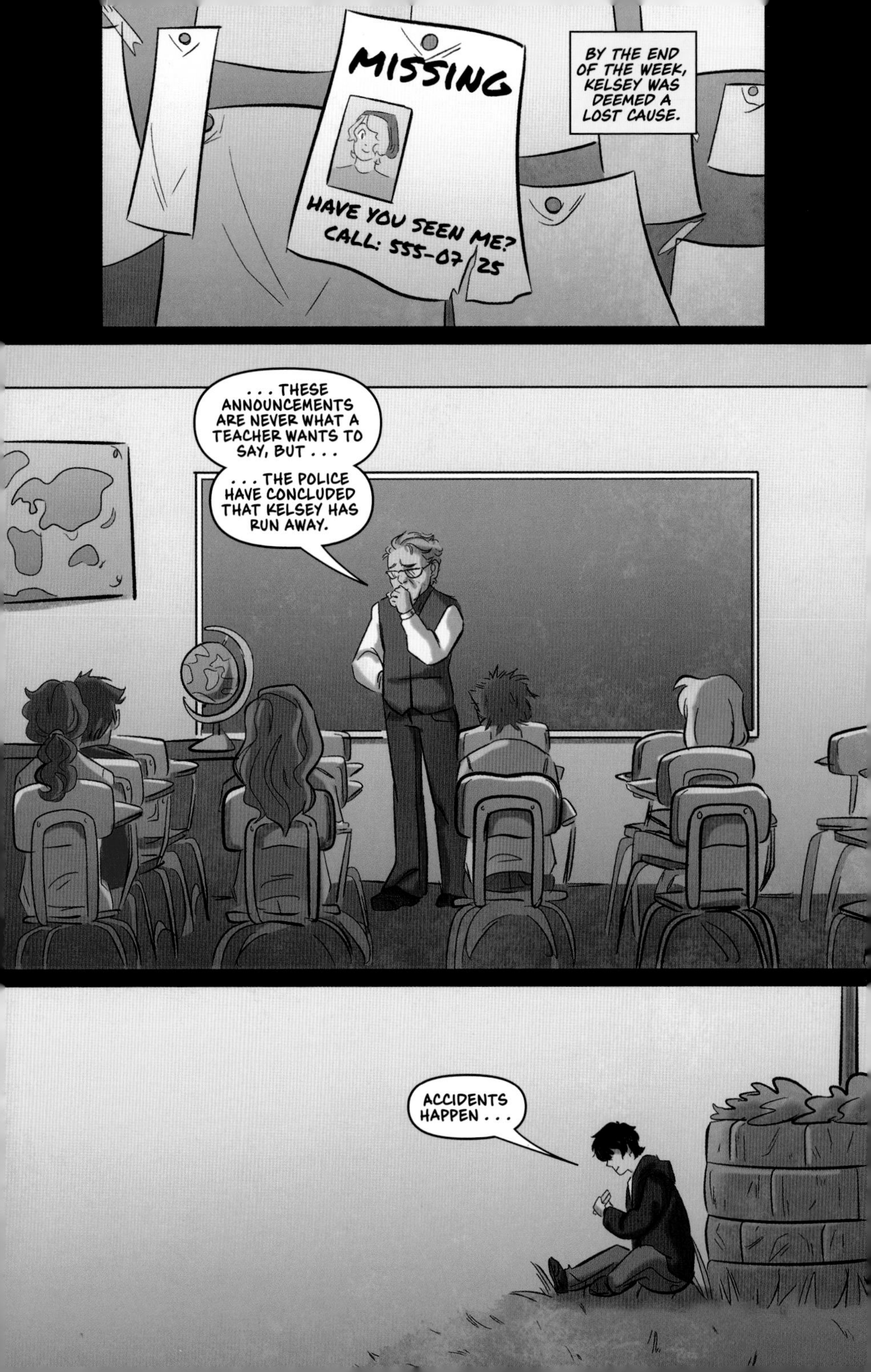
MISSING
HAVE YOU SEEN ME?
CALL: 555-07 25
BY THE END OF THE WEEK, KELSEY WAS DEEMED A LOST CAUSE.
. . . THESE ANNOUNCEMENTS ARE NEVER WHAT A TEACHER WANTS TO SAY, BUT . . .
. . . THE POLICE HAVE CONCLUDED THAT KELSEY HAS RUN AWAY.
ACCIDENTS HAPPEN . . .

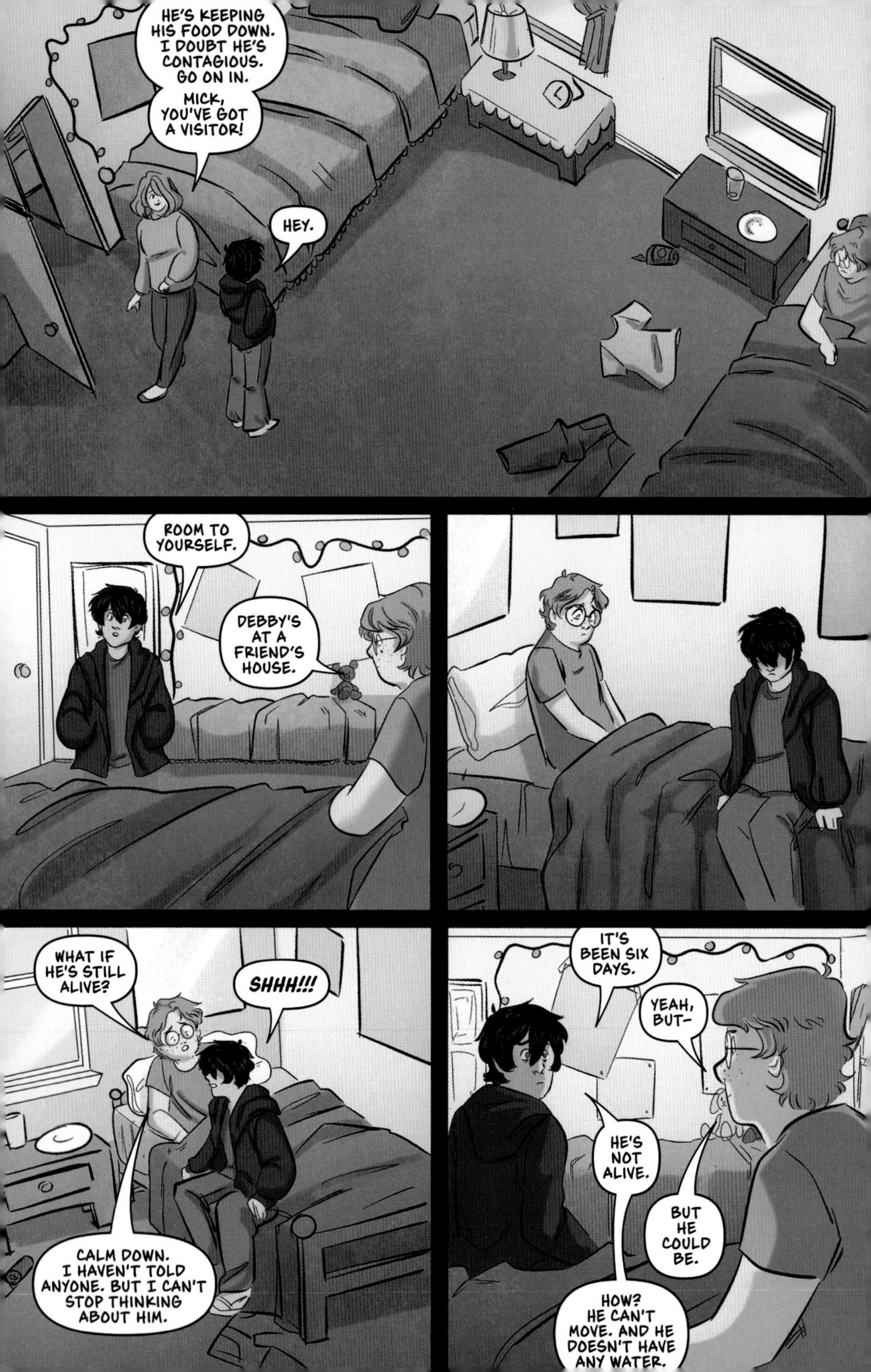
HE'S KEEPING HIS FOOD DOWN. I DOUBT HE'S CONTAGIOUS. GO ON IN.
MICK, YOU'VE GOT A VISITOR!
HEY.
ROOM TO YOURSELF.
DEBBY'S AT A FRIEND'S HOUSE.
WHAT IF HE'S STILL ALIVE?
SHHH!!!
CALM DOWN. I HAVEN'T TOLD ANYONE. BUT I CAN'T STOP THINKING ABOUT HIM.
IT'S BEEN SIX DAYS.
YEAH, BUT–
HE'S NOT ALIVE.
BUT HE COULD BE.
HOW? HE CAN'T MOVE. AND HE DOESN'T HAVE ANY WATER.

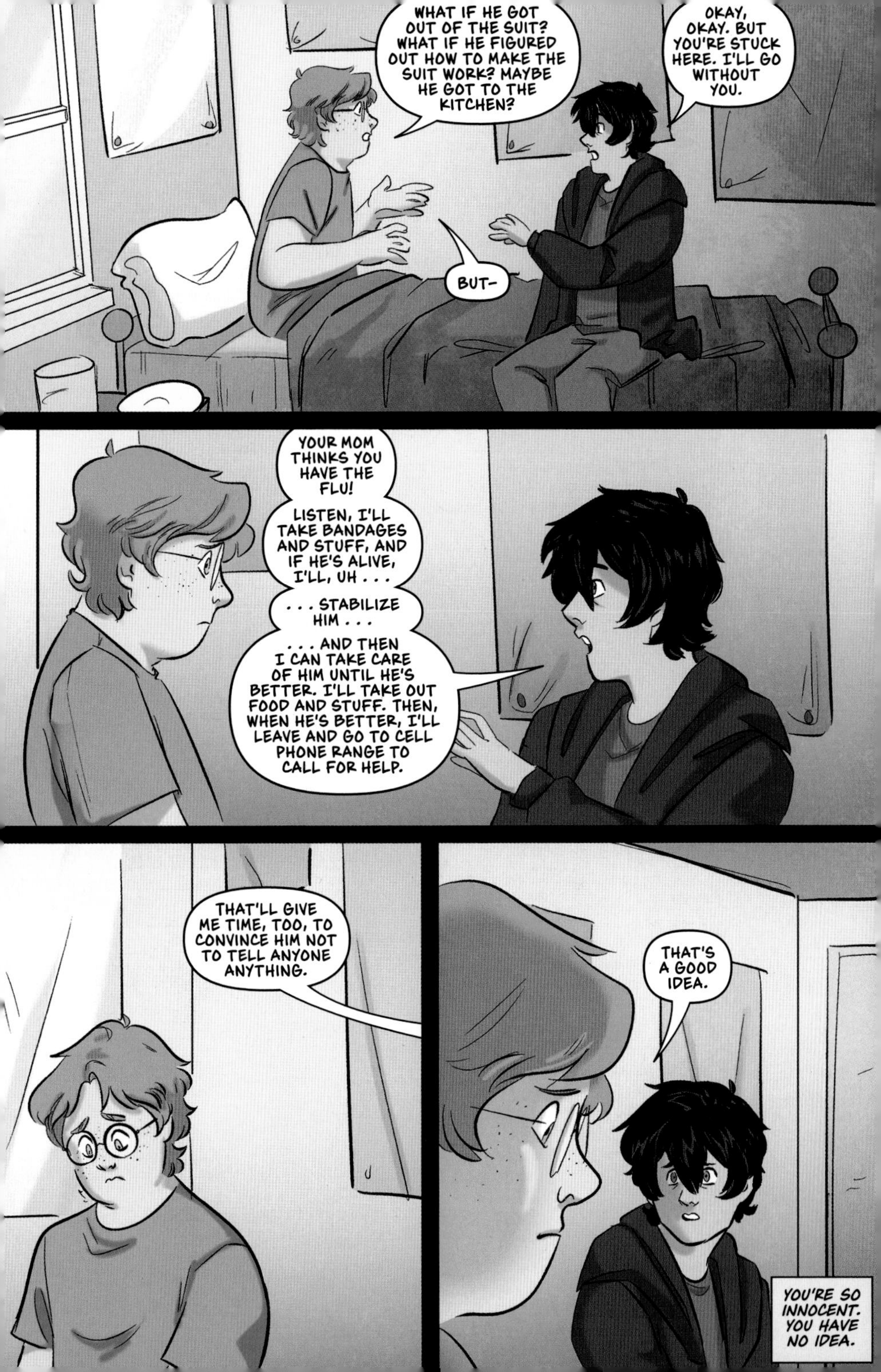
WHAT IF HE GOT OUT OF THE SUIT? WHAT IF HE FIGURED OUT HOW TO MAKE THE SUIT WORK? MAYBE HE GOT TO THE KITCHEN?
OKAY, OKAY. BUT YOU'RE STUCK HERE. I'LL GO WITHOUT YOU.
BUT-
YOUR MOM THINKS YOU HAVE THE FLU!
LISTEN, I'LL TAKE BANDAGES AND STUFF, AND IF HE'S ALIVE, I'LL, UH . . .
. . . STABILIZE HIM . . .
. . . AND THEN I CAN TAKE CARE OF HIM UNTIL HE'S BETTER. I'LL TAKE OUT FOOD AND STUFF. THEN, WHEN HE'S BETTER, I'LL LEAVE AND GO TO CELL PHONE RANGE TO CALL FOR HELP.
THAT'LL GIVE ME TIME, TOO, TO CONVINCE HIM NOT TO TELL ANYONE ANYTHING.
THAT'S A GOOD IDEA.
YOU'RE SO INNOCENT. YOU HAVE NO IDEA.

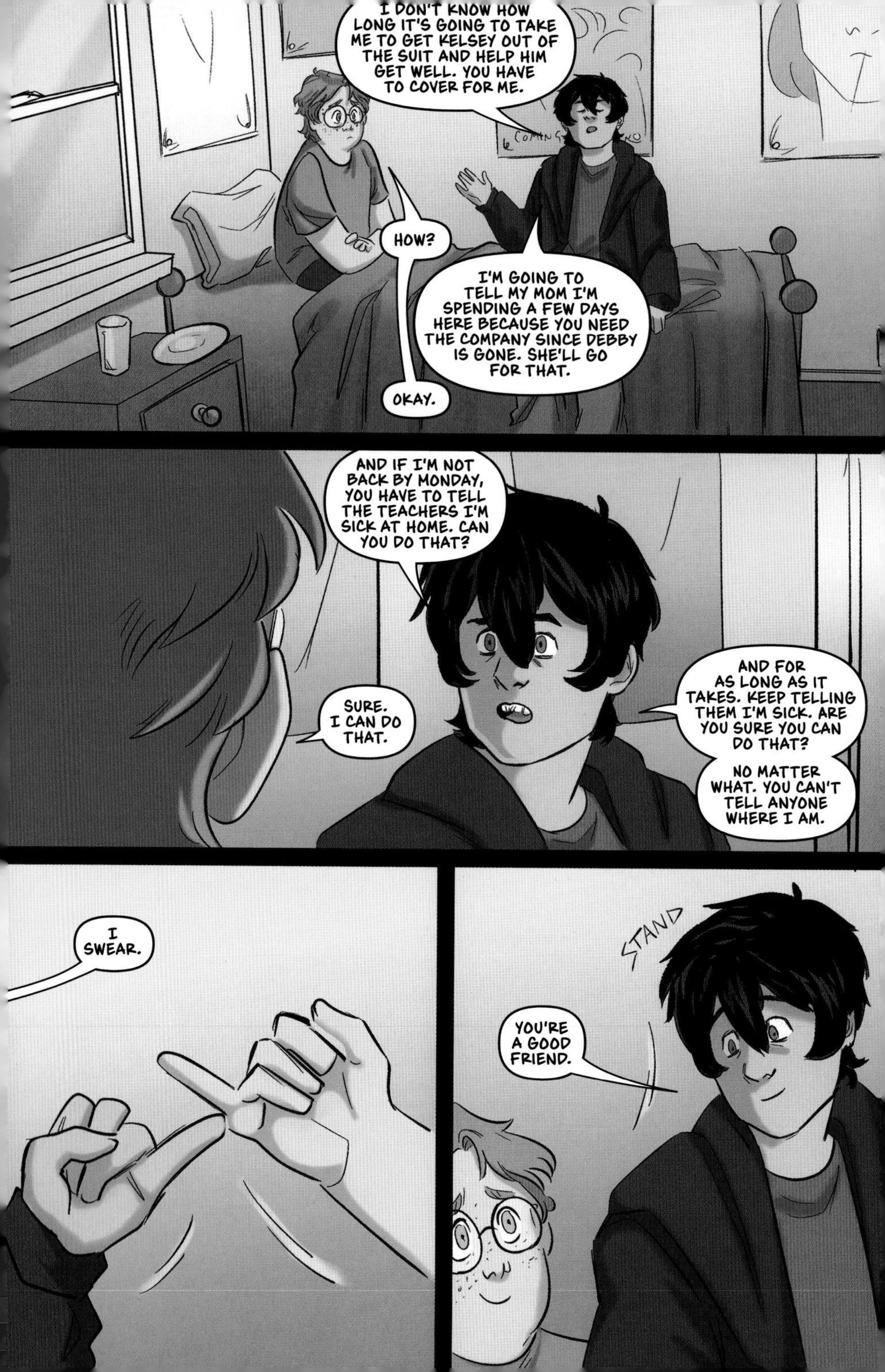
I DON'T KNOW HOW LONG IT'S GOING TO TAKE ME TO GET KELSEY OUT OF THE SUIT AND HELP HIM GET WELL. YOU HAVE TO COVER FOR ME.
HOW?
I'M GOING TO TELL MY MOM I'M SPENDING A FEW DAYS HERE BECAUSE YOU NEED THE COMPANY SINCE DEBBY IS GONE. SHE'LL GO FOR THAT.
OKAY.
AND IF I'M NOT BACK BY MONDAY, YOU HAVE TO TELL THE TEACHERS I'M SICK AT HOME. CAN YOU DO THAT?
SURE. I CAN DO THAT.
AND FOR AS LONG AS IT TAKES. KEEP TELLING THEM I'M SICK. ARE YOU SURE YOU CAN DO THAT?
NO MATTER WHAT. YOU CAN'T TELL ANYONE WHERE I AM.
I SWEAR.
STAND
YOU'RE A GOOD FRIEND.

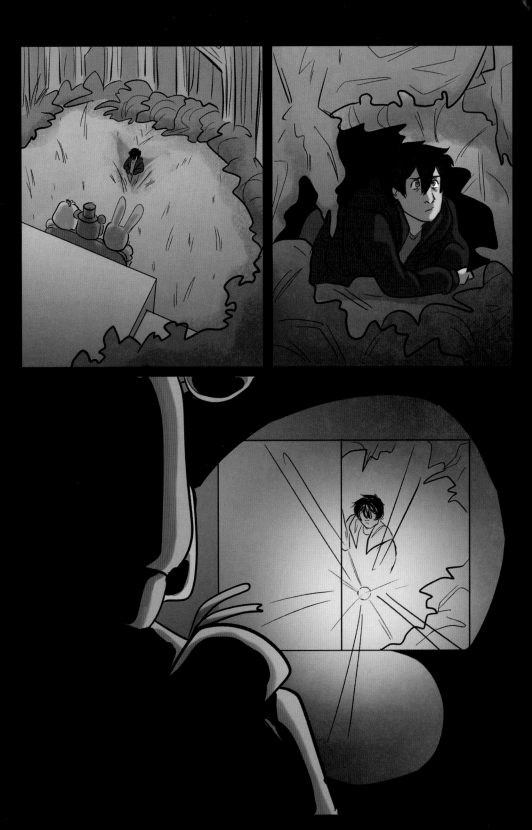

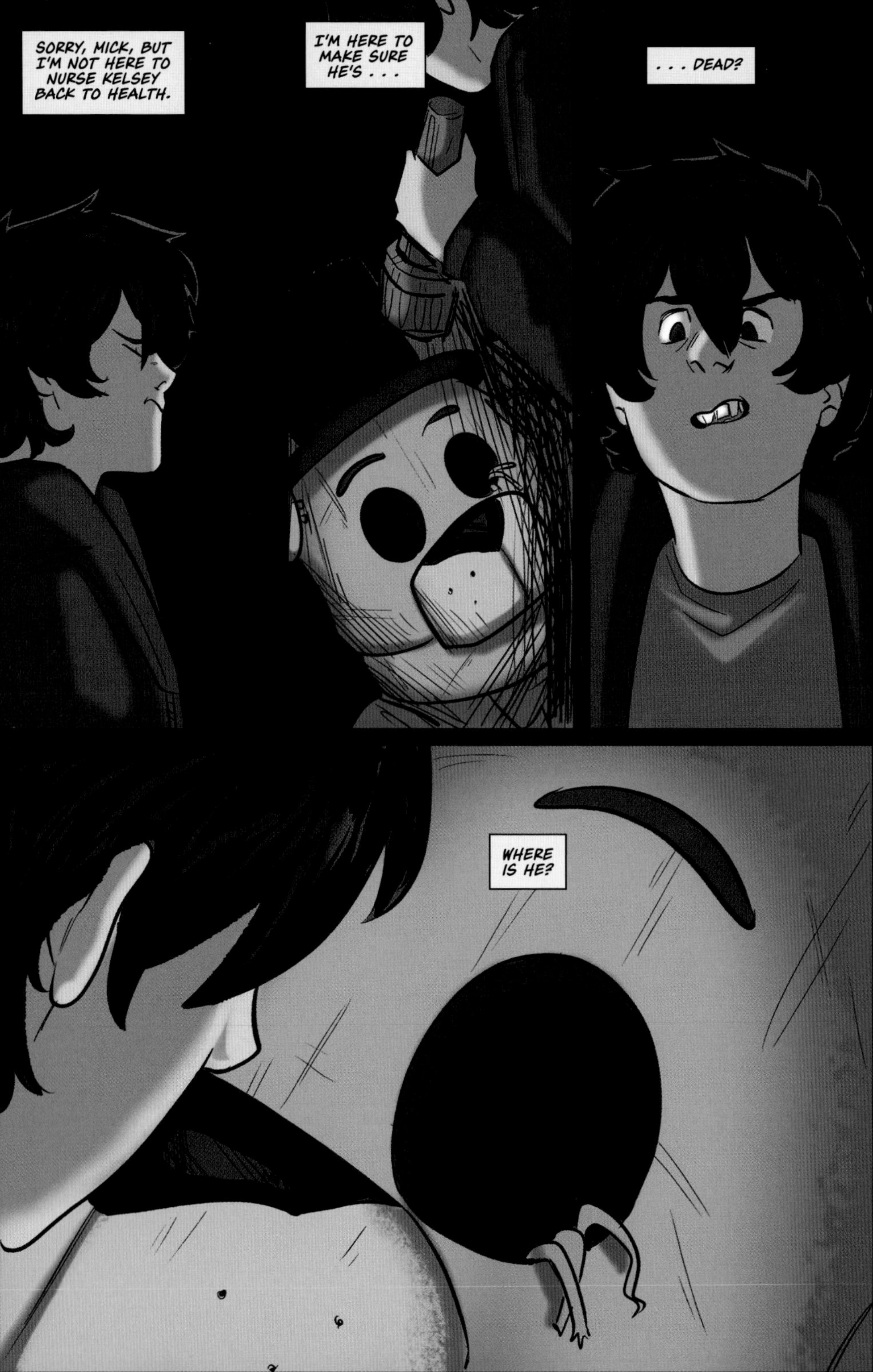
SORRY, MICK, BUT I'M NOT HERE TO NURSE KELSEY BACK TO HEALTH.
I'M HERE TO MAKE SURE HE'S . . .
. . . DEAD?
WHERE IS HE?

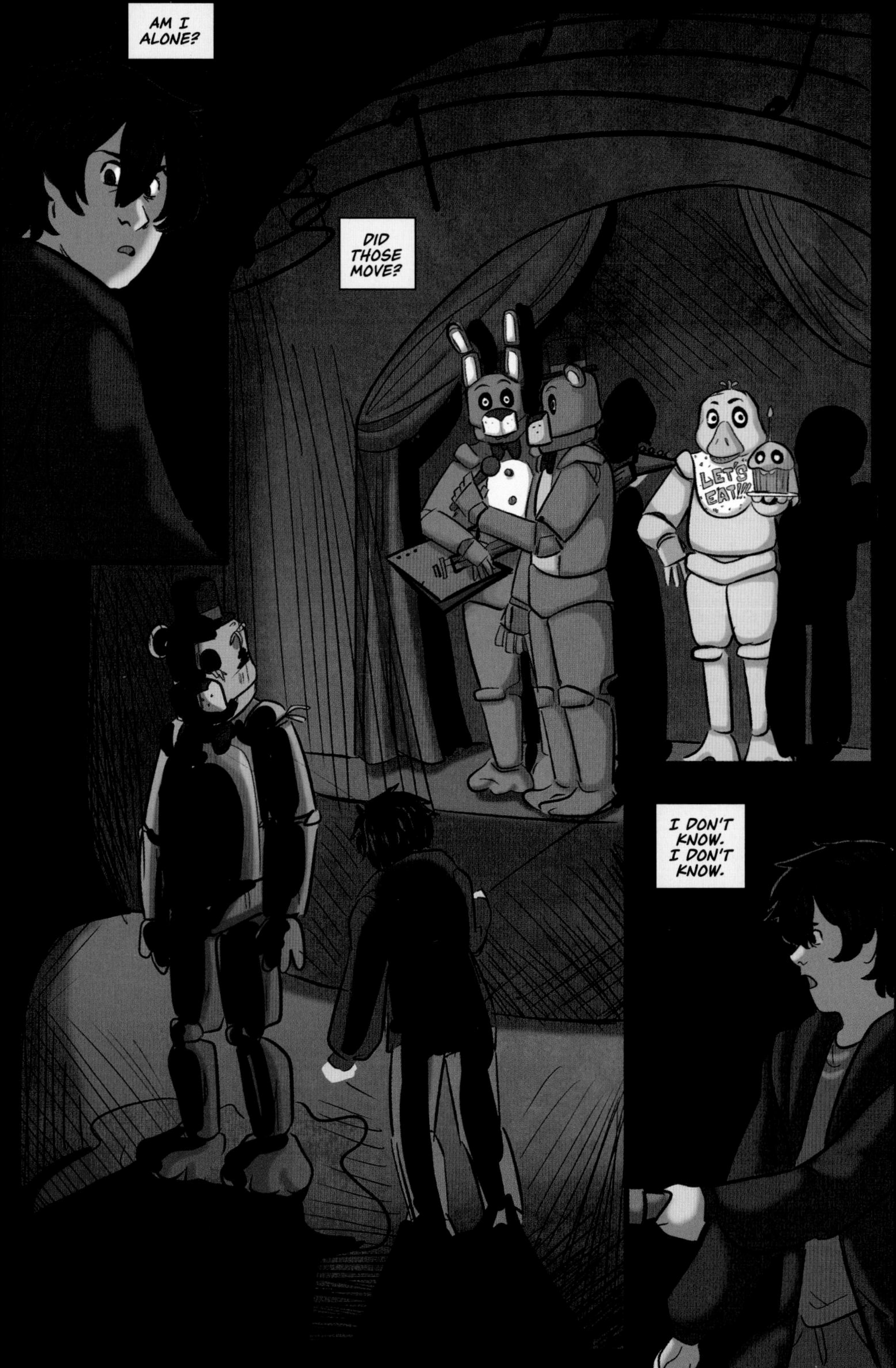
AM I ALONE?
DID THOSE MOVE?
LET'S EAT!!
I DON'T KNOW. I DON'T KNOW.

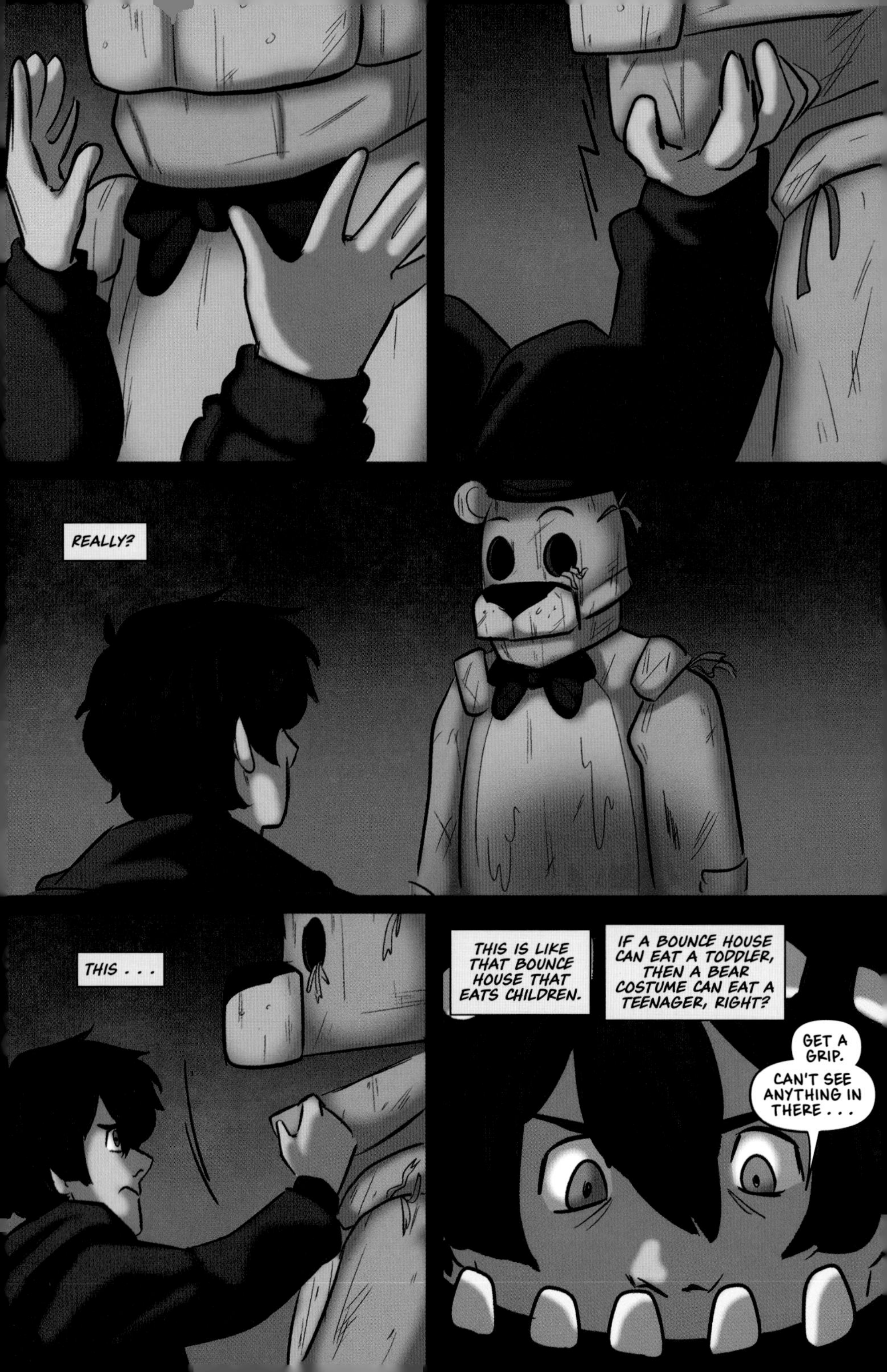
REALLY?
THIS . . .
THIS IS LIKE THAT BOUNCE HOUSE THAT EATS CHILDREN.
IF A BOUNCE HOUSE CAN EAT A TODDLER, THEN A BEAR COSTUME CAN EAT A TEENAGER, RIGHT?
GET A GRIP.
CAN'T SEE ANYTHING IN THERE . . .

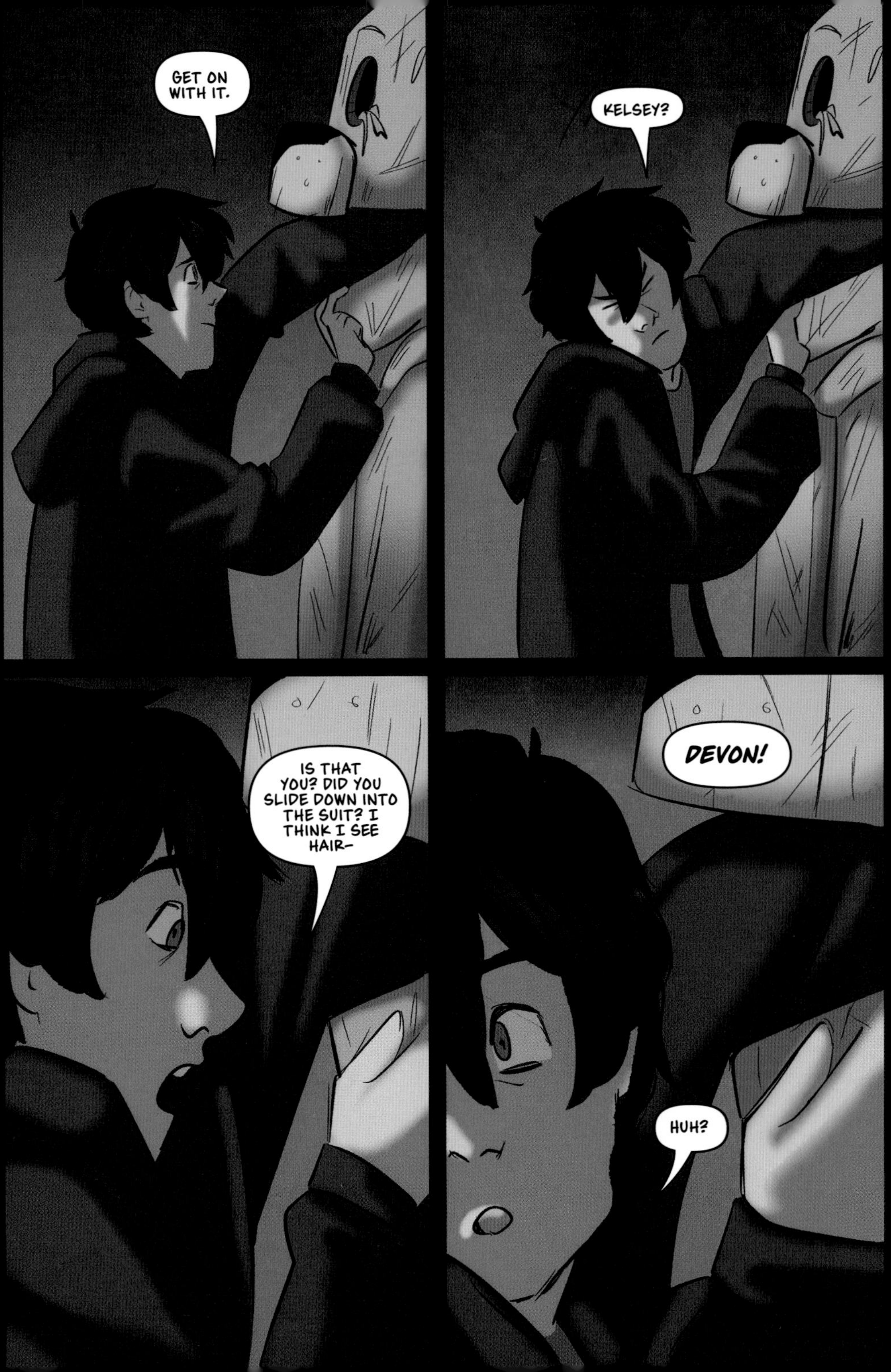
GET ON WITH IT.
KELSEY?
IS THAT YOU? DID YOU SLIDE DOWN INTO THE SUIT? I THINK I SEE HAIR–
DEVON!
HUH?

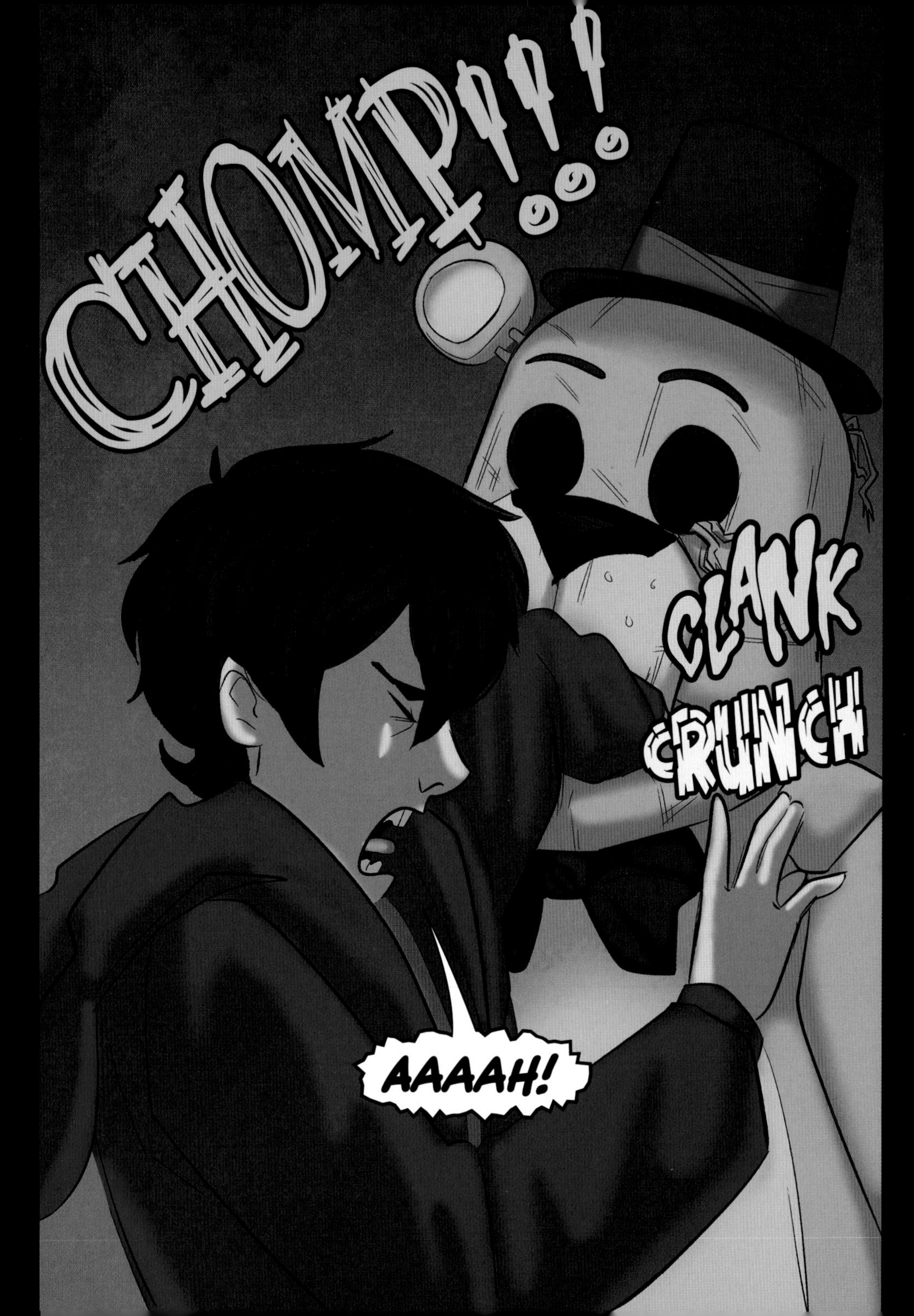
CHOMP!!!
CLANK
CRUNCH
AAAAH!

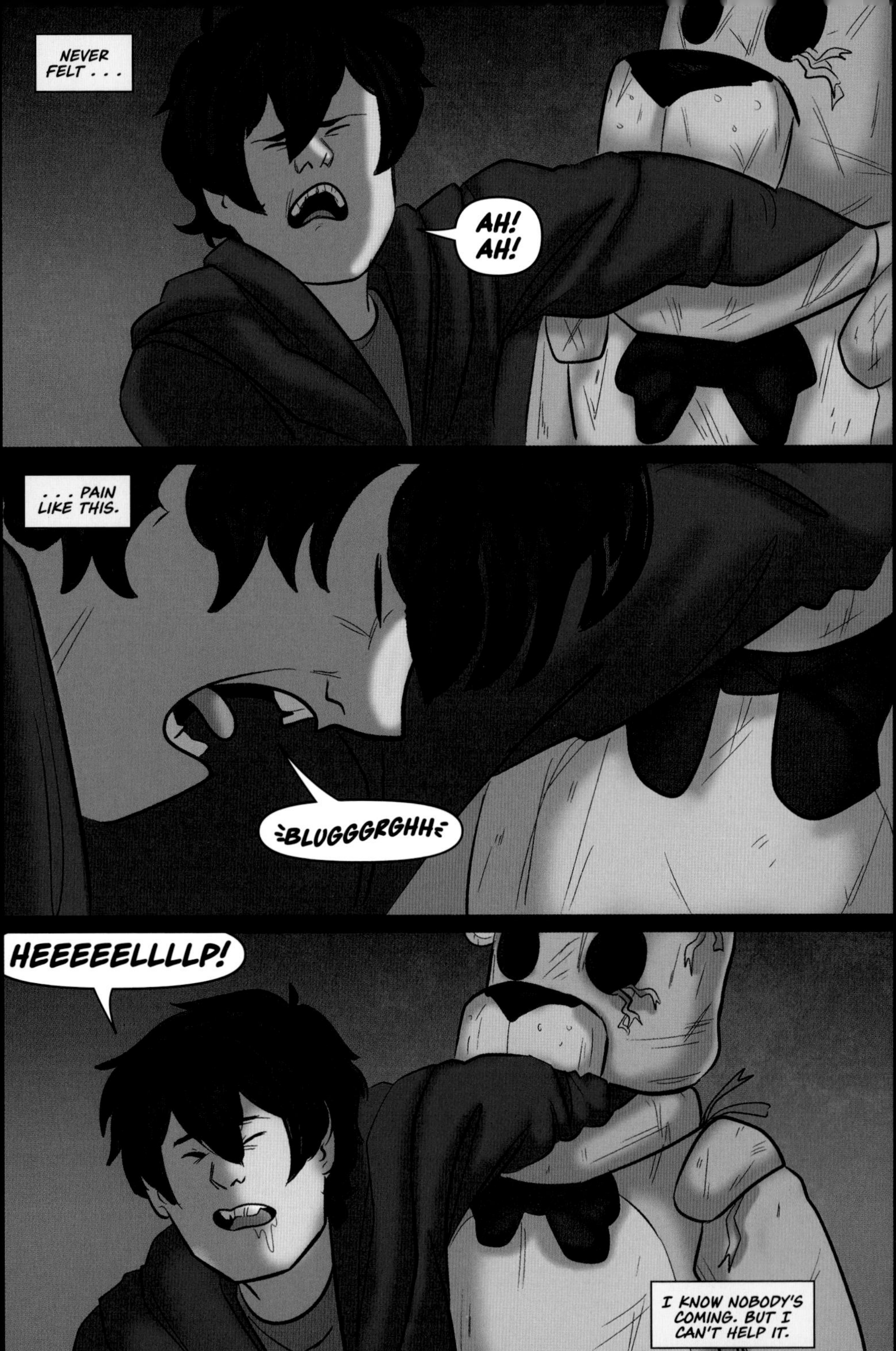
NEVER FELT . . .
AH! AH!
. . . PAIN LIKE THIS.
BLUGGGRGHH
HEEEEEELLLLLP!
I KNOW NOBODY'S COMING. BUT I CAN'T HELP IT.

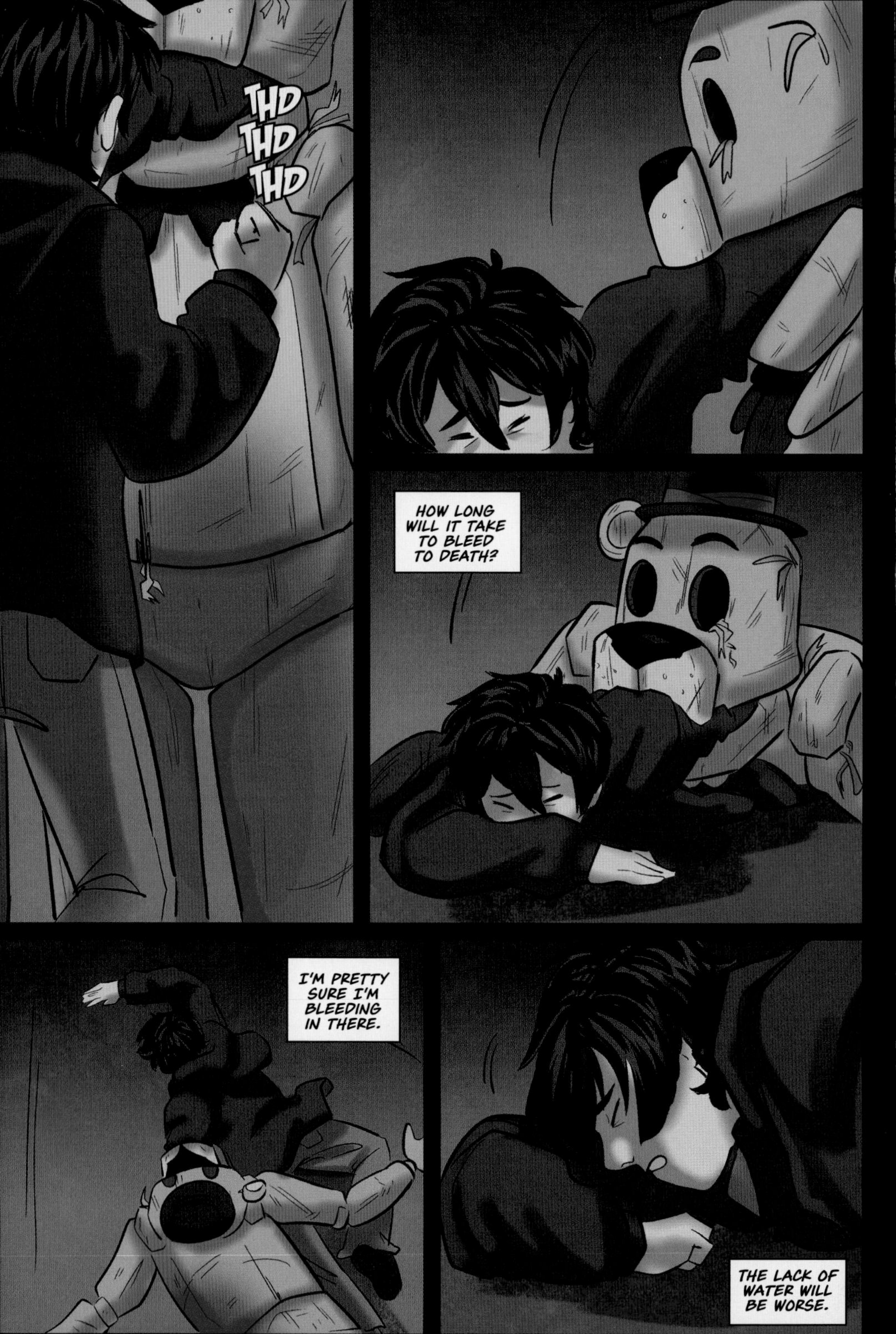
THD
THD
THD
HOW LONG WILL IT TAKE TO BLEED TO DEATH?
I'M PRETTY SURE I'M BLEEDING IN THERE.
THE LACK OF WATER WILL BE WORSE.

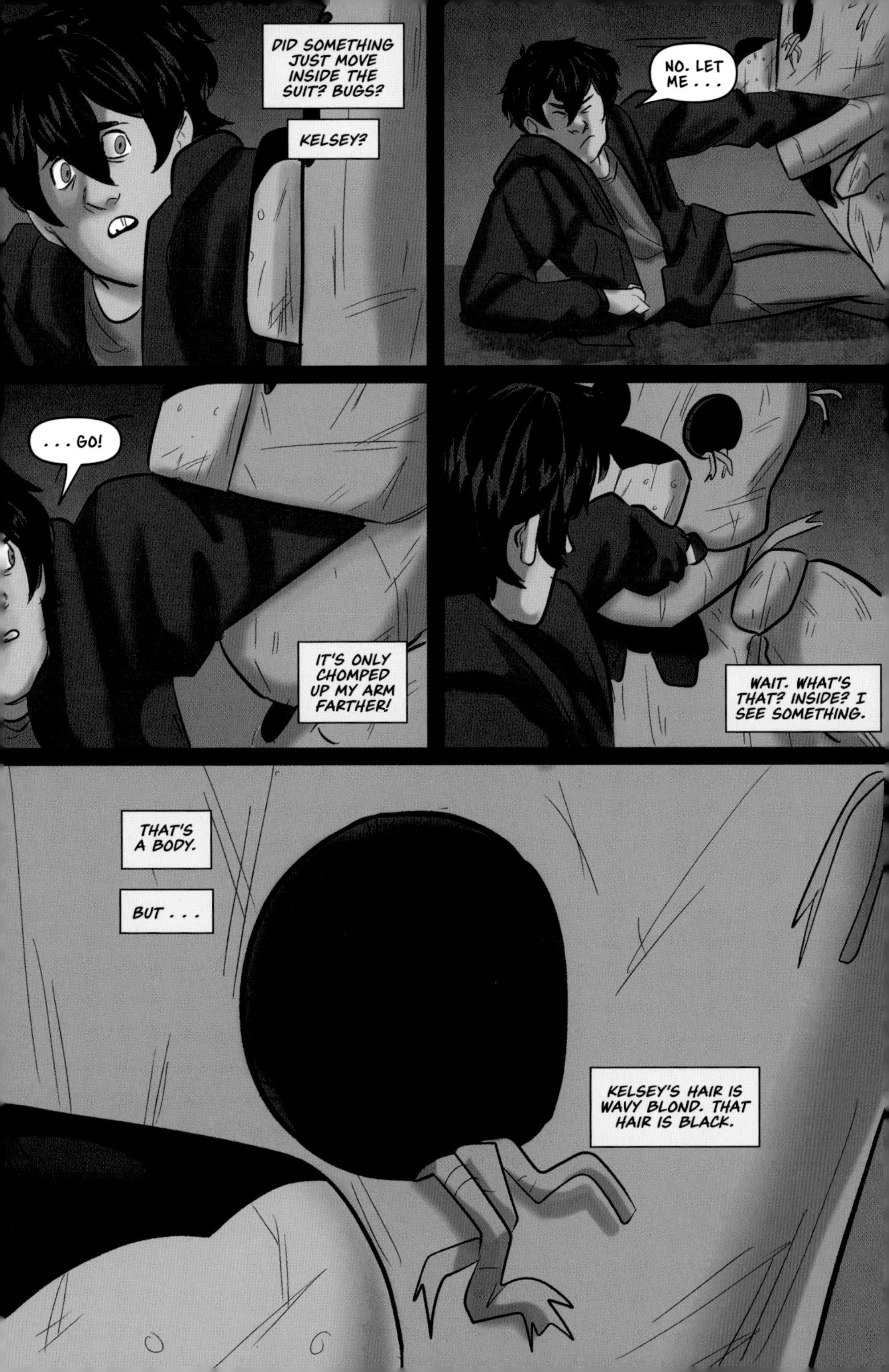
DID SOMETHING JUST MOVE INSIDE THE SUIT? BUGS?
KELSEY?
NO. LET ME . . .
. . . GO!
IT'S ONLY CHOMPED UP MY ARM FARTHER!
WAIT. WHAT'S THAT? INSIDE? I SEE SOMETHING.
THAT'S A BODY.
BUT . . .
KELSEY'S HAIR IS WAVY BLOND. THAT HAIR IS BLACK.

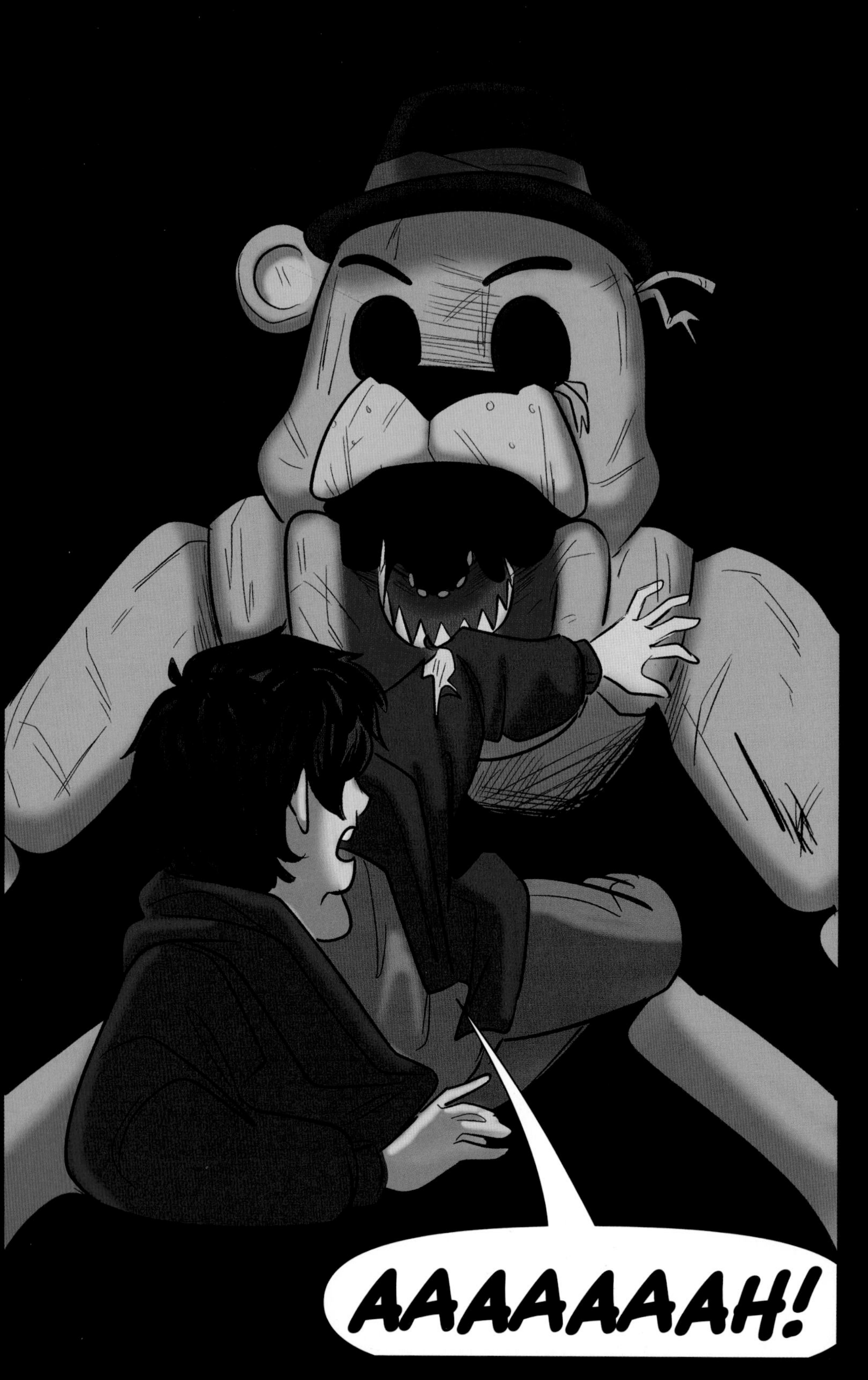
AAAAAAAH!

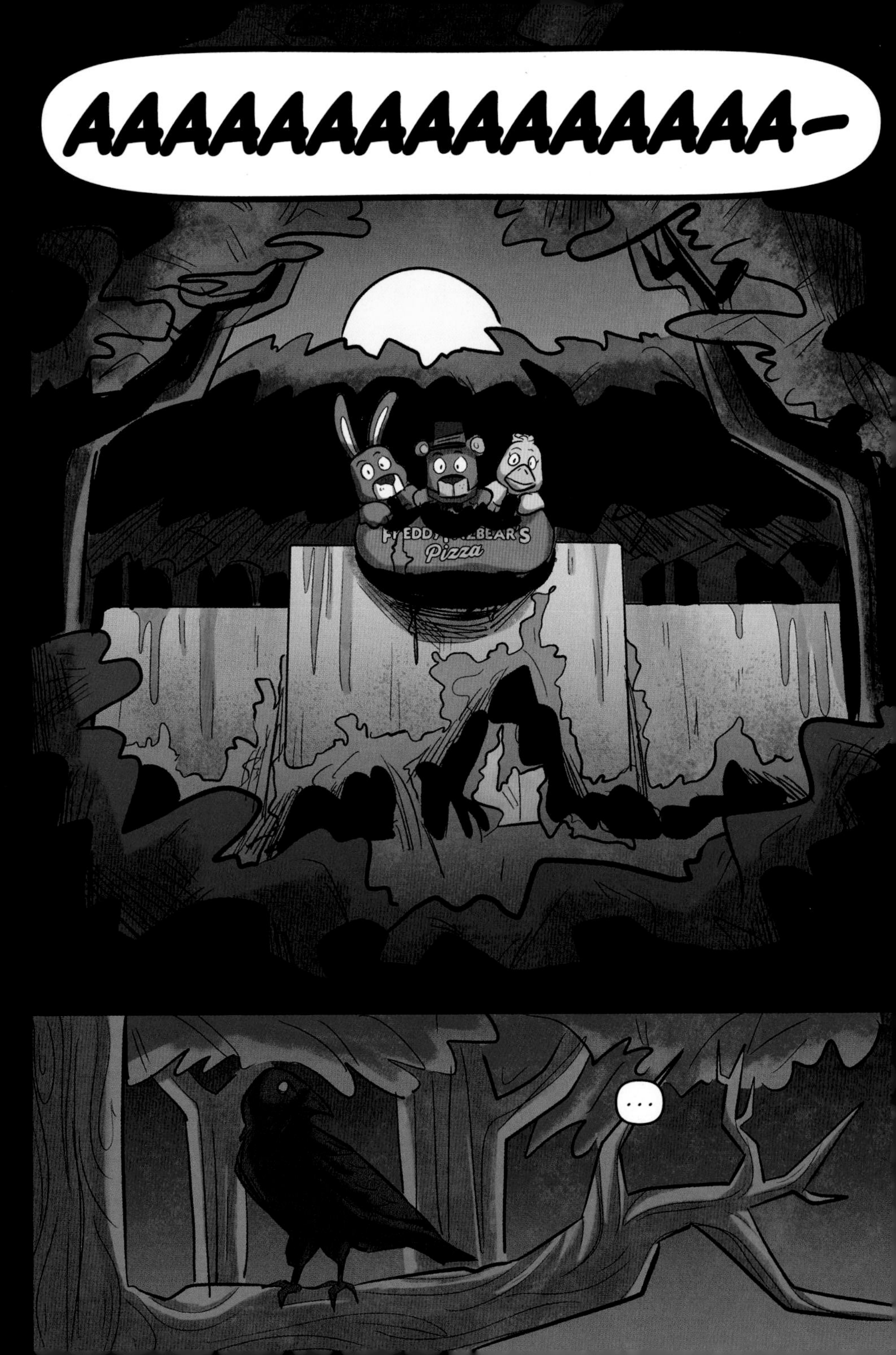
AAAAAAAAAAAAAAA-
Pizza
...

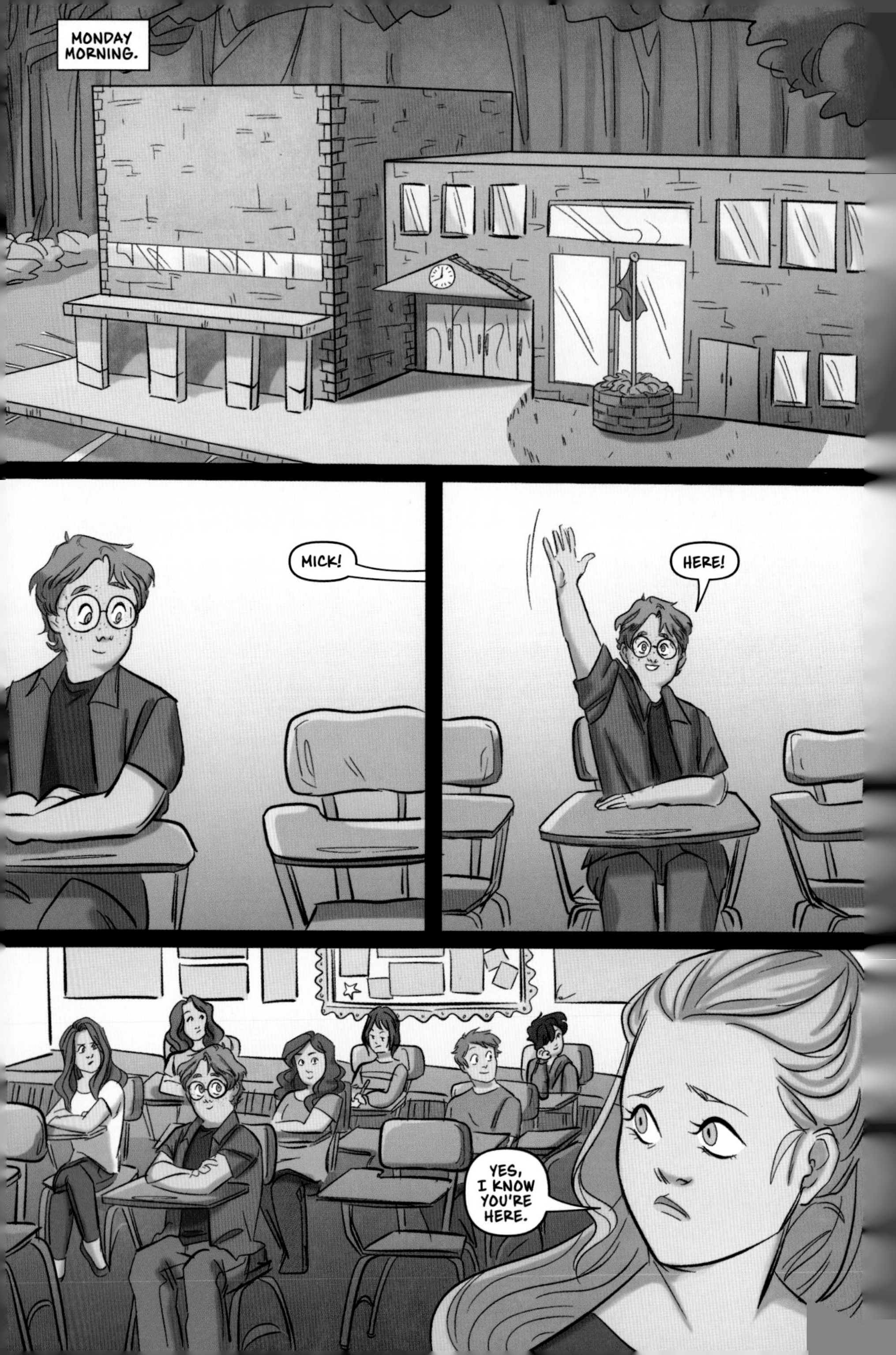
MONDAY MORNING.
MICK!
HERE!
YES, I KNOW YOU'RE HERE.

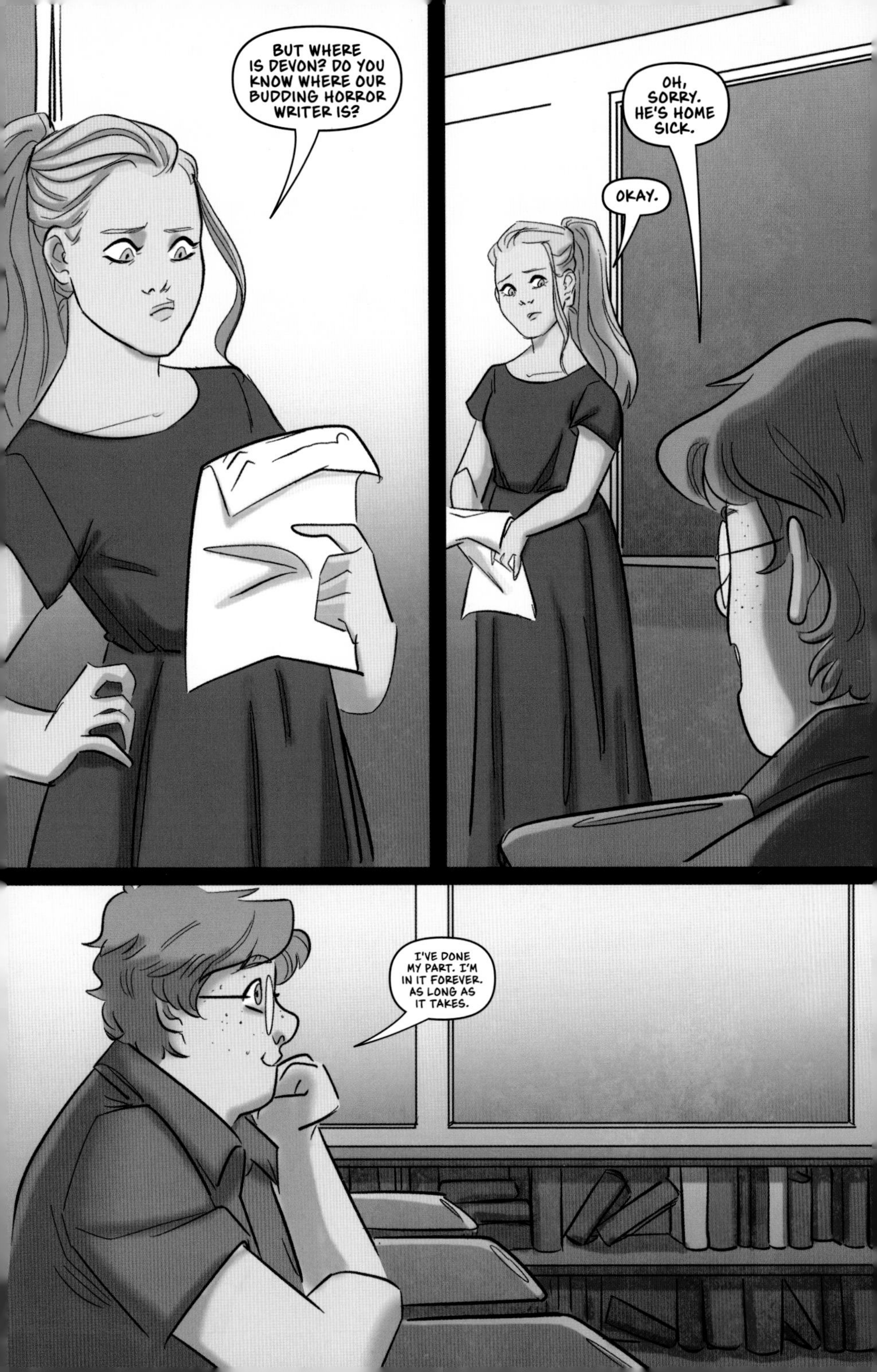
BUT WHERE IS DEVON? DO YOU KNOW WHERE OUR BUDDING HORROR WRITER IS?
OH, SORRY. HE'S HOME SICK.
OKAY.
I'VE DONE MY PART. I'M IN IT FOREVER. AS LONG AS IT TAKES.

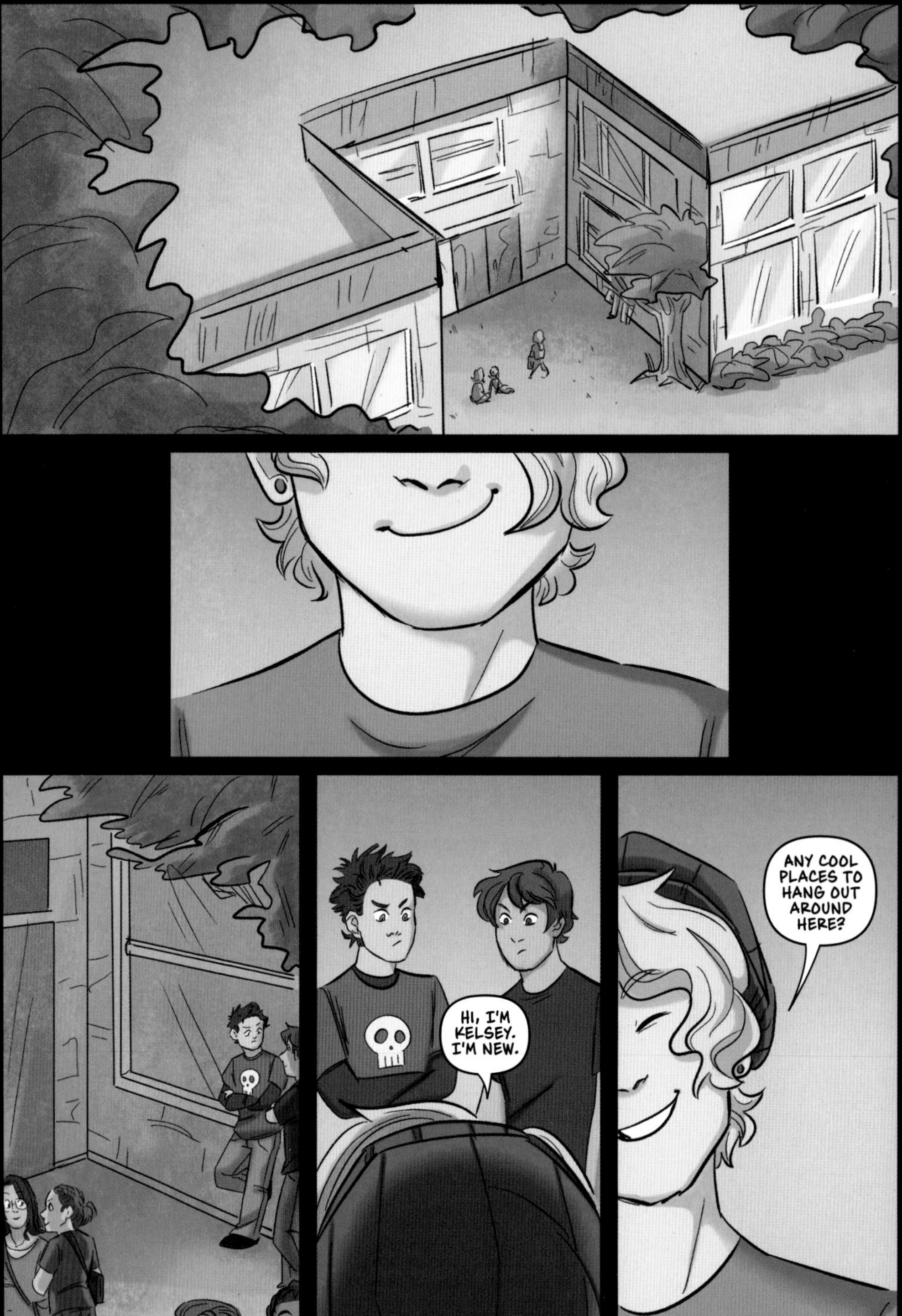
HI, I'M KELSEY. I'M NEW.
ANY COOL PLACES TO HANG OUT AROUND HERE?